PENGUIN BOOKS

The Trip of a Lifetime

Australian-born Dublin-based Monica McInerney is the
author of eleven best-selling novels. Monica grew up in
a family of seven children in the Clare Valley wine region
of South Australia and has been living between Australia
and Ireland for more than twenty years. She and her Irish
husband currently live in Dublin.

monicamcinerney.com
facebook.com/monicamcinerneyauthor
instagram.com/monicamcinerneyauthor
twitter.com/@monicamcinerney

Books by Monica McInerney

A Taste for It
Upside Down Inside Out
Spin the Bottle
The Alphabet Sisters
Family Baggage
Those Faraday Girls
All Together Now
At Home with the Templetons
Lola's Secret
The House of Memories
Hello from the Gillespies
The Trip of a Lifetime

MONICA McINERNEY

The Trip of a Lifetime

PENGUIN BOOKS

PENGUIN BOOKS

UK | USA | Canada | Ireland | Australia
India | New Zealand | South Africa

Penguin Books is part of the Penguin Random House group of companies
whose addresses can be found at global.penguinrandomhouse.com.

First published in Australia by Penguin
Random House Australia Pty Ltd, 2017
First published in Great Britain by Michael Joseph 2017
Published in Penguin Books 2018
002

Copyright © Monica McInerney, 2017

The moral right of the author and illustrator has been asserted

Set in 9.79/14.8 pt Sabon by Jouve (UK), Milton Keynes
Printed in Great Britain by Clays Ltd, St Ives plc

A CIP catalogue record for this book is available from the British Library

ISBN: 978–1–405–93281–3

www.greenpenguin.co.uk

MIX
Paper from
responsible sources
FSC® C018179

Penguin Random House is committed to a
sustainable future for our business, our readers
and our planet. This book is made from Forest
Stewardship Council® certified paper.

To my dear friend
Sarah Duffy,
a proud Australian and Kildare woman.

CHAPTER ONE

Bett Quinlan had a weekly ritual. Every Wednesday morning – the day the local newspaper she edited was published – she would walk up one side of the main street of the town of Clare and then down the other. She'd pass the bakery, the chemist, the charity shop, the hardware store, the butcher, the banks. Sometimes she even did the walk twice.

It delivered better feedback than any market research. On an average Wednesday, she would be stopped at least eight times, with townspeople expressing their opinions about the stories on the front page, or the back page or, indeed, any of the pages inside. Rarely was everyone happy. It was usually the unhappy ones who stopped her. But, without fail, it helped her with what she called 'taking the temperature' of the Clare Valley's citizens.

'Have you ever thought about wearing a bulletproof vest?' her grandmother Lola asked one week, when the front-page story was a particularly spicy one about council politics. 'Or a disguise?'

'I'm hoping you'll come with me next time,' Bett said. 'Who would pick on me if I was helping a frail, elderly Irishwoman stretch her frail, elderly Irish legs?'

'Your frail, elderly Irish grandmother is busy elsewhere most Wednesdays, fortunately,' Lola said.

'Out with the Golden Oldies?'

'We're not called that any more. We took a vote. We've got a new name now. The One-Footers. As in, one foot in the grave. There's nothing golden about being olden, in my eyes. Not that I can see too well either at the moment. Or hear too well. Or move too well. See how apt the new name is?'

'So what are you all doing this Wednesday? Apart from listing your ailments to each other?'

'Waterskiing, I think. Or maybe whitewater rafting?'

'In the puddle of water in the creek?'

'Perhaps. I can't remember. My memory's going too.'

Bett's latest weekly walk delivered the goods again. The previous evening, her assistant editor, Sam, had read the front-page headline – 'Fiery scenes in council chambers' – and given her a knowing look. 'That'll be one lighthearted stroll tomorrow,' he said.

He was right. She'd barely left the office the next morning before a passer-by stopped her. She had the story all wrong, she was told. Ten metres on, another person grabbed her hand and shook it vigorously. She had it absolutely right. Her approval ratings rose and fell as she walked along the street.

Halfway down the opposite side, she was glad to see a friendly face. An old schoolfriend, Jenny Randall. She was now the occupational therapist at the old folks' home.

'Have you got a minute, Bett?' Jenny asked.

'Do you want to abuse me?' Bett said. 'Then, no. Do you want to praise me? Sure, I've got hours.'

Jenny smiled. 'It's not about the paper. But if it was, I'd praise you. I think you got that story spot-on.' She dropped her voice. 'It's actually about your grandmother.'

Six months previously, Bett and Jenny had met for a confidential conversation about Lola. At the age of eighty-five, she had started dropping hints to Bett that she might, not immediately, not exactly now, but one day perhaps give some thought to moving into a room at the old folks' home. For now, she had assured Bett, she was more than happy sharing a house in the town with her friend Margaret. It was working beautifully. But just looking ahead . . .

Bett had spoken to Jenny about it, informally. Lola's name had – equally informally – been added to the waiting list. Bett had just as casually told her grandmother.

'"Waiting list"? As in, I move up a spot when someone dies?' Lola had said. 'That's the most sinister list in town.'

'Who died?' Bett said to Jenny now. 'Sorry, you know what I mean.'

'I do, and don't worry. It's not about a room.' She hesitated. 'Bett, is Lola okay at the moment?'

Bett thought about it. 'Okay' seemed far too ordinary a word to describe Lola. She pictured her grandmother. Tall, slender, straight-backed even at her age. White hair cut short, often decorated with a sparkly hairpin or an artificial flower or two. As for her unique approach to clothes . . . What would she be wearing today, for example? One of her daytime outfits, perhaps a leopard-skin cape with purple leggings and a jaunty feather-trimmed hat? Or something a little more festive, for midweek wear? One of her bright-orange ponchos – she had two – worn with a vertically striped pair of flares? Lola's volunteer work in the local charity shop aided and abetted her wardrobe choices, but Bett was sure she'd have no difficulty sourcing the outfits from elsewhere if necessary. There had been a suspicious number of parcels arriving at Lola's house recently, since she'd discovered online vintage shopping.

Jenny elaborated. 'How does she seem mood-wise to you?'

'Just the same,' Bett said. 'But I've only seen her briefly this week.' The start of the week was Bett's busiest time, juggling her editing with sharing the care of her twin son and daughter with her husband, Daniel. He worked in two jobs, as a weekend wedding photographer and a part-time production manager on a newspaper in Gawler, an hour away.

'I'm worried about her, Bett. She's not herself. You know I started holding those drop-in classes?'

Bett nodded. She'd written an article about the program Jenny had devised for her residents and any interested townspeople. Music afternoons. Craft sessions. Poetry readings.

'Lola's been to all of them,' Jenny said. 'Without fail. For the past three weeks. She's waiting outside the activities room before I open the door and she's always the last to leave.'

'Is that a problem? Has she been misbehaving? Upsetting the other residents? Insulting anyone?'

'No more than usual. It's just not like her to be there all the time. She's always had so much else going on in her life. The charity shop. Her friends. But now, it's as if we're all she has. She asked me if there was any possibility of weekend activities. She suggested a poker game on Saturdays. And a DVD night each Sunday.' Jenny paused. 'Bett, I think she's really lonely. Lonely and bored. And possibly depressed.'

Before Bett could insist that Lola wasn't any of those things, her phone rang. It was the office, her assistant, Sam. An urgent query. Was there any chance Bett could —

'I'll be there in five minutes,' she told him. She turned to Jenny. 'Thanks for telling me. Can you leave it with me and I'll ask her myself?'

'Of course. As I said, she's still a few people down on the waiting list, but if you think it's getting urgent, that it might be time for her to come to us full-time, I could —'

'Move her up a few spots? Jenny Randall, I don't even want to imagine how you'd do that.'

Jenny grinned. 'It'd make a great front page for your paper, put it that way.'

4

An hour later, the crisis dealt with at work, Bett stepped outside to make two private calls. The first was to her husband. On Wednesdays Daniel stayed home with the twins. It took him a long time to answer. When he did it was hard to hear him. Yvette and Zachary, nearly two years old, had recently discovered the joys of spoon-and-saucepan musical instruments. She and Daniel had a brief shouted conversation, Bett confirming she'd be home by six and would buy dinner on the way.

Her second call was to Lola. Her grandmother answered before the second ring.

'Bett! Are you coming to visit? Great! See you soon.'

'Don't you say hello any more?'

'It wastes time. Wonderful. I'm here. Come whenever you can. Come now. I'll put the kettle on.'

Without another word, Lola hung up.

A quick explanation to Sam, and Bett was on her way. She was glad she'd taken her coat, even for the short walk to Lola's house on the edge of the town. It was mid-April, an autumn chill creeping into the Valley as the vineyards all around transformed into warm reds and oranges. The trees lining Lola's street were also in full autumn glory. It was Bett's favourite time of year.

Lola had moved into Margaret's house a year earlier, an arrangement that suited them both. Margaret, a widow in her late sixties, had raised her three children there. It was spacious enough for her and Lola to have not only their own bedrooms, but their own separate living areas, one at each end of the house. They shared the cooking and cleaning duties.

As Bett knocked and obeyed her grandmother's call to come in, she heard the whistling of the kettle. Lola was in the kitchen preparing a tea tray. Bett had been close with her wardrobe guess. Lola was indeed wearing the orange poncho, although not with the striped flares. She'd teamed it with a green taffeta skirt. With her white hair she looked like a walking Irish flag.

'Nice outfit,' Bett said, kissing her grandmother's heavily rouged cheek. 'Happy Saint Patrick's Day.'

'You're a disgrace to your Irish ancestry. You know very well that was in March,' Lola replied cheerily.

She handed Bett the tray and the two of them made their way from the bright kitchen into Lola's even brighter living room. It was a riotous clash of colours, from the vivid-blue curtains to the rainbow swirls on the mat. The shelves were filled with books, coloured glass vases, ornaments and other bric-a-brac, all sourced from the charity shop. Family photos and framed prints and paintings, mostly of flowers, filled the space on every wall. The previous year Lola had gone through a phase of collecting paintings of seascapes. Before that, it was animals.

The windows were wide open, fresh air and autumn sunlight filling the room. The view was of the side garden, now full of late-blooming roses, a vibrant green hedge and a plum tree on which Lola had hung several bird feeders. Bett could hear birdsong, as well as the music coming from the ancient stereo. Her grandmother generally had a soundtrack to her day, either gentle piano music, old show hits or lavish orchestral arrangements. Today it was piano. Bett named it – Chopin's 'Minute Waltz' – and received a satisfied nod from Lola.

'That's my Bett. All those years of piano lessons paid off, didn't they?'

'If only listening counted. It's months since I've played a note.'

'It was such a shame you couldn't have the piano from the motel.'

'Don't worry. The only time I'd get to play it would be in the middle of the night. I'm not sure how Daniel and the twins would feel about that.'

'You could always play Brahms' "Lullaby", couldn't you? Or

6

Beethoven's "Für Elise". That always put me to sleep.'

Bett had grown up playing the piano, first as Lola's reluctant pupil, then because she loved it so much. The feel of the keys, the soothing sounds, the way she could lose herself in the familiarity of well-remembered tunes or in the concentration necessary to learn new pieces. When her parents had left their family motel in the Valley the previous year, she'd secretly hoped the piano in the function room wouldn't be part of the lease deal. She was disappointed. The new managers hoped to have occasional singalong sessions, apparently.

As they settled into the floral-patterned armchairs, Bett got to the point. 'I ran into Jenny Randall in the street today.'

'I hope you weren't in your car.'

Bett ignored that. 'She was talking to me about you.'

'I'll sue her for libel.'

'She was telling me you've been attending her classes at the home.'

'Is that a crime?'

'All her classes. Five a week. Most people only go to one a fortnight, if that.'

'I always was a keen student.'

'Jenny said you're first there and last to leave.'

'Good time-keeping is a virtue.'

'She said you asked her to put on extra classes.'

'She has a big mouth.'

'Lola, she's worried about you. And so am I, now. Jenny asked me if I thought you were okay. If I thought you might be —' Bett hesitated.

Lola stayed silent.

'A bit lonely,' Bett said. 'And a bit bored.'

'She's got that wrong,' Lola said.

'She has?' Bett said, relieved.

7

'I'm desperately lonely, not just a bit lonely. And I'm incredibly bored, not only a bit.'

'But all those classes you're doing —'

Lola made a scoffing sound. 'Nothing against your friend, but I may as well enrol at the kindergarten for the amount of mental stimulation I'm getting at that home. An hour's music, we were promised. You know what we got? Forty minutes of warbling "Shine on, Harvest Moon", over and over again. The poor old dears couldn't remember anything else, apparently. As for the craft class, I thought I might get a fruit basket or something to bring home. No. We painted ice-cream sticks. Dozens of them. I'm still not sure why. To keep the fire going at the crematorium, perhaps?'

'Lola!'

'I passed the Scouts' clubroom on the way home yesterday. I nearly joined up. At least I'd get a few camping trips. They have to let females in now, don't they?'

'I think so. I'm just not sure how they feel about 85-year-old females.'

Lola put her head back against the chair and sighed. 'It could be worse, Bett. I could be addicted to online gambling in an attempt to amuse myself.'

'As well as online shopping?'

'That's just a hobby. I don't buy anything. I try it on, then send it back. It gives me an excuse to go to the post office too.'

'Lola, what's happened? When did this all start?'

'My long glorious life? Bett, haven't you been paying attention? I was born eighty-five years ago in the county of Kildare in Ireland —'

'Not your life. This boredom. This loneliness. I'm so sorry, I know we haven't seen you as much as usual. Daniel's been busy with all those weddings, I've been busy at work too, and with the kids —'

'Stop that, please. If I wanted to be at your house, I'd invite myself, you know that.' Her smile took away any sting. 'Carrie said the same thing. Apologised for not having me over every day.'

'You've talked to Carrie about this already?' Bett was surprised by a sudden fizz of jealousy at the mention of her younger sister.

'Yes. She's always been my favourite of my three granddaughters. I had a séance and talked to Anna about it too.'

'Lola!' Anna, Bett's beloved older sister, had died of cancer five years earlier, leaving behind her young daughter Ellen, husband Glenn and her devastated family. Bett didn't think she'd ever be able to joke about her death.

'I'm sorry, Bett. I haven't spoken to Carrie or to Anna. I wouldn't be speaking to you either if it wasn't for Big Mouth Randall.'

'She's not a big mouth. She was concerned. I am too.'

'Don't be. All that's happened is I've realised something. I've known it for years, but lately it has really hit me.'

'What has? Are you sick?'

'No. Nothing new, anyway. The same aches and pains. The new hips that are now old hips. But I'm facing facts, Bett. I'm eighty-five. I can still walk, still talk, but for how much longer? I've been on borrowed time for years already. Look what happened to my Alex. Here one day, gone the next. Without any warning.'

Bett noticed a sudden tremor in Lola's voice. She knew Alex had been the love of her grandmother's life. After meeting him in her early years in Australia as a single mother, their brief, intense romance had been cut short when he'd had to return to his home country of Italy. They had been separated for fifty years, until a chance reconnection the year before had brought unexpected joy into both their lives. They had spoken daily on the phone, Lola in the Clare Valley, Alex in Melbourne, until Alex tragically died before he and Lola had been able to meet in person again.

'I can't avoid it any longer, darling,' Lola said. 'If there is anything left for me to do, I'm running out of time to do it. I need to seize the day while I still have a day to seize.'

'Draw up a bucket list, you mean?'

'Not a "list", exactly. More of an "item".' Lola stood up. 'But I need to give it some more thought. And you've a job to do. Off you go and find a scoop somewhere, there's a good girl.'

'I already did. It's on the front page.' She handed her grandmother a copy of the newspaper.

'Oh, very controversial. Excellent,' Lola said. 'Thank you, darling. I'll read it closely when I get back.'

'From where?'

'The library. I'm doing a creative writing course there every Wednesday afternoon. Last week was memoir writing. Today it's "How to make your love scenes sizzle". I can't wait.'

'How do you actually find the time to get lonely or bored?'

'It's just a knack I have. Goodbye, my darling. Close the door on the way out, won't you?'

Later that night, Bett had just convinced her son, Zach, to eat one more forkful of peas rather than mash them into his sister's hair when the phone rang. It was Sarah, another old schoolfriend. One by one, after years elsewhere, many of her classmates were returning to live in the Valley. Sarah had worked in London as a teacher before coming home the year before.

After a quick exchange about a forthcoming lunch date, Sarah hesitated. 'Bett, I'm not sure if I'm overstepping boundaries here, or if I should even say anything, but —'

'It's Lola, isn't it?'

'How did you know?'

'I just remembered you run the creative writing classes. And I know she was there today. Did something happen? Did she refuse to go home? Or refuse to do what she was told?'

'Nothing like that. She's my star pupil. It's just – Bett, I'm worried about her. Is she okay?'

Twice in one day. Bett was really beginning to worry now. 'I thought so. But I'm not sure any more.'

'Can I drop over and show you something?' Sarah said. 'It's not strictly ethical – I mean, not that anyone signed any confidentiality agreements – but I'd like you to read some of Lola's writing.'

An hour later, the two of them were sitting by the fire in the lounge room, drinking tea. Daniel was at the other end of the house with the children, trying to wrangle them into bed.

Bett looked up from the handful of A4 sheets Sarah had given her. She had tears in her eyes. 'Oh, Sarah. I had no idea. It's like reading her diary. It's so personal. And so sad.'

Sarah nodded. 'She told me it's flowing out of her. That she can't write it down fast enough. It's straight from her heart, she said. That's what worried me. Especially that final one, the one she showed me today, where she's —' Sarah stopped.

Bett said it for her. 'Writing about taking her own life.'

'I'm not imagining it, am I?' Sarah's words came in a rush. 'I had to show you. Maybe I'm wrong. I mean, she doesn't say it explicitly, does she?'

Bett read aloud. '"I have a choice, I've realised. I could end it all now. Do it myself. Some days I feel like I have already fallen apart physically. Why wait to go mentally too? I could leave now, while I am still sure of mind if not sure of foot. The idea grows more attractive every day. It would be so simple. So peaceful. A handful of pills, I think. My own bed. All done in my own time. In my own way." Sarah, are you sure it's about her? She wasn't writing in character?'

Sarah shook her head. 'It was part of our memoir class. That's why I thought you had to see it. Especially when you look at these as well.' She handed her two more sheets of paper. 'I'm sorry, Bett – these might be hard for you to read. One's about Anna. And Lola's old friend Alex. She's writing about wanting a reunion with them both. Soon.'

Sarah fell silent as Bett started to read. Lola had written about Anna. About seeing her beloved granddaughter again, in heaven or a place like heaven. Bett wasn't completely sure of Lola's religious beliefs, but it was clear that she believed she would see Anna again somewhere, somehow.

I still miss you so much, my darling Anna. A day doesn't go past without me thinking of you. I see something beautiful, I want to tell you about it. I hear something funny, I want to share it with you. I talk to your daughter, our darling Ellen, so often, and I want to tell you how proud I am of her, of you as her mother. But you are not here. I wish every day that I could see you, speak to you, laugh with you. I wish that I could have been the one who got that terrible illness. That I could have taken your place, and that you could be alive now, instead of me. It felt unfair five years ago and it is still unfair now. I talk to you and I want you to answer. And you can't. And that breaks my heart. It always will. I miss you as much today as I did the day you left us. And every day I wish we could be together again.

Lola had written to Alex too.

We didn't get to meet again on earth, Alex. It is one of the great sadnesses of my life. Oh, how we used to talk and laugh, my Alex. The dearest, kindest of men. I don't think you will ever know what good you did me. How you reminded me what love could be. How you showed me that there are still fine men in the world. Honourable men. Yes, I will always wish we hadn't had to separate all those years ago, but I will always respect your reasons. You put family first. And I knew the moment we somehow found each other again, that moment we spoke on the phone, that you hadn't changed. You had followed your life's path in the best way, but you still remained the man I loved. My heart broke for you fifty years ago, and it broke again last year when you left this world before we could meet one more time. But I've still imagined it. So many times. I know we would have talked, laughed and held each other close. I would have seen, once again, the beauty of your gentle spirit, your wit, your kindness. I would have felt cherished. Loved. My dear Alex. Every day I miss talking to you. Every day I wish we were together. Every day I wish it could happen.

Bett was silent for a moment after she finished reading. She rested her hand on the pages.

'I'm sorry if it's upsetting, Bett,' Sarah said. 'But I thought you needed to see it.'

'I'm glad I have. Thank you.'

Sarah left soon after. There wasn't the opportunity for Bett and Daniel to talk yet. She helped him settle the kids to sleep, did the dishes while he loaded the washing machine, put Yvette back to bed after she'd got herself up again, half-tidied the house, soothed Zachary when he had a bad dream, staying with him until he was fast asleep again. Finally, they sat down, at opposite ends of the sofa, Bett's feet resting on Daniel's lap. This was always her favourite part of the day, when work was over, their babies sound asleep, when she could talk to her husband, enjoy looking at his lanky body, shaggy hair, his dark eyes. He listened closely, as always, as she told him about her conversation with Lola and everything Jenny and Sarah had told her.

'Could Sarah be right, Daniel? Would Lola seriously be thinking about taking her own life?'

'Not Lola, of all people.' He paused. 'But then she has always done things her own way.'

Bett abruptly sat up straight. 'She can't. I couldn't bear it, Daniel. I can't imagine life without her. I'll tell her I know what she's planning and I won't allow it to happen.'

'That will work. She's always been so obedient.'

'Daniel, I mean it, this is serious —'

He reached over and hugged her, kissing the top of her curly head. 'Bett, come on. I think you're overreacting. What did Lola say to you today? That she was bored? Lonely? She's not the only person in town to feel like that sometimes, surely. And look what she's doing – filling her days with group activities. Writing about Anna. And Alex. I think that sounds healthy.'

'I wish I agreed.' Bett bit her lip. 'But she also said to me that there's something she needs to do. Something urgent, before it's too late. I'm worried now. I need to tell Dad. And Carrie.'

'Bett —'

She was already dialling her father's number. It went to voice-mail. She left a message, keeping her voice calm, not going into detail, saying that she wanted to have a chat to him about Lola. She rang Carrie next and explained the situation.

'Oh my God!' Carrie said. 'Bett, this is awful! We have to call the police. She might be trying to do it tonight. Hang up, quick, so I can dial triple-0.'

'Carrie, it's not that urgent. I just thought —'

'Of course it's urgent. You ring Dad again and tell him to get to Clare as fast as he can while I ring the police. Or the ambulance. Which should I ring first?'

'Carrie, stop it. She's not doing anything tonight.'

'How do you know? You're the one who said she was leaving suicide notes all over the place.'

'They're essays, not suicide notes.'

'Close enough. You said it yourself, they're like farewell notes, telling Anna and Alex she's on the way to see them. We need to do something, now, before it's too late.'

'Carrie, please, calm down —'

Their conversation went back and forth. Bett finally realised the only way either of them would get any sleep tonight was if they made sure Lola was okay. Carrie was home alone with her three kids while her vet husband, Matthew, was up north working. It would have to be Bett.

Daniel made one more attempt to soothe her. 'Bett, please —'

She already had the car keys in her hand. 'I have to go, Daniel. I'm sorry. I'll be back as soon as I can.'

It was only a five-minute drive from their house in the hills just outside Clare into the town itself. It had just gone ten as Bett knocked at Lola's front door. She knew Margaret was in Queensland visiting her daughter and grandchildren. Another reason to worry, or not to worry?

Lola opened the door, dressed in bright-pink pyjamas and a long silver dressing-gown.

'Bett! What a treat. Are you sleepwalking?'

'Is it too late? You do still stay up till eleven, don't you?'

'Every night. Why limit my excess gin drinking to the daylight hours?'

They'd barely sat down at the kitchen table before Bett explained her visit. 'I had a call tonight from Sarah. About you. About the essays you've been writing.'

'You really do run a spy network. Let me guess, Sarah has nominated me for the Pulitzer Prize?'

Bett hesitated, trying to find the right words. 'Sarah is concerned about your mental health. And after reading your essays, so am I.' She waited for a burst of laughter from Lola. For an amused denial. Nothing. She continued, still carefully choosing her words. 'She feels, and I agree, that everything you've been writing recently reads as if you can't wait to be reunited with people you knew and loved. And that you might want it to be sooner rather than later.'

'She's right. That's exactly how I feel.'

Bett felt a rush of panic again. 'Lola, please, no. It was hard enough when Anna died. I saw what Alex's death did to you too. Please don't put me through that kind of grief again. I can't do it.'

'Yes, you can and yes, you will, I'm afraid. There's no escaping it as a human being.'

'Lola, don't talk like this, please. What's happened? When did you get so morbid?'

'I'm not being morbid, darling. I'm just facing facts. My time left is limited. Please don't get upset. I'm fine about it. I told you, I've given this a lot of thought.'

'But the wrong kind of thoughts. Thoughts about finishing things yourself, and —'

'No, Bett, I won't do that. I promise. I was simply exploring all possible angles in my memoir writing, like the good student I am. When I do finally go, I want it to be as big a surprise to me as it will be to you. But there is something I want to talk to you about. Something I've been thinking about for some time now. I decided for sure tonight.'

Bett waited.

'There's something I need to do. As soon as possible, while I still can. And I would love your help.'

'Of course. Whatever it is. Just ask.'

'I want to go home,' Lola said.

'Home?' Bett was puzzled. 'Back to the motel, you mean?'

Lola shook her head. 'My home. My birthplace. Before it's too late.'

Bett stared at her. 'You mean . . .'

Lola nodded. 'Yes, Bett. I want to go home to Ireland.'

CHAPTER TWO

It was Friday. At any spare moment, in the office or at home, Bett had been researching guided tours to Ireland. She now hopefully had enough information to satisfy Lola.

After the surprise announcement two nights earlier, she and Lola had only had time for a short conversation before Bett's phone had rung. It was Daniel, accompanied down the line by loud screams from both Zachary and Yvette. Nothing urgent, he'd said, well, except that Yvette had fallen over in her cot and hit her head, and Zachary had panicked and started crying, and now he couldn't get either of them to settle and there was a lump on Yvette's head and he was just wondering should he put ice or ointment on it . . . Bett had stopped him there, reached for her car keys and apologised to Lola, promising to research flight packages to Ireland and get back to her as soon as she could.

As she walked up her grandmother's path now, at the arranged time of eleven a.m., she saw the front door was wide open. She could hear pop music playing as she came into the hallway.

'Lola?' she called. 'Hello?'

'In the kitchen, darling.'

Lola was sitting at the table. Two young women in their early twenties were on either side of her. A barely recognisable her.

'That is you under there, isn't it?' Bett said to her grandmother.

Lola opened one eye, peering through a thick paste of cream covering her face. 'Somewhere, yes.'

'I like the new hairdo.'

'Take a bow, Rachel,' Lola said to the young woman on her left. 'Dear Rachel wanted to do an old lady perm but I talked her into this instead.' 'This' was a spiky arrangement of Lola's short white hair. It wouldn't have looked out of place on the cover of a punk music magazine.

'Are those blue tips permanent?' Bett asked.

'What is permanent these days?' Lola said. 'We live in a fragile, ever-changing world.' She introduced both young women to Bett, then promptly ordered them away. 'Pop outside for a cigarette, darlings, or to check your phones or whatever it is young people do to amuse themselves. I need to have a confidential conversation with my granddaughter.'

Bett waited for them to leave before she spoke. 'Did you order them online as well?'

'Of course not. They're from the salon in town. Trainees. They needed guinea pigs to practise on. I said, "I'm more of an old sow than a guinea pig but if you're game, I am." We've had a lovely morning. I look adorable, don't I?'

'Alarming, but adorable.' Bett sat down. 'Lola, I've been doing a lot of thinking since we spoke the other night. About Ireland.'

Lola began to sing a warbling verse of 'Galway Bay'.

Bett ignored her. 'I've been doing lots of research for you. Looking up travel companies. The best times to travel. And travel insurance too.'

'Do they do insurance for people as old as me? Don't bother. If I die when I'm in Ireland, just leave my body there and come back on your own. I won't mind.'

Bett blinked. 'On my own?'

19

'You are coming with me, aren't you?'

'To Ireland?' Bett laughed. 'Lola, I can't.'

Lola's eyes widened through the paste. 'But I can't go alone, surely? An old lady, frail, defenceless, travelling solo across the world? How could you live with yourself if something happened?'

'Lola, stop it. We never even discussed me coming with you. It was all about you going back, not me. How can I possibly go? I've got work. The kids —'

'Such lovely children too. They're a credit to you and Daniel. I thought of asking Carrie to come as well. But that might be too hard, I decided, both of you away. So I tossed a coin. Carrie was heads, you were tails. Or was it the other way around? No matter. You won. Or lost, depending on your attitude to a fortnight in Ireland with your grandmother and your thirteen-year-old niece.'

'My niece?'

'I've invited Ellen too. She said yes immediately. I knew she would. Such a clever young girl.'

'Lola, seriously, stop this. First you decide I'm coming with you. Then you invite Ellen. All without any discussion. It's impossible anyway. Number one, I'd have to ask for time off —'

'You're the boss. Ask yourself. Do it now, if you like. I'll be your witness.'

'— and Ellen's got school too. She can't just take off for two weeks.'

'She can if her school principal gives permission. Which he has. He thought it sounded like a wonderfully educational trip for Ellen. We also agreed that next month would be the perfect time.'

'Next month? So soon? Lola, no. Look, I understand how important this is to you, I promise, but I was sure you were talking about a guided tour of Ireland. I researched a whole selection. I thought perhaps you'd go with one of your friends. Margaret loves to travel, doesn't she? Or even Dad.' She reached into her bag and took out a bulging folder. 'It's all here, brochures, itineraries —'

'Aren't you marvellous? No wonder you're such a good journalist. But let's forget about Ireland for now.' Lola lowered her voice. 'I've got a scoop for you.'

'No, you haven't. You're just trying to distract me. I know your tricks.'

'Of course I'm trying to distract you. You've become quite hysterical. But it really is a good scoop. Fine, though. I won't tell you. If you want someone else to write about it first, so be it.'

'I can't even tell if you're joking with all that cream on your face.'

Lola patted her cheeks. 'You're right. It should come off. I'll look like a baby if it's left on any longer.'

Bett had no choice but to wait as Lola called the two trainees back in. Ten minutes later, they had finished their work, been given generous tips by Lola, packed up their equipment and left.

Bett looked at her surprisingly fresh-faced grandmother. 'What was in that mask? Elixir of youth?'

'Crushed kittens and French champagne, I think. Now, back to my scoop —'

'Forget the scoop. Let's get back to Ireland.'

Lola beamed. 'I knew you'd come round. I truly can't wait. And the sooner we leave, the better, for all our sakes. I'm going to start packing tonight.'

Bett glared at her. 'I swear, if I didn't love you so much, I'd want to murder you sometimes.'

'After all the fuss you made about my alleged suicide notes? That's hypocritical, isn't it?'

'Lola, quite apart from the impossibility of me coming with you work-wise, home-wise, and at such short notice, I'm sorry to put the final dampener on it, but I can't afford it. I'm sure Glenn could pay for Ellen, but that's not the point.'

'You're right, it's not. And getting money out of Glenn is like getting blood out of a stone, we all know that, rich as he is. But you don't have to afford it. I'm paying for it all, darling – from your pre-flight gin and tonic to every glass of Guinness to your eye mask on the flight home.'

'How can you? You don't have any money either.'

'I won't have by the end of this, no. But I do have enough to pay for it now. I sold some shares.'

'Shares? Since when did you have shares?'

'I've had a long and serious life, dear Bett, and you don't know everything about me even if you think you do. Perhaps it wasn't shares. It might have been a diamond ring. Yes, it was a diamond ring. You didn't know I had one, did you? Either way, don't you worry your pretty curly head about it. All you need to know is that my bank account is full to overflowing – well, full to half-full – and I have this covered. So no matter what objections you raise, the financial one won't wash with me, sunshine.'

Bett put her hands over her face and gave a silent scream.

'But as I said, enough about Ireland for now,' Lola continued blithely. 'Back to my scoop. I'd lower my voice for dramatic value, but there's no need, we're the only ones here. I've got some breaking news for you. The mayor is making a big announcement today.'

'I know,' Bett said. 'About a road project or something. It's in my diary already.'

'It's not about roads. It's about something much more exciting than that.' Lola paused for effect. 'Hollywood is coming to the Valley, Bett. Well, not Hollywood exactly. But a film crew from Sydney and a whole cast of fine actors. And surely at least one of them has been to Hollywood at some stage. So at a pinch you could make that your headline, if you think it would fit.'

'Lola, what are you talking about?'

'A TV series. A murder mystery. Being made here, in the Valley.

It's been in the planning for months. There have been location scouts here and everything, visiting the wineries and choosing the different settings. Not that anyone knew it was for a TV series. They were told it was for a tourism video. A good cover story, don't you think? They'll be filming the main exterior shots for a start, I believe. They'll even be at the Gourmet Weekend next month. I understand the interior scenes will be shot in a studio in Sydney. Extraordinary, isn't it? Once it's edited you'll think it was all filmed in the same place, not here and there all over the country.'

'Lola —'

'The working title is *Murder in the Vines*, but that might change.'

'How do you know all this? More to the point, how come I don't and I'm editor of the local paper?'

'Better sources, I suppose. You'll find out soon anyway. I'm just giving you the – what's that saying? The heads up? So you can prepare your questions and not be caught on the hop.'

'How long have you known?'

'About a year.'

'And you're just telling me now?'

'It was a secret before now.'

'But I'm your granddaughter.'

'I was sworn to secrecy. See, I can be discreet.'

'Why is every visit with you like being in an industrial washing machine? Why can't you be like a normal grandmother? Pink-cheeked, baking apple pies and knitting woolly hats?'

'She sounds deranged. Now, off you go and write that scoop. Ring the mayor if you want to get the skinny —'

'The skinny?'

'And if he asks how you know what you know, tell him Deep Throat told you.'

'And the Ireland trip?' Bett said weakly.

'We'll discuss it later. Trust me, darling. It will work out. I'll also ring Carrie and tell her she lost out.'

'I can't trust you. And I haven't said yes to anything. But you're right, Carrie will be furious.'

'Oh, Carrie's always furious about something. But, as it happens, I've had another idea, tailored especially for her. It'll make her feel special and keep her busy, a win-win. It concerns you too, actually. But don't worry about that now. Off you go back to work. You need to be at that council announcement soon. No harm to run a brush through your hair, either. Unless that tousled look is deliberate?'

Bett had just stepped into the office when her mobile rang. She held the phone away from her ear as Carrie launched into a monologue.

'You're seriously going to Ireland with Lola? Next month? That's so not fair. You've already been to Ireland and lived in London and seen far more of the world than I have. All I've ever done is travelled through Asia, and that was a disaster. I was sick half the time and —'

Bett eventually managed to interrupt, keeping her voice calm. 'Do you truly think I had any say? I haven't even said yes. It might not happen anyway. She just needs something to look forward to —'

'It's Lola. It will happen. I can't believe she tossed a coin to decide between us. I bet she didn't even do that, just chose you. You've always been her favourite. If she was going to toss a coin, she should have done it under proper conditions, with an independent observer —'

'From the UN? Carrie, stop it, would you? I'm at work, I can't talk for long. I'm still getting to grips with it myself. How can I possibly go on an overseas trip out of the blue? God knows how

24

Ellen is feeling about it too, the thought of heading to Ireland with her elderly great-grandmother and nearly elderly aunt. Not exactly a thirteen-year-old's idea of a good time, I'm sure.'

'Ellen? Ellen's going too? Lola didn't even mention her. Oh, great. So it's a beautiful three-generational trip, a homecoming for Lola after a hundred years away, and I won't be there. Well, too bad – I'm coming, whether you all like it or not.'

'Carrie, do me a favour, would you?'

'What?'

'Look down.'

There was silence from Carrie.

Bett started to laugh. 'Can I remind you? You are nearly six months pregnant. It's your fourth. You have three other little kids at home. Their names are Delia, aged five and a half, Freya, aged four, and George, aged three.'

Carrie laughed then too. Bett did love that about her sister. Carrie could be petulant and spoilt and infuriating, but in an instant she could see the funny side. It had saved their relationship many times.

'I don't suppose Lola would wait until I've had the baby?'

'If Lola had her way, she'd be at the airport now. I have to go, Carrie. I'll talk about it with you later. I need to be at a council announcement in ten minutes.'

'I know! About that TV series! It's so exciting, isn't it?'

'You too? How come everyone knew about this except me?'

'Lola told me just now. She's also got a great idea for you about promoting it in the paper. Well, not you. Me, as it happens. She said it's a fantastic opportunity tourism-wise and I have to say I agree.'

Bett was back in the industrial washing machine. 'Hold on. You're going to promote this surprise TV series in my paper?'

'Exactly! Lola said she thought it would be great if you got me to write a weekly column about the filming, interview the actors, visit the locations, all that kind of behind-the-scenes stuff people love. She thought you could post it on the paper's website, that the film company would see it as good publicity. I know she also thought it would keep me busy and distract me from being jealous of you all being in Ireland. She's right, actually. And you wouldn't even have to pay me, I'd do it for fun. I know you're losing money at the paper as it is. How many words would you want for each column? And should I take the photos too, on my phone, or would you get Daniel to do those?'

Bett counted to five before she spoke again. 'Carrie, I'll call you back.'

Bett rang Lola as she walked down the main street to the council offices. 'Do you know the most annoying thing about you?'

'Heavens, where do I start? At least you only see me a few times a week. Imagine what it's like for me, with myself every minute of every day. For nearly ninety years. It's a wonder I'm still sane.'

'You're eighty-five not eighty-nine and yes, exactly. You deserve a long-service medal.'

'You've heard from Carrie, I gather? That column is a good idea, isn't it? And Carrie will be great at it. She loves all that film and TV gossip, and it will keep her busy while we're away.'

'And her children won't? But you're right. It is a good idea and she could do it over the phone if she isn't up to driving around. You've thought of everything, haven't you?'

'I do try. You know I didn't toss a coin either, don't you? It had to be you who came with me. Not only because I love you so much. You lived in Ireland far more recently than me. That insider knowledge will be invaluable.'

'I was in Dublin for less than six months, Lola. And I didn't see your childhood home because you sent me to the wrong part of the country, don't you remember? Over to Galway when all the time it was County Kildare you'd grown up in.'

'What a scallywag I am. But you do want to come with me, don't you, Bett?' The joking was gone. There was a different, vulnerable tone to Lola's voice. 'I'm sorry if it feels like I'm bossing you. But I'd love it so much if you and Ellen were there with me.'

Her words went straight to Bett's heart. 'I'll think about it, Lola, I promise. That's all I can say. I'll talk to Glenn about Ellen coming. I'll talk to Daniel about how he and the twins will get on without me for two weeks. I'll talk to my assistant about managing while I'm away.'

'That sounds like a lot of talking to me. Why don't you cut out the middle man and say "Yes, Lola"?'

Bett stopped walking and shut her eyes. There was no point sometimes in even trying to resist.

'Yes, Lola,' she said.

CHAPTER THREE

The following week, Bett's Wednesday walk took longer than normal. The news about the TV series being filmed in the Valley had been subject of the week ever since the mayor's announcement. Reading about it on the front page heightened everyone's excitement. As she walked, Bett fielded questions as if she were not just the paper's editor, but the TV series director, scriptwriter, casting agent and location scout.

'Are they looking for extras?'

'Will they say it's the Clare Valley or are they calling it something else?'

'Is it true Keira Knightley is playing one of the roles?'

She was just one of many actors Bett had heard mentioned. If the rumours were true, half of Hollywood would soon be in the Valley. Not only that, many of them would be staying in the Valley View Motel, Bett's old family business.

At least she'd been able to confirm that particular rumour. She'd spoken that morning to the motel's new managers. Yes, they said, every room had been booked two months earlier. 'We were told it was for a conference. They're very secretive, aren't they?'

They were. Bett and Sam had made many calls between them to try to add detail to their front-page story, but they hadn't learnt much more than Lola had told her, or the mayor had announced. Yes, the working title was *Murder in the Vines*. It was an eight-part series. A murder mystery set in the world of winemaking, with some comedy as well as drama. *Midsomer Murders* meets *SeaChange* meets *A Year in Provence*, someone dubbed it. It would be shown on the ABC at the end of the year, all going well. A tourism bonanza, the mayor had called it.

'Ha, sure,' one of the councillors had muttered at the announcement. 'We'll be fighting off the tourists. I can picture the slogan now: "Come to the Clare Valley, drink wine and be murdered".'

There was an unconfirmed list of the locations that would be used. Bett had spoken to three different people in the production office in Sydney, but had been told each time it was still under discussion. But even if only half the locations on the list were true, it was going to be an exciting time in the area. Three wineries had been chosen, apparently – one of the bigger operations and two of the small boutique ones. All three enjoyed beautiful settings, rolling hills and gum trees. The town hall would be used for one scene. So would the football oval.

It wasn't just the motel that would be booked out, either. Many holiday cottages too, and the caravan park. Bett's early research had indicated that a TV series required a big crew, as well as a big cast of actors. And if it was true that one or two famous names were in that cast, there'd be lots of daytrippers and autograph-seekers making their way to the Valley also. They'd need food, drinks, petrol. So many businesses would benefit. It would be wonderful for the Valley, everyone agreed.

Not quite everyone, of course. As a journalist, Bett knew there were always two sides to every story. Sometimes more. And for every positive reaction, there was always a negative. It was the case now. It would be so disruptive, she was told by one person. How will we find a car park to do our shopping, if they've taken over the main street? What about the other wineries, the ones not being used in the filming? Will people think there is something wrong with them because they weren't chosen?

An elderly woman, one of Lola's fellow volunteers from the charity shop, stopped Bett.

'Does someone have to be murdered? People might think the Valley is unsafe. Can't they just be badly hurt? Or not even badly hurt? Just a few bruises?'

'I don't think someone getting a few bruises would be that dramatic,' Bett said diplomatically. 'A series like this needs a big event to kick off the action.'

'So you've read the script?' the elderly woman asked eagerly. 'Is it as juicy as everyone says?'

Bett couldn't wait to read it. But the producers hadn't only been tight-lipped about the locations. They'd barely given her any information about the script, or the screenwriter. All they'd said was the person had written other successful TV programs and had a working knowledge of the wine industry.

'He or she used to be a winemaker?' Bett asked.

No answer.

'And why film it here in the Clare Valley? Why not one of the other wine regions?'

'The setting was non-negotiable. It was Clare or nowhere.' That was all they'd say, in rhyme or not.

Bett had tried to get more information from the mayor. Had the council paid the TV company to film it locally? It sometimes happened like that, she'd discovered in her crash course of online research into TV-series production.

'No comment,' the mayor said.

It was all some people needed. 'Outrageous! That money should be spent on our roads,' one councillor shouted. 'The TV crew will be here one day and gone the next. Our roads are here to stay.'

A fiery discussion began. Eventually, the mayor was forced to confirm no money had changed hands. 'We signed a confidentiality agreement, so I can't say more beyond stating categorically that the council did not pay them to come here. They invited themselves and we're very happy about that.'

'Invited themselves!' another councillor said. 'Who do they think they are? Marching in here, blocking our roads, booking out our restaurants and motels. What about us? Where are we supposed to eat?'

The mayor wasn't the only one to roll his eyes that time.

Bett had also talked more with Carrie about writing a weekly blog for the paper's website, an insiders' guide to the filming. Carrie was enthusiastic.

'I can't wait. Can I have a pen name?'

'Sure. Lois Lane?'

'Don't be silly. I mean a pseudonym so people wonder who I am and how I'm getting my stories.'

'But aren't you going to visit the set and interview all the actors and the locals about their reactions? Won't that be a giveaway? Unless you were planning on doing it in disguise.'

'Okay, forget the fake name. But can I get business cards? And call myself an investigative reporter?'

Bett found herself counting to five yet again.

It wasn't only the TV series making news in the Valley. As Bett did her weekly walk, Lola's trip to Ireland was hot topic number two.

'Isn't that fantastic about Lola going home!' she was told. 'At her age!'

Bett rang Lola midway through the walk. 'Did you put out a press release? I thought we were going to discuss the details before we told anyone.'

'I was too excited, Bett. I'm sorry. You haven't changed your mind, have you?'

She'd changed it one way and then the other a dozen times. In the end, it was Daniel who'd convinced her to go.

'How often does something like this come up?' he'd said, calmly, sensibly, infuriatingly. 'Lola's right. Going sooner rather than later does make sense. Ellen's got permission to go. You can take time off. You're owed weeks of leave. And of course I can cope. I may need to hire a couple of nannies, maybe a cleaner, perhaps a cook as well, but I'll be fine.'

Talking to Ellen had also helped convince her. Her niece was so excited already. 'Super-excited', as she put it. Bett had spoken to her via Skype several times in the past week, about the Irish trip and the TV series. Ellen was excited about that too. She seemed to be in a permanent state of excitement. The joy of being thirteen, Bett realised.

It still gave her a jolt to see Ellen on screen when they spoke. She was turning into the image of her mother, Anna. The same straight dark hair, cut in a bob. The same pale skin. She was already a young beauty, becoming more confident every year. The scar on her cheek that had made her life difficult as a little girl was now virtually invisible.

Ellen had also already travelled widely for someone her age – her father worked in the advertising business and often was posted to international offices – but she hadn't been to Ireland. Lola had asked her to draw up a wish list of places there she wanted to see. During their most recent Skype call, Ellen had called them out for Bett to write down. It was a long list.

How had she heard of all these places? Bett had asked.

'They've been used as film locations. I found a website about them. I've watched the films too.'

Bett knew Ellen had become a film buff. She'd recently announced she wanted to work in the film industry when she grew up. Not just as an actress like her mother, but as a filmmaker too.

Ellen had reeled off the place names. 'The Cliffs of Moher, used in *The Princess Bride*. And there's a castle in a town called Trim that was used in Mel Gibson's *Braveheart*. Oh, I'd like to go to the leprechaun museum too, even though it's not in a film. And I'd like to try Guinness.'

'You're thirteen years old.'

'Not even a sip? Under controlled circumstances?'

Bett had thought it was Lola who would be the handful. Not Ellen too.

She had Ellen's wish list in her bag as she visited Lola after work the next day. She had a whole folder of paperwork to share, including confirmation of their flights. She'd booked them online the evening before, wincing at the price as she keyed in Lola's credit card number. It was still a mystery how Lola could afford this, though Bett knew better than to ask for any more details.

Sitting in the bright sitting room again, she took Lola through their arrangements so far. They'd fly to Sydney, meet Ellen there, then fly on to Dublin. She gave Lola a printout with the details.

'Perfect, Bett,' Lola said, barely glancing at it. 'I still can't believe it's happening.'

'I still can't believe I'm coming with you. Now, I need to talk to you about where exactly you want to go, but in the meantime, here's Ellen's list.' She handed it over, waiting as Lola read through it.

It really was extraordinary this would be Lola's first trip home in sixty-five years, Bett thought. The young Irishwoman who'd sailed with her new husband, Edward, from Ireland to Holyhead in Wales, taken the train to London and then to Southampton for a five-week sea voyage to Australia could never have known what lay ahead. Or that it would be a new century before she returned.

She wondered if Lola had often been homesick. She'd always seemed so at home in Australia. She'd also rarely talked about her life in Ireland, except when it came to the songs she'd learnt as a child, many of which she'd taught Bett to play on the piano.

It was so different now for young travellers, Bett knew. Not just those from Ireland, but from England, Europe, Asia. Australia was full of them. All in constant contact with their friends and family back home, texting and tweeting and Snapchatting from the moment they landed. When Lola had emigrated, letters must have been the only possible communication. Phone calls would have been impossible or impossibly expensive. Perhaps Lola's parents hadn't even had a phone. Had they ever thought about coming out to visit her? It must have been an impossible dream. Back then, when you said goodbye you must have known —

'Thank you, Bett,' Lola said, handing back Ellen's list. 'I'll look forward to those places too. I've actually seen very little of Ireland. The museum sounds fun, too. I had a leprechaun as a pet when I was a child. Did I ever tell you that?'

'No. And don't tell Ellen either. She'll believe you.' Bett reached for her notebook again, feeling very efficient. She was beginning to enjoy this new unexpected role as travel planner. 'Now, I hope you don't mind, but I started planning our itinerary. I thought we should have a day or two in Dublin first to recover from the flight, and do a bit of sightseeing there, if that sounds okay with you?'

It did, Lola told her. Bett outlined her other plans. She'd mapped it out. They'd collect a hire car on the third day and drive to Kildare, Lola's home county. Bett had researched hotels in the area already. They'd go to the village of Ballymore Eustace first, of course, where Lola had grown up. Visit her family home. Her school. Lola nodded at each.

Bett hesitated. 'I've just realised something sad. You've never seen your parents' graves, have you?'

'No, Bett, I haven't.'

'Oh, Lola, that must have been so hard. Being across the world when they died, not being able to go to their funerals. We'll go to the cemetery as soon as we can, I promise. And you're sure there's none of your family left there at all? Even long-lost cousins you'd like to see?' She knew Lola had been an only child but perhaps there was still some extended family she'd like to meet.

'None that I know of, no.'

'I can try and find them for you if you like. It would be so easy.' Bett felt a shimmer of excitement. 'I could get in touch with the Kildare newspaper. There's probably a radio station too. We could spread the word online as well. It would make such a great story. "Kildare woman returns home after sixty-five years, in search of long-lost family and friends." You'd be a celebrity before we even arrived!'

'No, Bett. I don't want any of that.'

Bett was thrown by Lola's tone. 'But isn't that why we're going? To relive your memories, trace your roots?'

'I told you. There's no one left there that I know. I lost touch with everyone after I moved here.'

Bett persisted. 'But surely you'd know someone? Some of your old schoolfriends, even?'

'Five of them have died. The others emigrated.'

'You've looked them up already?'

'Not on my own. Luke helped me.' Her young computer guru, her friend Patricia's son. He'd recently become engaged to a local girl, Emily. Lola had matchmade them. One of her finest works of meddling, she called it.

'So you did want to meet up with them?'

'No. I wanted to find out where they were so I could avoid them.'

Bett couldn't hide her surprise.

'Ireland is a small country, Bett. And I'm from a very small village. Everyone knew everyone else. All the gossip, everyone's business. The last thing I want to do is run into someone who knew me back then. Who might want to know what happened to me since.'

'But you've had a wonderful life, Lola. A big, beautiful life. And I bet their lives have had ups and downs too. You might really enjoy meeting people from your past again.'

Lola shook her head.

Bett was taken aback. 'What about Edward's sister? The woman who wrote to you after Anna died?'

It was Bett who had inadvertently opened the letter five years earlier, thinking it was a condolence card for the family. They had been arriving in their dozens. It was from a woman called Margaret Hegarty, nee Quinlan, in County Kildare. She'd spotted Lola being interviewed on a quirky travel show about Australia on a cable TV channel, recognised her and got in touch to tell her that her brother Edward, Lola's husband, had recently died in Ireland. He had returned to live there after his time in Australia and then America, she had written. Bett could still recall the final paragraph: *Edward never explained the whole story of your separation but I wish you no ill will, Lola. If you find it in yourself to contact me, I would be pleased to hear from you.*

The letter had come as a terrible shock to Bett. She had grown up believing Lola's husband was killed fighting for the Australian Army during the Second World War. She'd realised then that Lola had been lying to her all her life. Lying to her own son too. To their entire family. She and Lola had fought about it. Over the course of a difficult evening, Lola had told Bett the truth. That she had left Edward soon after they had arrived in Australia, when she'd discovered he not only had a serious drinking problem, but was also violent. He had hit her one evening, after a drinking binge. She'd left him that same week. A month later, she'd discovered she was pregnant. After Jim was born, she'd decided it was better to tell people she was a war widow, rather than face prejudice as a single mother.

Bett was still the only Quinlan who knew the truth. She had kept the secret about Edward from her father, her sister, even from Daniel. It had been difficult, but she had finally understood that Lola had lied for all the right reasons, to protect Jim and to protect herself.

'I'm afraid it's too late to meet his sister,' Lola said. 'She died three years ago.'

'Luke researched that for you too?'

A nod. 'He found a website devoted to Irish deaths and funeral arrangements. It's been very helpful.'

'Did you ever write back to her?' Bett asked. 'After you got her letter?'

Lola shook her head. 'As I said at the time, there didn't seem to be any point.'

'Perhaps she had children. What if I tried to find them? I could do some research online myself.'

'No, Bett,' Lola said. Once again, her tone was firm.

The idea of this being a fun trip down memory lane was rapidly dissolving in Bett's mind. She'd imagined walking around Lola's home village with her, talking to people, hearing stories from the past. Not like this, as if Lola wanted to do it under a cloak of secrecy.

'Lola, I'm sorry, but have I misunderstood? Is this all going to be too difficult for you?'

'I have to go back, Bett, whether it's hard or not. I promised. The day I left. And I'm running out of time to keep that promise.'

About to ask more, Bett was interrupted by Lola's mobile phone ringing. Lola excused herself, answering the call from one of her friends, confirming the details for their next book club meeting.

As she waited, Bett glanced again at her draft itinerary, where she'd listed Lola's family home, her school, the church. She'd underestimated how difficult this homecoming might be for her grandmother. It must have been so hard for her to leave everything she knew in Ireland for a completely unknown life in Australia. She tried to imagine the final farewell to her parents, the tears, the hugs, with Lola promising to come back one day. How heartbreaking too for her parents to farewell their only child. None of them realising that it would be the last time they'd see each other . . .

Bett felt a rush of sorrow, and of guilt. No wonder this was difficult for Lola. She spoke as soon as her grandmother finished her phone call.

'I'm sorry if I was insensitive. It's so sad that you never saw your parents again. And that they never met Dad either. Their only grandchild.'

'That's just how it was, Bett, for so many people back then, not just me and Jim.'

'They saw lots of photos of him, though, didn't they?'

'Not many. Back then you had to go into a studio for photographs. It was none of this casual clicking with cameras and phones you do now.'

'Oh, Lola. You must have wanted to go home again long before now. I wish we'd all thought of it. We could have all clubbed together for your ticket —'

'It was never the right time, Bett. Not just financially. Jim and I were always so busy with our guesthouses. Moving so often. And then the three of you came along. The last thing I wanted to do then was go away, even for a trip overseas. I couldn't leave my beautiful girls.'

Bett didn't need reminding of how much Lola loved them, or how much they loved her in return. The wall of photos behind her was testament to it. As children, Lola had somehow moulded them into an amateur singing group, the Alphabet Sisters, named after the fact their initials were A, B and C. She had taught them show tunes, Irish laments, pop songs of the time. She'd driven them from country shows to talent quests. They'd performed for six years, from when Bett was ten until she was sixteen. Too long, Bett had often felt.

The photos on the wall spanned their entire career, showing the three of them in all manner of appalling costumes. Lola had made them herself. They'd always stood in the same formation – little Carrie on the left, with her pretty face, big smile, lovely golden curls. On the right, Anna, dark-haired, striking, tall and slender. And in the middle, Bett. With her wild curls and plump body that was still curvy now. She'd felt like piggy in the middle. That had been the end of them too, when a teenage boy shouted it at her during their final concert. Their nearly final concert. They'd managed one reunion performance, as adults, just months before Anna died. There had been many photographs taken that night. Bett still found them too sad to look at.

This time Lola consoled her. 'I know who you're remembering, darling. You'll never stop remembering her. And after I go, never stop remembering me either. Promise? Not for a second.'

'Lola, please, don't tease me —'

Lola reached over to tuck a wayward curl behind Bett's ear, as she had done so often. It was one of the most comforting gestures Bett knew. 'I'm sorry. I am an evil grandmother. But I'm truly happy to hear how upset the idea of me dying makes you. Can I stipulate in my will that you wear mourning clothes for a full year afterwards? And that you stand in the middle of the Clare main street every Tuesday at noon and howl at the sky like a dog? Would you do that for me?'

Bett was torn between wanting to laugh and to cry. 'If you wanted me to.'

'I insist. And now, you must go home to your handsome husband and adorable children. That's more than enough talking for one day. We'll have plenty of time on that long flight to cover every topic under the sun. You've done a wonderful job with the organising. I couldn't have wished for more.'

'I'm enjoying it, I promise.' Bett smiled. 'Now the shock has passed.'

'Thank you, darling.' Lola squeezed Bett's hand once again. 'For more than you know.'

After Bett had gone, Lola sat gazing out of the window. Normally this time of the day she would put on a piece of favourite music, make herself a gin and tonic, perhaps read, or even do a jigsaw puzzle. Not now. She simply sat in silence, glad to have the house to herself.

There was so much to think about. So much to prepare herself for. Bett was right. It wasn't going to be easy. Lola had hoped the most difficult of her Irish memories had lost their power by now. She'd had only twenty years there, after all, compared with more than six decades in Australia. But it was as if all her memories had been waiting. The trip had prised open a trapdoor in her mind, letting them out one by one.

Memories of her childhood.

Of Edward.

Of her parents.

She knew Bett had misunderstood her tonight. Before they were interrupted by the phone call, when they were talking about the promise Lola had made to return to Ireland, Lola knew Bett had assumed she was talking about her mother and father.

She should have told her the truth.

Not just about her parents.

She should have told her everything.

CHAPTER FOUR

It was now less than two weeks until their departure. Lola took a seat opposite the doctor's desk, adjusting her shirt.

'I do wish full-body examinations could be done without any examination of the body itself, don't you?' she said. 'Couldn't you get some sort of laser gun and wave that at me instead?'

'If we were in a sci-fi movie, sure,' Dr Lewis said.

'I don't know how you do your job. Every day spent poring over wizened collapsing bodies like mine.'

'You're neither wizened nor collapsing, and if I gave out gold stars, you'd get one for good health. You're doing remarkably well, Lola. I can write to your travel insurance company in good faith.'

'I told you years ago, it's all the gin I drink. It's preserved me from the inside out.'

'I'm glad to hear it. Bring me back a pot of shamrock, won't you?'

'Either that or a pot of gold. There is something else I'd like to ask. It's hard to answer. Impossible, really. So it's more of an idle enquiry. And I won't sue if you get it wrong, I promise.'

'Go ahead.'

'How long do you think I have left to live?'

Dr Lewis raised his eyebrows. 'That's your idle enquiry? Lola, how can I answer that? You might get hit by a bus when you step out of here today.'

'No, I won't. There aren't enough of them in Clare and I can dodge the few there are.'

'You could have another sort of accident. Or you might live happily for another twenty years without any mishaps at all. It might be me who gets hit by a bus.'

'Too ordinary. It would have to be a BMW, surely?'

'What's sparked this, Lola?'

'My trip. I'm scared.'

'You know statistically plane travel is safer than car travel?'

'I'm not scared of dying on the way. Or once I'm there. I'm scared of dying before I go. We're leaving in eleven days. Will I make it to then?'

'If I was a betting man, I'd put thirty dollars on it.'

'Only thirty? Your confidence overwhelms me.'

'I'll make it fifty. Don't worry. It'll be some trip home. You'll notice so many changes.'

'They have running water and motor cars now, apparently. It was wells and donkeys when I was there. I'm joking. We even had light switches in our house.'

'I was there for a week once. Back in the eighties. My wife and I loved it. Didn't see a drop of rain the entire time, though. Blue skies and sunshine every day. We wanted to complain about false advertising.' He stood up. 'You're in fine health. I think you'll make it there and back again. You'll also have Bett and Ellen by your side. Enjoy it, Lola. Doctor's orders.'

Back at home, with time to pass before her afternoon book club meeting, Lola made herself a cup of tea and took it out onto the

42

verandah. The sky was blue, the air crisp: a perfect autumn day. It was one of the prettiest times to be in the Valley, all the vineyards slowly changing colour, the thick green being smudged with outlines of red and orange, misty mornings giving way to clear fresh days. It was good timing for the TV series, too. Not just to take advantage of the wineries being busy with vintage, but as an opportunity to fill TV screens with great natural beauty as well. The Valley had been described once as the Tuscany of Australia. Lola had never quite got to grips with that. It was Australia, not Italy – celebrate it for its own charm, not as a copy of somewhere else, that was her opinion. But she did concede there were some similarities – the gentle rolling hills, small villages, stone buildings warmed by golden sunlight . . . The tourism folk should hire her to write their brochures, she decided, pleased with the image she was painting in her mind's eye.

The whole Valley was still abuzz with the news of the TV series. Bett had run even more stories about it. Carrie was telling everyone in town about her forthcoming blog. The producers were very happy with the publicity, Bett had told Lola, but were still unforthcoming with extra details.

'All they'll keep saying is it's written by someone with an insider's knowledge of the wine industry. And that it's an international cast. I'm dying to find out the names.'

Bett had been dying to find out more than the names. She'd asked Lola several times if she knew anything else. Even a snippet. Each time Lola had lied and said she didn't. The truth was, she knew exactly who had been cast. She'd known for weeks. So had the producers. They were just waiting for the optimum time publicity-wise to make the announcement. It would cause quite a stir, Lola knew. Especially the English actor in the leading role. Lola was old enough to be his mother – or his grandmother, in fact – but she did still hope there'd be an opportunity to have a close look at him. It wasn't every day a heartthrob came to town. He would be perfect in the role, she thought.

She knew all about the other roles in the series too. She knew the storyline. She had read all the scripts. If she had wanted to, she could even have had a credit as script consultant, she'd been told. She'd politely declined. Best to keep one's head down sometimes, she'd said to her source.

'But thank you all the same, darling,' she said last time they spoke. 'It's been such great fun.'

His initial phone call had come out of the blue, eleven months earlier. She hadn't recognised the Sydney number, but she'd known his voice the second she heard it. One of her favourite young men in the world. Well, young in her eyes at least. She'd been surprised when he told her he was now in his early forties. 'It only seems like yesterday you turned up at my front step, like a bedraggled cat. What were you then, seven years old? Eight?'

He'd laughed. 'Nineteen. I turned twenty while I was working for you. Don't you remember the cake you made me?'

'One of my finest creations.' She did remember it. Once she set her mind to it, she remembered everything about him. In all her time running hotels all over Australia, the Valley View Motel for the longest – twenty years – she had employed hundreds of seasonal workers, as waiting staff, cleaners, gardeners. This young man had always had a firm place in her memory.

His name was Tom Nikolić. His arrival – with him soaked through, hair and clothes – at the Valley View Motel reception one rainy afternoon hadn't been a surprise. The previous day, Lola had received a phone call from her friend, one of the priests connected with the Sevenhill church and winery. They were coming to the end of the grape harvest, about to farewell the team of travelling workers. Most would move on to another region or state and start picking other crops.

She and the priest had a short conversation. This young man came from a troubled background, Lola learnt. He was hardworking. He was trying to make a new start in life. He was travelling in a group, but the priest had guessed Tom would be happier away from them. They'd been in the Riverland for the past few years. Drugs were a problem there. 'He doesn't want that. He's bright. Did surprisingly well at school. If he had another job offer here in the Valley, it'd help him break away.'

Lola always needed an extra pair of hands at the motel. They had fifteen guest rooms, a busy restaurant and function room, a garden of sorts. Her son and his wife worked hard too, but they couldn't do everything. Anna, Bett and Carrie were all in their teens now, busy at school, with after-school pursuits. They helped out, but neither Lola nor Jim and Geraldine wanted them to be entirely tied to the motel. A new addition to their roster of casual staff was always welcome.

'Leave it with me,' she said to the priest. While Jim was officially the manager, it was still Lola's motel; they all knew that. A brief conversation with Jim sorted it out. She rang the priest again. The next day, Tom himself arrived.

Lola quickly saw that the priest was right. Tom wasn't the usual happy-go-lucky itinerant worker, saving up for overseas travel or being content to live without any real security. She brought him into the empty motel kitchen, made him a large sandwich and a mug of coffee. She was always quick to decide about people – a skill she'd learnt as a guesthouse manager. Within minutes she knew that she liked him. He was nervous, but he met her eye. He spoke quietly but firmly about being a hard worker, willing to try anything. She guessed that he didn't have anywhere to live. The vineyard workers either slept cheaply at the caravan park or camped. He'd been living with his fellow workers, he said, but they were moving on, taking their tents with them.

'One of the rooms here at the motel needs painting,' Lola told him. It was the truth. They'd had a leaking gutter, leading to paint damage inside. There hadn't been the chance to repaint yet. It had been out of action for guests. 'It also needs rewiring. If you can put up with flaking walls and faulty lights until we fix it, you can call that one your own, free of charge, while you're working here.'

'I could repaint it for you,' he said. 'Instead of paying rent.'

'Even better,' Lola answered. She told him the basic wage she could pay him. They agreed on a three-month trial period. He started the next day.

Her daughter-in-law, Geraldine, wasn't happy about it. 'We could have done his work between us. Can we afford another wage?'

Lola kept her temper. Years of practice dealing with Geraldine helped. She and her son's wife had never got on. Lola had reached the conclusion they never would. 'We'll all work better with some free time now and again. And much as I love climbing up and down ladders, Tom loves it even more. All these months picking apples and grapes, he's like a circus performer.'

'It can be as much work being in charge of a new employee,' Geraldine said. 'When am I going to find the time to look after him, with everything else I have to do, not just with the girls but —'

Lola interrupted. It was the only way she could deal with Geraldine, by limiting her complaining as much as possible. 'He's my protégé, Geraldine. You needn't give him another moment's thought.'

She – and Tom too, as it turned out – soon realised the word 'protégé' was a good one. Her instincts proved correct. He was a quick learner. What he didn't know he asked. In his first week, he brought all the undergrowth around the motel under control, mowing and weeding. In his second week, he prepared not just his room but all the rooms for painting. The third week, he did the painting itself. By the end of his fourth week, Lola called him in.

She didn't need to wait for the full three-month trial period, she told him. She was happy. They decided on the job description of handyman. That night, she gave him something more than a job title. A pile of books. She'd noticed he was spending his time in his room at night watching TV. He was saving, he'd told her. He didn't want to go into town and spend his money at any of the three pubs. He wasn't sporty, so he had no plans to join the football club or cricket club either.

He was grateful for the books. They weren't hers, she said. She'd borrowed them from the library on his behalf. A couple of literary novels, two thrillers, a non-fiction book on politics and a slim volume of poetry. She'd chosen them in conjunction with the librarian, an old friend of hers.

The next week he returned them to her.

'You didn't like them?'

'I loved them. Can I please have some more?'

She took him to the library with her the next day. From then on, he chose his own books.

When his father turned up two months later, Lola was ready. She and Tom had had enough conversations by then for her to know what to expect and also what support Tom would need. When he told her his father was on his way, she noticed the nervous version of him was back.

'Your father is very welcome,' Lola said. But she was glad the visit coincided with Jim and Geraldine's day off. They were taking the girls on a day trip to Moonta.

The father was drunk when he arrived. The abuse started soon after. Lola made it her business to be cleaning one of the rooms up from Tom's. The older man was asking for money. He switched between English and Croatian, swearing. When Lola heard the first sound of violence – a slap – she decided it was time to act.

She opened the door to Tom's room and drew herself up to

her full height. Years of dealing with drunk patrons gave her the confidence and steel she needed.

'Enough!' she shouted.

The shock of a female Irish voice stopped the older man, his arm raised. Tom was shaking, she noticed. There was also a red mark on his face.

'You have two choices,' Lola said to his father. 'Leave now and don't come back. Or stay here and talk to the police I'm about to call.'

'This is my business. Get your nose out of it.'

'This is my motel. Your son is my employee. Under article seventeen, item fifteen of the Workers Rights Act of 1973, I am duty-bound to step in on behalf of any of my employees when I feel their safety is being threatened or unreasonable demands are being made of them.' There was no such Act, as far as she knew, but the tone and the stream of officialese worked.

Tom tried to make the peace. Lola guessed he'd tried many times over the years with his father. It didn't work, if it ever had. In front of Lola, his father started to pull open the cupboard drawers beside the bed, clearly looking for money.

At that moment, a siren sounded. It was the weekly trial run of the town's fire alarm, sudden and loud enough to make most people jump, no matter how used to it they were. Lola saw the father take a step back, to hesitate. It was the opportunity she needed.

'I'm calling the police now. They're just down the road. They'll be here in a minute.'

She walked swiftly back towards the office. She wasn't going to ring the police. She knew from experience that they could take some time to reach her. But her hunch paid off. Minutes later, she heard the sound of a car starting. Tom's father's car. She watched through the office window as he drove away.

Tom didn't come to her immediately. She respected him for that, as she respected him even more that evening when he did come.

He wanted to offer his resignation. It wasn't fair for her to have to see scenes like that, his private life getting mixed up in his working life. His father had left without any money today but chances were he'd be back.

'Fine,' Lola said. 'And when he comes, we'll ask him politely to leave again. And the next time. And the next time. Until he stops bullying you and threatening you.'

Tom didn't answer. He just stared at her.

'Why are you helping me?' he said, finally.

'Because I can.' There was more she could have said but it wasn't the time or the place for her own story. 'Tom, does your father hit your mother?'

A nod.

'And he's hit you often? Since you were a little boy?'

A long pause and then another nod.

'I don't know how I can help your mother,' Lola said. 'I wish I could, but —'

'She's got good friends,' he said, interrupting. 'They've been telling her for years to leave him.'

'Please tell her to listen. If she needs outside help, give her my number. But you don't have to put up with it any more. You're your own person, not just his son. You're a hard worker, a bright young man. You're a handyman now, but you can be more than that. I know you'll be more than that.'

Over the next few months, he relaxed. If his father got in touch with him again, Lola didn't hear about it. She saw his confidence growing, in the way he worked, the way he spoke to her. He kept reading. A conversation with the priest put the idea in her mind. She sent away for the brochures and one night, during one of their regular, casual catch-ups, she gave Tom a padded envelope.

He opened it, frowning, looking at the bundle of forms. 'University?'

She explained. It was in Adelaide, in the city centre. The church had a boarding house nearby. They chose several scholarship students each year. 'Our priest has recommended you. I'll write you a reference.'

'What would I study?'

'Anything you want.'

He chose history and literature. When the university students went back in the following February, Tom was among their ranks. As the three years of his degree passed, he kept in touch. He flourished on campus, joining clubs and associations. The film society. A drama group. He was a terrible actor, he told Lola – she had to agree, after travelling to Adelaide to see him in one production. But it turned out his quietness, his observation skills, his watchfulness, honed during the years of reading his father's moods, had given him the skills he needed to start writing himself. A play first. He didn't go far from his own life for subject matter. It was a drama between an emigrant father and his son. After that, it was as if he had written the darkness and violence out of himself. His next play was a comedy. His shy exterior disguised a wry sense of humour, a quick wit. The following year, he moved to Sydney. Within three months, he met and fell in love with a TV actor called Lawrence.

Lola wasn't at all surprised Tom was gay. She'd guessed years earlier, possibly even before he had known for sure. Lawrence was from a wealthy Sydney establishment background. Plenty of funds were available for them to start their own production company. In the past ten years, Lola had watched proudly as friends talked about this TV program or that series they had enjoyed watching. She never mentioned that she knew the writer. But she passed on every compliment to Tom.

It was Tom who'd offered her a credit as script consultant on the forthcoming TV series. 'Half of the ideas came from you, Lola. More than half. You deserve it.'

'And get chased out of town by people waving pitchforks? No thanks. I'm happily hiding behind the cloak of anonymity. I loved helping you. That's all the payment I need.'

It was true. When he first got in touch and told her he was writing a comedy–drama series set in the wine world, the action sparked by a murder in episode one, her interest was immediately ignited. She was even happier when he told her he was basing it on his memories of working in the Valley.

'Please tell me the star is an elderly Irishwoman running a motel?' she said. 'I'd like Maggie Smith to play me, if her Irish accent is good enough.'

There wasn't an Irishwoman in the cast, he told her regretfully. But there were lots of winemakers in the story, and international wine buyers, and other characters – a restaurant owner, a shop owner. One of them would be bumped off in the first episode, and it would turn out at least six people had good reason to be the killer.

In a series of phone calls over the next few months, she shared the stories she'd heard since she arrived in the Clare Valley. She told him tales of winemaker egos running unchecked, expressed in the old joke: 'What's the difference between God and a winemaker? God doesn't think he's a winemaker.' She told him of the jealousy when one won an award, and another didn't. Of sabotage. Of wine thefts. Of extramarital affairs. In the 'real' world, she was discreet with her insider knowledge of the Valley's shenanigans. This was different. This was research. It was also great fun.

Tom sent her the script when he finished it. She laughed in places. She held her breath in others, as the tension built. She marvelled at how spare the writing was, how just a few lines on a handful of pages would be turned into a whole episode. She was thrilled when he rang her to say the investor funding was in place, and the series was definitely going ahead. When he told her he would do his best to have it filmed in the Valley, she happily – and, once again, confidentially – supplied him with a list of key people to speak to. It wouldn't be called the Clare Valley in the series, of course. It was a drama, not a documentary or tourism promotion. But it would still benefit them all. The street used in *Neighbours* welcomed thousands of visitors each year, after all. So did the town in Cornwall used for *Doc Martin*.

She found it surprisingly easy to keep the news to herself. Only after Tom gave her the go-ahead did she tell Bett, and even then Bett had been about to find out. It was a shame she would miss some of the filming while she was in Ireland, but it couldn't be helped.

Ireland.

In less than a fortnight she would be back home in Ireland. A shiver passed through her.

She still didn't know if it was nerves or excitement.

CHAPTER FIVE

As soon as Lola walked into her friend Patricia's living room later that day, she knew every member of the book club had been talking about her.

'Hello, everyone. Am I planning to take my own life? No, I'm not. Am I going home to Ireland to take my own life? No, I'm not. Am I the scriptwriter of this TV series everyone's talking about? No, I'm not.'

'Damn,' said Patricia. 'I was sure I'd got three out of three.'

'Oh, Lola. Give us a bit of fun,' Kay, another of her friends, said. 'Couldn't you have pretended?'

'She's right,' said Joan, another friend. 'You could have kept us titillated for weeks.'

Patricia nodded enthusiastically. 'I heard you were planning on turning the motel into a right-to-die headquarters. That doctor, the one they call Doctor Death, was taking over the lease.'

Kay lowered her voice. 'I heard that the TV series won't be going ahead because one of the winemakers insists the main character is based on him and that's libellous.'

It was based on him, as it happened, Lola knew. And it had been carefully checked by lawyers for potential libel. A few changes had rendered it legally harmless.

Joan spoke again. 'I heard you've got a big inheritance waiting for you in Ireland, a castle or a big manor house, and you're going back to claim it.'

'I heard that one too,' said Kay. 'It had been used by the IRA or something but now that there's peace there they've given it back.'

Lola wished Tom was there. He'd be getting enough ideas to fuel another six TV series.

'All lies, I'm afraid.' She sat down. 'So, who wants to start? Is Anna Karenina a victim or a heroine?'

Afterwards, as was their custom, Lola, Joan, Patricia and Kay went for tea and cake. They moved their business around town, trying out the different restaurants or the new winery cafes. Today they decided on a visit to an old favourite, Lorikeet Hill Winery on the main road. It was a chilly afternoon so they gladly took a seat inside by the open fire. Outside, the vineyards glowed red and orange.

They began as they had for some years now, raising their teacups to the memory of departed friends. The list grew longer every year. Lola added a silent extra toast to Alex and Anna. Not that Lola needed tea or this ritual to be reminded of either of them. She would feel Anna's presence even more strongly soon, with two weeks in Ellen's company. Thank God for her great-granddaughter. A living link with Anna, with her own sparky personality.

She tuned back in in time to hear Kay talking about her neighbour's daughter. She'd got into trouble at school, apparently. Taken suggestive photos and posted them online, against school guidelines. A lively discussion began, the merits and problems of social media vigorously debated.

'The kids of today live their entire lives through a screen.' Patricia sighed. 'It makes childrearing and babysitting easier, I'm sure, but it can't be healthy.'

'Oh, speaking of babysitting,' Kay said. 'Look at these photos

I took of my grandson at the playground last week. Isn't he a pet!' She pulled out her phone and showed them the photos.

It prompted Patricia to take out her iPad and show a funny YouTube clip of a dog on a swing. That reminded Joan of a video she'd made of her cat Boo-Boo chasing a toy mouse around the living room.

Lola sat back, her phone tucked away in her bag, and said nothing.

In her house two kilometres away, Bett was in the middle of a fight. Not with Daniel, or any friends, or even with Carrie. She was having a stand-off with her toddler daughter. Bett wanted Yvette to wear her yellow dress. Yvette was having none of it. Bett's phone rang, interrupting the argument. She was glad. A bit of breathing space wouldn't do either of them any harm.

Moments later, she was wishing she hadn't answered. It was her friend and predecessor as editor of the *Valley Times*, Rebecca Carter. In the past year, Rebecca had moved from being a working journalist to taking on a full-time position in the journalists' union.

'It's bad news,' Rebecca said, straight to the point as always. 'The *Valley Times* is going up for sale. The owners are selling their entire newspaper portfolio. Six regional papers. I've seen the proposal documents. If they sell or even if they don't, they're going online only by the end of the year.'

Bett had half-expected the news. The confirmation still gave her a jolt. 'So they won't close completely? They'll still need editors and reporters?'

'Half as many, according to what I read. The ads will be sold from a central office interstate. The editorial content will be shared between newspapers.'

'But then it won't be a local paper any more. People won't read it.'

'They say that people aren't reading it as it is.'

'But they are. If they saw how many times I get stopped each week on the street —'

'They don't care, Bett. It's all about circulation and advertising. And the figures aren't good enough. I'm sorry.'

Normally she and Daniel waited until the twins were in bed before they had any serious discussions. That night he was barely in the door from work before she blurted out her worries.

'I can't go to Ireland, Daniel. My job's at risk. I can't just up and leave in the middle of —'

'"Hello, Daniel. How was your day?" "Good, thanks, Bett."'

'Sorry.' She gave him a sheepish smile.

There was a squeal from the living room, followed swiftly by a squeal from the twins' bedroom. Bett ran in one direction, Daniel in the other.

It was nearly nine before they could talk again. Bett explained all that Rebecca had told her.

'You knew something like this was on the cards, didn't you?' he said. 'And they still have to get a buyer. Nothing will change until then. You can't cancel your Irish trip because of "what-ifs".'

'But what if —?' She stopped. 'Sorry. You're right. Thank you. Enough about me.' She asked him about his day. It had been his turn to visit his mother in the care home in Adelaide. Mrs Hilder had been diagnosed with Alzheimer's ten years earlier. In the beginning, Daniel had done his best to care for her in their family home, returning from Melbourne for that reason. But her condition had deteriorated rapidly. For the past two years she had been in a home in Adelaide. Daniel drove to see her twice a week, sometimes more, alternating with his sister Christine.

He rubbed his eyes. 'No change. The nurses say Mum's calmer

after my visits, but they're being kind. She doesn't know if I'm there or not, or who I am most of the time. She called me Teddy today.'

'Who was Teddy? Your mum's brother? I thought his name was Kevin.'

'Teddy was the family dog. I know I need a haircut but . . .'

Bett bit back a smile. 'I'm sorry, Daniel.'

'Me too.'

Soon after, they sat down to dinner, a hastily prepared pasta meal. They clinked their glasses of shiraz. 'So, is your Irish itinerary all sorted?' Daniel asked.

'Not yet. I'm still waiting on some addresses from Lola. It's so strange. I thought she'd want to come back in the flashiest way possible. Hire a bright-yellow convertible, sit in the back like a queen, waving at everyone. But it's like she wants to come in under cover of darkness, then slip out again. She's like a different person. Vulnerable, somehow.'

'She's eighty-five years old, Bett. She's not an Amazonian warrior queen.'

'She is to me. I always felt like she was the one protecting me. This time, I'm in charge of her. I'm nervous too. What if something goes wrong?'

'As in what if she dies while you're away? You'll deal with it, Bett.'

'But what if she gets sick? What if Ellen gets sick? What if I get sick?'

'You'll get firsthand experience of the Irish health system, I suppose.'

'And what about the road signs? How will I follow them, and drive? I mean, I only lived in Dublin a short while. I barely got out into the countryside when I was living there, but everyone told me it's impossible to find your way around once you get off the motorways, that the signs are all pointing in the wrong direction and sometimes they're in miles and sometimes in kilometres and —'

'Why don't you hire a driver?'

'— I'm not the most confident driver anyway. I drove straight off an international flight once before and I nearly crashed. It's so dangerous to drive with jet lag, I can't believe it's legal. Are you laughing at me, Daniel Hilder? What's so funny?'

'You and your overactive imagination. I haven't seen it at full-tilt like this for a while. I'm also trying to get a word in. Why don't you hire a driver? It would take all the pressure off you.'

Bett laughed. 'Sure. Very Hollywood. We swan about in a black limousine with tinted windows trying to be as inconspicuous as possible?'

'It doesn't have to be a limousine. Or have tinted windows. A friend of mine did it in Italy once, when he took his mother back to her homeplace. He said it was the best money he ever spent. No looking up maps or worrying about parking. They sat in the back and talked, and saw things.'

'It would be so expensive. We can't afford it.'

'No, we can't. But Lola might be able to. She told you, no expense spared. Talk to her about it.'

'What a marvellous idea!' Lola said immediately when Bett phoned and explained. 'Dear, thoughtful Daniel. I've been worrying about you and your driving, ever since we started talking about the trip.'

'What's wrong with my driving?'

'Nothing. You're a very capable driver. Very enthusiastic. I'd just prefer you kept to bumper cars rather than the open road.'

'Then maybe you should have asked Carrie to go with you, not me. She's a great driver.'

'And maybe you should grow up and stop sulking or I'll cancel the whole trip.' Bett could hear the smile in Lola's voice. 'You never cease to amuse me, Bett Quinlan. I know you're a grown woman but you sometimes sound exactly like your five-year-old self. We don't change inside, do we? Only our outer shell ages. I used to feel about twenty-two inside. I think I'm back to being nineteen now.'

'Nineteen? The age you were when you left Ireland for Australia?'

'Nearly correct. I was twenty. Not quite a child bride. We left for Australia the day after the wedding.'

'So soon? Did I know that? Why —'

Lola interrupted. 'I told you, we'll have the entire flight to go over the minutiae of my fascinating life, darling. In answer to your main question, yes please to a driver. I love the idea. Ask for one with a nice ordinary car, though, please. Nothing flashy.'

'Drat. I was thinking of a motorbike with three side cars. One for each of us.'

'All right, then. Make mine silver, will you? Now, off you go and leave me and my gin in peace.'

Five kilometres away, in their recently renovated farmhouse, Carrie was following Matthew around.

'But Caroline Quinlan does sound better, doesn't it?'

'You've never called yourself Caroline in all the years I've known you.'

'This is different. This is a career move. I'm a journalist now.'

'A journalist? You're writing a few blog posts for Bett's newspaper, not infiltrating the White House.'

'Don't be patronising. This could be the start of a brand-new career for me.'

'Another one? How is it different to all your other brand-new careers? The online angel dolls? The makeup parties?'

'That's so mean of you to dwell on my failures. Do you know J. K. Rowling got rejected four hundred times before she published *Harry Potter*? That loads of people turned down The Beatles? Failure is the stepping stone to success. In fact, I might put that on my website as an inspirational quote.'

'What website?'

'I'm getting my own website. To host all my columns and blog posts.'

'I thought you were just putting them up on the newspaper site.'

'To begin with, sure. But people will want to read my writing on other subjects as well. I've been researching it. I need to get my own hook apparently. My USP, it's called. Unique Self Personality, or something like that. I read about an American woman who married an Irish farmer and wrote about the culture shock and got a book deal and everything. And I found another blog by a high-flying businesswoman who moved to the country. She was so hilarious about picking up a pig for the first time. Or maybe it was a rooster. I could so easily write those kinds of "eek-an-animal" articles too.'

'Carrie, I'm a vet. Remember those things I work with every day? That you help me with sometimes? They're called animals.'

'I know that, Matthew. That subject's been done anyway. Maybe I should become a vegetarian. I could write about my internal struggle between wanting to live an ethical life and what you do for a living, helping farmers keep their animals as healthy as they can before they kill them for food.'

'I think my job is a bit more complicated than that.'

'Or maybe I should write about being a town girl who turned into a country girl.'

'We live five minutes outside the town. It's hardly the outback.'

'Or maybe the kids? People love reading about funny things kids say. What's the funniest thing any of ours have said lately?'

Matthew stared blankly at her.

'I'll have to start writing them down,' Carrie said. 'Maybe I could ask my friends and borrow some of their kids' sayings instead, until I can remember ours. Our kids are funny sometimes, aren't they?'

'Maybe you could just write about the TV series for starters. The way you've been asked to do. And see what happens after that.'

'Okay. But I'll still ring Luke now, and get him to set me up.'

'Luke?'

'Lola's friend. That geeky guy who knows everything about computers. I was thinking I might even record some videos for my blog, me interviewing the actors, walking around the set. That's got a name too. Vlogging. As in video and blogging put together, isn't that clever? I could become a vlogger and a blogger. Maybe we could do a joint website, Matthew. That could be my USP. We could call it "The Vet and the Vlogger". What do you think?'

'I'll be in the shed,' he said.

Luke was at Lola's when Carrie rang him. Lola had been having trouble with her internet connection in the past week. As usual, Luke had diagnosed and fixed it within a few minutes.

'You truly are an angel of modern technology, Luke,' Lola said. 'What would I do without you?'

'Probably learn how to do it yourself. Is there anything else you need?'

'Not at all. Off you go to Carrie. But don't take any nonsense from her, will you? I adore her, as I adore both my grandchildren and all my great-grandchildren, but she's inclined to be a bit giddy. She asked me yesterday what she should wear to her book launch. "What book launch?" I asked. The book she would write about her experiences doing blogs and vlogs, she told me. All this before she's written a single word. Whatever a vlog is. It sounded like something nasty you might find growing on your heel.'

Luke grinned. 'It's an online video blog.'

'Is that all? I might start a vlog myself. I could vlog about my trip to Ireland, couldn't I?'

'I'd watch it. So would Emily.' His fiancée was one of Lola's biggest fans.

'Thank you, Luke. And please thank Emily too. Now, off you go. I have to do some secret rummaging and it's really not something you'd want to see.'

CHAPTER SIX

Lola made herself a gin and tonic before settling by the fire in the living room. It was fake, lit by the flick of a switch, but with realistic glowing logs and a real flame. Margaret had installed it, declaring she was too old to be worrying about the mess of wood, kindling and ashes. Lola had to agree.

As a child, she'd spent too many cold mornings ferrying ashes out in a large tin bucket, or bringing coal in from the big scuttle in the shed at the end of their garden, hearing the crunch of frost underfoot as she ran back into the comparative warmth of the kitchen.

She could almost hear the frost crunching, see the kitchen now. It was happening more often, these sudden, vivid memory flashes. Memories of her home life. Of her primary school days in their small village, then at the secondary school she'd attended in the nearby town of Naas. The previous day she'd had a memory of cycling to school while balancing a poetry book on the handlebars, doing her homework at the last minute yet again. She'd had memory flashes of rare days out in Dublin too. Even the one summer holiday she and her parents had taken to the seaside town of Bray in County Wicklow, where miraculously the sun had shone every day for the entire week. She remembered an afternoon on the beach, playing with the daughter of another holidaying family, the two of them burying their legs in the sand and sculpting mermaid tails. The memory had been so strong, it was as if she could feel the sand on her skin.

Going home would be a shock, she knew that. She'd read enough articles, seen films, heard interviews with emigrants. She'd imagined it enough times herself in the early days too. Pictured herself standing in front of her family house. Imagined seeing her parents again.

Her parents.

She had only two photographs of them. She didn't need to go to her dresser and retrieve them to remember them. Both black and white, taken long before colour photographs were common or even possible. Both formal, as photographs from that time usually were. One of her as a five-year-old, standing between her parents. All in their Sunday best. She was the only one smiling. The other had been taken fifteen years later, again in formal clothes, her a girl of twenty standing between them in a two-piece suit. She looked solemn. Her father's expression was stern, her mother unsmiling. It had been her wedding day.

Her father was the principal of the primary school in Ballymore Eustace, her home village, better known simply as Ballymore. She'd attended his school. Her mother taught piano students, either at the well-polished upright piano in their house or, occasionally, visiting students in their own homes, the few who had their own pianos. Lola – or Louisa, as she had been christened and was still called by her father – had been expected to study hard too.

It was her mother who'd first taught her the piano, drilling her in scales, insisting she practise at least an hour a day. She'd then been handed over to an elderly piano teacher who visited twice weekly. Her parents hoped Lola would become a teacher too, of music as well as other subjects. They didn't just hope it, they expected it. They'd expected many things in regard to her. That she would be better behaved than she was. That she would be less disobedient. Less outspoken. Less opinionated. A different person altogether.

They definitely wouldn't have approved if they'd discovered through village gossip that she was 'doing a line', as dating was called then, with Edward Quinlan. She'd too easily been able to imagine her father's reaction if he had heard.

'You're seeing one of the Quinlans? The gardener's son?'

She'd always been aware of the class divide in their village. It was obvious on many levels, from the houses people lived in, the clothes they wore, their occupations, the way they spoke. At the top – if that was how you looked at it, which Lola never had – was the 'gentry'. The families that lived in the grand estates in their part of Kildare. The Anglo–Irish families, living in many-roomed mansions, their children taught by tutors or sent up to Dublin or back to England to boarding schools.

The irony was that it was through her father that she had met Edward. Under normal circumstances, they might never have crossed paths. Her father kept a too-close eye on her and her mother. Lola never understood how her mother put up with it. The questions each day about what she had done – in an accusing, not an interested way. The criticism of the cleanliness of the house or the meals she cooked. The constant stories of his own excellence as a teacher, as a headmaster, subtly painting himself as a superior member of their small community. Lola had attended his school only for her primary years, before going to the nuns at the convent school in Naas. Her father was clever, but he wasn't respected. He was feared. The other children had always been wary of her too, as his daughter.

It was no wonder she had become rebellious. For as long as she could remember, she'd hated being told how to behave, how to dress, how to talk. She didn't want to be a good, kind, obedient young woman if it involved never speaking her mind, always feeling suppressed. If she'd been her father's son, not his daughter, would life have been easier? Only if she was prepared to be his mirror image, she suspected.

She always knew that he wasn't happy with her the way she was. That he wanted her to be more like her mother. Petite, quietly spoken. Obedient. Instead, Lola was the cuckoo in the nest. Tall, five foot nine before her sixteenth birthday. Dark-red hair that wasn't obedient either. Even at the convent she was regularly told off about it. She often threatened to cut it off. Long hair took too much looking after, she'd decided. It wasn't until she had moved to Australia, after she'd left Edward, when Jim was two or three, that she finally did it. She still recalled the freedom of it. She'd kept it short ever since, long before Judi Dench or Mia Farrow made such haircuts fashionable. When her hair turned not grey but white, the year she was sixty, she liked it even more.

The nuns in Naas had tried to manage her. She was an excellent student, so they forgave her some transgressions in behaviour as long as they didn't impact on her studies. She was busy outside of school too. Her father tutored children after classes and Lola had started to assist him. Her idea, not his. She enjoyed it. She was sociable from an early age.

Music was her real passion. Something special happened when she was at the piano. There was no one controlling her then. She could play whatever she pleased, let whatever mood was inside her pour out onto the keyboard, as she played to release any frustration or upset with her parents. When she was feeling happy, she would play jigs or cheerful Irish melodies. She could sing too, not brilliantly, but she could hold a tune. She learnt all the songs people loved to hear at social gatherings. She was often invited to parties for that reason. Record players were still an item of the future back then. Music was homemade. Lola could move easily from a jig or a reel to a parlour song to a classical piece. Her father was often proud, if suspicious, of her gifts.

When word came through to her father that the children of the upper-class family in the nearby Bayfield estate needed a piano tutor over the summer, he'd thought that it was Lola's mother they meant. No, he was told. It was the daughter they wanted. They had heard she was very proficient.

Which was how Lola, at the age of nineteen, found herself walking past the high walls of the property up the driveway to the Bayfield mansion. It was truly a different world. She'd heard countless stories about the estate already. Many of the children she had gone to primary school with had ended up working there, as domestic servants – maids and kitchen staff. Large estates needed plenty of staff to keep running, not just indoors but in the stables and grounds too.

That morning, before she left, her mother had fussed over her appearance. Her father briskly outlined his rules of behaviour. No answering back. No insolence. Respect at all times. She stood still, expressionless. She realised with a flash of insight that he saw her entry into Bayfield as a possible introduction for him. Even as she thought it, he spoke. 'Should the subject be raised, I am available to tutor in French, science and mathematics.'

It wouldn't come up, Lola would make sure of it. She was grateful for this opportunity of even a measure of freedom and independence. The last thing she wanted was for her father to join her. Since completing school, she had come to realise how limited her options were. She knew her father had been making enquiries on her behalf about teaching work or perhaps clerical work in Naas or Newbridge, the only career paths for young women of her age and education. But in the meantime, she would have this unexpected job over the summer, teaching piano for two hours a day, each Tuesday and Thursday. She'd enjoy every minute of it, she decided.

She hated it.

From the first morning it was clear that she was a new servant.

Not a welcome one, either, judging by the chilly reception she received from the family's housekeeper. The children – two young sisters, aged ten and twelve – were bad-tempered and spoilt. They could almost manage a song or two each, but it was clear to Lola that they'd already been taught to hate the piano. There was no joy in their playing. One of them even flinched when she moved close that first morning.

'I'm not going to hit you,' Lola said in astonishment.

'Our music teacher at school does.'

'Well, I won't.'

By the second lesson she could see why their usual teacher might have resorted to violence. It was impossible to get the pair of them to concentrate. No wonder, Lola thought. The pieces she had been instructed by the housekeeper to teach them were solemn, ponderous and gloomy. Their mother – Lola never saw their father – came to listen once. Lola knew she was under scrutiny. She would have made her own father proud with her respectful words and near-obsequious behaviour. To her surprise, the children's mother was quite polite. Nicer to Lola than her housekeeper had been.

At the third lesson, they were again joined by the mother. After listening from a corner of the room, she informed Lola that she and the children's father would be away for the following fortnight, on a business trip to England. The children would remain at Bayfield and continue their music studies. As she was leaving, Lola dared to ask a question: could she possibly teach them other pieces too?

'I'm not musical, I'm afraid,' the woman said in her refined English accent. 'What do you mean?'

Lola knew not to suggest Irish jigs and reels. Instead, she named songs popular at the time: 'Pennies from Heaven', 'Tea for Two', 'The Last Rose of Summer'.

The children's mother gave a sudden, sweet smile. 'I'd certainly prefer to hear them instead.'

At the next lesson, Lola removed the classical sheet music and produced her own. She played the pieces first, as they listened.

'We can't play that,' the older, sulkier one said.

'Why not?'

'It's too . . .'

Lola waited.

'Happy.'

'That's exactly why you should play it. It is happy. I'll teach you both to play it.'

For once, the girls fought over who got first turn on the piano stool.

It was on her way home from that almost enjoyable lesson that she ran into Edward Quinlan. Literally ran into him. She'd taught for longer than her scheduled two hours. She was due back at home to help her mother prepare for guests, friends of her father's from his native Cork. She'd walked briskly until she was out of sight of the house and then she had started running down the path, moving through the trees from sunlight to shade. The gate was in sight when she ran right into him.

If theirs had been a storybook romance, she would have fallen gracefully to the ground and been helped up manfully by him. Instead, she sent him flying, even though he was taller and broader than her. He hadn't seen her coming as he stepped out from behind a tree with an armful of clippings. The branches and leaves also went flying.

They spoke at the same time. 'I'm so sorry.' 'Where did you come from?'

She helped him up, taking his hand, as if it was the most natural thing in the world to do. Afterwards, she wondered whether she had imagined the sudden charge of electricity between them, the feel of his work-roughened hand in her own softer one. She'd replayed that moment so many times over the years, always wondering if it could have possibly gone any other way between them, or if it had been fate at work —

Her mobile phone ringing interrupted her memories. A name flashed up on the screen. Jim. The one wonderful thing to have come out of all that followed that day at Bayfield.

'Darling!' she said, delighted as always to hear from him.

It wasn't Jim. It was his wife Geraldine, calling on his phone. 'Jim's asked me to call you.'

Implicit in her sentence was that she would certainly never have called Lola herself. Lola rarely phoned her either. It had long been silently acknowledged between the two of them that there was little or no mutual affection. A year earlier, Geraldine had gone one step further and brought the unspoken into the open, telling Lola in the most certain of terms how she felt about her. Lola had hated hearing it, even if she grudgingly respected Geraldine for speaking her mind.

Families were unfathomable, Lola had often thought. A village of sorts, a disparate selection of people somehow expected to get along just because they happened to live in close proximity. It was more of a miracle if any members did get on, let alone enjoy each other's company.

'How are you, Geraldine?' Lola asked now, doing her best to sound sincere. 'All going well with the guesthouse, I hope?'

A year earlier Jim and Geraldine had left the Clare Valley and their family-run motel. They now lived in the Adelaide Hills, several hours away, managing a small five-bedroom guesthouse.

'Everything's fine, thank you,' Geraldine said.

'I'm sure you're very busy. Autumn is so beautiful in the Hills.'

'Yes, it is.'

Lola sighed inwardly. The two of them talking as if they were actors in an English-language video. So stiff and polite. Lola allowed herself a moment to imagine if they did speak the truth to one another: *How are you, Geraldine, you buttoned-up, cold-hearted woman, who I still can't fathom why my son married?*

Geraldine's answer sprang just as easily to mind: *I'm fine, Lola, you interfering old cow of an Irishwoman. I'd have hoped you'd have died long before now but here you are still hanging around causing mischief, even though we've moved away from you and I thought we were out of your reach. But no, you spring this idea of a trip to Ireland on everyone. And not only is Jim not invited to come, even though he wouldn't be able to, but you're clearly disrupting Ellen's schooling, not to mention Bett's working life and home life, just to satisfy some half-baked selfish urge to go 'home', when in all the time I've known you, you've never expressed the slightest interest in seeing Ireland again.*

It took Lola a moment to realise Geraldine hadn't said those things. She tuned in again as her daughter-in-law continued to speak.

'— so we were hoping to drive up on Monday morning to see everyone, if that suits you as well?'

'We? You and Jim? Of course. Wonderful. Do you want to stay here?' She already knew the answer.

'No, thank you.' Geraldine's answer couldn't have come any quicker. 'We'll stay at the motel. Jim wants to look over the books there while we're in town.'

They still owned the motel. They'd leased it out rather than sold it, keeping a watchful eye on it from afar. As did Lola, from not so afar. She liked the new managers very much, and fortunately they didn't seem to mind her dropping in to have a cup of tea with them once a fortnight or so. She didn't approve of all the changes they were making – personally, she wouldn't have installed a barbecue, why would people eat in the motel's restaurant if they could cook their own dinner more cheaply? – but to her own surprise she'd managed to stay quiet.

'I can't wait to see you both,' Lola said.

I can't wait to see Jim and I will do my best to be polite to you, she thought.

CHAPTER SEVEN

The next day, Bett sat back in Lola's armchair and watched as her grandmother read through the latest lot of paperwork. She would have been able to make the decision herself but instinct told her to run everything, even something as simple as choosing their driver, past her grandmother.

'All three quotes look good to me,' Bett said as Lola read. 'They're all experienced. They'll all collect us at the airport. Similar-sized cars. Around the same price. I just hope it's not too expensive for you.'

'I'd have paid double,' Lola said. 'It was a brainwave of Daniel's. No fighting over maps. No getting lost. We just sit in the back and get driven around Ireland like three little babies in a pram.'

'Three pretty big babies,' Bett said.

'Don't you think that's what old folks' homes should offer, Bett? Adult-sized prams. Old people like me could lie back, tucked up all snug under a blanket and get pushed up and down the street, looking out at the world. People would poke their heads in at us to say hello and have a chat. And if they got boring, we could pretend to fall asleep mid-conversation. What a marvellous idea. I think I should patent it, don't you? Adult-sized prams. We could call them Lolamobiles.'

'You're trying to put off a decision, aren't you? Can't you close your eyes and point?'

'It's more complicated than that. How much did you tell any of them about me?'

'I just gave them the basic information.'

'Did you give them my full name? My age?'

'Lola, are you wanted by the Irish police? Is that why you haven't been back before now?'

'Of course not. I was living at home until I got married, remember. It was hard enough to get up to what I got up to without bringing criminal elements into the equation.'

'What did you get up to?'

'Curiosity killed the cat, Bett. Haven't I always taught you that?'

'No, you always taught me to be curious.'

'Did I? Imagine that. So what did you say about me?'

Bett could barely remember. She'd written a lot of emails since those ones. 'Just the basics, as I said. That I was coming to Ireland with my Irish-born grandmother and young niece —'

'Did you say where I had grown up? Give my parents' names? Their occupations? Did you say anything about Edward? About him dying in the war?'

'No. I didn't think those things were relevant to getting a quote for a driver. Lola, of course not. I googled "Ireland" and "chauffeurs". I liked the sound of these three and their websites looked good. I can track down people who hired them, if you want references, but anything like this is a gamble, isn't it? It's like the hotels we'll be staying in. I'll research them and book us into the ones that seem the best but the hotel chef might be having a bad night the evening we're there, or it could be stormy and the wind rattling the window might keep you awake all night.'

'You are making this complicated. Of course the wind won't keep me awake. Gin is the best sleeping tonic in the world.' She held out one of the pages. 'I'd like him, please.'

Bett read the name. Desmond Foley. 'Dare I ask why?'

'I didn't know anyone with his surname when I was growing up.'

'That's a good thing?'

'It means the chances are better that he won't know me, or anything about me.'

'Lola, as you said, you've been away for years. What are the chances of anyone knowing you?'

'This is Ireland, Bett. Irish people can scent a connection within seconds. They'll talk and talk and ask questions until they make a connection if they have to. It's in our blood.'

She was right, Bett knew. During her time living in Dublin, she'd witnessed many conversations like that. Two Irish people narrowing down which county each came from, which town, which street, or who their neighbours were, until there was a link between them. Once, in Bett's hearing, the questions continued until the pair were able to happily discover they'd once shopped in the same supermarket. In her experience, Australians were the opposite. They hated meeting other Australians on their travels, wanting their big overseas adventure to belong to them alone.

'Right, then,' Bett said. 'I'll email this Desmond Foley tonight. So, any more insider news for me about the TV series or should I wait for the next official press release?'

As it happened, Lola did have news. Tom had phoned her that morning. The lead actor playing the key role of the UK-based wine importer had agreed to fly out to Australia earlier than expected. He'd be making a flying publicity trip to the Clare Valley. It was quite a coup all round, Tom had told Lola. Not only had the actor been nominated for two BAFTAs, he was also currently in the news for his complicated personal life. He'd recently left his second wife for a new woman, not a younger, prettier version as expected in his industry, but for a well-known stage actress fifteen years his senior. Lola told Tom she thought it showed very good taste on his part.

'He can't wait to get here, apparently,' Tom had said. The actor's cheated-on wife was furious about the affair. So much so that she'd cut all the legs off his trousers, the sleeves off his shirts, the toes off his socks and posted the whole lot to the hotel he was staying in with his new love. 'Cash on delivery. He's supposed to be mean with his money, so that would have really stung.'

'I know something but I can't tell, I'm sorry,' Lola said to Bett. 'You'll find out soon, darling. Be patient.'

'Can you at least give me a clue?'

Lola mimed zipping her lips shut.

'Not even who your deep throat in the TV company is?'

'Who said anything about the TV company? I could be sleeping with the mayor for all you know.'

'I'm holding the front page if you are,' Bett said.

As Bett gathered her bag and folders, she had a longing to share her concerns for the future of the paper with Lola. She decided against it. Voicing them might make it worse. She didn't want to add to Lola's worries, either. She'd seemed livelier, more herself, in the past few days.

'I'm talking to Ellen again tonight too,' she said as Lola walked her to the door. 'She's so excited.'

'I know. She's messaging me every day too. Thank you again, Bett. I know it's a big thing to ask of you, leaving Daniel and your children behind, when you have so much on at work too. Not to mention all those worries you must have about the newspaper possibly being sold —'

Bett opened and shut her mouth. But of course Lola would know about that.

'— but it means so much to me,' Lola continued. 'More than you could imagine.'

The discussion about the paper could wait. Bett kissed her grandmother goodbye. 'Any time, Lola.'

The next morning, Bett was just walking into the office when she heard the ping of an email on her phone. It was from Ireland, from Desmond Foley of Desmond Foley Chauffeurs. He was most delighted to have won the job, he told her:

> I will do my utter utmost to make the homecoming and possible family reunion as smooth and enjoyable as possible. If there is anything I can do on the ground for you before you arrive, you only have to ask.

Bett frowned. Had she said anything about it being a possible family reunion? She quickly read through her previous emails, guiltily recalling Lola's request to be discreet. She must have been in a fulsome mood the night she'd written them. She'd explained to all three possible candidates that she was looking for a driver:

> for my grandmother Lola Quinlan (nee Delaney), my niece and myself, to visit childhood places in and around Ballymore Eustace in Kildare as well as other places that might emerge as the trip unfolds. My grandmother (aged eighty-five) hasn't been back to Ireland since she emigrated sixty-five years ago, so it's a very special trip for her.

On the bright side, at least she hadn't mentioned Lola's parents' names. Or Edward Quinlan.

She wrote a quick email back to Desmond Foley, downplaying any idea of there being a family reunion. *It is a private visit home*, she wrote, *and I'm hoping you are able to keep these details confidential.*

There was an almost instant reply:

My sincere apologies, Ms Quinlan. I put two and two together – an elderly lady returning to her roots, showing her country to her granddaughter and great-granddaughter – and just assumed you would be meeting up with long-lost family members. My wife always says I leap to conclusions. She also says I'm inclined to talk too much when I'm driving. But I assure you I only talk when spoken to and if you prefer the entire journey to be made in silence, I will certainly follow your instructions. I aim to please and am here to serve, as our slogan says.

Bett glanced at the bottom of the email. The slogan was: *Sightsee Stress-Free*. Perhaps he'd changed it recently. She decided to reply to him later. As she switched on her computer, another email arrived on her phone. It was from Carrie. The subject line was *Publicity photo*.

Hi Bett,
Just thinking you'll probably need some recent photos of me to help promote my blog. I got Matthew to take these. Please choose which one you think is best. I like them all. Cxx

Bett scrolled through them. She was smiling at the first one, laughing out loud by the fifteenth. She and Carrie definitely didn't always get on, but sometimes – like now, when Bett's anxiety levels were higher than she'd like – Carrie would somehow make her laugh or distract her in the funniest way. The photos were hilarious. She could imagine Carrie and Matthew amusing themselves too.

Carrie had sent through a variety of different photos and poses.

Bett's favourite was Carrie in serious journalist mode, pen to her lips, wearing glasses. They had to be Matthew's – Carrie had perfect eyesight. In another, she was laughing uproariously and, clearly, fakely. She was also wearing full makeup. Bett was certain her hair had been blowdried too. Half the photos were taken indoors, at the desk or leaning on the mantelpiece like an American president. The outdoor ones showed Carrie against a wide range of clichéd rural backdrops – fences, shed doors. She even had a piece of straw between her teeth in one. The final photo was a shot of her sitting on Matthew's ride-on lawn mower, one hand on the wheel, the other holding a phone to her ear.

Bett was still laughing as she rang her. 'Carrie, thanks so much. You've really cheered me up.'

'I have? How?'

'Your photos. The joke ones.'

'Oh, the laughing ones, you mean? I wondered about those. Delete them, would you? Let's go with one of the serious ones. The ones with me and the glasses, I think. I don't look my prettiest but I think they give me the air of intellectual seriousness we need, don't you?'

Bett realised then the photos were genuine. Oh, God. She chose her words carefully. 'Carrie, it's a fun blog about the TV series. A few hundred words whenever you've got something to say. It doesn't have to take over your life. I just want you to enjoy doing it and everyone else to enjoy reading it.'

'They're going to love it! You've got no idea how many people are waiting for it already. I was telling all the girls at our exercise class last night and they're so jealous! There was a bit of meanness at first about it being nepotism, you being my sister and everything. But as I said, I'm not being paid, even though I probably should be. I looked up freelance rates but I decided I'm prepared to do this first series for free, to help get my name out there.'

'Out where?'

'Cyberspace. I've decided to take a slightly – hold on, let me check the word again – "snarky" tone. Apparently that's the way bloggers speak these days. It's a mixture of sarcastic and funny, as far as I can make out. So I'm going to try and write like that, and hopefully I'll go viral.'

'Carrie, you don't have to be snarky. And great if you go viral but that's not the idea either. It's just a way to help promote the Valley and the TV series too. It would be better if you weren't snarky.'

'Really? I'm so glad! I spent last night trying to be snarky to Matthew and we nearly had a fight. He said I was just being mean, that there was nothing clever about it. So, which photo will you use?'

There was no point spoiling her excitement. 'One that looks most like you,' Bett said diplomatically.

'Make it one of the pretty ones then, won't you? No glasses. They don't really suit me.'

'No glasses,' Bett agreed. Oh, God, she thought again as she hung up. She'd created a monster.

Two nights later, Bett was on her way to Lola's again. Her Irish trip notebook was already half full and they hadn't left Australia yet.

Once again, Daniel was looking after the twins. She'd helped him put them to bed first, and even put on a load of washing, but she'd had to go before the dishes were done. In the car, about to drive away, she was hit with a wave of guilt. Daniel would be sole carer for the two weeks she was away. He was practically sole carer at the moment too. She knew she'd been too distracted – about the paper, Lola, Ireland. She'd barely asked him about his own work recently, or his mother.

She decided Lola wouldn't mind if she was a little bit late.

He was in the kitchen at the computer when she came back in. He had music playing, not too loud to wake up the twins, but loud enough that he didn't hear her. She crept up behind him, put her arms around him and leaned down to kiss his neck.

'Bett!' He swore, hurriedly spinning around, deliberately – she was sure of it – covering the screen.

'Caught you!' she joked. 'Didn't I tell you not to look up Russian dating sites until I'm well gone?'

'Very funny,' he said. He still didn't move from the computer. He leaned back even further.

'Are you looking at Russian dating sites?' she said.

'No. Ukrainian. Their hair is blonder. They're supposed to be more amenable too.'

'What are you looking at?'

'I told you, Ukrainian dating sites. And Korean dating sites. I'm very multicultural.'

'Daniel, come on —' A sudden howl from the twins' bedroom stopped their conversation. She ran in first. It was Yvette. She'd dropped her favourite doll off the side of her cot and wasn't happy about it. Bett tucked it in beside her, stayed until she was peaceful again. By the time she came back out to the kitchen, the computer was closed down.

Bett raised an eyebrow. 'Anyone would think you were feeling guilty about something. That you'd taken the opportunity while I was out of the room to quickly get off a website or something.'

'Would they?' Daniel said, smiling. He glanced at his watch. 'You're late. Lola will kill you.'

'She'll understand when I tell her I had to get to the bottom of a mystery in my marriage.'

'Bett, go. Please. Quickly, before the kids wake up again. I was doing some work, that's all. And I knew you'd tell me off for working at home.'

'You're right,' she said. They were both trying not to bring their work home.

'Is that why you came back?' he asked. 'To check if I was working?'

'No. It was to tell you I love you.' She kissed him goodbye again, promising to be back by eleven at the latest.

During the short drive to Lola's house, she did her best to damp down the soft, suspicious voice that was trying to make itself heard. Daniel hadn't been on his work website. She'd only seen a flash of the screen before he deliberately blocked her view but it had been a chat room of some kind. Since when had her husband frequented chat rooms?

Within minutes of arriving at Lola's, she had plenty else to occupy her mind. Lola's housemate, Margaret, had returned from her long holiday in Queensland that morning. She and Lola were not just happy housemates. They both liked to turn any small gathering into an occasion. Bett had expected a biscuit at the most. There were platters of homemade brownies, an assortment of sandwiches and a freshly made lemon cake, drizzled in white icing. It was all beautifully laid out in their dining room, on a linen tablecloth, with a vase of roses from their garden as the centrepiece. They'd brought out their best china and finest teapot, a large silver one big enough for ten people.

Bett gazed in admiration. 'I feel like I'm in *Home Beautiful* magazine. Who else is coming?'

'Just you, Bett,' Margaret said. 'Blame me. I was in a baking frenzy today.'

'She always is when she gets back from holiday. She says it's how she "grounds" herself.' Lola made quote marks with her fingers.

'I needed "grounding".' Margaret did the gesture too. 'I love my daughter and grandchildren, Bett, don't get me wrong. But some-times I am very grateful that hundreds of kilometres separate us.'

'Margaret's grandchildren are free-range,' Lola explained. 'Or hippies, as we used to call them.'

'Your grandmother's being polite, Bett. They are wild savages. No rules, no manners. Not that I'm allowed to point that out. I only have half a tongue left, I had to bite it so many times.'

Bett farewelled her latest attempt at a diet as she was offered a sample of everything. The brownies were melt-in-the-mouth. The lemon drizzle cake had a perfect tang. The sandwiches were made with pillowy white bread, real butter, three fillings apiece. How could she possibly say no? It would be rude, surely, even if she had already eaten a full dinner.

It was nearly nine-thirty by the time they got down to business. Tonight's visit was to choose their accommodation in Kildare.

Bett produced the latest bundle of paperwork from her bag. 'I found three big hotels not far from your village, and lots of B&Bs too. I'm sure there's probably Airbnb places too, if you want me to try for something quirkier. Actually, I hadn't thought of that before now. Your childhood home was a two-storey house in the country, wasn't it? Wouldn't it be brilliant if that was on Airbnb now? You might even be able to stay in your old bedroom.' She found Google on her phone, excited now. 'Lola, tell me the exact address again, and I'll see.'

'Oh, that would be so special,' Margaret said. 'When a friend of mine went to the UK recently, she stayed in those kinds of places all the time, manor houses, even a castle. The owners had to do it to be able to afford the maintenance. How many bedrooms did you have in your house, Lola? I don't think I'd ever realised you were one of the landed gentry.'

'Lola?' Bett asked again, finger poised on her phone. 'The address?'

'I can't remember.'

'You can't remember your childhood address?'

'We didn't have street names and numbers. The house was outside the village.'

'Then that would make it easier to find, wouldn't it?' Margaret said. 'Did the house have a name?'

'I can't remember.'

Bett smiled. 'Lola, are you joking? You can't remember the name of your own house?'

'No. Isn't that terrible?' Lola's voice was defiant. 'I wouldn't want to stay in someone else's home anyway. Except yours, Margaret. I love it here. Why travel all that way across the world to stay in an ordinary house and not a lovely hotel?'

Margaret and Bett exchanged a look.

'I don't even need to see your shortlist, Bett,' Lola said. 'Surprise me. Pick the nicest one. Hang the expense. Now, how long did Desmond Foley say it would take us to drive from Dublin to Kildare?'

It was a deliberate change of subject. Bett had no choice but to go along with it.

Bett left just before eleven with another To Do list. Margaret and Lola both waved her off from the front door, then returned to Lola's sitting room.

'So now she's gone, tell me the truth,' Margaret said as she took her seat by the fire. 'You do remember the name of your childhood home, don't you?'

'Of course,' Lola said. It was called Leixcraig House, she told Margaret. A two-storey house in its own small grounds, on a country road several miles from the village of Ballymore Eustace.

'Why didn't you tell Bett?'

'Because I knew she would google it. And if she googled it, she would find it is a guesthouse now. We could stay there. And I don't know if I could cope with that.'

'It's a guesthouse? How do you know?'

Lola stood, went to her bedroom and returned with a piece of paper, folded three times. It was a photograph of a beautiful two-storey house, with a large oak tree in the front garden. To the side of the gate an elegant sign was visible: *Leixcraig House. Bed & Breakfast. Dinner available on request.*

'I found this last year,' Lola said. 'Luke was showing me how to use Google Street View and Google Earth. We had a most enter-taining afternoon keying in all our friends' addresses, seeing their houses. I couldn't believe it. There was even an aerial shot of Mrs Kernaghan's house here in Clare. And guess who was sunbaking nude in the back garden, caught forevermore by their cameras?'

Mrs Kernaghan had been their nemesis in the charity shop the previous year. Lola and Margaret were just two of many in the town who'd secretly rejoiced when she announced that she was moving to Perth to be closer to her grandchildren.

'Not Mrs Kernaghan?'

'The very woman. Completely in the nip. No wonder she wanted to move. I tried other addresses. Yours. All our friends. The motel. The detail was extraordinary. I could even see Bumper, our sheep, in one of the photos.'

'But Bumper's dead.'

'That's what surprised me. I thought I was seeing ghosts. Ghost sheep, if such a thing exists. Luke explained that the images aren't always current. It depends on when their satellites or video cars or whatever they use drove past. Before Luke left, I keyed in my old Kildare address. Not the name of the house. The name of the road. And there it was, in front of me.'

Margaret looked down at the printout. 'So how old is this photo?'

'I don't know. Luke wasn't able to find out. I lied to him too, to my shame. I said it was a photo of a penpal's house.'

'It looks beautiful. Don't you want to stay in it? Wouldn't that be a wonderful way to return home?'

Lola shook her head.

'But surely the owners would love to meet you too?' Margaret persisted. 'It looks like they've been faithful to the original look of the house, doesn't it? Did the guesthouse have a website? Did you get to see inside?'

'I didn't look.'

'You didn't? Lola Quinlan, the most curious person I have ever met in my life, turned down an opportunity to sit in front of her computer on the other side of the world and peer in at her child-hood home? I can't believe my ears. Let's do it now. I'll protect you if the memories get too overwhelming. Where was your bedroom, on the ground floor or the first floor?'

'No, Margaret.'

Margaret tried again, more gently. 'Lola, you don't have to stay there. I can understand that might be difficult. Well, actually, I can't understand. I think it would be fantastic. But can't you at least show their website to me, one of your oldest friends? I'd love to be able to picture where you grew up. It seems incredible, all these years we've known each other and it's as if I always took you being Irish for granted, the way Mr Kouris is Greek or Mrs Gavinski is Polish. We're all just Australians now, aren't we? But this is so exciting, your trip, the whole going home after all these years —'

'I'm sorry, Margaret, but no.' To her friend's astonishment, Lola ripped up the photo.

'Lola! Luke will have to print another one for you now.'

'I don't want another copy. I'm starting to think this whole trip is a terrible mistake. I wonder, would we lose much money if Bett was to cancel the tickets now?'

'But you leave in less than a week. Ellen is so excited, you told me as much. So is Bett. All the organisation she's done for you, not just the trip itself, but so she could take time off work, be away from home, all the arrangements with Daniel and the twins. You can't cancel it now.'

'They'd have to cancel if I died suddenly. I might die tonight.'

'So might I. And it's my turn to do the breakfast dishes. Lola, what's happened? What's wrong?'

'I don't know.' She shut her eyes briefly, and massaged her temples. 'Yes I do. I'm scared, Margaret.'

'I can see that. But of what?'

'Of what's waiting there for me.'

'People from your past, do you mean? Your family in Kildare?'

Lola shook her head. 'My father was from Cork, a different part of the country. I never knew his family. I always had the feeling he was ashamed of them.'

'And your mother?'

'An only child, like me. It was only ever the three of us. The smallest Irish family in history.' It had never been spoken of in her family home, but Lola had always suspected her mother had suffered several miscarriages at least.

'I don't think I ever asked you this before,' Margaret said, 'but how did your parents die?'

Lola told her. Her mother had gone first, an aneurysm. Her father just months later. Cancer.

'You didn't go to the funerals? No, of course you didn't. You haven't been back there.'

'Their funerals were over before I even knew they'd died. It took a month at least back then for mail to travel between Ireland and Australia. That's how I heard about both deaths. By letter, from a friend of my mother's, a lovely woman called Elizabeth O'Connell. I used to help mind her children. She and I kept in touch after I left.'

'Oh, Lola. What a way to find out such sad news.'

'It's just how it was back then, Margaret. Not like today, where people could watch their loved ones pass away on Skype if they wanted.'

'Do people do that?' Margaret was shocked.

'Probably. They do everything else online, don't they? Perhaps I'll offer myself to Google or Yahoo or whoever the big corporation is these days, and they can stream my death live on the internet. I'll let them know when I start to feel a bit poorly and they can send in the cameras.'

'Lola!'

'It'll come to that, don't you think? People will do anything for a moment of glory. Why stop at sex tapes? Don't look shocked, Margaret. I go to the doctor. I read those magazines in waiting rooms.'

Margaret picked up her iPad. 'Even if you don't want to look at your old house, can I?'

'No. I've forgotten the name again. You could google "guest-houses in Kildare", I suppose.'

Margaret slowly keyed in the words. 'There are hundreds. Hundreds!'

'That will keep you busy while I'm away,' Lola said.

'If I didn't love you so much, you'd drive me mad.'

'And I love you too, dear Margaret. Which is why I'm hoping you won't go searching. I'll show you a photo of my house when I get back, I promise. I want to see it in person first, in real life, not on a screen. I spent too long as it was looking at that image.' She gestured to the torn paper. 'It didn't do me any good. If I can take a virtual tour here in my living room, why even bother going there?'

'Is that why you've asked Bett not to contact anyone in Ireland before you get there?'

'Exactly,' Lola lied. 'I want it to unfold in its own way. If I'm meant to meet someone from my past, then so be it. But I have to leave some room for surprises, Margaret.'

'What if it's a bad surprise?'

'I'll worry about that when it happens.'

CHAPTER EIGHT

In a small suburban house on the northside of Dublin, Des Foley was sitting in front of the laptop computer on his kitchen table. His wife, Breda, was at the stove, stirring a Thai curry she'd spent the afternoon making. The two of them didn't just enjoy their food. They loved it: eating out, cooking, reading about it. Once a year they went on a week-long trip to a new city in Europe, building their holiday around their passion for food, touring produce markets, researching the best restaurants.

Their three adult children found it very funny. 'It's far from this we were reared,' the oldest said one Christmas, as they sat down to roast goose with pear and cranberry stuffing. It had been prepared, step by step, from repeated viewings of Nigella Lawson videos.

Des had the draft itinerary for his latest booking beside him. Three visiting Australians wanting a driver for ten days. He was dealing with the granddaughter. She'd been quite forthcoming at first but then had suddenly stopped saying anything about the purpose of their trip. No bother, he thought. Perhaps they were famous in Australia and didn't want him tipping off the paparazzi or anything. He'd driven an actual Hollywood star around Ireland once and the paparazzi had been a nightmare, cameras flashing, cars and motorbikes following them. They always seemed to know where they'd be, even though he was only told the itinerary himself each morning. It had been a Top-10-Highlights-of-Ireland kind of trip: Glendalough, the Giant's Causeway, the Cliffs of Moher . . . It wouldn't have taken a genius to work out where they'd go, but even so. It wasn't until afterwards that he'd twigged. The Hollywood star herself – or at least her PR people – had been tipping off the photographers.

Des's kids had pored over the magazines online afterwards, delighted to find their father in at least three shots.

'You look like a fugitive,' his daughter had laughed, enlarging one of the photos on her phone screen.

'So would you if you had flashes going off as you tried to drive. They're lucky I didn't crash.'

'She gave you a big tip, I hope.'

'In my dreams.' He showed them what the actress had given him. A DVD of her last film. She'd signed it: *To my driver.*

'She didn't even know your name?'

They'd all found it hilarious.

It was no coincidence that Des started wearing a name tag after that. Not that he'd had any film stars since. His clients were mostly visiting business people, conference delegates, politicians from Europe occasionally. Usually it was just a few hours' work. Occasionally a longer run, a trip from Dublin to Cork, or up to Belfast. The dream bookings were ones like this. Ten full days' work. It would pay for his and Breda's next holiday. Spain, they were thinking. Malaga, to be exact. They were keen to try all sorts of tapas.

'Dinner in ten minutes, Des,' Breda said. 'Can you cut up the limes? And chop the coriander?'

He packed away the laptop and began on the limes. The sharp fresh smell blended with the coriander waiting on the chopping board, the spices from the curry already making the kitchen as fragrant as a Thai restaurant. That was their long-term travel plan:

a month in Asia. They'd already researched cooking schools in Laos, Cambodia and Thailand.

'There goes our inheritance,' their son had said. 'What's wrong with the chipper down the road?'

Des filled Breda in on the latest correspondence from the Quinlan booking. They always discussed his work, and her work as a district health nurse, in detail.

'How will you live without me for ten whole days, petal?'

'You'll be back most nights, won't you? Unless you and the older lady run off together? What did you tell me her name was?'

Des checked the printout. 'Lola Quinlan, nee Delaney. Travelling with her granddaughter Bett Quinlan and great-granddaughter Ellen Quinlan-Green.'

'It's a mobile harem. And that Lola one is nearly ninety, did you say? That's some age to go travelling. You might need to research a few hospitals along your route as well. Be prepared.'

'Forget hospitals. You mean funeral homes, don't you?'

'Des Foley!'

'We're mostly travelling around Kildare, I think. That's an easy enough run home each night. Though I'd drive home to you even if it was across hot coals, you know that.'

Breda rolled her eyes. 'And ruin your beautiful new tyres? Bet you wouldn't. Sounds like it's a real homecoming. Has she much family left here, did she say?'

'I asked the granddaughter, but I got short shrift. A private trip, she said. Much as I'd like to know, I have to respect their wishes.'

Breda put the lid on the pan and laughed. 'Listen to yourself. As if you won't pepper them with questions the second you meet them at the airport! Tell me their names again?'

Des repeated them and watched as Breda took out her iPhone and tapped on the keyboard.

'Breda, I said I wouldn't ask them for any more info.'

'Yes, you said that. But I didn't. You think I'm sending you off with a mysterious old lady and her relatives for ten days without knowing as much as I can about them?' She spoke into the voice-activated search engine. 'Lola Quinlan. South Australia.'

Des couldn't resist. He came over and stood behind his wife as the first of the entries appeared on the phone's screen.

In Clare the next day, Bett and Carrie were supposed to be having an informal meeting over coffee in one of the cafes on the main street. It wasn't going well. Bett had just told Carrie that she wanted to see Carrie's blog posts before they were posted on the newspaper's website or in the paper itself. Carrie had taken offence, declaring it as proof that Bett didn't trust that she could write.

'Of course I trust you,' Bett said. 'That's why I agreed with Lola's idea to ask you to do it. But every writer gets edited, especially when it's for a newspaper, when the space is limited.' Bett reached for her bag and pulled out a printout of an article she'd subbed earlier that day. She'd had a hunch she might need to show Carrie what she meant. 'Like this, for example. It was too long so I had to cut it back. But it's still that writer's work, not mine.'

'But look what you've done to it. That poor person might have spent hours writing that. And you've just gone slash-slash-slash with a red pen as if it means nothing.'

'Carrie, this is what I do for a living. I read articles, edit them where needed and then move on to the next one. You think I have time to linger on every word of a cricket match report, testing it for scene-setting or character development? People skim-read these days anyway. I don't even edit on paper any more. It's done on screen. I just thought it would be helpful for you to see an example on paper.'

'Helpful? I think "disheartening" is the word you're looking for.'

How did her sister do this to her? Bett prayed for patience. 'It's up to you, Carrie. If you don't want to do the blog, say, and I'll ask someone else. But either way, I need to have it set up before I go.'

Carrie stayed silent for a moment. Bett knew she was weighing up her options. She also knew there was no way Carrie would let someone else do it. Bett had already heard around town that Carrie was making a big deal out of it. 'So you've hired a showbiz correspondent for the paper?' one person had said to her in the supermarket.

The questions she'd been asked about the TV series and crew had given Bett another idea. Deciding to take her sister's silence as agreement, she outlined her new idea. At the end of every blog post there could be a section for comments and questions from readers. Perhaps Carrie could also answer those, to keep a lively online communication going, Bett suggested.

'What if I don't know the answer to their questions, though?' Carrie said, still sulking. 'I'm not like you and Anna, remember. I didn't go to university.'

'It won't be questions about politics or the solar system. I mean questions about the TV series. The producer said she's happy to be your contact person. She also wants to see the blog before we post it, which I normally wouldn't agree to, but I had to make an exception in this case. They want to keep some details under wraps until the show goes to air.'

'Do you know who the murderer is?'

'No. I don't even know who gets murdered. They won't tell me anything.'

'They'll tell me, won't they? I'll have to know.'

'Not necessarily. You're writing what's called a feature piece, Carrie. How many people in the crew, what the actors think of the Clare Valley, how many times they do each scene, that kind of thing.'

'It sounds like you could just write it yourself, if you know what you want so clearly.'

Bett took another deep breath. 'Yes, Carrie. I'd love to write it myself but it's going to be tricky doing that when I'm on the other side of the world in Ireland.'

'Being "The Chosen One".'

'Carrie, stop it, would you? You couldn't travel even if you wanted to.'

'Or if Lola had wanted me to.'

'It's not going to be all fun and games, you know. Lola's being so strange about it, I'm convinced we'll do most of our sightseeing in the middle of the night. All Ellen wants to do is visit film locations and send photos to her friends. She's asked me three times if her phone will work in Ireland.'

'She's got a phone? She's just a kid.'

'She's thirteen years old. Of course she's got a phone.'

'I'm not letting my kids have phones until they're at least sixteen. It's breaking down the fabric of family life. People spend more time on their screens than they do talking to each other.'

'By the time your kids are sixteen, phones will probably be implanted in their fingertips.'

'Speaking of photos, the ones I sent you for my blog were only taken on Matthew's phone. Would it be better if I went into a studio and got them done professionally?'

'That would cost a fortune. And it's really not necessary.'

'We can afford it and it's groundwork for my new career. You have to spend money to make money.'

Bett wished Carrie wouldn't always make it so clear that she and Matthew had much more money than she and Daniel. For a mean moment, she was tempted to say to Carrie that yes, she should go in and get studio photos taken; let them waste some of theirs. Then her kinder side assured her sister that the iPhone photos were just fine.

Carrie flicked her blonde curls back over her shoulder. She had lots of habits that annoyed Bett, but that was number one on the list.

'You're right, I guess,' Carrie said. 'I'll wait until my blog goes viral and then get proper photos taken. It probably doesn't really matter yet when it's just for a local audience. Everyone here knows what I look like in real life. Photos never do me justice anyway, Matthew says.'

As always, Bett was taken aback at her sister's vanity. Not to mention her ability to slip in throwaway insults under the guise of normal conversation. 'Just a local audience', when those readers were the lifeblood of Bett's paper, already in real danger of closing. As for the casual allusion to her good looks, Carrie had always had that confidence, even as a teenager. Bett had spent her younger years constantly self-conscious: about her face, hair, weight. Even now, at thirty-seven, Bett found more to criticise than praise about her own appearance. Somehow Carrie had missed out on the self-critical gene. She knew she was pretty. She knew other people found her pretty. That was the way it was.

It was time to go, Bett decided, before her patience wore out. As she walked to her car after saying goodbye, she wondered whether it would be too childish to draw a moustache on Carrie's byline photo.

That night after the kids were in bed, Bett and Daniel sat down with a calendar and a glass of wine each. There were still a lot of arrangements to put in place. The childcare at least was organised – their neighbour Jane already occasionally looked after the twins and had assured them she could step in whenever Daniel needed. Daniel had also been in touch with his sister, Christine, in Adelaide. While Bett was away, Christine would do Daniel's share of the visits to their mother too.

When Bett had first met Mrs Hilder, she had already been in the advanced stages of Alzheimer's. Sometimes the older woman had seemed to vaguely recognise her. Most often she ignored her completely. Bett had taken the twins to see her when they were babies. It hadn't gone well. Mrs Hilder had loudly and repeatedly insisted on holding them. They'd carefully placed the babies in her arms, staying close by. There had only been time to take a quick photograph before she'd lost interest and they'd nearly fallen to the floor. Bett and the twins had only visited her a few times since she'd been moved to the specialist care home in Adelaide. She and Daniel had realised that there was, sadly, no point coming more often. New people only confused her. If it was Daniel or Christine on their own, there was always the hope that she might recognise them, even for a few seconds. It hadn't happened recently, Bett knew. Daniel had tried to sound fine about it, but Bett had seen the hurt underneath. It had broken her heart. Bett had had occasional difficulties with her own mother, but at least they could still communicate, even if Geraldine wasn't always capable of being demonstrative.

It took twenty minutes to compare diaries, to make sure Daniel had the details of play dates, medical appointments and other arrangements that tended to fall into Bett's responsibility. She'd battled against that when the twins were young, feeling overwhelmed enough by motherhood, and still deep in grief about Anna's death. In the past few months, though, she'd felt they were finding a kind of rhythm. It helped, too, that the twins were endlessly entertaining. That was going to be the hardest part of this trip. Missing special moments with them.

It was as if Daniel read her mind. 'We'll Skype every day if you want. Or if they're asleep, I'll wake them and get them to do something for you. I'm joking, Bett, I promise. If and when I ever do get them to sleep while you're away, I will rejoice and open beers, not wake them up.'

She'd already thanked him dozens of times. She thanked him again.

'Bring me back a can of Guinness and we're quits. This is for you, by the way. While you're away.' He held out a memory stick.

'Can I look at it now?'

'Sure,' he said.

She plugged it into her laptop and clicked it open. It was a video file.

'Is it you on loop telling me how much you adore me?'

'Kind of,' he said. 'Hold on. Before you look, let me get you another glass of wine.'

'Why, how kind,' she said, holding out her glass.

Watching him go, Bett decided if she had to sum up her husband in one word, that would be it – kind. She had a sudden longing to be away with him, just the two of them. Even for a night. Would it be possible before she went to Ireland? No, she realised. But when she got back. A night for the two of them, to talk without interruption. To make love without interruption.

It was a terrible thing to admit, but she couldn't remember the last time they'd had sex. There never seemed to be the time. Or if there was time, they were both too exhausted. She'd gone on to an online parenting forum recently, seeking advice about what to do when twins started mimicking each other, as theirs had started doing. Instead, she found herself following a long thread about getting the physical side of a relationship back on track. It had been a comfort to realise she wasn't alone. Forget hiring a nanny, one woman had written. I'm thinking of hiring him a lover – the more

97

sleep I get, the better. Anyone know any good Russian dating sites they can recommend? There'd been great hilarity about that. Bett wished now they hadn't mentioned dating sites. It reminded her of Daniel's behaviour the other night. And of her own behaviour the following day, once he'd left for work. It felt shameful to even think of it, as she heard him now, whistling in the kitchen, pouring her another glass of riesling. But she had gone to their laptop and checked his recently visited websites and search history. Both were blank. As if they'd been deliberately cleared.

'Here you go,' he said, coming back and handing her the glass.

She took a sip and then pressed play. It was a homemade video. Daniel was in it briefly at the start, but mostly it was the twins. Edited highlights of the twins, taken from all the videos Daniel had made since they were born. He'd set the images to a soundtrack of 'It Takes Two' by Marvin Gaye and Kim Weston. The two of them kicking their legs in unison. A hilarious minute of her trying to change Yvette's nappy while also trying to stop Zachary from wriggling away. Her asleep, and the twins in her arms, all of them snoring. He'd exaggerated the sound in that section. The two of them eating solids for the first time, faces covered in pumpkin puree, Bett covered in pumpkin puree, their kitchen covered in pumpkin puree. Image after image of them, her two beautiful babies. Not babies any more. Her two beautiful children.

'It's for when you're away and missing them,' he said. 'So you remember just how messy they are.'

She surprised both of them by bursting into tears.

CHAPTER NINE

In Dublin, Des Foley was at a Gaelic football match. Dublin versus Kildare at Croke Park. He was a longtime supporter of the Dublin team. He didn't get to their matches as often as he'd like, his work often taking up the weekend, but today's charity match was an exception. He'd made a day of it, taking sandwiches and a flask, arriving in time for the earlier minor match too. He'd even got some work done. That iPhone really was a great old invention. He'd confirmed another job for the following weekend, supplied quotes for three possible jobs and done more research for his Quinlan booking.

His wife would have rolled her eyes if she'd known. She'd caught him googling again recently and not been happy about it. 'Des, leave them alone. I feel guilty enough for doing a bit of it myself. They've made it clear they want just a driver, not a tour guide or a private investigator.'

'I'm just getting organised. I haven't driven around Kildare for a few years. It's professional of me to know the best restaurants and cafes if they get peckish. Lola is in her mid-eighties, remember. Food is important when you're that age.'

'Food is important at our age, but I'm worried you're not stopping at that. I know you, Desmond Foley. I know when you get a bee in your bonnet.'

'I'm a bee-free zone, I promise. Just researching the best seafood chowder in a twenty-mile radius. Visitors always want seafood chowder. And brown bread.'

Breda's googling the previous week had been very interesting too, as it happened. Quite a few online entries about Lola had appeared, with photos, mostly on a Clare Valley newspaper site. Des had since discovered that the newspaper was edited by the very Bett Quinlan he was liaising with! The internet was a wonderful thing, even if nothing was private these days. Lola Quinlan went to lots of fancy-dress parties, Des and Breda had decided. In every photo they found she was wearing the most extraordinary outfits. They'd also discovered she'd taken part in an offbeat travel program for a UK-based cable TV channel some years earlier. Unfortunately they'd been unable to watch the program itself. It had been removed from the channel's website, annoyingly.

It seemed like fate that here he was at a Dublin–Kildare match today too. At half-time he wandered into the bar, got himself a pint and wandered just as casually to where a Kildare supporter of about his age was standing, also wearing his club's colours, also nursing a pint.

'Grand match,' Des said.

'If we win, sure.'

'You're just up for the day?'

'I am.'

'What part are you from?'

'Naas.'

'Is that right? Lovely town. I'm headed that way soon myself.' He said it as if Kildare was a thousand kilometres away, not forty minutes down the motorway. It was an icebreaker all the same.

Five minutes later they'd exchanged names, occupations, and deduced they knew three people in common.

'I'm doing some family-tree research of my own, as it happens.

Quinlans and Delaneys, from the Ballymore Eustace area.'

The other man shook his head. 'Can't say I know any Quinlans, off the top of my head. Or Delaneys. What are you trying to find, someone in particular?'

'It's for an old client of mine.' That was true enough. This Lola was a client and she was old. 'Emigrated back in the late 1930s, keen to find any remaining family. She was going to pay one of those genealogy agencies to do it but I said I'd ask around a bit first.' He would make a great spy, Des thought with pleasure.

'They're both common enough surnames. Give me your number and I'll let you know if I hear anything. Your client is over in America, did you say?'

Des hadn't said. This fellow was as wily at getting information as Des himself, he realised. He had a sudden image of Breda telling him off: *Des, keep your nose out of other people's business.*

Too late now. 'Australia, actually,' he said.

The man nodded. 'A Quinlan or Delaney who went to Australia in the 1930s from near Ballymore Eustace. Shouldn't be too hard to find out something.'

'You're a gentleman. Can I get you a pint?'

'I won't say no.'

Unfortunately, it was Breda who answered the man's call the next morning. Des was in the shower. She answered his phone, as she always did in his absence, in case it was a work booking.

He was washing the shampoo out of his hair and singing loudly when she came in.

'Petal!' he said as she appeared. 'Come to see me in all my naked glory?'

'All your naked interfering glory, you mean.'

'Hop in here with me, love, and explain yourself.'

She stayed where she was, talking loudly over the sound of the running water. A call had just come in, she explained. From a new friend of his in Kildare. He'd found out a bit of news about his client, old Mrs Quinlan. Breda's arms were crossed. She wasn't happy.

Des turned off the water. 'It just came up. We met at the match, got chatting —'

She handed him a towel. 'Why can't you just garden and watch box-sets like most fellas your age?'

'Come on. You're curious too, I can see it. What did he say he'd found out?'

'He wouldn't tell me. I think he thought I was your secretary. Put him right about that, won't you?'

With the towel tied around his waist, Des rang him back. He listened, took a few notes, said a warm thanks, made a promise of another pint next time Dublin were playing Kildare, then hung up.

Breda was nearby, waiting. 'Well?'

'Well what?' Des said, fighting a grin. 'You're right. I shouldn't have gone digging. It was no business of mine. I'll forget he told me anything.'

Breda rolled her eyes. 'You're loving this, aren't you?'

He nodded. 'And so are you.'

'Come on, then. Tell me what he said.'

Des did.

In Clare the next day, Lola was waiting for the sound of her son's car. He'd phoned from Adelaide as they were leaving. Expected time of arrival, ten a.m. It was a minute to ten when she heard the crunch of gravel under car wheels. Darling Jim. Always so punctual.

With the help of a stick – her arthritis had been at her that morning – she was at the front door as he and Geraldine came up the path. A polite hello and a barely felt hug from Geraldine, a close tight embrace with Jim. He never ceased to cheer her up, just the sight of him.

Five minutes later, they were in her bright sitting room with tea and biscuits. Lola listened with great interest as they – mostly Jim, but with some contribution from Geraldine – filled her in on life in their new guesthouse. It was in Aldgate, one of the prettiest towns in the Adelaide Hills, in Lola's opinion.

It was a pleasure to run, Jim enthused. Jim was generally enthusiastic. It only took an hour or two each day to clean, he said, not all day like the motel. There was time to talk to guests, to research interesting dishes for breakfast. Geraldine rolled her eyes as Jim described the latest addition to his menu – homemade raspberry and rhubarb jam – but Lola knew it was an act. Geraldine was devoted to Jim and proud of him, as he was of her. Theirs was the happiest marriage Lola had seen, even if it constantly baffled her. Again, she said a silent thankyou to whoever was in charge of these things. She'd worried often in the early years that Jim might have somehow inherited his father's temperament. It had been a relief to watch him become the calm, gentle man he still was.

'Enough about us,' Jim said. 'Tell me everything about this trip to Ireland. I still can't believe you're going and I still can't believe you're not taking me with you.'

Lola had just patted his hand, about to explain her reasoning again, when Geraldine's phone rang. It was a friend of hers a few streets away, wanting to change their afternoon coffee to now if possible.

'That's fine, Geraldine,' Lola said, hoping her pleasure wasn't too obvious. 'Off you go. I'll take good care of Jim, I promise.'

She watched as her son and his wife exchanged a quick kiss goodbye. They were going to be separated for less than two hours, for God's sake. Geraldine was hardly boarding the *Titanic*. Lola kept a bland smile on her face until her daughter-in-law had gone, then settled back into her chair, far more relaxed now. It always astonished her that Jim never seemed to pick up on the tension between his mother and wife. Perhaps it was for the best.

'So, back to Ireland,' she said. 'This is just a reconnaissance mission, darling. I want you to come there with me next time.'

'You're going to make a habit of international flights in your nineties, are you?'

'I'm nowhere near being in my nineties, you young pup.'

'Are you sure you're well enough? Not just physically —'

'Not you as well. How many people have told you?'

'About your precarious mental state? Three so far, but I also had a missed call from Len the butcher this morning, so I'd say it will be four when I call him back.'

Lola explained yet again. She was fine. Perfectly fine. She had no intention et cetera, et cetera.

Jim was satisfied. 'That's what I told all of them. If I hear rumours you're thinking of strapping yourself to a rocket and being blasted into outer space for your final moments, then I'll worry.'

'There's an idea. Jim, you don't really mind that I didn't invite you to come to Ireland, do you?'

'Do you want the truth?'

Lola nodded.

'I did at first. For less than a minute. Then I looked out the window of the guesthouse and saw how beautiful the autumn leaves are, and I looked in our bookings folder and saw we are full for the next two months. And I realised I couldn't go with you even if I wanted to. I'll enjoy hearing about it as much as being there. And I don't like long flights, remember.'

'No, you don't.' The longest one he'd been on was from Melbourne to Perth when she'd taken a temporary job managing a guesthouse there. Jim had cried the entire journey there and back. Six hours' worth. At the age of seven. Presumably he'd got over that now but she was grateful he'd given her an out from any residual guilt.

He poured some more tea. 'So, are you going to meet up with any of my father's family?' he said.

She tried to keep her voice casual. 'I doubt it. I don't know where any of them are.'

'It would be easy enough to track them down, wouldn't it? Bett could do it for you, put all her journalist skills to work. Or your friend Luke. He found Alex for you, didn't he? Do you want me to ask him, if you have too much else to organise?'

'No. No, thanks, Jim. It's been so long, I don't know if any of them would still be in the area, or even alive.'

'He had a sister, didn't he?'

Lola tensed. 'How did you know that?'

'You told me. Years ago. Remember? When I had to draw that family tree at school and all the other kids had dozens of branches? And I had just the two of us?'

'I'd forgotten that.' It came back to her now in a rush, a memory of helping him do that homework. It was the loneliest family tree she could ever have imagined for herself.

Jim had been sad too. He'd seemed to accept his father and his grandparents on both sides were dead. But not even one aunt or uncle? The boy he sat beside at school had needed to get another piece of paper to draw in his aunts and uncles, he had so many.

Lola had made a decision. Surely one truthful detail wouldn't hurt. 'You do have one aunt. In Ireland. Your father's big sister. Her name's Margaret, but people called her Peggy.'

That was enough for Jim. She'd watched as, tongue poking out in concentration, he drew a line from his father's name and in his best handwriting, spelt out A u n t   P e g g y.

'Did Peggy marry, have kids?' Jim asked now. 'Have I got a tribe of Irish cousins I never knew about?'

Lola had thought Jim was past caring about any long-gone Irish cousins. 'I honestly don't know,' she answered truthfully. 'She and your father had a big falling-out just before we left for Australia. They never spoke again.' That part was a lie. 'She died recently, I believe.' She added just enough detail, briefly explaining about the website Luke had found, listing recent Irish deaths.

'Was there anything on the site about her family? If you want me to do some extra research, I'm happy to. If you want to meet up with any of her children —'

'I don't think so, darling. But thank you all the same.' Lola inwardly cursed the internet. It made this information too accessible. She should never have mentioned that website to Jim. Or mentioned Peggy in the first place.

She hoped that was the last of it for now. Shortly afterwards, as they were finishing their tea, Jim surprised her again.

'Geraldine and I are planning a driving trip later in the year. Just for a fortnight or so. Up to Canberra, we thought.'

'That will be nice, darling,' she said.

'I was thinking of going to the Australian War Memorial. To do some research.'

'Really? Into what?'

'My father's war record. I heard a radio documentary about it. Eventually everything will be online but even now there are records of nearly every soldier who ever fought for Australia. Details about their age, when they enlisted, where they trained, any injuries suffered, where they were killed, if they were one of the men who didn't come home. Edward died the same year he joined up, didn't he?'

'I think so.' She did her best to keep her tone of voice neutral.

'You think so?'

106

'It might have been the following year. Sorry, Jim. I'm getting muddled so easily these days.'

'I won't worry you for it now, but when you get back from Ireland, maybe we could sit down and you could tell me everything you remember about his war record.'

'Of course, Jim,' Lola said, hesitating only briefly. 'Now, I know I'm long retired from the business and you and Geraldine will be doing your official tour later together, but take me for a drive up to the motel, would you? Just to have a little look. And on the way, perhaps you'd come with me to Anna's grave? Just the two of us. I know you and Geraldine would have called into her on the way to me but —'

Anna's grave in the Sevenhill cemetery was always the first place they visited on any return trips home to the Clare Valley. He told her he'd be happy to go back there again. 'It's a bit early for champagne, though, isn't it?'

'Is it ever too early for champagne?' Every year on Anna's anniversary they had a ceremony at Anna's graveside, toasting her, remembering her, missing her. Lola often raised a glass to her even if it wasn't the time of her anniversary. 'We'll use water today instead. Or juice. She won't mind.'

Jim gently helped his mother to her feet. 'No, I'm sure she won't,' he said.

They didn't stay long, the two of them there at the hillside cemetery, surrounded by rows of autumnal vines. A cold breeze was blowing. Lola pulled her jacket in close around her. There was a softly spoken prayer from each of them, a quiet minute of remembering her, as if they ever needed reminding. Anna was always there, part of them all these days. It would always be that way.

After the cemetery, their visit to the Valley View Motel felt lighthearted. At Lola's request, Jim didn't stop the car, simply drove slowly as Lola peered across at the two rows of rooms, the central building with its dining room, kitchen and function room. It had been Lola's home for nearly two decades. Lola knew the new managers sent monthly email reports to Jim and Geraldine. She'd have loved to have been included on the mailing list but knew without asking that it would make Geraldine unhappy. Still, there were other ways of finding out information. Asking straight out, for example.

'How is their occupancy rate?' she asked Jim as he drove slowly past the forecourt a second time, again at Lola's request. Very good, Jim told her, reeling off figures from the last report he and Geraldine had received. Lola nodded in approval. She could see about half-a-dozen cars parked in front of the units, including numbers four and eleven, two of her favourite rooms. She and Anna, Bett and Carrie had taken great delight over the years in sleeping in empty available motel rooms rather than crowding in with Jim and Geraldine in the manager's small house at the edge of the motel property. It wasn't common knowledge – Lola knew some people felt uneasy about such things – but Anna had died in her favourite room, number seven, with her family around her. People presumed she had died in the manager's house, Lola knew. If they were unable to feel comfortable with the facts of life, this was one situation where she wasn't going to try to change their minds.

'Did we ever have a birth here?' Lola asked. She knew she didn't have to explain her thought processes. They always thought of Anna's death when they were here at the motel.

'I don't think so. Nor in any of our guesthouses. We'd remember, wouldn't we?'

'I hope so. I know we were unshockable, but a new baby would have registered with us, wouldn't it?'

'Would you have charged the guest extra for double occupancy?'

Lola laughed. 'No, I'd give the baby its first night on earth free of charge. I was always fair.'

'Formidable, but yes, fair.'

'Me? Formidable? I'm a pussycat.'

'I'd go with lion rather than cat.'

'A lioness? Yes, I like that. Can you put that on my grave? "Here lies Lola 'The Lioness' Quinlan".'

'People will think you were a heavyweight boxer.'

'Let them. Can you put a sculpture of two boxing gloves on my headstone too?'

'Of course.'

They had been having conversations about Lola's gravestone for years. Geraldine never approved. The girls were often quite taken aback. But Lola knew it mattered. She didn't want the Lioness line, that was definitely a joke, but she did know what she wanted. A simple gravestone. Her plot was already booked – just a curve of the hill away from Anna's. She also knew what songs she wanted played at her funeral. What readings. She was having it in the Sevenhill church, she'd decided, not for an each-way bet heaven-or-hell-wise, but for architectural reasons. It was a beautiful building, and so peaceful inside. Plenty of seats too. She hoped there would be a big turnout for her when the time came. She'd considered adding 'complimentary G&Ts to first 100 arrivals' to the funeral notice. She'd written that out too, with blank spaces for the dates to be filled in. She'd crossed out the G&Ts, though. She'd rather the money went to the local pub.

Jim was just about to drive back onto the main road when his phone beeped. Geraldine, texting him to say she was ready to be collected. Drat, Lola thought but didn't say. She was loving this extra unexpected time with her son. She declined when Jim invited her to join them.

'Thank you but no, darling. I still have a lot to do before I go away. Now, be a good boy and drop me off home and then you two lovebirds can have a bit of time to yourselves.'

Back home, she stood on the verandah waving until his car was out of sight. Her lovely Jim. He truly was the apple of her eye. And at least she hadn't lied to him then. She did have something she wanted to do.

She'd been working on it for five years. Not every day, just whenever it felt right.

It was for her great-granddaughter Ellen. She called it her Anna Book. Handwritten, in an ordinary notebook, it was half-filled with all the little details about Anna that Lola could remember. Not just funny things she had said as a child, or memories from her days performing as the Alphabet Sisters singing trio with her two sisters, though there were plenty of those stories in it. It was slowly filling up with Lola's many other memories of her oldest granddaughter, from the day she was born, right through her childhood, her teenage years, her work as an actress, a voiceover artist, her wedding to Glenn . . .

Lola hadn't decided yet whether she would put anything in it about the breakdown of that marriage. She still didn't know how much, if anything, Glenn had told Ellen about that time in their lives. Anna's diagnosis had been so sudden, her final weeks so fast-moving, that there had been no time and it felt as though there was no need to explain the truth to Ellen – that her parents had been on the verge of separation. Thankfully Glenn and Anna had still had a bedrock of love between them, due to Ellen. He had travelled directly to Clare when he heard the news of Anna's cancer diagnosis. He'd stayed there to farewell his wife and be close to their daughter through the hardest time of her young life.

In recent years, as Ellen grew older, she had become more knowing. When Glenn had started seeing Denise, now his second wife,

Ellen had reacted badly, misbehaving towards both Denise and her daughter, Lily, one year her junior. But that had settled down too in the past year, Lola had been proud to see. Occasional pep talks via Skype helped. Ellen was inclined to be dramatic. She hadn't licked that off a stone, as the Irish saying went. What was the other saying along those lines? The apple didn't fall far from the tree? Ellen loved to wring as much drama from any situation as Anna had. Indeed, Lola herself hadn't been immune to the temperamental temptation over the years. That was one reason she was able to nip it in the bud as often as she could. It took a drama queen to know a drama queen, after all.

In their recent conversations, and from what she'd learnt during Ellen's most recent short but wonderful visit, all was fine at home.

'Denise will never be as good as Mum but she's okay,' Ellen had announced. And she liked Lily, she'd decided. 'She's actually fun, even if she is younger than me.'

That would be a wonderful side treat of this trip to Ireland, Lola knew. Getting to know Ellen even better, and helping Bett and Ellen bond even more, most importantly. Bett had her twins, Carrie had her three with a fourth on the way. It would be easy – too easy – for the girls to get swept up in their own families and children. It felt important that Ellen have strong relationships with her aunts. Bett, especially. Carrie had different talents to offer – skills in makeup, an interest in fashion, a love of entertaining. They'd come into their own as Ellen grew older. For now, Lola wanted Ellen to watch and learn from Bett's generous spirit, her sensitivity, her warmth. She would not only be a good friend and a loving aunt, but a good role model to her little niece.

Yes, this trip to Ireland was necessary for so many reasons. Lola was realising that more and more as it grew closer. For now, though, she had memories to write down. A story she'd recalled about Anna, her first audition as an actress. It had gone disastrously. Anna had

CHAPTER TEN

In the Clare Town Hall three days later, a flurry of last-minute cleaning was underway. The mayor stood in the doorway, keeping an eye on proceedings. He'd made the right decision. The town's largest building was definitely the best venue for this photo call to welcome the TV company to the Valley. Not that it would be the entire crew, he knew. Only one of the cast and the head producer would be here today. The other actors, along with the technical crew, wouldn't be in the Valley for days yet. But he was determined to use every opportunity available to promote not just the TV series but, more importantly, the Clare Valley itself.

The producer, fortunately, was obliging. The mayor had got to know her quite well over the past month, as the final arrangements were put in place. He'd been amazed at how familiar she seemed to be with the Valley, naming different areas – Armagh, Polish Hill River, Billy Goat Hill – and pronouncing all the placenames correctly too. That was a particular bugbear of his. It was the village of Min-tair-o, not Min-tahr-o, for example. He'd offered to arrange a tour of the Valley's many wineries, big and small. She'd already seen them, the producer said.

'All of them?' he asked.

She nodded. 'I remember the first ten. It gets a bit hazy after that.'

The early days of filming would coincide with the annual Clare Valley Gourmet Weekend, one of the biggest events on the Valley's social calendar. It marked the end of vintage, the end of the busy season. Each winery linked up with a restaurant in the area or one from further afield, offering a range of different tastes of food and wine, to a backdrop of the autumnal vines. Many of the wineries hired bands, from pop combos to classical musicians to jazz. Thousands of people would spend the weekend in the Valley, at the tasting event on the Saturday and then the food and wine celebrations on the Sunday. It would be perfect footage for the TV series, the producer explained. All the colour and activity of a busy winegrowing area. Hundreds of people helping to set the scene. But even more people than those would be needed.

That was the other reason for today's event. It wasn't just to introduce one of the stars. The producer would be inviting a number of locals to be paid extras during filming in the area. The mayor expected a big response.

'What scene are you shooting during Gourmet Weekend?' he asked. 'The murder scene?'

'I can't remember offhand,' the producer had answered.

Any time the mayor asked for plot details, he got the same non-committal answer. There was nothing to be found online, either. He had tried, as had most members of the council staff (during working hours too, he suspected). The librarian had also told him there'd been a rush on the use of the public computers when news of the series was announced.

He still only knew what he'd been told in the beginning. That the TV series was a murder mystery, mostly dramatic but with some comedy elements, set in a wine region very like the Clare Valley but not called the Clare Valley. The characters included a visiting delegation of wine buyers from overseas. A very successful but unpopular winemaker. A restaurant owner. Much scandal was promised.

Would it be an affair, or perhaps some sort of industrial sabotage? Tainted wine, perhaps? A key character appeared to be the detective sent up from Adelaide – not called Adelaide in the series, but the closest capital city, in any case – to investigate the crime, while battling secrets of his own. But as for who got murdered or who'd done the murdering, they were none the wiser.

The mayor had found himself stopped more often than usual during his walks around town. Some older residents seemed particularly confused by what they had heard on the grapevine. An apt term in this case, the mayor realised.

'What's wrong with our own police investigating this murder?' one old man had asked him. 'Are they implying that our police are incompetent, if they have to send up a fellow from the city?'

'It's not real,' the mayor explained kindly. 'The detective is being used for extra dramatic tension.'

'I'd be tense too, if I thought people believed I wasn't doing my job properly. If I was the local policeman, I'd go on strike. Let them find their own murderer.'

Others had been more worried about the rumours there was an extramarital affair in the storyline.

'It's all very close to the bone for something that's apparently "made up", if you ask me,' one of the councillors said after a recent meeting.

'Really?' the mayor said, deliberately misunderstanding. 'There's been a murder here in the Valley I didn't know about? I am losing touch.' His joke fell flat. He tried again to pour oil on gossipy waters, explaining that in drama there were just a few plots: love, death, betrayal. That there were always unintentional echoes in real life. That's why TV dramas were so popular, he said. People could always identify with at least one storyline or character.

'I still think someone's told the scriptwriter all our secrets,' another councillor said, unimpressed with the impromptu lecture.

'All they've done is change the names. What do they take us for, fools?'

That morning, the mayor had asked the producer again if there was any chance of seeing a script.

'I'm afraid not,' she said, as cheerfully as she had answered him the other times.

'And you still can't remember the name of the scriptwriter?'

'I've a terrible memory for names.'

That wasn't true. He had been amazed at her recall. She'd remembered the names of the councillors and staff members with ease, each time they had met.

She took pity on him now, smiling. 'It'll all be great, I promise. Please don't worry. That's my job.'

He felt only slightly calmed by her words.

There had been some discussion about staging this announcement in one of the vineyards or wineries. But they needed a crowd and there was every chance people would get lost on the way, or tramp on the vines or trip over something in the wineries. Or others would get upset that one winery was being favoured over another. The mayor finally decreed that it would be held in this neutral venue. They'd done their best to cheer it up, draping the stage in artificial vine leaves, pinning up lots of tourism posters, arranging displays of wine on long tables. Someone had even brought in a couple of bikes and left them on the stage to highlight the Riesling Trail, the cycling and walking path that followed the route of the old railway line through the Valley. The mayor was privately concerned the whole effect was of a jumble sale, but there was no time – or budget – to call in a professional set decorator.

Again, the producer told him not to worry. 'It'll be Larissa they want to photograph, not two old bikes, trust me,' she said.

The mayor himself was secretly looking forward to meeting Larissa de Lorenzo. Famous from a two-year stint on a popular

TV soap opera, she would be playing one of the main roles. In her early twenties, with a blue-eyed-blonde beauty, she was tipped for imminent overseas stardom. It was a coup to have her in the cast, so the media release from the TV company had informed him.

An hour later, they were ready to go. Larissa had arrived on time, accompanied by her parents. She'd kindly interrupted a family holiday in the nearby Flinders Ranges to appear in this photo call. The mayor was instantly charmed by her, if slightly intimidated by her parents. They were guarding their daughter as if she was an Oscar winner draped in millions of dollars' worth of diamonds, not a young Australian actress dressed in jeans and a red duffel jacket. She was very pretty, there was no denying that. He had never seen teeth quite so white, either.

The hall was nearly full. The entire council was in attendance. A good representation of media – the assistant editor from the local newspaper and a radio crew from nearby Port Pirie. Even more excitingly, there were two camera crews from Adelaide.

Everyone in the area had been invited. To make sure the town hall didn't look empty, the mayor had also asked the principals of the Valley's schools to send fifty students each. It looked as though they'd sent one hundred each. The hall was jammed with chattering kids, so many it was getting hard to hear himself think. Every one of them seemed to have phones. They were taking selfies or staging pouty group shots. The boys were as bad as the girls.

He could see Bett Quinlan's sister Carrie, with a notebook in one hand, her phone in the other. As he watched, she took photos, then wrote something in the notebook. She seemed very serious. Perhaps she was following in her sister's footsteps and taking up journalism? Not a great time to do it. He had been hearing disturbing rumours about the future of Bett's paper. Then he remembered Carrie was doing a blog about the TV series.

'All set?' the producer asked him.

'Ready when you are,' he said.

They were going to begin by introducing Larissa. She was already being besieged by autograph hunters. Next, the producer would invite people to leave their names if they'd like to be extras. She also had another trick up her sleeve, the mayor knew. There was still one uncast speaking role. Not a big role, but a pivotal one, and with a fee attached too. A young person – male or female – would notice something on the night of the murder that would seem unrelated but turn out to be integral to the investigation.

'It will add authenticity if it's a real Clare Valley person, don't you think?' the producer said.

'But you don't call it the Clare Valley, do you?' the mayor said.

'Oh, you're just splitting hairs,' she said cheerily.

There would hopefully be one person in the town who could deliver their lines well. The mayor had uneasy memories of the last big dramatic production in the town, Lola Quinlan's musical *Many Happy Returns*, based on the story of the Second World War American General Douglas MacArthur's famous wartime speech, 'I will return', uttered in nearby Terowie. Lola had written it herself while in the grip of a feverish nightmare, from what the mayor could tell. It had been one of the most ramshackle if unexpectedly entertaining nights in the town's memory. Perhaps one of the actors from that show might try for the role? Hopefully not, he thought, recalling some of their performances.

Which reminded him . . . Where was Lola Quinlan? He gazed around the hall, finally spotting her towards the back, flamboyantly dressed as always. She was with a group of other elderly women – her 'crew' as he'd heard her call them once. He recalled she was off to Ireland any day. Good for her. A big trip for someone her age. As he watched, one of her friends took out a phone and they posed for a group selfie. They were as bad as the schoolkids. As he watched, they started to wave at one of the TV cameras.

There really was a most excellent media turnout. More than he'd expected, in fact. These interstate TV companies really did know how to run an event.

'Ready?' the producer asked beside him.

'Ready,' he said.

At home later that night, Bett was trying to juggle five activities at once. She had two casseroles simmering on the stove. Her plan had been to fill the freezer so Daniel wouldn't have to worry about cooking and could concentrate on twin-wrangling. So far, there were only two meals in there. She'd be better off sticking the name of a pizza delivery service on the fridge. She was also trying to finish her packing. They were leaving the next day. May in Ireland was officially early summer, which in reality meant temperatures not much warmer than the current autumn in South Australia. But there might be a couple of sunny days. She'd pack two dresses, just in case, as soon as she'd finished the cooking. She also had her laptop open on the bench beside her. She was answering work emails and trying to edit several articles that had come in that day from her community correspondents. From the twins' bedroom she could hear Daniel trying to simultaneously read a bedtime story and keep two lively kids in their beds.

A chime from her laptop alerted her to a new email. It was from Carrie. Subject: *First blog!!!!!!!!*

Bett felt a dart of alarm at the row of exclamation marks. Perhaps she should have asked Carrie to write a sample blog for her. It had been years since she'd read anything her sister had written, she realised. Carrie had been a good student, but more interested in practical subjects than academic ones. Of the three sisters, she'd also been the only one who'd declared an interest in working in the family motel business. Which she'd done until she and Matthew started having children and she'd decided to be a stay-at-home mum instead, trying several other activities as a money-earning sideline. Not that any of those had been too successful, if Bett remembered rightly. She recalled a children's party-planning company. A makeup line. And the short-lived attempt to make and sell handmade dolls. Bett had only ever seen one. It was more 'voodoo' than 'cute'.

She washed her hands and prepared to read Carrie's blog. Bett was constantly in need of fresh content for her paper, print and online, but had never been given a budget to pay for it. She wouldn't have dared ask anyone but her sister to do it for free.

She'd been paying for it in other ways, however. Her time, mostly. Carrie had rung her at least eight times since the town hall event to ask questions.

Bett's patience had finally come to an end. 'Carrie, please, just do the best you can. I told you, it's a colour piece. My assistant's written the facts. I want you to be more informal. As if you were telling a friend what happened.'

'A good friend or someone I don't know that well but still consider a friend?'

Bett shut her eyes. 'Either.'

'Great! And how many words again?'

'As many as you need. It'll be going online so you've got more space than if it was in the paper itself.'

'Got it! Roger, over and out!'

There were more exclamation marks waiting in Carrie's email itself.

Here it is!!!! I hope you like it!!!!!!!!!! she'd written.

Bett gave the casseroles a quick stir before she started reading. From the bedroom came the sound of a range of farmyard animals. Either Daniel had tipped over the edge sanity-wise or he'd succumbed to the twins' insistence he read their farmyard story again.

And again. They were obsessed with it. She quietly closed the hall door.

Halfway through Carrie's blog she spoke aloud. 'Oh my God.' She kept going to the end, then read it again, hoping she'd read it too quickly the first time and it was better than she thought.

It wasn't.

It was as if Carrie was back in primary school, doing a 'What I Did on My Holidays' assignment. Not only that. It was peppered throughout with many enquiries to Bett herself:

My exciting day began in the Clare Town Hall. It was built in 1926 and is made of sandstone. Inside there was a strong smell of furniture polish and approximately four hundred chairs. *(Note to Bett – I didn't get time to count them all, sorry. Do you want me to check with the council exactly how many there were?)* Some were empty, some had people sitting in them already. More and more people arrived, including a lot of schoolkids. *(Bett, did their parents know they were being taken out of lessons? Should I check with the parents' association?)* Up on the stage there were a few tables and a few posters of vineyards and a couple of bikes. There were also lots of leaves. I don't know if they were real or artificial. They looked quite real, I thought.

I was not the only journalist there. I counted two cameramen *(I'm not being sexist, Bett, they were both men. Are there female cameramen? Or camerawomen?)* and someone from the local paper *(your paper, Bett!!)*, someone with a microphone who I guess was from the radio station in Port Pirie. There were lots of people – mostly men, again, it really is a man's world sometimes – in suits too. I think I recognised one of them as a politician, but I'm not sure.

We'd been told it would start at eleven but by three minutes past it still hadn't started. I could see that everyone was there ready and waiting, including the actress, the pretty one from that Seahorse Bay TV soap opera who is absolutely tiny. Apparently that's often the case that film and TV stars are much smaller in real life. The actress's parents – her name is Larissa de Lorenzo, by the way – were there too, I think, unless they were bodyguards. Oh, the series is definitely called *Murder in the Vines*, by the way! They announced it at the start (it finally began at eight minutes past eleven). We still don't know who gets murdered. The mayor talked a bit about how good this will be for tourism, which I have to say he says about most things, new roads or bike races or anything and then the producer who is a woman (at last!!!!!) aged about fifty or maybe a bit more, short hair, red lipstick, also in jeans and a kind of sleeveless jacket, with a really lovely voice. *(Bett, it reminded me of Anna's, that beautiful warm deep voice she had.)*

Bett stopped there for a moment. Even now, she would sometimes hear her sister's voice unexpectedly on the TV or radio. Anna had worked as a successful voiceover artist until a few months before she died. She'd put voices to everything from new car ads to dish-washing sponge commercials. In the first year after she died the family had turned off any of her ads. Now, it was a comfort. It was even, occasionally, quite funny to hear her.

Bett continued.

The producer said that they were very glad to be filming in the Clare Valley, it's so beautiful, so picturesque, etc etc. She also said they'd need lots of paid extras for the crowd scenes, with one role even having a bit of speaking. All the kids stopped taking selfies for a minute at the sound of that. *(I'm serious, Bett, that's all they did the rest of the time, either took photos of themselves or their friends, all with these weird pouts. Not just the kids, either. Lola and her friends were at it too.)* Heaps of the kids and lots of other people then rushed over to register as extras. I think the best word to describe it would be stampede. And that was it, pretty much. *(Sorry, Bett, I'm not sure what else happened after that as I had to leave to pick up the kids from the babysitter. C xx)*

Carrie had also attached ten photos. She was in eight of them, smiling at the camera, the crowded town hall behind her. She'd taken one photo of the young actress and her parents but unfortunately from the back of the hall. It was like playing 'Where's Wally?' to spot her.

Bett stared at the screen in silence. She had three options, she realised. She could ring Carrie and say she'd have to start writing it all over again, that this was too stream-of-consciousness, not factual enough. There would be tears, an argument, drama. Option two, she could try to rewrite the whole blog herself. That could take hours. She didn't have hours. Or option three – she could simply do a quick edit, take out all the queries directed to her, and publish it online. As it was. Tonight.

She'd readily agreed with Lola's idea to ask Carrie to do the blog, after all. Not only because it would distract Carrie from being jealous. Not only because Carrie would really enjoy doing it. She loved TV and gossip more than anyone Bett knew. But Carrie was also extremely popular in the Valley. She was – generally – so bright, open and chatty. This report was exactly what it was like to listen to her when she was in full flight about something she'd seen or done. She gave all the detail. She wasn't a hard-nosed investigative reporter. She was a local mother of three-nearly-four, putting into words what she'd seen in the hall. Which was exactly what Bett had asked her to do.

As for the photos . . . Bett decided she'd have to talk to Carrie about those before any future posts. It would help if she got closer to people rather than standing a kilometre away. And she didn't need to be in all of them. Not with her photo there on the byline. But none of that mattered this time. Bett could easily download a publicity shot of Larissa. She had hundreds of photos on file of the mayor. Carrie had somehow got a close-up shot of the producer as she was walking by. There were also lots of shots of local people, which was what her readers most wanted to see, after all.

Bett made her decision. Option three. She wrote back to Carrie. *I love it.* No exclamation mark.

And she nearly meant it.

CHAPTER ELEVEN

In Dublin, Des Foley was in front of his computer again. Breda was out with friends. He certainly wouldn't dare do this if she was home. The kids weren't due to call over tonight, fortunately. But if by chance they did, he'd say he was just doing a bit of research for a client.

It was true too. That's exactly what he was doing.

But without being asked! He could almost hear Breda saying it. *Desmond Foley, stop poking your nose into other people's business!*

But it was his business, wasn't it? Part of the full customer service experience he did his best to provide. The granddaughter had said in her latest email that it would be two days in and around Dublin at first, then at least a week in Kildare and a few side trips elsewhere. *Details to be confirmed*, she'd written. He was glad to hear that. Why come all the way from Australia just to see two counties? And wouldn't it be a bonus for them if their driver had all sorts of handy tourist information already researched? Or, for example, if they happened to say, if only we'd done a bit more research into the Quinlan and Delaney family histories before we got here? At which point Des would be able to pretend he had overheard them, and then dazzle them with his own findings.

He always listened to the conversations coming from the back seat. That was one of his favourite parts of the job. It was like being a waiter. People forgot you were there, or thought you were deaf or something. The things he'd heard discussed over the years would curl his hair, if it wasn't curly already. Political secrets. Business gossip. Kildare was one of his favourite counties for eavesdropping, as it happened. He'd occasionally driven horse trainers or breeders or even wealthy punters from the airport to the thoroughbred auction house or racecourses there. He'd sat at the wheel, quiet as a mouse, polite as can be, yet kept his ears wide open. Over the years he'd picked up a tip or two that had proved quite valuable, the rare times he placed a bet. He knew Breda thought he did nothing but drive and chat. She'd be surprised if she saw him. He did have some self-control. He'd long discovered that you often learnt more by staying quiet than you would by asking questions.

He'd begun tonight by reading several more issues of Bett Quinlan's newspaper. The Clare Valley seemed like a nice place to live. Lots of community spirit. Lively politics. Excellent sporting facilities. Lots of connections with Clare in Ireland too, he'd discovered. There seemed to be plenty of excitement about a TV series soon to be filmed there. He'd also read with great interest about a big event called the Gourmet Weekend. He'd hopped over on to the event's own website, literally licking his lips as he read some of the menus. Wouldn't Breda love to go to something like that one day? Continuing his googling, he'd also found Bett Quinlan's name at the bottom of some media releases from a now defunct record company in London. It might have been a different Bett Quinlan, of course, but these young Australians travelled as much as the young Irish kids did. He and Breda were half-expecting and dreading one of their three to announce they were emigrating. America or Canada would be bad enough. Australia or New Zealand was worse. Too far away.

The youngest of the Quinlan party, Ellen Quinlan-Green her name was, was on Facebook but he was pleased to see that only her friends could access it. He'd heard a disturbing program on the radio one day while waiting for a client outside Government Buildings. Unscrupulous men were preying on young girls via their Facebook pages, befriending them, stealing their photos. It didn't bear thinking about.

He glanced at the clock. It was nearly nine. Breda would be back by ten. He'd better get a move on. The task he'd set himself tonight was to find out what he could about Lola Quinlan nee Delaney *before* she had left Ireland for Australia. His friend at the football match had given him an excellent lead. He'd told Des that he'd asked around, casually, in his local pub in Naas. Did anyone happen to know of a Quinlan or Delaney who had gone to Australia back in the late 1930s, probably just before the war? No one knew any of them specifically, he said, but one man had a recollection of there being a teacher at the school in Ballymore Eustace years back called Delaney. Another had heard that a lot of the national school records were online these days. Not just names, but examples of their schoolwork and all, as part of an online history project. They were very good starting points. Des had thanked his new friend. He definitely owed him a pint at the next Dublin versus Kildare match.

Using two fingers to type, he keyed in 'Delaney school Ballymore Eustace' and pressed return.

An hour later, he glanced at the clock. Five minutes to ten! Where had the time gone? He'd been lost in a world of fascinating information. His friend's friend was right. There had been a principal of the national school in Ballymore Eustace in the 1930s called Delaney. It had to be Lola's father. He'd also visited the website packed with school records from that time. He hadn't been able to find a Lola Delaney or Quinlan, but there had been mention of a Louisa Delaney. Perhaps Lola was a nickname? He'd ask Breda what she thought later. He'd tried to find class photos, but had been disappointed. He hadn't been disheartened for long. There were too many other fascinating links to follow about life in Kildare at that time.

As a born and bred Dubliner, he'd had no idea until tonight about all the private estates that existed in Kildare back then, occupied by Anglo–Irish families with their impressive mansions and teams of domestic staff. It was all very *Downton Abbey*, it seemed. Clicking through to other sites, he'd discovered that three of the estates near Ballymore Eustace itself were now prestigious horse studs owned by the Aga Khan, the multimillionaire spiritual leader. The current Aga Khan's father had been married to the American actress Rita Hayworth. She might even have visited Kildare! What would it have been like to live or work on one of those estates when they were still privately owned? he wondered. It must have taken a small army to run them. Wouldn't it be incredible if this Lola was a long-lost member of one of the old gentry families and was coming home to reclaim her share of it? There'd be the minor matter of kicking out the Aga Khan but, still, what a story!

He could imagine Breda's voice: *Desmond Foley, have you lost the run of yourself again?*

'Yes, Breda, I think I have,' he said aloud. It was all the fault of the internet. It made this far too easy. Perhaps it was time to be purely businesslike again.

He checked the time. If his calculations were right, the Quinlans would soon be on their way to the airport. He sent Bett an email to wish them bon voyage, and then shut the computer down. Breda would be home soon. She was always a little merry after a night with her best friends, and he didn't want to spoil her good humour. He picked up his latest detective novel. He was mad for them. They were to blame for his overdeveloped curiosity, Breda often said. He did have a gift for hunting out clues, he thought. The last three thrillers he'd read, he'd guessed whodunnit long before the detective had got a sniff of it. Either the author hadn't hidden the clues well enough or Des really was blessed with a cunning, curious criminal mind.

Maybe he should write a book himself. His detective could be a down-on-his-luck, ex-alcoholic racing-car driver who had sobered up and now earned his living as a chauffeur. Until one day, in the back of his car, his old sidekick appeared, a rookie driver who now headed up a wealthy but corrupt racing team . . .

Not bad at all, Des Foley, if he said so himself. Certainly as plausible as the one he was reading. And tonight had proved he was good at research, hadn't it?

He'd just finished reading a chapter when Breda came in, aglow with red wine and the company of friends. She related the entire night to him, what the four of them had eaten, drunk and talked about.

'And what about you, love?' she said. 'Did you have a good night?'

'Quiet enough,' he said. 'I read, mostly.' He had to ask. 'Did you know the Aga Khan owns three horse studs in Kildare? And that his father used to be married to Rita Hayworth?'

'Desmond Foley, forget about the Aga Khan. You've been googling the Quinlans again, haven't you?'

He gave a sheepish nod.

She raised her eyes to heaven. 'What are you like? That poor family will rue the day they booked you as their driver.'

'Of course they won't,' Des said, offended. He might be a bit nosy, yes, but he was a professional too. 'I bet they're looking forward to meeting me as much as I'm looking forward to meeting them.'

Checking her emails at Sydney Airport, Bett was beginning to wonder if they'd chosen the wrong driver. He seemed to be taking an overly enthusiastic interest in their trip. In his latest email he'd mentioned he'd be tracking their flight online, so they weren't to worry if it was delayed – he'd be there waiting whether they were early, late or on time. Still, that was better than a lack of enthusiasm. And it was still a relief to know someone else would be doing the driving.

She glanced over at Lola. Her grandmother was browsing in the duty-free section, trying out different perfumes, making the young assistant laugh. Lola was always ready to chat to strangers, to find out about their lives. She'd seemed much happier in the past few days too. More excited than anxious about what the trip might be like.

Lola returned, smelling like a perfume shop herself.

'How many samples did you try?' Bett said, waving her hand in front of her nose. Her eyes began to water too.

'Just a dozen or so. I might make this my signature scent. What do you think?'

'I'll let you know once I can breathe again.' Bett smiled. 'So, are you excited?'

'Deliriously,' Lola said. 'Thank you again, darling. You weren't too sad saying goodbye today?'

'A little.'

Daniel and the twins and Jim and Geraldine had all come to the airport to see them off. They'd farewelled Carrie and Matthew and their kids in Clare. Not that Carrie had paid them much attention. She'd been too busy checking for comments on the bottom of her blog.

'Another ten comments, Bett!' she'd said, even as they were hugging. 'People love it!'

It was true, Bett knew. Carrie's informal chatty style had hit the mark. Even if she didn't know any more about the filming than anyone else, she also had an air of authority now. 'I got stopped five times in the main street yesterday,' she'd told Bett. 'People are dying to know if I've heard any more about who the lead actor is. I said my lips were sealed. Hinting I know but can't say, do you see?'

Bett had also reminded her to send any future blogs to her before she posted them.

Carrie still wasn't happy about that. 'It could take you hours to get back. It'll lose its spontaneity.'

'I'll live with it, if it's a choice between spontaneity and being sued for libel.'

The big hug from her mother surprised her. Geraldine usually reserved her physical affection for Bett's father. The two of them still often held hands. As teenagers, the three girls had always been embarrassed to see their father even give their mother a kiss as he passed her in the kitchen or bar.

Her dad had hugged her so tightly the breath had nearly been squeezed out of her. Bett had smiled to watch him hug Lola too.

'They are so cute,' Ellen had said on her last visit. Cute wasn't exactly the word for the two of them, both being so tall, but Bett agreed there was a very special mother–son bond.

Most surprisingly, Geraldine had even hugged Lola. Briefly. A landmark event, in Bett's opinion.

Bett's final farewells had been with her husband and children.

'I love you. We all love you. Now, go away and forget we exist,' Daniel had whispered in Bett's ear as he held her close. 'You are carefree, childfree Bett for the next two weeks.'

'I'm in charge of Lola and Ellen, remember.'

'No, you're not. The driver is in charge of the three of you. You're just another passenger. Enjoy it.'

She had long hugs with Yvette, and Zach, and then Yvette again and then Zach again, and then Daniel once more. Then with one final wave to them all, she and Lola had moved out of sight.

Now, after a quick flight, here they were in Sydney.

'One flight down already,' Lola said. 'So far, so good. I'm not even jet-lagged yet.'

'You're incredible,' Bett said. 'You bounced back from that

two-hour flight as if it was a two-hour flight.'

'I'm sorry my largesse couldn't stretch to business-class seats, Bett.'

'I'm still embarrassed you're paying for everything. I'll repay you one day, I promise.'

'I don't want your money,' Lola said, patting her on the hand. 'What use were those shares to me?'

'I thought you sold a diamond ring?'

'That's what I meant. What use was that old ring to me anyway?'

'Bett! Really-Great-Gran!'

There was only one person who called her great-grandmother by that name. Any more discussion was swept aside as a beaming, dark-haired girl ran up and flung herself at them. It was Ellen.

Across the departures hall, they saw Glenn carrying all of Ellen's luggage. Beside him, his wife, Denise, and stepdaughter, Lily. All three were waving.

During Anna's marriage, Bett had never liked Glenn. She'd found him overbearing, overconfident. But Anna's death had changed him too. Softened him. She now liked him very much. There was no disguising how much he loved Ellen, and how good a father he was.

Bett thought Denise was good for him. Low-key, smart. She was good with Ellen too. Calm but firm – just what Ellen needed. Bett adored her niece, it was impossible not to. But Ellen was also a wily teenager. Bett knew she'd need to keep her wits about her on this trip.

Right now, Ellen was more excited-child than precocious-teen. She showed Lola and Bett her new backpack. Her new suitcase. She was most proud of her latest model iPhone.

'Dad bought me a new one especially for this trip, so I can keep in touch with my friends while I'm away.'

'Keep in touch with us, I said,' Glenn corrected, ruffling her dark hair.

'Whatever,' she said in a singsong voice, throwing her father a cheeky grin. For a second she looked so like Anna that Bett felt the punch of grief again. She glanced at Lola. She'd felt it too.

They walked to the international check-in desk together. It wasn't until they reached the long queue for economy check-in that Glenn revealed his surprise. With a flourish, he directed them to the business-class area.

'No arguments,' he said. 'It's all arranged. I've had you upgraded, there and back.'

'Glenn, no!' Bett said. 'It's too expensive.'

'Glenn, that's very generous, but no,' Lola said. 'This is my trip, I told you. Ellen's my guest.'

'Lola, Bett, are you serious?' Glenn laughed. 'You're going to fight me over the choice between a cramped seat for twenty-two hours or a luxurious armchair that reclines into a bed? With gin and tonics on demand?'

Ellen spoke then. 'I'll be fine in business class on my own, Dad, really.'

Bett knew from Ellen's grin that her line had been rehearsed. Glenn had known they'd object. He was enjoying this, she could tell. She also felt a shimmer of guilt that she and Lola had recently talked about Glenn being mean with his money.

'Ladies, please,' he said. 'I haven't paid for a cent of it, I promise. I used my work frequent-flyer points. You're taking Ellen off my hands for two weeks, after all. Such peace, such quiet. I should be upgrading you to first class.'

'Dad!' Ellen said.

'I'm going to miss you every second of every day and you know it,' Glenn said, holding his daughter close. 'So, any more arguments, Lola? A lady of your height, it would be criminal to put you in cramped conditions.'

'Glenn, I accept, on behalf of Bett and each of my ancient bones. Thank you.' She kissed him on the cheek.

Beside her, Bett wanted to make a high-pitched noise of excitement. Business class! Both times she'd flown across the world she'd spent hours of the uncomfortable trip dreaming what such luxury would be like. Any dread of the long journey was swept away. She kissed Glenn too.

At the departure gates, there were tears from Ellen as she hugged her father one last time. Her eyes were dry the moment he was out of sight. The three of them emerged into the airside duty-free area, a brightly lit, highly fragrant array of shops.

Ellen stopped abruptly. 'Sorry, I just need to check my phone.'

'Again?' Lola said. 'You checked it outside about five minutes ago.'

'Lily might have posted photos of our farewell.'

'But you were there yourself. You don't need to see photos of it.'

'Oh, Really-Great-Gran, of course I do! I won't be long.'

Bett and Lola exchanged a look as Ellen took out her phone. She gave them both a brief glimpse of the screen, showing a photo of Ellen and her stepsister posing for a selfie minutes earlier. 'Lily's almost as quick at posting as me, look!'

Less than a minute later her phone cheeped again. Ellen stopped to check it. Again. And again.

By the time they reached the airline lounge at the end of the hall, they'd stopped six times for Ellen to check her phone. Bett was becoming irritated and trying not to show it. Lola was very irritated and not shy about showing it.

'I do hope this isn't going to be your modus operandi for this entire two weeks, Ellen Quinlan-Green. I'm bringing you with us for the benefit of your scintillating company, and to give you an indelible experience, not to give you new backdrop scenery to your phone's screen.'

Ellen pouted. 'But I have to check it. Otherwise I might miss out on something.'

'What could you possibly have missed out on during the past ten minutes, for example, during which you've checked your phone at least four times?'

'Six times,' Bett said.

Another frown from Ellen. 'Heaps of things. What my friends are doing. A new music video. Snapchat. Instagram —'

'Stop talking slang to me please, Ellen. Speak English.'

'I am, Really-Great-Gran.' Her eyes filled with tears. 'This is how it is with us these days. Just because you didn't have this technology when you were my age doesn't mean it's wrong that I do. You're just jealous because all you get to do is talk to each other and look at ordinary things like, I don't know, trees and sky and' – she threw out an arm towards the floor-to-ceiling windows – 'planes. We get to look at movies and photos and wonderful things, whenever we want, in the palms of our hands!'

Bett was taken aback by the sudden speech. Lola gazed at her great-granddaughter. She seemed to be trying not to laugh.

'Very passionate, Ellen. Yes, poor us, with nothing but sky and trees and planes to look at.' She held out her hand. 'Your phone, please.'

Ellen hid it behind her back. 'No way.'

Lola's voice chilled a degree. 'Your phone, please, Ellen.'

'It's mine. Dad gave it to me.'

'Do you really think it's polite to talk to me like that? Do you think your father, or your mother, or Denise, or Lily, would think that is a decent way to address your great-grandmother who has invited you to come on a trip to her home country?'

'Dad paid for my seat.'

'I paid for your seat. And a loyalty program devised by a marketing department paid for the fancy part of it. And I will have no compunction marching the three of us back to the desk and asking that nice lady to cancel the upgrade and return us to economy.'

135

Bett shot Lola an alarmed glance. Surely not?

There was a row of empty seats in a nearby waiting area. Lola turned to Bett.

'Darling, go for a walk, would you? Go and look at those lovely souvenir koalas and kangaroos in that shop over there and tell me how many of them are made in Australia. Ellen and I are going to sit down and have a little chat, aren't we?'

Ellen nodded, but her expression was mutinous.

Bett moved away, out of earshot, but close enough to watch them. She could tell Ellen was in a fury. Beside her, Lola seemed so relaxed she could have been meditating. She was talking softly, though, Bett could see.

Lola was a kind of child whisperer, she thought. She'd had years of first-hand experience of it. Lola had always had a multitude of ways to calm down her three granddaughters – jars to catch their tears, truth sticks to point at them to extract the whole story, or endless terrible jokes, delivered one after the other until they'd had no choice but to laugh.

It looked like she'd reached into her joke armoury now. As Bett watched, Ellen uncrossed her arms. The brows looked less knitted. A moment later, she even seemed to be giggling.

Bett heard a ping from her own phone. A text from Daniel: *Love you. Missing you already.* A photo of the twins fast asleep. She suspected that wasn't the case yet. He probably had a store of those photos ready to send to keep her worries at bay. She typed back a quick reply, telling him about business class with a long row of exclamation marks.

Fantastic! To the manner born, he replied.

She clicked on to Facebook. Then Twitter. Instagram. Her emails. She frowned at a work one, quickly tapped out a reply, copying in her assistant, Sam. They'd had a handover the previous day and she had promised not to check her work emails during this trip but she hadn't technically left the country yet. It would be simpler to reply herself than have Sam try to figure it out. Another email caught her eye. Then a ping from Messenger, a message from Carrie – a screenshot of even more comments at the end of her blog, with a *Woooohoooooo!* written beside it. Bett sent a thumbs up back, deciding not to mention the business-class upgrade yet, to keep Carrie's jealousy to a low hum.

Ten minutes later, she glanced up. Lola and Ellen were still side by side. Lola gave Bett a faint nod. A signal to return.

'So, is it good news or bad news?' Bett said, keeping her tone light. 'Economy or business class?'

'Business class, of course,' Lola said. 'As if we'd turn that down. Isn't that right, Ellen?'

'That's right, Lola,' Ellen replied with a big smile.

'"Lola"?' Bett asked.

'It was one of the conditions of our agreement,' Lola said. 'She can call me Lola from now on.'

'And the phone crisis?' Bett asked in an undertone once Ellen skipped – actually skipped – ahead.

Lola patted her jacket. 'In my pocket, where it will remain except for two hours a day. One hour in the morning, one hour in the evening.'

'How on earth did you manage that?'

'Threats of physical violence.'

'Seriously?'

Lola shook her head, then mimed zipping her lips.

'You're really not going to tell me?'

'Not yet, no.'

'Why not?'

Lola looked pointedly at the phone in Bett's hand. 'Because I'm about to use the same tactic on you.'

CHAPTER TWELVE

In their Adelaide Hills guesthouse, Geraldine was finishing the end-of-day tidy-up of their kitchen while Jim went through their accounts in the room next door. She loved their new kitchen. It was so compact, so modern, a pleasure to clean compared with the one in the motel. She cooked for a maximum of ten people here. At the motel she'd sometimes catered for one hundred. Moving here was the best decision she and Jim could have made, for so many reasons.

She'd had to leave Clare. It was hard enough to live with the knowledge that Anna had died, without seeing reminders of her every day, everywhere she looked. Having to pass the room where she'd spent her final days. Walk by the bench she and Anna had sat on together, in the brief moments she had been well enough. Geraldine had needed peace to grieve. Selfish peace. She wanted to mourn with Jim, as Anna's parents. She couldn't share it any longer with Lola, with Carrie, with Bett. She had slowly realised that everything about grief was selfish. She needed to mourn Anna purely as her eldest daughter, not see the others mourning Anna as a sister, a granddaughter.

Thank God Jim had understood. He'd agreed to this move to a new place, a new business, a new life. Of course she missed her grandchildren, her other two daughters. She and Jim both did. But they saw them often, and received photos or texts almost daily, from Carrie especially.

Geraldine hadn't explained her true feelings to Bett or Carrie. It wasn't her way. She only talked about her innermost fears and worries with Jim. It had always been like that between them, even if not everyone understood it. Lola, especially. Geraldine had long known she would never be the daughter-in-law Lola wanted her to be. Lola had always made it clear she found her wanting, as a wife, as a mother, as a daughter-in-law. Geraldine had finally stood up to her the previous year. Nothing had felt as good. She'd somehow kept her temper as she told Lola how it had felt to have someone as domineering, as interfering as her so close by, year after year. How suffocating it had been. Oh, she knew she was in a minority. She knew Lola was practically a national treasure in the eyes of many people in the Valley. Her flamboyance, her sense of fun, her musical talents . . . All of it drove Geraldine crazy. Lola drove Geraldine crazy. To think that her Jim, her quiet, kind, gentle, steadfast, generous, supportive, adored husband could have been that woman's son . . .

As she wiped the counter a final time, she wished once again that she had met Jim's father. Perhaps that would have shed more light on Jim's personality. But she hadn't. And why not? Because of Lola.

Lola and her lies.

Geraldine and Jim had been married for a year before Jim told her everything about his family background. When they first met, when Geraldine was working in the kitchen of their guesthouse at the time, it was Lola who'd told her about her husband dying during the war. How Lola had found herself a pregnant young widow, raising her son alone, across the world from her family in Ireland. Such a sad story. At first, Geraldine had admired Lola, even enjoyed her. As she and Jim grew closer, fell in love and married, she heard more about his peripatetic childhood. He and Lola had moved often, saving hard, upgrading to better premises each time. It was always clear to Geraldine how much Jim admired his mother. Lola was obviously and justly proud of him too. As she should be, Geraldine knew. But he was no longer a child. He was a man in his twenties when Geraldine met him. Lola should have let him lead his own life. But she'd never given him that chance.

'Oh no, you can't move away,' she'd said to them the year they were married. 'We work so well together. Business is booming. Let's keep it as it is for the time being.'

She'd said it the next time a possible move came up. And the next. After that, the idea of them moving away was somehow never raised again.

It had made sense in the beginning. There hadn't been enough money to rent and run two guesthouses. The three of them did make a good team. But as time passed, Geraldine realised something. Lola was simply always there. Before work. At work. After work. There was no escaping her, all of them living in the staff quarters. Lola had been as big a personality back then. Interested in all things, in all people. Geraldine had slowly realised that if she was to have any privacy or independence at all, she had to close down around Lola, to keep things from her. She had to put up a barrier, or it would be Jim-and-Geraldine-and-Lola, a trio not a couple.

It was when Geraldine learnt she was pregnant with Anna that Jim started talking about his father in more detail. The two of them liked to lie in bed at the end of their long day, Jim holding her close, both of them talking about their baby, what he or she might be like, who he or she might look like, what he or she would become.

Even now, nearly forty years later, Geraldine could recall those times. The memory made her smile, the joy followed swiftly, sharply, with a stab of grief. How could her beautiful Anna be gone? How could she possibly be dead? If she and Jim had known back then, talking with such happiness about their first baby, if they could have known that the year she turned thirty-four she would —

No. No, she couldn't start crying. They had guests staying. She might need to go out and talk to them. She forced herself to think of something else. Do something else, before the grief overwhelmed her again. It had always been her way of coping. Work through any pain life throws at you. Keep busy. As busy as possible.

As she came into the living room twenty minutes later, having scrubbed all the counters one more time, Jim looked up from the computer. It doubled as a public computer if guests ever needed it. They rarely did. Everyone used their own phones these days.

He noticed the dust cloth in her hand. 'I thought you were finishing up for the night?'

'I'll just sort out this cupboard first.'

'I'll keep going here too, then,' he said, returning to the screen.

He was researching their planned driving holiday, she knew, as she pulled out the glassware in the cupboard, reorganising the shelves she'd reorganised barely a fortnight before. Jim liked to keep busy too, for the same reason. He needed to plan ahead, have something to look forward to. In recent months, he'd even organised passports for them both, just in case they took a notion to travel overseas one day, he said. His latest project was this trip to Canberra. For the Floriade flower festival, they'd decided. But for other reasons too.

On the recent drive back from Clare, Jim had reported his entire conversation with Lola. Geraldine hadn't been happy about it.

'She didn't say anything new about your father at all?' Geraldine said. 'Not even when you mentioned the war records?'

'No.'

'I can't understand it. When is she going to tell you the truth?'

'When the time is right.'

'Jim, she's eighty-five years old. How much more time has she got left?'

She saw from the sudden fix of his jaw that she'd upset him. Any conversation on this topic always left one or both of them upset. They drove in silence for ten minutes before Jim spoke again.

'I trust my mother, Geraldine. I still believe she told me what she told me for all the right reasons.'

'But she lied to you. She's still lying to you. To all of us.'

'Not all of us, Geraldine. It's between Mum and me. That's all.'

Even recalling that conversation made Geraldine's temper rise. She stopped cleaning the cupboard and sat still for a moment. She had to bring it up with him again. It was gnawing at her. It had been like that since this idea of the trip home to Ireland had come up, since the farewell at the airport. They'd all behaved as if it was a normal, happy homecoming trip, Lola going back to Ireland for the first time in sixty-five years, back to her home county of Kildare. Yes, Geraldine had thought. Back to where she and Jim's father had grown up, met and got married. The father she had been lying about for years. The father she had conveniently not discussed with her son. Still.

She needed to choose her words carefully, she knew that.

'Jim, what if something happens to Lola while she's away? A stroke, or worse?'

'We'll deal with it. But I hope nothing does happen,' Jim said, evenly. She could see his hands had stilled on the keyboard, though. After a moment, he spoke again. 'Geraldine, don't ask. Because I'm going to say the same thing I say to you every time this comes up. Yes, perhaps Lola and I should have spoken about this before she left for Ireland. We didn't. No, Lola still hasn't told me the truth about my father. No, I haven't been honest with her either. But that's been for good reasons on my part. I believe she's stayed silent for good reasons too.'

She'd heard this from him too many times over the years. 'When you were a little boy, yes. But now? How can she keep lying?

142

How can you not have told her —'

'For the same reason I've told you every time. What good would it do Lola to hear it?'

'I still think she should know. Before it's too late.'

'Before she dies, you mean? Why? If she does die, it won't matter either way, will it?'

Geraldine wanted to curse out loud. They fought so rarely. But they always fought about this. Would they never be able to escape from Lola's influence?

She tried one more time, from a different angle, one she had never tried before, not out loud anyway. 'I think it's a terrible shame. The girls would have loved to have had a grandfather.'

'Perhaps.'

His one-word answer was a signal. Stop talking about this, Geraldine. But something in her wouldn't let it go tonight.

'Just think of Bett over in Ireland. What if she meets some of his relatives? What if she starts talking to them about him dying in the war?'

'I'm sure Lola's thought of that.'

'What about Ellen? Everything she knows about her great-grandfather is a lie.'

Jim turned in his chair then. His voice was firm. 'No, Geraldine, it's not. She knows he was Irish. That he and Lola were married and came to Australia just before the war. All true. Beyond that, I don't think a thirteen-year-old would be interested in the facts of her great-grandfather's life, especially when she never met him. She knows she's lucky to have even one great-grandparent, I'm sure.'

That note of steel in his voice. Unusual but effective.

She gave up then, even though she had to clench her fists to stop herself asking more questions. 'I'll leave the cupboard until the morning,' she said.

'I'll lock up,' Jim said.

'Goodnight,' she said, in a voice as cold as she could make it.

'Goodnight,' he replied, in a falsely cheery voice.

Lying in bed alone twenty minutes later, she was still angry. It was a ridiculous situation. If something did happen to Lola in Ireland, the chance of a full exchange of the truth would be gone. It wasn't just about Lola any more. Carrie and Bett deserved to know the truth too. And if discovering their grandmother had lied to them all their lives, had lied to their father – well, if that was to shatter their illusions about their saintlike grandmother even slightly, then perhaps that was no bad thing.

Geraldine was wide awake now. How could Jim not tell Lola all he knew? It was inexplicable. She loved her husband dearly, but she would never understand his behaviour in regard to his mother. How could Jim not see how important it was for everyone to know the whole story? He was burying his head in the sand, when it would be so simple to start the conversation, for him to simply sit down with his mother, and say, 'Mum, something happened forty-five years ago, something important, and I think it's time you knew about it.'

It was getting to the stage that if Jim didn't say something, then Geraldine herself would. Jim would be angry at first, she knew that. But surely then he would see that she had done it for all the right reasons? As he always insisted Lola had done what she'd done for the right reasons too.

Geraldine turned in the bed, her mind too full of imagined conversations for sleep. She could picture the different possibilities so clearly. She and Lola, just the two of them, talking. She imagined the expression on Lola's face if Geraldine told her what she and Jim had known, all these years . . . Or would it be better if Jim had that conversation with his mother over the phone, while she was in Ireland? Or should they wait until all three of them were together, face to face, after Lola returned? Round her thoughts went, as she imagined every possible scenario, becoming angrier with each minute that something so important had been left ignored for so long.

When Jim came to bed an hour later, quietly moving around the room, changing into his pyjamas, saying her name in a soft voice, wanting to make amends as he always did after any disagreement, she didn't respond. For the first time in their long marriage she pretended she was fast asleep.

CHAPTER THIRTEEN

There was also tension that night in a renovated farmhouse outside of Clare. After calling out for help three times without a response, Matthew had resorted to modern technology and phoned his wife instead. Through the closed door of the study, he heard Carrie's phone ring six times before she finally answered.

'Carrie, I need some help here.'

'Sorry, I can't. I'm busy researching.'

'Carrie, come on.'

'No, Matthew. I manage them every day while you're at work so you can manage them now while I'm at work. And it's even harder for me, remember. You're not pregnant.'

'Carrie, yours is a hobby, not work. You're not even being paid to do this blog for Bett.'

'How dare you be so patronising. And you call yourself a feminist?'

'You call me a feminist. I'm not even sure what that means any more.'

'That men and women are equal. It's as simple as that.'

'What's equal about this situation? I'm in the kitchen trying to feed three kids and do the washing and speak to you on the mobile phone because you won't answer my cries for help in person,

146

while you're there in the office with your feet up looking at gossip websites.'

Carrie hurriedly put her feet down and closed the SoapStarsToday website. 'I am not just looking at gossip. I'm researching background on possible cast members of the TV series. I can't turn up on the set and say, "Hi, who are you and why are you famous?" That would be so embarrassing. I want to be able to refer to specific projects, ask them challenging questions. And as for having my feet up, you try being this pregnant with puffy ankles and see how you feel.' She put her feet back up.

There was a long sigh from Matthew. 'Carrie, I can't be pregnant, no matter how much I want men and women to be equal. All I really want is for you to stop ogling soap stars for five minutes and come and help me scrape the baked beans off the wall before they harden. Is that too much to ask?'

'How did the baked beans get on the wall?'

'It's a mystery. Ask your kids. They're too busy laughing at me to tell me.'

'Five minutes. But then they're all yours again.'

'I'll set the stopwatch.'

It took both of them an hour to finish feeding their kids, clean the wall, somehow get all three in and out of the bath in twenty minutes and into bed by eight p.m. Carrie decided to forgo her research until after dinner. The bean explosion had made her feel a bit guilty. Yes, they were Matthew's kids too and he should do his share, but the truth was he didn't have her expertise. They'd never have tried the old 'whoops, we've thrown the food at the wall' trick if she'd been in charge.

'Any more word from Lola and Bett?' Matthew asked as they sat down in front of the TV – finally – to eat their own dinner. Not baked beans but a defrosted casserole made by the Baby Squad – friends of Lola's – months earlier and still proving to be not only edible but delicious. 'They'd be nearly halfway by now, wouldn't they?'

Carrie glanced at her watch and did a quick calculation. 'Nearly. I know I said I'd like to go too, but I don't think I could bear that long flight, pregnant or not.' She stretched her legs out and wiggled both feet. 'We're much better off here on the ground. Imagine the three of them, stuck in cramped aeroplane seats eating lukewarm mush out of foil containers. Poor things.'

'The poor things,' Matthew agreed.

Thirty thousand feet in the air, Bett leaned back in her roomy business-class seat, took a final sip of her French sauvignon blanc and decided against one more bite of her chocolate fondant dessert. How had she not known that air travel could be like this?

She had just enjoyed a delectable three-course meal served on a tray off real plates with real cutlery and a white cloth napkin. She'd been invited to have her bed made up whenever she was ready, so she could stretch out – full length! – and sleep. Sleep! It would have been a luxurious treat to sleep sitting up with the neck cushion she'd brought. But to lie down? On a bed in the sky someone else had made for her? She sent Glenn another fervent psychic thankyou and sent Daniel a fervent psychic apology. If she had the time correct, he'd probably be trying to coax the twins into bed around now. And here she was, being treated like the Queen of Sheba, whoever she may have been.

They'd been greeted with wide smiles from the moment they showed their business-class boarding passes at the gate. They were personally shown to their seats, Lola fussed over as if she was royalty, even more so when Ellen cheerily informed everyone that she was her great-grandmother, that she was eighty-five and going home to Ireland for the FIRST time in SIXTY-FIVE years! Ellen herself was fussed over too, her enthusiasm and obvious bond with her great-grandmother bringing smiles to fellow passengers' faces, as well as the flight attendants'.

Bett was happy for Lola and Ellen to be seated side by side, while she sat across the aisle. She watched Lola quickly adapt to the sudden luxury, pressing this button and that button as directed by Ellen, who'd obviously flown business class before. She demonstrated the personal TV screen, the fold-up table, unwrapped Lola's soft blanket for her, showed her where to store her glasses, her book. Bett was glad of the lesson – she found all the buttons baffling, but was too embarrassed to ask the flight attendant and make it obvious she was unused to high-end travel. She glanced at their fellow passengers – mostly businesspeople, she assumed, all settling into their seats, one man already asleep before they'd even taken off.

Ellen was the only child, Lola easily the oldest passenger. The pair of them were soon the pets of the flight attendants. Lola's travelling outfit was also drawing attention.

'I read it was best to be comfortable,' she said.

'You certainly look it,' their personal flight attendant said with a smile.

Lola was wearing a velour tracksuit she'd found in the charity shop. Bett was sure it was comfortable, but the pattern would take the eye out of you, to use one of Lola's Irish phrases. It was covered in rainbows and unicorns. Lola had speculated it had once belonged to a member of a dance troupe. Very possibly, Bett agreed. Lola had teamed it with a bright-yellow pashmina and her silver lamé eye mask, which was now perched on her forehead. She looked like Ziggy Stardust's mother, Bett thought. Beside her, Ellen was the model of a seasoned traveller, also in comfortable travelling clothes, though without any garish patterns. As Bett watched, Ellen took out a little tube of hand cream and offered some to Lola.

'Flying can be very drying,' she said solemnly.

'Thank you, darling,' Lola replied. 'Do I eat it or put it on my skin?'

Ellen's laugh made Bett smile. Ellen laughed like Anna too. Being with her really was like travelling with a mini version of her sister. It was a sudden beautiful thought.

For a moment Bett considered looking through their itinerary again. But she already knew it off by heart. She wasn't ready to watch any films. She felt a twitch in her fingers, a longing to check her emails, the internet, her Facebook page, the newspaper website —

As if she'd read her mind, Lola leaned across the aisle.

'Darling, do you have the internet in your seat?'

'I don't think so. But I could ask —'

'No, don't. What about your phone? Can you receive calls or send texts?'

'I doubt it. In an emergency, probably. Is something wrong?'

'No, nothing at all. I want to tell you a secret about the TV series but I need to be sure you can't tell anyone for at least eight hours, until the official announcement.'

'Lola! How do you know all these things?'

'I told you I can't tell you. But that's fine, if you don't want to know this one —'

'Of course I do.'

Lola checked Ellen was happy beside her. She was engrossed in a *Harry Potter* movie, a blanket pulled up to her chin, a picture of contentment. Lola leaned back across to Bett and said two words.

'Rafe Ascot.'

Bett's eyes widened. 'He's here? In business class! Where?'

'Not here. He's going to be in Clare. For the TV series. He's playing the lead role. It's being announced today.'

'Rafe Ascot! Are you sure? But he's huge! A megastar! I mean,

I know he's been hit by scandal lately – didn't he have an affair with his nanny or something?'

'No, his co-star, who is fifteen years older than him.'

'How did they manage to get him?'

'He knows a friend of the producer, I think. He liked the role. Liked the idea of time away from the UK, out of the glare of publicity.'

Bett secretly loved that her grandmother was using a term like 'glare of publicity'. 'But that will bring paparazzi to Clare, won't it?'

'I should think so.' Lola smiled.

'And tourists?'

'Probably.' A bigger smile.

'And I'm not there for the announcement. A big story like this and who have I left in charge? Carrie.'

'She's only in charge of the blog. Your assistant will cover the news aspect, surely?'

'Yes, but Carrie will go bananas. She's had a crush on him for years. I have to talk to her —' She stopped. 'I can't talk to her. I can't talk to Sam either.'

'No,' Lola said. 'Clever timing on my part, wasn't it?'

'Have you known for long?'

'A month or two. I was sworn to secrecy. I'm like a steel vault, aren't I?'

'Is that the only secret you have up your sleeve? Some warning would be nice if you're going to spring anything else on me this trip.'

'I think that's it. But my mind is definitely going, so I might be wrong. Happy flying, darling.' With that she pulled down her silver eye shade and slowly reclined her seat.

*

At home in Dublin, Des was busy at his laptop. He'd just keyed in the Quinlans' flight details. The modern world really was extraordinary. He'd been able to see that their flight had left Sydney on time and was due to arrive at the halfway point of Singapore five minutes before schedule.

'You're now an airline stalker as well, I see?' Breda said, coming into the kitchen from the hall. She took off her coat and put the morning newspaper on the table in front of him.

'Technology is here to serve us, my sweet. I was checking they haven't installed a rocket booster or anything like that. So, something to eat?'

'Yes, please. I'll just shower.'

Breda worked three nights a week doing night shifts with a nursing agency. Her hours suited them. Des's jobs often didn't start until mid-morning. He liked being home to welcome her and make her something light and delicious to eat, before she went up to bed. This morning he'd decided on a cheese and herb omelette. He mixed up the eggs, grated the cheese and chopped the fresh herbs.

As he waited for the kettle to boil, he leafed through the newspaper. It was one of the tabloids, heavy with gossip and headlines, light on news of substance. A comic more than a newspaper, he thought. How much longer would print news last? He made a mental note to ask this Bett Quinlan about the newspaper industry in Australia. His own kids got all their news off Facebook or online sites. Des liked to think he was well informed too, but that was from hours spent in the car listening to the radio, not newspaper reading.

This paper was as scandal-filled as usual. Some Irish news – politics, cigarette smuggling, a drugs bust, gangland threats. Nothing unusual. It had a double-page spread devoted to some English actor who was having an affair with a much older woman. There was a side column of quotes from people interviewed on the street about him. Thumbs up all round, especially from mature women. 'Print my phone number, would you, in case he gets sick of her? I'm ready when he is!' Her age was under her photo. Seventy-nine. Des smiled.

Breda returned. 'I hope you're not smiling at the page-three girl, are you?'

'Of course not. I only read this paper for the hard-hitting news.'

Breda yawned. 'I was thinking, this family you're collecting, do you want to invite them over for dinner here? They're in Dublin for the first two nights, did you say?'

Des nodded. 'Getting over the jet lag before we go to Kildare, that's right. Invite them here?'

'I'm off for the next few nights. Maybe they might like to come to a real Irish home for dinner rather than a restaurant. A lady of that age, first time back after all those years. It feels right to be hospitable, don't you think?'

'You're some woman, Breda Foley. I thought the same thing myself but didn't want to say it, in case you thought I was sticking my nose into their business too much again.'

'You are. But I'm intrigued now too. They might say no, and no problem if they do. But I was thinking I could do that marinated chicken —'

'With the rosemary-infused mashed potatoes?'

She nodded. 'And the broad bean puree and spinach and almond side dishes.'

'I'll ask them as soon as I pick them up.'

'Maybe let them get in the car first,' Breda advised.

Fifteen hours later Des was waiting in the fancy new terminal at Dublin airport. The Quinlans' flight had landed twenty minutes earlier, right on time. He'd estimated thirty minutes for the three of them to go through passport control and collect their luggage. He waited in line with the other chauffeurs, some in suits like him, holding up iPads bearing their clients' names, others in casual clothes, with names scrawled on pieces of paper. There was room in the industry for everyone, but Des preferred his own businesslike approach. He adjusted his chauffeur's cap. He'd been teased about it, but he always laughed off their comments. He liked his cap. It looked professional. It also hid his bald spot.

The first of the passengers from their long-haul flight began to emerge. A mixture of ages, men and women. He smiled at a family reunion, a young couple with a baby being greeted in a mass of hugs, all clearly meeting a grandson or granddaughter for the first time. He watched another arrival, a woman in a smart trouser suit, met by a nervous-looking young man. He heard snippets as they marched past him, talk of spreadsheets and cash flows.

He'd emailed Bett and told her he would be there waiting with a sign. It wasn't needed. He spotted them immediately. They made a striking trio. A young girl, dark hair, pale skin, a pretty little thing. Beside her, a woman in her thirties with a mass of dark curls. But it was the tall, white-haired woman in between them who truly caught Des's eye. She was dressed in an extraordinary brightly coloured tracksuit. She was wearing not just one long necklace but at least ten. Her posture was regal, even if she did seem to be relying on a stick for some support. Lola Quinlan, Bett Quinlan and Ellen Quinlan-Green. Des named them all in his mind.

He stepped forward. As he related to Breda later, still amused at his own behaviour, he took off his cap and bowed deeply. 'Welcome to Ireland. Desmond Foley, at your service.'

*

Ten minutes later, they were all settled in his car. No, Lola had told him firmly but with a smile, she was perfectly happy to walk to it. She didn't need a wheelchair. Yes, it had been a lovely journey, Bett told him.

'I slept for hours,' the girl said. 'And I watched five movies. Five!'

'It's a difficult flight, I believe? So long, of course.' He wanted to say he and his wife were hoping to fly to Asia themselves one day, but bit his tongue. Breda was right, he had to be friendly but professional, welcoming but not too talkative.

He'd parked – illegally – as close to the main doors as possible. He knew the traffic police well and made it his business to slip them the odd fiver.

'Your chariot awaits,' he'd said, pointing proudly at the car, washed and polished the previous day. He helped them in – the back seat was roomy enough for three – before loading their luggage.

'So, to the hotel first?' he asked. Bett had been his contact, but he now felt it was Lola he should be speaking to. She seemed to have a natural authority, and not only because of her height or age.

He saw Bett glance at her grandmother. He was right.

'Yes, please, Desmond,' Lola answered.

'Please, call me Des,' he said.

He pulled away from the kerb, wanting to ask a dozen questions. He could hear them talking softly in the back. He usually played classical music at a low volume, for atmosphere and privacy for his clients. He decided not to turn it on yet.

Through the rear-view mirror, he could see the older woman looking left and right as they drove down the motorway.

'Is it all completely different so far, Lola?' the girl asked from her middle seat.

'I was never at the airport before, Ellen,' Lola said. 'I went to Australia by ship.'

By ship! Imagine that, Des thought. All the questions he'd like to ask about that journey!

There were two routes he could take from the airport to their hotel near Ballsbridge. One would skirt the city, one would take them right into it. He directed his question at Lola this time.

'We'd love the city route, Des,' Lola said. 'In fact, please take your time and show us the sights. We're in no rush to get to the hotel, are we, my darlings?'

'It's your trip, Lola,' Bett said. 'Whatever you say goes.'

'I do like hearing that.' Lola leaned forward. 'We're in your hands, Des, thank you.'

'The Des Foley Scenic Tour it is,' Des said, smiling. This would be a great job, he knew it.

CHAPTER FOURTEEN

Fifteen minutes after leaving the airport, Des wasn't feeling so confident. He'd had to apologise twice for the fact they hadn't moved more than one hundred metres along the motorway from the airport. Lola had told him not to worry. There must have been a serious collision somewhere. The traffic seemed to be backed up for kilometres. Not the best welcome to Ireland after sixty-five years away, Des thought.

As they inched forward, he listened in again to their conversation. Ellen was remarking on the green fields. Bett was recalling her own arrival in Dublin. She'd come in on the airport bus, late at night.

Again, Des had to bite his tongue. Bett had been here before? When? For how long? Why hadn't she mentioned that in her emails?

Fortunately Ellen asked all the questions Des wanted to ask. He listened as Bett explained that she had lived in Dublin and then London for nearly three years.

'How old was I?' Ellen asked.

'You were four when I left and seven when I came back. Do you remember? For Lola's eightieth birthday party?'

'Just before Mum got sick.'

'That's right, darling.'

In the rear-view mirror Des saw Lola and Bett exchange glances.

'That was the saddest time of my whole life,' Ellen said.

'Ours too, darling,' Lola said, kissing the top of her head. Bett did the same.

Des longed to ask more. So Ellen's mother had been sick. Had she got better or . . . ? *Mind your own business*, he imagined Breda saying.

Five minutes later they were moving properly again. Dublin never looked good on a grey day like today, but his passengers – or his guests, as he liked to call them – didn't seem to mind about the weather. The focus was on Ellen's reaction so far, not Lola's. She was full of observations. 'Look at the two languages on the road signs! Why are the houses all joined up like that? Look, an Irish flag!' Des named the suburbs as they passed through them: Whitehall, Drumcondra.

'Did you ever come here, Lola?' Ellen asked each time.

'Never. This part of Dublin is all new to me too, darling,' Lola said.

She sat up straighter, Des noticed, as they drew closer to the city centre. He pointed out Croke Park on their left, the stadium for the GAA, the Gaelic Athletics Association. To their right, the Royal Canal. If they looked quickly, they'd see a statue of the writer Brendan Behan on a bench. Three men were beside it. They were all drinking. It wasn't noon yet. Des didn't mention them.

He had a few literary quotes up his sleeve for moments like this. He tried one now. 'Brendan Behan was not just a writer, playwright and wit, he was also unfortunately one of Ireland's most famous alcoholics. As he said, "I only take a drink on two occasions – when I'm thirsty and when I'm not."'

He expected a laugh and received two brief smiles. *Careful, Des*, he could imagine Breda saying.

They continued along Dorset Street, a raggle-taggle stretch of takeaway shops, a car yard, charity shops . . .

Bett spotted them too. 'Look, Lola. You can volunteer there if you get bored with us.'

A left turn moments later and there was far more to see. 'And here we are in O'Connell Street,' he announced. 'Dublin's main thoroughfare, once a beautiful boulevard, now not quite as glamorous. Home to the GPO, the general post office, the main focus of the 1916 Easter Rising, during which —'

Ellen interrupted him with a shout. 'Look, a leprechaun!'

'She's right, there is,' Bett said, laughing. 'After me telling her there was no such thing.'

A man in a leprechaun costume stood on the footpath, holding a sign pointing to a nearby souvenir shop. As they stopped at the traffic lights beside him, he put down the sign, took off his leprechaun head and lit up a cigarette.

'And that's why they disappeared,' Lola said to Ellen. 'I told you smoking is bad for you.'

'Would you like me to show you anything in particular?' Des asked, taking the opportunity. 'Sorry to have overheard, I know you lived here for a while, Ms Quinlan, and you're from here, Mrs Quinlan —'

'No titles, please, Des,' Lola said. 'We're going to be together for two weeks. I'm Lola, this is Bett and this young lady beside me is Ellen.'

'I'd actually like to be called Miss Quinlan,' Ellen said. 'Though officially I'm Miss Quinlan-Green.'

'Miss Quinlan it is,' Des said. 'And Lola and Bett. And I'm Des. I'm only called Desmond when I'm being told off by my wife. Which is most of the time, ha ha ha!'

Again, Lola and Bett smiled politely.

'Please do be our guide, Des,' Lola said as they moved again. 'The shops look like the shops used to look, but wasn't there once a pillar in O'Connell Street? Where that spire is?'

'The IRA blew that one up, Lola. The Spire was erected on the same spot to mark the millennium. Except there was a bit of a delay. So it marks 2002 instead. A fine year in itself, I suppose.'

He drove as slowly as he could without risking the ire of other drivers. He was in his element. If he hadn't been a chauffeur, he'd have loved to have been a guide on one of the tourist buses. He knew his Irish history, or enough of it. He knew a good few Irish songs too, especially the ones the visitors liked to hear: 'Molly Malone', 'The Foggy Dew', 'Whiskey in the Jar'. . .

He told them more about the GPO, gave a brief history of the 1916 Easter Rising, pointed out the bullet holes which may or may not have actually been bullet holes but why spoil a good story? He pointed down the River Liffey towards the docklands, explaining it was a tidal river so the levels went up and down each day. He told them about the annual Liffey Swim, when brave 'or foolhardy, if you ask me' swimmers competed each year. 'Not until the council have flooded it with clean water first, mind you. It's not sometimes called the Sniffy Liffey for nothing.' He named the bridges. They were one of his favourite features of the city, all of different designs, lit in different colours at night-time. They'd have to be sure to walk across the Ha'penny Bridge, he said, a true landmark of Dublin.

On they went, past Trinity College. He mentioned it was home to the Book of Kells. He pointed out Grafton Street. Roadworks slowed their progress, but the delay this time was perfect for his tour-guiding purposes. He explained about the northside and south-side of the city, how the Liffey divided them, how the northside was considered the shabby side, the southside the 'posh' side.

'Where's our hotel, Lola?' Ellen asked.

'Southside, of course, darling,' Lola said.

Ten minutes later, he was parked in front of their hotel. It was a well-known one, three storeys high, built of red brick, in its own grounds. There was even a turret or two. Des opened their doors and took out their luggage as they stood and gazed around. Ellen seemed delighted. Bett was trying to get her to stand still long enough for a photo.

'I can be official photographer as well as driver, if you like?' Des said. 'You want to document every moment of this trip, I'm sure.' He had a flash of Breda telling him off and backtracked. 'Not that I know anything about the reasons for the trip. But it must be special, three generations of one family back home.' He stopped and sighed. 'Sorry. My wife says I am incurably inquisitive and she's right.'

'I'm a great believer in curiosity myself, Des,' Lola said. 'Yes please to you being our occasional official photographer. Come here, my girls. Bett, dear, please give Des your phone.' She beckoned. Ellen stood on one side, Bett on the other, their arms around one another.

Des took his time, down on one knee, changing positions, getting the hotel at the right angle.

'Just to remind you, I'm eighty-five years old, Des,' Lola said. 'You might want to get a move on.'

Biting back a grin, Des finally took the photo.

'So, do they want to come to dinner?' Breda asked him.

After Des had carried in their luggage and showed them to the reception desk, he'd come back outside to his car and phoned his wife. 'I haven't asked yet. They've gone in to freshen up after the journey. Lola's asked me to take them for another sightseeing drive this afternoon.'

'Lola? Not Mrs Quinlan?'

Des explained how friendly they were. 'And tonight I'm taking them to an Irish dance show. They said they all slept well on the flight, so they don't need an early night. They've insisted they can get a taxi back to the hotel, so I'll be home after I drop them off. Young Ellen can't wait. She said she tried Irish dancing at school once but kept getting told off for waving her arms around.'

'Ask them about dinner soon, won't you? That chicken is even better if it's marinated a day early.'

They were all on the second floor of the hotel. Lola had a room to herself. Bett and Ellen were sharing a room across the hall. Ellen started exploring, opening and shutting the curtains, opening and shutting every drawer, turning on the large TV, trying out the little safe, inspecting the lotions and soaps in the spacious marble bathroom. She was showing no signs of jet lag. Bett checked the time. It would be around ten p.m. in Australia. She quickly uploaded the photo Des had taken of the three of them to her Instagram and Facebook accounts. She messaged Daniel privately to say they'd arrived safely and she'd ring him as soon as she could. She emailed the photo to her mother and father too. It was probably too late for them to be online, but they'd see it first thing in the morning.

There was a quiet knock at the door. Bett had left it open. It was Lola.

'I've come to make sure your room's not better than mine. Nearly, but not quite. Excellent.'

Bett glanced up from her phone. 'Sorry, I'm just sending that photo home. I won't be a second.'

Lola held out Ellen's phone. 'I promised you could have it for a while each day. It's a while now.'

Ellen snatched it. 'Thanks, Lola!' She was soon engrossed, her fingers rapidly tapping on the tiny keyboard.

Lola waited, watching for one minute. Then two. She stood in the doorway and deliberately waited for five minutes. When she spoke, her voice was low and calm.

'So we fly across the world. We enjoy tiptop luxury due to Glenn's kind gesture. We happen to hire the world's friendliest, though possibly verging on overly friendly, driver. We are in a new city, full of new sights for all of us to explore. But both of you would prefer to sit there looking at your screens.'

'I was just checking work emails,' Bett said. 'And sending that photo of us to everyone.'

'I was just checking Instagram,' Ellen said. 'And watching a music video.'

'Watch away. Email away. I'll go outside and look at Dublin on my own,' Lola said, turning.

'Lola, wait!' Ellen said.

'Lola, stop, please!' Bett stood up. 'Don't you want everyone to see what we're up to over here? Everyone will be dying to know how it's going.'

'I'm sure they will. But can we do it first and then tell them about it later? If they see and hear everything instantly, they won't want to see or hear us when we get home.'

'But they'd love to know now.'

'Let them wait. Until we've had a chance to experience it and reflect on it and talk about it ourselves, instead of – what do you call it? Live-tweeting it.'

'"Live-tweeting"? You are up to date.'

'Why are you always so surprised at my modern mind? I don't live in a vacuum, Bett. I even know people younger than you.'

'But do you mean you don't want me to send any photos back home the entire time we're here? Everyone will think we've been kidnapped.'

'You can send a few sentences each day. You're a journalist, after all. Use words. I won't relax if I know every single thing I do is being photographed and beamed back to Australia. Besides, I want to approve any photos of me. Photoshop them if necessary. And yes, I know about Photoshop too.'

Ellen wasn't happy. 'What about my dad? He'll miss me if he doesn't see a photo of me every day.'

'He'll miss you even if he does see a photo of you every day. I'll make an exception, Ellen. Bett can send one photo of you to your dad every day. Only of you. To show that you are alive and well.'

'No scenery in the background?'

'Perhaps with a leprechaun, if we see any with their heads on. Otherwise, no, or you won't have anything to show him when you get home either. I'd also like you to start keeping a travel diary.'

'I can't. I'd need my phone to do that. And you said I can only have it twice a day.'

'Let me give you something.' Lola reached into her bag. 'There's a remarkable invention called paper, Ellen. And something called pens too. If you put them together, it's called writing.'

Ellen had her hands on her hips. 'I have seen paper before.'

'I'm glad. I hoped your father was sending you to a good school. So, then, give me back your phone and pick up that pen. I want you to write down your impressions of the flight. Bett, you too, please.' She produced another notebook and pen.

Bett took it, fighting a smile. 'And what about you?'

'I don't need a notebook. Not with two beady-eyed scribes like you girls doing my work for me.'

'So what will you do while we're doing our homework?' Bett asked.

'Go down to the bar for a refreshing gin and tonic,' Lola said, smiling. 'See you in half an hour.'

*

The bar on the ground floor was a welcoming combination of wood-panelled walls, deep-red carpets and plush sofas. Lola found a seat by the window. A young man in the hotel uniform came over and took her order. His accent wasn't Irish. Polish or Russian, perhaps, she thought.

She had stayed in this hotel once before. She hadn't been completely sure when Bett first suggested it. She was sure now. She'd remembered it as soon as she saw the fountain in front, the curved windows of the bar. Of course, the rest of it was so different. It must have changed hands many times over the years. Been modernised. It had been expensive then and was expensive now. Lola was happy to pay. Especially now she was sure she'd remembered it correctly.

It had been a special occasion. The wedding of one of the female teachers from her father's school in Ballymore Eustace. Lola had just turned seventeen. The teacher was marrying into a well-off Dublin family. The ceremony had been held in a church nearby, in the upmarket suburb of Ballsbridge, Lola recalled. How extraordinary to be remembering all these placenames from her past. There were more than three hundred people at the church and the reception afterwards, held in the ballroom of this hotel. A vulgar display of wealth, her father had said. Lola had adored every single moment of it.

She, and her mother, had been astonished when her father had not only accepted the invitation but insisted they get new outfits made for the occasion. They visited a dressmaker in Newbridge. Fabric was chosen. Lola wanted the brightest colours possible, with tassels and bows and ribbons – the more the better. She had been talked out of it. 'It's a wedding, not a circus,' her father had said. Lola could still recall her feeling of disappointment as her mother chose a dull fawn shade for her dress instead. Lola had made up for those bland days since. In every way, every day she could. Even today, she thought, stroking her bright-pink wool jacket.

She had danced with a man for the first time at that wedding. She even remembered his name. Oliver. He'd approached her, a glass of beer in his hand. He was taller than her. That didn't happen often with young men of her acquaintance.

They had a dance. Then later that evening, another dance. She could see her father watching them. Her mother looked nervous. She often did. Lola had slowly started to realise that, watching as her mother held back in social situations. She was shy but it had somehow turned into a reputation for being stuck-up or standoff-ish. Lola had overheard three of the ladies at Mass talking about her mother once. That Mrs Delaney was a snob, they'd decided. She thought she was better than them, living in that grand house outside the village, her husband the school principal.

Lola had wanted to set them right. To explain her mother was shy. That she didn't think herself better than anyone. That Lola had caught her crying many times, had worried often that her mother didn't have any friends except for Elizabeth, that she spent too much time on her own. As for the big house, it was rented, not owned. And if her parents ever had visitors, they would soon see that there was little luxury inside, either. She'd been about to say all of that to them, when she had felt her father's presence in the churchyard beside her. She'd been hurried away.

Once they were home again, in private, she was given a stern talking-to, reminded that she had to watch her behaviour. 'I saw that bold expression on your face, Louisa,' he said. He never called her by her preferred name of Lola. She'd stood in front of him, head bowed, listening but not responding. Nothing he was saying was news to her. She'd grown up hearing all the things she wasn't and all the things she should be.

She had danced with two other young men that night. She loved every moment: the feel of their hands on her back, the music filling the room, the silk of her dress, its dull colour lit into more exciting shades by the combination of candlelight and mirrors in the ballroom.

She was surprised and happy to see her parents dancing once too. She knew – had known since she was a child – that it wasn't the best of marriages. But her mother's face was glowing as she looked up at her father, and her step was light. Lola hoped the mood between them would last. Too often, there was a chill in their house that went beyond the weather.

The next morning in the hotel breakfast room, her head was still filled with the colour and glamour of the evening before. She joined her parents at their table, looking forward to discussing the style of the guests, the music, the beautiful decorations in the room. Imagine, not eighteen yet and she had already been to a fancy wedding in Dublin! She wished it wasn't the school holidays and that she could be going back to her final year of school at the convent in Naas on Monday, able to describe every minute of it to her classmates, not just the food, the clothes, but the dances she'd —

'You made a show of yourself last night, Louisa Delaney.' It was her father's greeting to her.

She stared at him, incredulous. She glanced at her mother. She was gazing steadfastly at her plate.

'I did? In what way?'

'You know in exactly what way.'

'I don't, Father. Please tell me.'

Lola could feel her back straighten, even recalling that conversation.

In a low voice – because God forbid he draw any more unwanted attention to himself and his wife and daughter – he listed all her transgressions from the evening before. She had danced too much. Laughed too much. Talked too much. Thrown herself at not just one boy, but others.

'They asked me to dance, Father,' Lola said in a voice as low and as cold as his.

Her father ignored her. 'I saw you, laughing and being ridiculous on the dance floor. Talking the entire time.'

'Yes, Father. I was asking them to come outside and kiss me.'

Her mother's head shot up at that. 'Lola —'

'That's what you mean, Father, isn't it? When you say I was making a show of myself? Because I was talking to people? Enjoying myself? Should I have done what you did all night? Looked like you were having a terrible time? That you'd have preferred to be anywhere else? That is better manners, is it?'

'That is enough.'

'Yes, Father, you're right. It's enough.'

She ate her breakfast in silence. All three of them did. Even when their host, the father of the groom, came into the breakfast room to a cheer from some of the other tables, the Delaney family sat in total silence.

'Another drink, madam?' The voice of the young Eastern European waiter brought her back to the present.

'Thank you, but no,' Lola said. One gin had already sent her further down memory lane than expected. She needed to travel this road home as slowly and carefully as she could.

'I'm all finished, Lola. Bett is still writing hers.'

Lola turned and smiled at her great-granddaughter. She had changed from her travelling clothes and was wearing a bright-red dress with a blue cardigan. 'Hello, Ellen. You look lovely.'

'Thank you. So do you.' Ellen perched herself on the armchair opposite Lola. She had a serious expression on her face. 'Lola, I've been thinking about your phone ban. I'm not happy about it. So Bett said I should talk to you face to face about it. That you would prefer that to me being mean about you behind your back. My question is, why can't we all just do what we want while we're here? I know it's a big trip for you, and Dad said it will definitely be your last one, but I might get back here again another time so it wouldn't matter if I missed things this time. I'd see it the next time, wouldn't I?'

'Possibly. But don't you think there's a difference between seeing things only on a screen and seeing them in real life?'

Ellen shrugged.

'But that's not the only reason I want you to stay off your phone,' Lola continued. 'The truth is, I need your help. You see, Ellen, my eyeballs are eighty-five years old. Imagine that. I have the same eyeballs now that I had when I was born, here in Ireland, all those years ago. My bones have grown and regenerated, my skin has too, so has my hair, but along with my heart and my lungs, my eyeballs are the very same ones. They've been looking all around me every day for all those years. For thousands of days. And miraculously they are still working, and apart from having a few cataracts removed over the years, they should keep working while we are here. But I need help. Lots of help. Not just walking and being driven around by that nice man Des, but I need help noticing things. I've brought you with me as my official noticer.'

'What do I have to notice?'

'I don't know. That's your job, not mine. You have to be on the lookout all the time. For example, look out that window for me. Now, I can see a large green shrub, but what else can you see?'

'Nothing. Just the bush. And a few birds.'

'What birds?'

'A little one with a red breast.'

'Lovely, a robin.'

'Actually, there's two. And a cheeky little brown one that's all speckled. It's teasing the robins.'

'A starling! My favourite bird. The naughtiest of birds, I always thought. Thank you, Ellen. I wouldn't have known they were there.

What about inside the bar? Can you describe two customers to me while I shut my eyes and have a little rest?'

Ellen glanced around before deciding on an elderly couple in the corner. 'The man is old, with large red ears. He's wearing a blue jacket, yellow trousers —'

'Yellow!' Lola said. 'Are you sure?'

'Very sure.' Ellen lowered her voice. 'They are a bit too bright. He looks like a clown in them. His shoes are a kind of light-brown colour.'

'Does he have bells on the toes of his shoes?'

Ellen giggled. 'No! They're just shoe-shoes.'

'He's probably not a clown, then. Go on.'

'I'll describe his wife now. She's —'

'Just a moment. Are we sure it's his wife? Could it be his girl-friend? Are they on a date?'

'They might be. They're holding hands! Even though they're so old! Maybe it's a first date?'

'They're getting on exceptionally well if that's the case,' Lola said. 'Go on. What's the lady wearing?'

Ellen itemised it. A blue shirt with a pear brooch. A tartan skirt. An orange-and-red-striped scarf.

'Oh, dear. Doesn't it all clash?'

Ellen glanced at Lola's pink jacket and orange trousers, but said nothing. Through her half-closed eyes, Lola noticed the glance and also said nothing.

'And she's wearing sensible shoes,' Ellen continued. 'Like school shoes.'

'Good for her. I'm a great believer in sensible shoes. Not for me but for anyone else.'

Again, Lola knew Ellen was glancing down at her own bright-green pumps with the kitten heels.

'The lady is laughing at something the man is saying. He's

looking at us. Are they laughing at us?'

'I hope so. I love being the centre of attention, don't you?' Lola opened her eyes. 'Beautifully done, Ellen. You are a first-class noticer. I made the right decision bringing you on this trip, that's for sure. But do you see, if you had been on your phone . . .'

Ellen raised an eyebrow in a gesture beyond her years. 'I get it. I wouldn't have noticed anything.'

'Nor would I. And I adored hearing you describe it all. Which is why I need your full attention each day. You can still have your phone twice a day, as I said. When you're in your nice but boring hotel room and there's nothing I need you to notice for me. How does that sound?'

'Annoying, but okay.' Ellen grinned. 'Bett warned me about you. This is exactly what she said, "Now, Lola will listen but then she'll turn it upside down so you find yourself agreeing with everything she says before you know what you're doing."'

'She had me in a nutshell. And you have your mother's art of mimicking in a nutshell too.'

'I'm glad.'

'So am I, darling. So am I.'

'All sorted?' Bett said, appearing beside them.

'Beautifully,' Lola said.

'Beautifully,' Ellen echoed in a perfect Irish accent.

CHAPTER FIFTEEN

At home in the Clare Valley, Daniel was giving his twins a pep talk.

'Okay, kids. Delia, Freya and George and their mum and dad will be here in about five minutes. Whatever you do, don't let the side down. I need you to look happy and clean and well fed, okay?'

'Okay,' Yvette echoed, waving a tower of Lego blocks. She was surrounded by a colourful pile.

'Okay,' Zachary said as he leaned down to touch his toes, over-balanced and fell.

Daniel caught him just in time. 'Not bad, both of you. Just try and look a bit more angelic, would you? And super-intelligent? And also don't forget to laugh at everything I say?'

They both stared solemnly at him.

'What was I thinking?' Daniel said to himself as he opened the fridge for the fifth time to check on the chops and sausages. Bett had suggested it would be good if they all caught up while she was away. He'd thought a picnic in the park later in the week. But when he'd rung Carrie about it, the conversation had somehow ended with him inviting them over for a barbecue. Tonight.

He liked barbecues. But only when Bett was around. She was better at entertaining than him. She could somehow greet people, keep up a conversation, pour drinks, offer food and keep an eye on the kids, all at the same time. He usually found himself standing awkwardly with a beer beside the barbecue itself, talking about sport with the other men and trying not to burn the meat. He'd half-thought about pre-cooking the barbecue tonight, so he could hand out sausages in white bread to Carrie and Matthew and their kids as they walked in. There'd be none of the fuss of waiting, none of the awkwardness of trying to make conversation while keeping the food edible. If he handed them drinks at the same time, the whole evening could be over in less than twenty minutes. It sounded like the perfect scenario. He wondered whether he could start cooking the sausages now.

There was the sound of a car outside. At that same moment his phone rang. He checked the screen for the name. Audrey, at last. He cursed under his breath. He'd been waiting for her call all day and here she was, just as Bett's sister was about to walk in the door. He hesitated for a second, eager to speak to her. No, reason won. He could only hope that Carrie and her family would leave early enough for him to be able to call her back tonight.

Through the window he watched Matthew park their new people carrier – a recent purchase – beside his and Bett's old, secondhand car. He turned back to the twins. 'Here they are. Good luck, everyone.'

'Good luck, Dad,' Yvette said.

He met them on the verandah as they clambered out of the car. Carrie was dressed as if she was on the way to the races: lots of makeup, plenty of jewellery. She was wearing a sort of flowing blue dress, he noted, knowing Bett would ask him about it later, even though it would probably upset her. All these years later, the competitiveness between the two sisters still surprised him. Matthew was wearing what Matthew always wore: moleskins, a blue shirt and a jumper around his shoulders.

Their three kids, Delia, Freya and little George, were also

beautifully dressed. 'She buys them designer clothes,' Bett had said once. 'For kids! What a waste of money, don't you think?'

'Aren't all clothes designed by someone?' he'd replied.

'We could send both twins to a private boarding school on her kids' clothing allowance alone.'

'It's not too late for me to go back and study as a vet, if that's what you want,' he said mildly.

She'd been immediately contrite. 'I wouldn't swap you with Matthew for a million dollars. Two million. Who wants to send their kids to a private boarding school anyway? We'd never see them.'

'Exactly. They'd hate it. And they're happier dressed in rags anyway,' Daniel said.

'And one meal of gruel a day is enough for anyone, isn't it?'

'It was for me. And who needs toys when there are sticks and leaves outside for them to play with?'

'Exactly,' she'd said, smiling.

He loved that smile of hers. And those lively eyes of hers. He loved everything about her, as it happened. Which was why he was trying to do what he was trying to do. And why it had been so frustrating that he hadn't been able to answer Audrey's call tonight . . .

He greeted his visitors. 'Matthew! Carrie! Great to see you. Hi, kids. Great to see you all too.' Daniel waited, knowing it was coming. She'd said it both times they'd spoken since Bett had left.

'So, Mister Mom!' Carrie said. 'Still surviving?'

'Thriving and surviving,' he said, smiling weakly.

'You're a poet and you didn't know it,' Matthew said as they followed him inside. There was an awkward pause, then Matthew held out a bottle of wine and a six pack of beer. 'For you, mate.'

'Thanks. Mate,' Daniel said. He headed for the kitchen, leaving Carrie cooing hello to the twins while simultaneously telling her own children to behave themselves, sit down quietly and not touch anything. To Daniel's astonishment, they did exactly that, sitting in a row on the couch, hands on laps.

Three robot children, Daniel thought. He badly needed Bett right now. She'd whisper something to him that would make it okay. 'You know all her kids are on tranquillisers,' she'd said once.

It wasn't true, of course, but it relaxed him that time. Their social gatherings were always strangely tense. Not only because of their unorthodox history. That was old news, the fact that Matthew had once been engaged to Bett, until Carrie returned home from overseas and she and Matthew met and fell almost instantly in love. Bett and Matthew's break-up had led to a big fight between Bett, Carrie and Anna, and a three-year feud, mended only by Lola's interference.

Daniel had known Bett before those events, occasionally working with her, always liking her company. He hadn't heard about the broken engagement or the fight until he ran into her in Melbourne. They'd had a memorable night together. But she'd left his flat before he woke up the next morning, to his disappointment. It was only when he came back to the Clare Valley to help take care of his mother, his return coinciding with Bett's return from overseas, that they'd started working together again, and falling in love. It seemed such a gentle term for how it had felt to realise he wanted to be with Bett for the rest of his life. She still delighted him. She entertained him, supported him, encouraged him. Understood him. He was a father because of her. She made his life better in so many ways. He wished again that she wasn't so far away, that she was about to come in and help him get through this evening.

It wasn't that he didn't like Carrie or Matthew. Carrie was Bett's sister, after all. They had been through so much. He'd seen at close hand how devastated they both were by Anna's death. The shockwaves still rippled. But Carrie was so, well, annoying at times. Spoilt. It drove him mad when Bett would say she was jealous of her sister, or wished she had her slimmer figure, or her blonde hair or her striking blue eyes. 'If you did, I wouldn't be here,' he'd say. 'You're much more beautiful. And smarter. And kinder.' He could never say it often enough, though.

Thank God he had just one sister and they'd never had cause for rivalry. They got on fine, sharing the visits to their mother, speaking once or twice a week. They rarely socialised but he knew she liked him and he liked her. There was none of the tangling he saw between the two Quinlan sisters.

He'd talked to Bett that morning, briefly, when she'd rung to say they'd arrived safely and that business class had been incredible. She'd been amazed to hear about this barbecue.

'You're having them over already? I'm barely gone. Did you get talked into it?'

'I think so. I still don't know how.'

'Just make sure the house is reasonably tidy, will you? Or I won't hear the end of it from Carrie. And that the kids are in reasonably clean clothes?'

The clothes. Hell. He hadn't changed their clothes since lunch. A lunch of spaghetti out of a tin. Which had ended up as spaghetti on two T-shirts. Three T-shirts. He'd changed his, but —

'Daniel? Is everything okay?' It was Carrie calling from the living room.

'Coming,' he called. He joined them again. 'Sorry about that. The, um, fridge door got stuck.'

Matthew stood up. 'Want me to take a look at it, mate?'

'No, I fixed it. Thanks, mate.' Mate? Why did he keep saying that word? One, Matthew wasn't his mate, he was his brother-in-law. Two, when did he ever use the term 'mate'?

He wished again for pre-cooked sausages.

'So!' he said, clapping his hands, startling his own children and making one of Carrie's well-behaved angels jump. 'Anyone hungry?'

'You're going to start cooking already?' Carrie said. 'I thought we might have a drink first.'

Bett appeared in his mind again. *You didn't offer them a drink? Oh, Daniel . . .*

'A drink? Great idea! Wine, Carrie?'

'Just sparkling water for me, thanks.' She gestured towards her stomach area. How had he forgotten she was pregnant?

'Matthew? Beer?'

'No, I'm driving, but thanks anyway, mate.'

'No worries.' The 'mate' was trying to squeeze out of his mouth but he bit it back. Was he imagining a hurt look on Matthew's face?

Great, he thought, as he went back into the kitchen to get Carrie's water. Not even any alcohol to help smooth the tension.

'So, kids,' he said again as he came in, 'what about you lot? Coke? Fanta?' He noticed Carrie about to protest and got in first. 'I was joking, Carrie, promise. Sugar is evil, I know that. Clean healthy tap water all round?' he asked the three of them. Three nods.

They were all still sitting in a row on the couch. The stained couch. The couch he was supposed to have covered in a throw rug before Carrie and company arrived. Still, at least the three of them sitting there meant the worst of the stains were covered. By their designer-clothes-clad bottoms, as it happened. It was unsettling how well behaved they were. Especially compared to his two, who were having a silent but ferocious tussle over a toy fox they both adored. Was he imagining it, or had Yvette just growled at Zach? Actually bared her teeth? That was a new developmental milestone. Carrie's children seemed transfixed, as if twin-fighting was some kind of spectator sport.

Tranquillisers, remember, his imaginary Bett whispered.

Carrie gave him one of her dazzling white-toothed smiles. ('She's definitely had them bleached,' Bett had said recently. As the light bounced off them, Daniel agreed.) 'So, Daniel, you're coping okay?'

'It has only been a couple of days. But sure. Great. We're going great.'

Carrie gave what Daniel would have described to Bett as a tinkling laugh. 'Lola's unbelievable, isn't she? Overseas trips on the spur of the moment like this. You had to use up your holidays, I suppose?'

'Some of them. Mostly it's parental leave,' he said.

'Oh. Right.' She turned to Matthew. 'If I hadn't been pregnant and had gone away with Lola too, could you have taken parental leave?'

Matthew looked confused. 'But you are pregnant. And you said that Lola wanted Bett to go, not you anyway.' He turned to Daniel. 'Carrie's got it into her head that Bett is Lola's favourite.'

Daniel knew for certain that Bett was Lola's favourite. Lola had told him once when he'd been driving her home from a late-afternoon lunch. She often got very indiscreet after a few gin and tonics. It was one of the many things he enjoyed about her.

'Really?' he answered, hoping it was vague enough. 'So, let me start cooking.'

Matthew sprang out of his seat again. 'Need a hand?'

'Great. Sure. Can you get it started and I'll be out there soon?'

Matthew must have been feeling awkward too. He was out the back door in an instant, whistling as he fired up the barbecue.

'So, did you read my blog yet?' Carrie asked.

'Not yet, sorry. But congratulations. Bett said you'd had heaps of comments already.'

'Did she? When did she say that? What else did she say?'

Uh-oh. 'Just that it had had a great response.'

'She didn't say it was too long, did she? Or that I'd gone into too much detail? Or not enough detail?'

How did women live with these highways of doubt in their

minds? 'She said it was great,' he said.

'She said that to me too but I don't know if she meant it or not.'

'She meant it, Carrie, I'm sure.'

'I hope she doesn't feel I'm trespassing. I mean, she's the journalist and now I'm a writer too.'

'I think she's okay with it. She asked you to do it, didn't she?'

'Well, Lola suggested it, but yes, it is on her paper's website. But it could lead to all sorts of things. I could go viral, or get a book deal. Do you think Bett would be okay if that happened?'

'I'm sure she would,' he said. *I'll kill her if that happens*, his imaginary Bett said.

'I'll put these on, Dan, will I?' Matthew said, appearing with a tray of sausages.

'Thanks, mate.'

'No worries, mate.'

Carrie glanced over at the children. The five of them were on the floor in a huddle, happily occupied with the Lego. Daniel was glad to see Carrie's children hadn't picked up any stains from the couch. He was also relieved to see her eldest, Delia, sneakily pinch Freya, the middle child, who gave her a slap back. They were real children beneath the tranquillisers, then. Fortunately Carrie hadn't noticed. She was too busy looking around the room. He kept waiting for her to run a finger along a shelf to check for dust. She'd find plenty, that's for sure.

She gave him another of her dazzling smiles. 'Now, Daniel, is there anything we can do to help with the kids, before it all gets too overwhelming for you? Have them for a sleepover, for example?'

One of Bett's final cautions sprang to mind: 'If she asks if she can have them for a sleepover, say no.'

'No,' Daniel said.

Carrie frowned. 'Really? Why not? You don't want a night off?'

Bett's voice came to mind again. She'd felt strongly on this subject, he'd discovered. 'It'll be her way of hinting you can't cope, that she can handle five children and we, or at least you, can't even handle two on your own.'

'I can handle two on my own.' He winced inwardly at how blunt that sounded. 'But thanks anyway.'

Carrie didn't give up easily. 'I thought you might like a break.'

'No, it's all great. We're getting on great.'

Right then, Yvette started to cry. As often happened, Zachary started up too.

Delia held up her hands like a surrendering criminal. 'I didn't do anything. I was just sitting here.'

'I know you didn't do anything,' Carrie said. 'The twins are just missing their mum, aren't you, twins?'

Daniel hated it when she called them twins in that collective, dismissive way. 'They love their dad as much as their mum, thanks, Carrie.'

If she heard him, she didn't show it. She bundled Yvette and Zachary into her arms. Daniel took a strange satisfaction in them continuing to wail. He took Yvette from her. She instantly went quiet. Zachary reached out both arms. The second Daniel was holding him, he stopped crying too. He planted an enthusiastic, grateful kiss on their heads.

'What about bread?' It was Matthew, poking his head in. 'And sauce?'

'Great idea, Matthew,' Carrie said, too quickly and chirpily in Daniel's opinion. Of course, he'd been meaning to put out bread and sauce. 'And how about salad?' Carrie continued, following him into the kitchen. 'My kids love salad. They can't get enough of it.'

Daniel couldn't help but notice Delia and Freya pull faces and mouth 'Yuk' behind their mother's back.

'I try to make sure they get at least five portions of fruit or vegetables a day,' she said.

'Good for you,' Daniel said. 'Do you want to count my salad ingredients?'

That tinkling laugh again. 'Don't be silly! I know you and Bett have a very different approach to nutrition. So, where is it?'

'Where's what?'

'Your salad.'

He'd had every intention of making one. He'd even gone so far as buying a lettuce and some tomatoes and cucumber. He just hadn't put them in the same bowl yet. Or cut them up. He decided to tell the truth.

'It's a work in progress, as it happens. They're still what I'd call "vegetables".'

'Oh, Daniel!' Carrie said, with that laugh again. It was starting to grate on him. 'Here, let me do it.'

Why not? he decided. 'That'd be great, Carrie, thanks.'

After checking the children were back happily playing and not attacking one another, Daniel and Carrie moved to the kitchen bench, hurriedly and jointly making the salad. He'd just finished chopping the tomatoes when his phone rang. It was on the bench beside the salad bowl.

Before he had a chance to reach for it, Carrie picked it up. She glanced at the screen. 'I thought it might be Bett. It's someone called Audrey.'

Daniel couldn't stop himself. He snatched at the phone, toma-toey hands and all. It kept ringing.

Carrie stared at him. 'Aren't you going to answer it?'

'No. Not now. I'll call her back later.'

'Who's Audrey? A work colleague?'

Daniel thought quickly. 'Yes. One of the other photographers. She's doing a job for me. Really helping me out, actually. She's good like that.'

'Isn't that great?' Carrie said. 'What age is she?'

It finally stopped ringing. Thank God, he thought. 'What age?' he said.

'Yes. What age? How old?'

There was too long a pause. The phone was on the counter between them. A beep sounded. A voicemail message.

'About my age,' he said, finally. 'A bit younger maybe.'

Carrie gave a slow nod. 'If she's doing a job for you, shouldn't you ring her back? In case it's urgent?'

'No, she'll understand.'

'Understand? That you're busy entertaining your wife's sister . . .'

He knew from the way she emphasised 'wife' exactly what she was thinking. For God's sake. He decided not to play her game. 'So, is that enough salad, do you think?'

'Plenty,' she answered briskly.

He ignored the look she gave him. He also ignored Imaginary Bett in his head, whispering that he hadn't heard the last of that.

They all moved outside, where Matthew was expertly laying out the cooked sausages. Carrie was soon just as expertly preparing sausages in bread with sauce. She fed her three children first, and then Daniel's two. They both nearly snatched the food out of her hands.

'Oh, they were starving, the poor kids,' Carrie said. 'Poor little Yvette and Zachy. Did Daddy forget to feed you today?'

He decided he hated the voice she used when she spoke to his children as much as he hated her fake laugh. He hated anyone calling Zach Zachy too. 'They had a full can of spaghetti each for lunch,' he said, hearing the chill in his own voice.

'Canned? You know that's full of sugar, don't you?'

'Oh, we love sugar around here. We eat it all the time. Sometimes I don't bother with the spaghetti. We just eat sugar out of the packet. Cut out the middleman.'

'Ha!' Matthew said, through a mouthful of sausage and bread. 'Good one, Dan.'

After they'd finished eating, Daniel organised a game of chasey through the house with all five kids. They were much easier company, he decided. Carrie's three had also turned into nearly normal children, with tomato sauce stains on their clothes, and louder voices. The tranquillisers were obviously wearing off. Matthew and Carrie seemed happy to sit back and watch as he let them do whatever they wanted – clamber over him, or take turns jumping up and ambush-piggybacking him. At one stage he was lying on the carpet with all five piled on top of him. The twins were pulling at his hair, while the older three were shrieking as they tried to make a human pyramid.

'Careful, children,' Carrie called. 'Don't hurt yourselves.'

Daniel waited for a warning about hurting him.

'Don't get your dresses dirty, Delia and Freya. Or your jeans, George.'

'Too late for that,' Daniel called back cheerily.

What about dessert, Daniel? Imaginary Bett hissed.

Daniel leapt up, causing the children to slide off him with even more excited shrieks. 'Ice-cream in cones, anyone?' There were five enthusiastic cries of yes. A 'No' from Carrie. The sugar, he guessed.

'No thanks, mate,' Matthew said, patting his slightly rounded stomach. 'I'm under strict supervision.'

'Matthew's watching his weight,' Carrie said. 'He shouldn't have had that sausage tonight but we made an exception.'

'That' sausage? Daniel had seen him eat at least five. And who knows how many more while he was out there on his own cooking them.

All five kids finally finished their ice-creams. Daniel had one too. He was starting to wonder how much longer they'd stay when Matthew's phone rang.

He had a quick conversation, then gave a regretful smile. 'Sorry, mate. The farmer down the road from our house needs a hand with his sheep. Carrie, you and the kids could stay and I —'

'No.' Daniel hoped he hadn't shouted. 'No, you all head off. I need to put the twins to bed anyway.'

'Do you need a hand?' Carrie said.

'No.' Another near shout. 'No, go tend your sheep, Matthew.' Tend? What was he, a shepherd? Little Matt Peep. Imaginary Bett started to laugh.

It took ten minutes but they were finally gone. He walked into the living room and fell onto the carpet again. In seconds, both twins had toddled over and were lying on top of him, laughing as if it was the funniest night of their lives. Imaginary Bett was smiling too. *You did it*, she said.

He rolled onto his back, pulled his son and daughter into his arms and gave them the squeezy hugs they loved so much. He loved those hugs too.

'We did it,' he said.

In their car a kilometre down the road, Carrie turned to Matthew.

'I think Daniel's having an affair,' she said.

CHAPTER SIXTEEN

It was just as well they'd flown business class, Bett thought, as she showered and got ready for that evening's outing. They hadn't stopped since they had arrived in Dublin. She'd sent a brief words-not-photos report to her parents, Daniel, Carrie and Glenn in Australia, as instructed:

It's all great. No jet lag so far. (Thank you again for business class, Glenn, from all three of us!!) Our driver is very helpful and very friendly – so friendly in fact that he invited us to have dinner with him and his wife, at their home. Lola accepted immediately. Ellen is very impressed with Irish hospitality. We've been sightseeing during the day and went to an Irish music and dance show last night. Ellen loved it, especially when she got chosen to come on stage and join in on one of the dances! (Yes, I have photos. I have a short video of it too. I'm just not allowed to share them with you yet.) Dublin is even livelier than I remember it. Tourists everywhere (we don't count, we're with Lola, she's a local). Miraculously, the sun has shone both days too. Dinner tonight with Des (our driver) and then off to Kildare tomorrow. Love to you all from the three of us, Lola, Bett and Ellen xxx

She'd barely pressed send before a reply had come in.

Carrie: *Business class??????!!!!!!!!!!!!!!!!!!!!*

Oops, Bett thought. She'd forgotten she hadn't told Carrie yet. She wrote back quickly, keeping it brief. *A surprise upgrade from Glenn!* She quickly logged out before she heard back.

It seemed extraordinary that they'd only left Australia three days earlier. So far it had been Bett, not Lola, who'd travelled down memory lane. Lola's idea. She wanted to see exactly where Bett had lived and worked in Dublin.

It hadn't taken long. She'd only lived in the city for a few months when she first went overseas, working behind the bar of a music venue before being offered a job with a record company in London. It wasn't a happy time for her. Still reeling from the fight with her sisters, she'd also been trying to ignore the fact she felt more relief than sorrow about the break-up of her engagement to Matthew. She'd drowned her feelings in too much alcohol, too many late nights and all the live music she could find.

She'd lived in a share house on the North Circular Road, not far from the Phoenix Park, Europe's largest enclosed park, as she announced in a tour guide's voice to Ellen and Lola.

'It was that house there.' Bett pointed at one of the four-storey houses on the road to the park. 'The one with the red door. Hold on – no, it wasn't, it was the one next to it. Or was it that one with the green door?' she said.

Des drove them around the park, then down through Smithfield, the old fruit market area, and across town, following the route Bett used to take to her job at the music venue. It was still there, a long list of forthcoming gigs written on a blackboard outside.

'Can I take a photo, Lola?' Bett asked.

'Of course, darling. Take all you like. You just can't send them to anyone.'

Lola stayed in the car while Ellen turned photographer, getting her aunt to pose in front of the venue, the two of them laughing as Bett struck more elaborate poses. It was while they were busy doing that that Des had invited them to dinner, they'd learnt later from Lola.

Des had been very shy about it, apparently. 'This might be forward of me, Mrs Quinlan —'

'Lola, please, Des.'

'Lola, my wife Breda and I would be honoured if you'd like to join us for dinner at our house. Now, the house itself is nothing fancy, but Breda is a fantastic cook and I'm not bad myself, and we thought you might like a home-cooked meal. But if you'd prefer I recommended some restaurants instead, that is absolutely grand too.'

Lola had smiled at him. 'I knew I made the right decision choosing you, Des Foley. You're not only a very safe driver, with an impeccably clean car, you're a gentleman. Thank you. We'd be delighted.'

He'd picked up his phone, dialled his wife and said two words. 'Start marinating.'

Bett came out of the shower to find Ellen dressed and ready, lying on her bed, writing in her notebook. She had taken to the idea of a travel journal with more enthusiasm than Bett expected. She'd asked if she could read Ellen's first entry and been surprised when she told her no.

'You can read mine,' Bett said.

'I don't want to, thank you anyway. I might get your memories mixed up with mine. You can read mine at the end of the trip, and I'll read yours. We can compare notes then.'

Fine, Bett had said, biting back a smile. She was finding Ellen great company – a constant mix of enthusiastic young girl and precocious teenager. After dressing and applying light makeup, Bett crossed the hall and knocked on her grandmother's open door.

Lola was sitting in the armchair at the window. Her eyes were shut tight.

'Lola? Are you okay?'

'Healthy as a trout, darling, thank you.' She still didn't open her eyes.

'Are you exhausted? Do you want me to ring Des and say you're not up to it after all?'

'I wouldn't dream of cancelling. I suspect he and his wife have already gone to a good bit of trouble.'

Bett sat down on the edge of the bed. Des wasn't due to collect them for another forty minutes.

'But are you coping okay? You're not finding any of this too hard?'

'Will I tell you something truthfully?'

Bett nodded.

'I don't feel anything yet,' Lola said.

'Nothing at all?'

'Nothing real. I feel like I'm in a dream somehow. Or a tourist ad for Ireland. Dublin looks like it should look. The Irish music sounded as it should last night. The Irish dancing was wonderful. So was the Irish food, the Irish coffee. But I don't feel I have any connection to it.'

'Perhaps it will be different when we get to Kildare. Perhaps it's because we've only been doing the touristy things so far.'

'That's what I am, Bett. I'm a tourist here.'

'No, you're not. This is your home.'

'It was. I don't know if that's true any more.' Her voice was almost desolate. Then she smiled. Bett could see it was an effort but she was glad to see it all the same. 'Ignore me, darling. I'm fine, I promise. I can also hear your phone beeping and I know you're dying to check it.'

'It's that obvious?'

Lola nodded. 'You're as bad as Ellen. Worse.'

It was a text from Daniel, just four words: *Love you missing you.* And a photo of him with the twins, all three of them waving at her. She did a quick calculation. It was only five a.m. in Clare. They were up early. She tapped back a quick reply: *Love you all so much too.* She'd only been away from them for three days and she'd already watched the video Daniel had made for her half-a-dozen times.

She showed Lola the photo and then clicked on to another website. 'You were right about the news of that actor causing a fuss,' she said. 'He's our cover story on Wednesday too but look at this.' 'This' was the front page of the statewide newspaper, featuring a large photo of Rafe Ascot and a big headline: *Love Rat Heading Our Way!*

Bett told Lola she'd also had an excited email from Carrie. The TV producer had promised her a face-to-face interview with Rafe as soon as he arrived in Clare. *I've done loads of research for it already. My friends are SOOOOO jealous,* Carrie had written. *Best Job Ever!!!!*

'It's great for her,' Bett said to Lola, trying to ignore her own pangs of jealousy. 'Hopefully that'll distract her from getting too upset about us flying business class.'

'I wouldn't bet on it,' Lola said with a smile.

They were downstairs waiting in the foyer for Des when Bett's phone pinged again. And again. A third time. She quickly read the emails. They were all from the TV producer. The irate TV producer.

'Oh, bloody hell,' Bett said. 'I'm so sorry, Lola, but I need to call Australia.'

'But Des is about to arrive,' Lola said.

'It's urgent, I'm sorry. I have to ring Carrie.'

'She's having the baby!' Ellen said.

'I wish she was. It would be less trouble than this.'

In a quiet corner of the foyer, she rang her sister, trying hard to keep her temper. 'I know it's early, Carrie, but this is serious. What on earth were you thinking, posting that about Rafe without showing me? I told you to run everything past me first.'

'I didn't want to bother you,' Carrie said. 'Anyway, I didn't write it. I copied it all off the internet. That's why I didn't think you had to see it.'

'Carrie, people make things up on the internet the whole time. And I told you, I only gave you the site log-in details in case I couldn't do it from here for some technical reason. I can't believe this has been up since last night. No wonder the producer is furious. You have to take it down. Right now.'

'But I'm getting so many comments about it. People are loving it!'

'Yes, because it's full of scandalous lies. Carrie, I promised the TV people that we would work with them, not recycle old rubbish about their star actor like this.'

'Are you saying my blog is rubbish?'

'No. Yes. Seriously, did you read any of it before you did your cut-and-pasting? How do you know for sure that Rafe once had a ménage à trois? Or that he has a gambling addiction? Or that he once asked Pippa Middleton out?'

'I read it —'

'On gossip sites on the internet. Exactly. But you've reported it as fact. Please, take it down right now. Before anyone else sees it. You'll be able to do it quicker there than I can from here.'

'Can't I wait and see how many comments I get first?'

'No! Do it now! If you don't, I'll call the office and get the whole website taken down.'

'No way!'

'Now, Carrie. You've got ten seconds. And you'd better start praying the producer isn't sending that link to her lawyers as well as to me.'

Bett glanced across the foyer. Des had arrived and was talking to Lola and Ellen. She signalled to say she'd be just a minute. After saying goodbye to Carrie, she quickly typed an email to the producer: *The blog post in question has been deleted. My sister has received a rapid lesson in factual reporting. Our apologies. It won't happen again.*

In the back of Des's car shortly after, Bett filled Lola in, glad that Ellen had chosen to ride in the front seat, out of earshot.

'So much for editorial independence,' Bett said in a low voice.

'Put it out of your mind, darling. You're a long way from Clare now.'

'I'm a long way from Carrie. That's more worrying.'

Alone at home in Clare, Carrie was not happy. Everything had been going so well until Bett rang. She'd woken up early especially to check for any comments on her blog. She'd posted about Rafe just before midnight the night before. The response had amazed her. Comments started appearing within moments, all saying similar things. *He sounds horrible! Lock up your daughters! Ewww, what a creep!!* Overnight, dozens more had come in. Carrie had decided to reply to them all. *I know! I agree!* She'd been having a great time until Bett rang and ruined all her fun.

She'd had no choice but to delete the post. What a waste. The whole point of the blog was to reach out to readers, wasn't it? Give them what they wanted? She'd started a real conversation too, going back and forth with all the comments, which the online advice had assured her was the key to being a successful blogger. It was so unfair.

She regretted not fighting her corner more. Was it too late to call Bett back? What if she reposted the story but added an introduction saying, *Hey, everyone, look at this info I found about Rafe Ascot on the internet, I've done you a favour and gathered it for you, happy reading!* She knew without asking what Bett would say. There'd been no mistaking the tone in her voice. That bossy tone. Talk about overreacting.

What a waste of a day to herself. She'd been thrilled when Matthew decided to take the kids to work with him to see the new horses that had arrived at a farm north of Clare. She reached for her phone and re-read the message Bett had sent about their trip so far. She was so jealous, she couldn't pretend otherwise. But she wouldn't give her sister the satisfaction of knowing. Not yet anyway. She was still too mad.

It came to her then. There was something she'd meant to do. Something that had been nagging at her since the barbecue with Daniel, even though Matthew had instantly rejected her suggestion that Daniel was having an affair.

'When would he get the time for one?' he'd said in the car, keeping his voice low so the kids didn't overhear. 'And he's not that kind of guy.'

'That's what guys always say about other guys,' she'd whispered back. 'He'd make time if he had to.'

'For God's sake, Carrie. He has one after-hours phone call from a woman, tells you straight out that it's a work colleague and you put two and two together and make two hundred.'

But Carrie knew she hadn't been imagining it all. Daniel had behaved strangely. And if he ever was going to have an affair – not that she was definitely saying he was, not yet, not without any proof – but wouldn't now be exactly when he'd do it, when Bett was on the other side of the world?

The more Carrie thought about it, the more she could see it was possible. But was it better to pretend she hadn't noticed anything? What was the right thing to do in a situation like this?

Normally she would ask Lola for advice, but that was impossible at the moment. She couldn't call her in Ireland, not when her grandmother was at the start of such an emotional journey home. At least Carrie assumed it was emotional. Bett had been very unforthcoming with photos or many details of their trip so far. On Lola's orders, apparently. That was unfair too, in Carrie's opinion. It was hard enough being left behind. They could at least share what was happening there, not make them all wait until they got home again.

Should she ring Bett instead? Ask her casually about this Audrey? No, Bett might already have concerns. She might get even more upset, already separated from Daniel and her twins. And she was already upset by Carrie's blog, even if she shouldn't have been. No, she couldn't ring her. Not yet, anyway. Not until she had the facts, seeing as they seemed to matter so much to Bett. She'd make a few subtle enquiries first. It would be good practice for her journalistic career.

She looked up the phone number in Gawler. She'd have to wait until the office opened at nine a.m. She knew Daniel only worked part-time there these days. The rest of his working time was taken up with freelance photography. He was busy nearly every weekend at weddings, apparently. She hoped he wasn't working at the newspaper today. If he did answer, she'd hang up.

At exactly one minute past nine, she dialled. As her call was answered, something made her change her voice, just in case. The best she could do was an American accent. A terrible American accent.

'Hi there! I'm wondering if I can speak to Audrey.'

'Sorry, who?' It was an older man, gruff-voiced.

'Audrey. One of your photographers.'

CHAPTER SEVENTEEN

It was clear within seconds of stepping into Des and Breda's small semi-detached house on the northside of Dublin that they'd gone to a lot of trouble. Des introduced them proudly to his wife, then brought them into the front room. The good room, he called it. Was there a bad room? Ellen wanted to know.

It was spotless, with fresh flowers on a sideboard, two lamps glowing and even an open fire lit against the May evening chill. Photos of Des and Breda's three children filled the main wall, from childhood to adulthood, in First Communion dresses and suits, then later in their wedding photos. A corner was devoted to their grandchildren. One apiece and another on the way, Des told them proudly.

Tantalising smells drifted in from the kitchen. Breda, a petite woman with short dark hair and a big welcoming smile, was chief cook, she told them. She'd join them all in a moment. She turned down all their offers of help. 'You're our special guests,' she insisted.

'Do you always invite your customers home like this?' Lola asked, taking the seat of honour beside the fire as directed and accepting a small glass of sherry from Des.

'Only special ones,' he said. 'It's not every customer who's here on such a homecoming.'

'Lola said it doesn't feel like home yet, though,' Ellen said. 'She thinks she's just a tourist now.'

Bett was taken aback. How did Ellen know that? Had she been eavesdropping?

'Home's not just about places, though, is it?' Des said. 'It's about people, memories of family. It'll feel different once you've met up with everyone in Kildare, Lola, I'm sure.'

Lola stayed quiet.

Feeling awkward, Bett stepped in. 'Unfortunately, most of the people Lola knew are long gone, Des.'

'But there'll still be plenty of people who remember Lola's father, surely? It's not often someone is a headmaster in a school for more than forty years, after all,' he added.

The mood in the room suddenly changed.

'I beg your pardon?' Lola said. Her voice had cooled.

Bett tensed, sure they hadn't said anything about Lola's father in Des's earshot. She was puzzled too. She'd known Lola's father had been a teacher, but a headmaster? In the same school for forty years? Why hadn't Lola told her that? And how did Des know?

'So my great-great-grandfather was a headmaster?' Ellen said. 'Wow. In the same place you went to school, Lola? Did the other kids pick on you? Can we visit it? Is it still there?'

'I don't know,' Lola said, shifting in her chair.

If Bett was acutely aware of Lola's discomfort, Des wasn't. 'It sure is, Ellen! It's a business premises now, but you can still visit it. Not only that, you can read all about it online. I found a website with mentions of your father, Lola. Charles Delaney, that's him, isn't it? And there were scans of the students' workbooks and everything, from right back in the 1930s and '40s. You might even be in there yourself! I couldn't find a Lola Quinlan or Delaney but I did find one mention of a Louisa Delaney. That had to be you, I decided. Am I right? Is Lola a nickname? I've got the laptop next door. Do you want me to show —'

'Dinner will be served shortly,' Breda said cheerily, appearing at the door. She stopped and looked around, taking in their serious expressions. 'What is it? What have you done now, Des?'

Probably lost his job, Bett thought miserably.

An hour later, it was as if nothing had happened. Anyone who didn't know Lola – Des and Breda, in this case – wouldn't have known Lola was acting. But Bett had grown up beside her grandmother. She knew her every mood, every tone of voice. She also knew how much value Lola placed on good manners, on being gracious in difficult situations.

Des had started to stutter and stumble an explanation, that he was addicted to Google, and research, that he'd keyed in Lola's name and home village and it had been incredible how much information had come up . . . On he'd gone, until Lola put up her hand.

'Perhaps we might leave it there, Des.'

It worked, as that calm, firm tone had always worked over the years, in rowdy motel dining rooms or with misbehaving granddaughters. Des stopped talking.

Lola smiled. 'We're not here tonight to talk about my school days, Des. I was never a good student. Far too naughty, but you didn't hear me say that, Ellen. I'm sure we don't want to hear about my ancestors either. Nothing quite as boring as someone talking about their family tree, isn't that right, Breda? Tell us about Dublin, Des. Your home city. Has it changed much around here over the years?'

As smoothly as that, she soothed the situation.

Before dinner, there'd been time for Des to take Lola and Ellen outside to point out the Poolbeg chimneys, a Dublin landmark visible from their garden. Inside, Breda was swift to apologise.

'I'm very sorry, Bett. He always gets carried away. And he got so excited when he heard your grandmother hadn't been home in sixty-five years. He was just trying to be helpful, I promise.'

'I know. But it's not a normal trip home, Breda. I think Lola's finding it harder than she expected.'

'I can imagine. I told him to stop but he kept finding bits of information. He fancies himself as something of a detective too, unfortunately.' Breda sighed. 'Bett, we'd be so disappointed, but we'll understand if you want to cancel his contract. It would be such a shame, because he really is a good driver, so safe. And that car is his pride and joy. But we'd respect your decision.'

It wasn't up to Bett. 'I just think Lola would have preferred that Des hadn't done that research without being asked,' she said, carefully choosing her words.

'I can't blame her. I could have cut the tension in the room with a knife. Look, he'll kill me but I want to kill him too, so we're even. It's all here.' She reached across to a cupboard and picked up a folder. 'Des's research. It's better you have it than him, no matter what your grandmother decides to do.'

Bett could hear them coming back in. Lola was laughing at something Des was saying. So was Ellen. A good sign, she hoped. She quickly pushed the folder into her bag.

Two hours later, back at the hotel, Des insisted on helping Lola out of the car. He apologised again.

'Des, please, that's enough,' Lola said, with an imperious wave. 'Put it out of your mind. So you'll be here for us tomorrow at ten a.m.?'

'You're not sacking me?'

'For some harmless research? Of course not. Not until I get the recipe for tonight's chicken, at least.'

Up in their hotel room, Bett took the daily photo of Ellen and sent it to Glenn in Sydney, before helping her niece get ready for bed. She texted Daniel, sending her love, saying she'd call in the morning. She made sure Ellen was tucked up under the covers with a book before she went across the corridor and gently knocked on the door, once again left ajar. She'd deliberately left the folder of information behind.

Lola was again in the armchair by the window, slowly rubbing lotion into her hands. Without any words needed, Bett sat on the bed beside her, took her hands and began to massage in the cream.

Lola shut her eyes. 'If I could purr, I would. Thank you, darling.'

'So did you enjoy tonight?' Bett asked.

'Very much. Those crème brûlées were delicious. Breda has her own blowtorch, did you see that? I'd quite like one myself. Do you think Margaret would mind if I started cooking everything with the aid of a naked flame?'

'And Des's detective work?'

'He had been busy, hadn't he?'

'I'm sorry. It's my fault. I found him. And I sent through too much information at the start.'

'I chose Des. So if it's anyone's fault, it's mine.'

Bett waited, continuing to massage in the cream.

Lola still didn't open her eyes. 'I'm not going to say anything more, Bett. If that's what you're waiting for.'

Bett bit back the questions she wanted to ask about Lola's father. 'Breda gave me all his research. She thought it was better we had it than Des.'

'And have you read it?'

'It's not for me to read first. It's your history, your family.'

'It's your family too.'

199

Lola was right, Bett realised. This was her great-grandfather they were talking – not talking – about.

'Do you want me to drop it all over to you?'

There was just a moment's hesitation. 'I'm too tired to read tonight. You hold on to it, Bett.'

She didn't say if Bett could read it or not. Bett didn't ask. Instead, after finishing her massage, she kissed her grandmother goodnight on top of her white head, and quietly closed the door behind her.

The next morning, Bett woke, stretched and looked across the room to say good morning to Ellen. Her bed was empty. The bathroom door was open, the light off. Bett checked the time. Seven-thirty. She heard a noise in the corridor outside. A slamming of a door. Ellen must have woken early and gone over to Lola.

Bett pulled on her dressing-gown and padded across the carpet in her bare feet. Three gentle knocks on Lola's door, then her grandmother appeared.

'Good morning, darling. Are you bringing me breakfast in bed?'

'If you want it, I will. Actually, I'm looking for Ellen.'

'Why? Where has she gone?'

Lola always had been good at this game. 'I can't imagine,' Bett said, smiling.

'Isn't she in your room?' Lola said.

'She's not with you?'

'Not last time I looked.' Lola opened the door wider. She was alone in her suite.

Within a few minutes, Bett was in the corridor again, fully dressed, wide awake. Lola had rung reception. No, there were no thirteen-year-olds alone in the foyer, the receptionist said. Or in the breakfast room.

Bett ran down the stairs. The lift was too slow. The hotel's leisure centre was in the basement. Surely that's where a teenager would go, for a swim, or a turn in the spa? There were four people in the pool, doing slow laps. All adults. The spa was empty. She looked in the sauna and steam room. Also empty. As one of the swimmers came up for air, she startled him.

'Excuse me, have you seen a young girl? Here, on her own?'

The man was foreign, and didn't understand her at first. Bett apologised and repeated her question.

'Sorry, no, just us,' the man said.

Bett checked the change rooms. No Ellen.

She couldn't search the entire hotel on her own. She went back to reception. She had to wait impatiently for a guest to settle his account before she explained once more. Yes, she was told, there were CCTVs but it was too early to review the footage, or call the police.

'But a thirteen-year-old is missing. It's not too early.' Her voice betrayed her panic. She'd expected mishaps with Lola, a fall, illness, even exhaustion, but not Ellen. Think, Bett, where could she be . . .

The kitchen.

That was it. The kitchen. Ellen must have woken up hungry, gone down to the dining room, got chatting with the staff and been invited into the kitchen. She'd spent hours in the motel kitchen in Clare. It would feel normal for her to wander in and say hello to the chef.

Ellen wasn't there.

Disastrous scenarios were appearing in Bett's mind. Ellen had woken up and gone for a swim. On the way back a predatory man had seen her, a young pretty girl on her own. There were hundreds of hotel rooms. Who knew who or what could be lurking behind them?

Or had Ellen gone outside exploring and got lost? She could be anywhere in Dublin by now. She caught the bus to school in Sydney on her own, but this was different. She didn't even have her phone.

Lola had it. Oh, God. If something had happened —

Her phone.

Bett stood still. She'd thought of something. She went to the receptionist again.

'I've spoken to housekeeping,' the woman said. 'The porters are looking for her too.'

Bett thanked her. 'Do you have a business centre? With a computer?'

'Of course.' She gave directions, up the stairs, first room to the right.

Bett ran at first, and then slowed as she came near the small business office. There, at the sole computer, was Ellen. Fully dressed, not a hair out of place. She was on Instagram.

Relief coursed through Bett. Words leapt into her mind: *For God's sake, Ellen. We've been worried sick*. She bit them back. She was the adult. She had to stay calm.

She changed her mind. 'For God's sake, Ellen. We've been worried sick. We had no idea where you were, if —'

Ellen calmly interrupted. 'But I left you a note.'

'What?'

'By your bed. Saying I didn't want to wake Lola for my phone but I wanted to talk to my friends.'

'Why didn't you wake me?'

'You looked too peaceful.'

Bett was a long way from peaceful now. 'I thought you'd run away or been snatched or drowned.'

'No. I've just been here. Waiting for you and Lola to wake up.'

Bett ran her hand through her curls. 'If Lola didn't have your phone, this wouldn't have happened.'

Ellen had a glint in her eye. 'So will you ask her for my phone back full-time or will I?'

'We'll both kill you first. Then we'll discuss it.'

Bett phoned Lola's room with the good news. She was waiting there for them when they returned via reception. The search party had been called off.

'Time for a Quinlan meeting?' Lola said in a deceptively cheery tone.

Once they were all seated, Lola began. 'Now, Ellen, do I need to explain why we were so worried?'

'But I left a note.'

'Be that as it may. You are thirteen. You can't go wandering around a big hotel on your own.'

'Dad would let me.'

'I don't believe that.'

Ellen's expression turned mutinous. 'Some trip this is. No phone. No freedom.'

Bett saw Lola's lips twitch. 'A fine political slogan for a teenage rebellion, Ellen. I'd like you to apologise to Bett and to me, please.'

A sullen look at the floor. Silence.

'Or we won't have any breakfast. Or go to Kildare today. I can see you trying to decide whether to sulk and display all those uncharming traits teenagers are renowned for, and also spoil my first and last trip home to Ireland, or whether you're going to be a grown-up about this. Can you decide quickly, please? My stomach is grumbling. I'm sure I can smell that delicious full Irish breakfast from here. Eggs, bacon, little sausages, perhaps even a hash brown or two, though they do seem to be more American than Irish. Still, they are made of potato, I suppose . . .'

Ellen continued to look at the floor but she was fighting a smile too, Bett could see. Once again, it was good to watch Lola in action.

Lola continued to talk. 'Or perhaps those are pancakes I can smell? And maple syrup. Or fruit salad? Ah, no, it's toast. Fresh toast. And coffee. Am I right in thinking my sulky great-granddaughter is allowed to have a weak coffee now and again? Or is that my addled old brain deceiving me? I might be confusing her with my usually well-behaved adorable great-granddaughter, who seems to have been invaded by a speechless kind of tribe of zombies.'

Ellen looked up. 'You don't have "tribes" of zombies, Lola.'

'No? What is the collective term? Did you know the collective term for crows is a murder? And the collective term for emus is a mob? Coming down for breakfast, Ellen? We'll leave the sulking for later, will we?'

Ellen smiled properly then. A little sheepishly too, Bett was glad to see. She wondered whether she'd be able to replicate Lola's tactics with Yvette and Zachary in the years to come. No. She'd never be able to summon up Lola's perfect blend of jokiness and benign menace.

'I'm sorry to worry you, Lola,' Ellen said. 'And you too, Bett.'

They assured her she was forgiven.

'But can we please come to an agreement?' Ellen asked, turning to Lola, solemn again.

'Perhaps. What's your proposal?'

'I get to keep my phone all day. Even if I only use it in the morning and the evening, as we agreed. In case of emergencies.'

'I'll think about it. It will depend on how well behaved you are today. Deal?'

'Deal,' Ellen said. She held out her hand. She and Lola shook on it.

As they walked down the corridor, Ellen looked up at her great-grandmother, mischief in her eyes. Both Bett and Lola could see Anna again: her grace, her sense of humour.

'You strike a hard bargain, Lola,' Ellen said.

Lola winked at her. 'Your mother used to say that exact same thing.'

'Did she really?'

'She really did,' Lola said.

They continued down the corridor, still holding hands.

CHAPTER EIGHTEEN

At ten a.m., as arranged, they stepped outside with their luggage to find Des waiting by his gleaming car. It was a beautiful May day, the sky a soft blue.

Lola greeted him. 'And no more apologies necessary regarding last night, Des. Each day is a new day as far as I'm concerned. Each new day is a miracle, to be frank, at my age.'

He tipped his chauffeur's cap. 'Thank you, Mrs Quinlan.'

'Lola, please.'

'Lola,' he said again. 'Good morning, Miss Quinlan. Good morning, Bett.'

'People think we're royalty. Or film stars,' Ellen said, enjoying the attention from a group of people standing outside the hotel. 'It's because of you, Lola.'

'Me? Surely not,' Lola said, smoothing down her golden flared trousers and adjusting the six strands of beads adding extra colour to her rainbow-covered kaftan top. 'It's Des's fancy car, isn't it, Des?'

'That's right, Lola,' he said, proudly opening the doors. 'So, off to Kildare we go.'

'Yes,' Lola said. 'Off we go.'

*

Bett felt the tension rising in Lola as they drove through the Dublin suburbs. She'd heard her grandmother ask Des to take the route to Kildare via Wicklow. In the front seat again, Ellen chattered to Des about her favourite pop star, her favourite TV program, her favourite books, a constant burble that created a strangely soothing soundtrack. Des was happy to chat back, even surprising Ellen – and Bett – with a burst of a recent Taylor Swift song and a spirited discussion about Justin Bieber. He also listened with what looked like genuine interest when Ellen spoke at great length about her school's campaign to save the orangutans of Borneo.

Lola was far away, Bett could tell. Staring out of the window, not reacting to anything Ellen was saying, not even joining in on any of the songs.

'Are you okay?' she asked her grandmother in a low voice.

'Grand, darling, thank you.'

Grand. The catch-all Irish word for every occasion. Bett had picked it up herself in the short time she'd lived in Dublin. Lola rarely used such Irish terms at home in Australia. Bett had noticed them emerging in the past few days.

'Let me know if you want Des to stop at any time, won't you?'

'I will, Bett, thank you.'

The road continued past housing estates, shopping centres, apartment buildings, car yards, a football stadium.

'Nothing like this in your day, Lola, I'm sure,' Des said over his shoulder.

'Nothing at all, Des.'

'None of these buildings were here?' Ellen asked. 'It must have been so boring.'

'We liked it,' Lola said, smiling. 'It was all green fields and mountains back then.'

Ellen pointed. 'You can still see the mountains – look.'

'So you can,' Lola said, before lapsing into silence again.

Bett decided to leave her in peace. Was it any wonder she was deep in thought? This trip had happened so quickly. Here they were in Ireland less than a month after Lola had first announced her wish to come home. She was feeling disorientated enough herself. Right now, she should have been home trying to feed the twins, talking to Daniel about work, not sitting here in the back of a chauffeur-driven car . . .

She'd had the briefest of calls to him that morning after Ellen was found. All was fine at home. The barbecue with Carrie and Matthew and their kids had gone well, he told her. Then Yvette had called out – roared, in fact – and he'd had to go.

'Welcome to County Wicklow!'

Ellen's shout from the front seat broke into her thoughts. A sign told them they'd crossed from County Dublin into Wicklow, the county that lay between Dublin and Kildare. The scenery outside was changing, the road narrowing and winding, the tall trees on either side turning it into a tunnel of green light. They were rising up into the foothills of the mountains, the city of Dublin visible behind them. They passed pine plantations and small farms, fields of a deep green so unlike the shade they were used to in Australia.

'Did you come to Wicklow a lot, Lola?' Ellen asked, turning around again.

'For my holidays once, Ellen, yes. To a seaside town called Bray. The sun shone the whole week.'

'That's what the sun does.'

'Not necessarily so in Ireland, darling.'

'Do you want a detour, Lola?' Des asked. 'We could go to Bray now?'

He was constantly alert to their conversations, Bett noticed.

Lola shook her head. 'No, thank you, Des. On to Kildare, please.'

The trees and the hedges now lining their route were all lush with new growth. Shafts of sun filtering through the leaves sent splashes of light onto the road ahead. Bett kept waiting for a change in mood from Lola, for her to become ebullient, excited, more like the normal Lola. Surely she knew a song or two that would match the moment, the one about the forty shades of green, even? Bett had grown up hearing them. But there was only silence from Lola. It was unsettling. She knew many versions of her grandmother, but not this one. She tried to find the word.

Melancholy.

That was it. She was melancholy. Sad, even.

Ellen was enjoying trying to pronounce the place names in English and Irish on road signs they passed. Enniscorthy. *Inis Córthaidh*. Tullow. *An Tulach*. They drove through the busy town of Blessington, again with no reaction from Lola. Bett glanced at her. Her grandmother was sitting so still, gazing out the window.

Ellen broke the silence, pointing at a new sign. Poulaphouca. 'How do I say that one?'

Lola answered. 'Pool-ah-foo-ka,' she said. 'Des, could you please stop near here if you can?'

'No problem at all, Lola.'

Moments later he drove into a parking area. A wide silver lake rippled in front of them for as far as they could see, against a backdrop of mountains. The sky looked huge above it. They all got out of the car.

'It's beautiful,' Ellen declared. 'Bett, can you take a photo of me to send to Dad tonight?'

Lola watched as Bett took the shot. 'I remember all the talk about making this lake,' she said.

'They made a lake?' Ellen said, amazed. 'How did they do that?'

Lola explained. Back in the 1930s, Dublin was a growing city, needing fresh supplies of water. A decision was taken to flood the valley and create a reservoir here at Poulaphouca. 'It means "The devil's hole",' Lola said.

'That's creepy,' Ellen said. 'Did they tell the people they were going to flood it?'

'They did, darling, yes. But some of the houses are still under there somewhere.'

They looked out in silence, imagining an underwater village.

'We used to come here for picnics,' Lola said. 'There was a tearoom down the road.'

'With your friends or your parents?' Ellen asked.

'My parents once or twice. Other people too.'

As Ellen wandered over to where Des was standing, Bett waited, but Lola didn't say anything more. Was it Edward she had come here with? Bett tried to imagine it. Her grandmother as a nineteen-year-old, walking hand in hand with Edward, or sitting on the grass picnicking with him and friends . . .

Nearby, she could hear Des explaining to Ellen more about the flooding of the valley. She was fascinated with the idea of the underwater houses.

'Did they take their furniture out before the water came in or is that all there too? And what about their pets? How did they let the cats and dogs know the water was coming? They wouldn't have been drowned, would they? And do they know for sure that everyone got out? What if there were kids playing who didn't hear the bell or the siren or whatever they did before they flooded it?'

'It didn't happen that suddenly, Ellen,' Des said. He explained there had been plenty of warning, following years of planning.

Ellen was impressed. 'How do you know all this? Did you learn about it in school?'

'I researched it on the internet this morning,' he admitted with a sheepish grin.

Back in the car again, Des told Ellen to keep her eyes peeled for the sign for Ballymore Eustace, Lola's village. 'We're just on the border of County Kildare now,' he said.

She was excited, leaning forward. 'There it is!' she called. 'Look, Lola!'

Des slowed the car, giving them all time to read the sign. 'I can stop for a photo anytime you want, Lola, just ask,' he said. 'Or we can go straight on to your village and do the photos later.'

Lola's reply surprised them all. 'I'm sorry, but I need to change our plans. I hope you don't mind. I don't feel well. I'd like to go straight to our hotel and lie down.'

'Now?' Bett said. 'But we're nearly at Ballymore Eustace.'

'It's been waiting for me for the past sixty-five years. I'm sure it will be there tomorrow.'

'But we're so close, Lola,' Ellen said. 'Can't we just drive through and look at your house? And then come back and do it more slowly tomorrow when you're less tired?'

'I don't feel well enough, Ellen. I'm sorry.'

Des read the mood correctly for once. 'That's absolutely fine, Lola. Your hotel isn't far away. You'll be having your lie-down before you know it.'

Something in Lola's expression stopped Ellen from protesting further. Bett stayed quiet too.

If their Dublin hotel had been fancy, their Kildare one was even grander. Des followed the long driveway into the landscaped grounds. It had once been a hunting lodge, he told them. Then an exclusive boarding school run by French nuns for years. And now, this fine four-star hotel.

'It's like a castle,' Ellen breathed. 'Wait till my friends see it. Lola, please can I take a photo?'

Lola didn't reply.

'Lola?' Bett asked.

She blinked and came back to full attention. 'Sorry. Yes, Ellen.'

'That was easy,' Ellen whispered to Bett.

Des drew up in front of the hotel. Before he got out to open their doors, he turned.

'So, a rest break for you all? I can come back this afternoon, or in the morning; just say the word.'

'No, Des,' Lola said. 'You, Bett and Ellen go to Ballymore Eustace as planned. I'm fine on my own.'

Bett was confused. 'Lola, we can't go to your home town without you. We'll stay here with you.'

'No, Bett.' Her voice was firm. 'I'll be happier on my own. We can all check in now, but then I'd like you to go for a drive with Des. You can come back around six p.m. and tell me what you've seen.'

'But I don't understand,' Ellen said. 'What will we look for? You haven't told us anything yet.'

'Ellen's right,' Bett said. 'We're happy to wait till you feel up to it, Lola. All of us together.'

'Thank you, but no,' Lola said.

Bett knew that tone. She wouldn't be changing her mind.

Ellen still wasn't happy. 'But you'll come with us all tomorrow, won't you?'

'Of course. Unless I stay here the whole ten days. What a wonderful hotel. Well chosen, Bett.'

'I'm glad you like it.' There didn't seem to be anything else to say.

Bett and Ellen were back with Des at the car before long. They'd all checked in. Bett and Ellen's room was still being cleaned, but Lola's room had been ready. Bett and Ellen escorted her, accompanied by a porter carrying their luggage.

Her room was beautiful, spacious and elegant, overlooking the hotel's extensive gardens, the many trees in full soft-green leaf. Closer to the hotel building itself were several statues, another fountain, more flower beds. A large comfortable armchair was set up in the bay window. There was a wedding about to take place down below. A sign in the foyer had declared the hotel to be one of Ireland's most popular wedding venues. A small marquee was set up beyond the fountain. Guests in fine dress were strolling nearby. A bride and groom were visible to the far right of the grounds, having their photograph taken under a big chestnut tree. There was even a string quartet playing under another tree. At Lola's request, Ellen opened the window wide, letting in not just a gentle breeze but the soft sound of classical music. 'Well, Bett?' Lola asked.

After a moment's listening, Bett named it. Pachelbel's 'Canon in D'.

'That's my girl.' Lola settled herself into the armchair and sighed. 'I couldn't have asked for more if I'd rung ahead and ordered. So much to watch and listen to, as well. No need to worry. I'll be fine.'

Fine? Lola was far from feeling fine, Bett knew that. 'Ellen, would you please run downstairs for me and let Des know I'll be another five minutes or so? Can you wait there with him?'

'Am I allowed to? Should I call for a security guard to escort me?'

'Very funny. Go on. I'll count how long it takes you.'

'I'm thirteen,' she said haughtily. 'That doesn't work any more.'

Once she was gone, Bett sat down opposite Lola. 'What is it, Lola? Was it something you saw? A place you remembered? The lake? This hotel, even?'

Lola shook her head. She hesitated, then spoke. 'It's a funny thing, Bett. I always thought memories were unchangeable. Set in stone, shaped by the years. But there are always others too, ones you haven't let yourself remember. I didn't expect those to be waiting here for me too.'

'I don't understand.'

'I'm not sure I do yet either. Darling, off you go. Please, think of today's drive with Des as a reconnaissance mission. It doesn't matter that you're seeing it all before me. I'll see it myself tomorrow. If my sight lasts that long. That was a joke, Bett.'

Bett had never felt less like laughing. 'But it feels wrong. I don't even know where your house is. And what if we go to the wrong school? We might go to all the wrong places.'

'Then tomorrow will be like a brand-new tour. Away you go. Get to know your niece better. Talk to her about her new stepmother and her stepsister. Her schoolwork. Her dad. You know you can't compete when I'm around, so seize the moment.'

'You promise you'll be okay? That a nap is all you need? I can get a doctor if you're worried.'

'A doctor? My dear one in Clare would be heartbroken if I went behind his back. Please, Bett. Go. Leave me in peace. I've got a wedding to watch.'

Bett reluctantly obeyed her.

CHAPTER NINETEEN

For half an hour, Lola didn't move. She sat in the armchair, looking out the window, watching the wedding activity unfold below. Her room was perfectly situated, allowing her to see new arrivals at the front of the hotel too. She briefly considered calling reception to ask if they had any binoculars.

She especially enjoyed the bride and groom's photo session. They must have struck at least fifty poses, from serious and romantic to giddy and, yes, embarrassing. Would they really ever display a photo of the two of them leaping in the air, aided by a small trampoline the photographer's assistant had magically produced? Lola could only imagine how forced their smiles were becoming. Perhaps it was good preparation for the years of marriage ahead. Not only the ups and downs, but also the necessity of keeping a smile on your face, even if it was sometimes the last thing you felt like doing.

How long would this couple last? A year? Five years? Forever? Would there be children? Just one, or many? Or none at all, by choice or for sadder reasons? How would their families get on? Did their parents approve of their child's choice of life partner? Would all sorts of tensions come out tonight during the wedding reception in that splendid marquee, with its array of fairy lights inside, the entrance bright with winding garlands of flowers, the smartly dressed guests all gathered together to wish the young couple a happy future?

Lola's tears came from nowhere, shocking her. Her hands trembled as she brought them to her face, covering her eyes, trying to calm herself. It didn't work. She leaned forward, rocking as if she was a child, back and forth, as she realised the truth.

She didn't want to be here.

This had been a terrible, silly mistake. She should be home at Margaret's house in Clare, not here in Ireland, chasing something that was long gone.

There was nothing here for her now. She had felt it at every step of this journey. Landing in Dublin airport, seeing joyous reunions all around them. Who had been there to welcome her home? No one but a hired driver. Who was waiting to hug her, to say, 'At last, you're home'? No one. The person whose hug she had longed to feel, all those years she'd been in Australia, was gone.

She couldn't think like this. She was being ridiculous. She spoke aloud. 'Stop this, Lola. Stop it now.'

It didn't work. Her sobs kept coming, more painful now. Her face was wet with tears. Why hadn't she come back earlier? Because of her pride. Because she had wanted to prove something, to show her parents that she didn't need their approval, that they had no control over her any more.

And she had done that, hadn't she? She had started again, emotionally, and geographically. She'd done everything possible to make a success of her life, to rise out of the ashes of her family life and the mess of her ill-fated marriage. Not on her own, either. With Jim. With her granddaughters. They loved her, didn't they? As much as she loved them? She knew they did.

Yet here she was, every part of her hurting, aching, wishing everything was different. But it was too late. Years too late. She

would never hear the words she'd yearned to hear: *I love you, Lola.*
I'm proud of you, of what you have done, of who you have become.

The tears overcame her again.

It was as if all her barriers had been torn away. All the sadnesses of her life came rushing at her. How could God, the universe, whoever was in charge, be so cruel? Not just in her own life, but all around her. To think of Ellen, little Ellen, going through life without her mother. All of them having to go on without their Anna, Jim without his daughter, Geraldine too. It wasn't just their family that was suffering. She thought of Alex. Of his family, all missing him. So many people felt like this. She thought of tragedies in the Clare Valley, young men and women killed in car accidents. Lives lost at work, on farms. She'd seen the effects of all those and more at close quarters, the shock and grief and horror and despair.

There was so much heartache and sorrow out in the wide world. Too much. Children killed by their parents. Women in violent situations, facing abuse every day. Lola held her hands to her head, willing the bad thoughts to stay away, trying to summon the moments of joy and grace that had sustained her all her life. They'd disappeared out of reach. All she could think of was the despair in the world. Those poor refugee children and their parents locked in those detention centres off Australia. All those families in camps in Europe . . . Where was the humanity, the kindness? What kind of life was that for any of them, adults and little kids growing up without hope of a future?

She couldn't stop the distressing images. Thought after thought of sadness and futility filled her mind. The world was a hopeless mess. Human beings were cruel, savage. And what had she decided to do while all these terrible things were happening all around her? Waste money on this futile trip. She'd had no shares or a diamond ring to sell. Bett would never know the truth, but Lola had sold the one valuable item she had ever owned in her life. A small painting of a forest scene. She'd found it in a charity shop, forty years earlier. It had cost her less than twenty dollars, a lot for her at the time. She'd been drawn to the beauty in it, a whole landscape depicted in a few lines of colour, in layers of different shades of greens. It was only small, not even thirty inches across, but she had loved it. It had come with her on all her moves, from guesthouses to motels, and finally to Margaret's house, where she'd hung it among her other, ever-changing framed prints and paintings.

If anyone ever remarked on its special qualities, she'd always proudly declared it as a print, or an amateur copy. For years she'd thought that's all it was. Until one evening, three years previously, she'd been watching a TV program on the ABC. An imported BBC show, an antiques program. An almost identical painting was under excited discussion. The artist had recently died. It was valued at ten thousand pounds.

She had done nothing about it then, just held the knowledge to herself like a secret. It was only this year, when she'd found herself unable to stop thinking about coming back to Ireland, that she'd decided to find out more. She asked Luke to help. Luke and his marvellous internet research skills. The painting she had was a print, she told him, but she'd always wondered what an original might be worth, if someone was lucky enough to own one.

He'd copied down the details from the corner of the painting, a date, a signature. Leave it with me, he'd said. She hadn't had to wait long. He'd phoned her that same day.

Thirty thousand dollars.

More money than she had ever dreamt of having in her life.

She should have left it to her family in her will. Surprised them with her one item of value, for them to sell and divide the proceeds, or for one of them to keep. But what had she done?

She'd sold it. The gallery owner in Melbourne could barely believe his luck. The deal was done within days, negotiated through a lawyer Lola hired in Adelaide. And what had she done with all that money? Spent it, foolishly, on this trip, on airfares for three of them, on fancy hotels like this one, even a driver, trying to prove something to whom – herself?

It had to have been to herself. There was no one else here in Ireland who cared what Louisa Quinlan nee Delaney had become, or how her life had turned out.

If Bett or Carrie had come to her for advice, telling her they wanted to do something so impulsive, Lola knew immediately what she'd have said. That it was a fool's errand. 'You can't go through life trying to impress other people, trying to seek other people's approval. You have to be content with yourself and your own decisions.'

Where were the wise words when she needed them herself?

As they'd driven into Kildare today, she'd realised the truth. She'd had a growing unease since arriving in Ireland that the trip had been a mistake. She'd done her best to ignore her instincts, hoping it would somehow become a lighthearted homecoming, with Bett and Ellen by her side, two of her favourite people in the world. She had thought they would protect her in some emotional way, be the proof of the good things in her life, the proof that out of sad times happiness had flourished. That her lost relationship with her parents, her disastrous marriage to Edward, were counterweighed by the positive parts of her life.

But that hadn't happened. Rather than feel stronger as each hour passed in Ireland, she had felt herself grow more fragile. As if one by one, all the layers of self-sufficiency and independence and experience that had grown around her during her sixty-five years in Australia had slipped away. She'd found herself stepping back in time in her mind, in her memories, back to her childhood, to her teenage years. She had felt powerless. Suffocated. That she was in the wrong place, as she had felt so often, so strongly, all the years she had lived here. Always knowing her father didn't approve of her. That her mother wasn't strong enough to support her, to believe in her, to be proud of her. That she had disappointed her parents. Was there anything more soul-destroying than knowing you'd let down the very people who had brought you into the world?

She had thought about Edward too.

She'd always felt sure it would never last with him. She had gone into their marriage with her eyes wide open. There had been no love between them, she had known that too. What there had been, what she had hoped might almost be enough, was physical attraction. That had been one of the best, most unexpected surprises of their relationship. She had been taught by the nuns, by schoolyard whispered conversations, that sex was to be endured, that it was dangerous, that any pleasure came at a price. She had listened to it all with mild interest, never having had it tested, not knowing then that everything they said was wrong, that the pleasure could be worth any pain. That sex could be joyous, and fun, and overwhelming. That it could also be empowering. If her body could make her feel so good, what else was possible in life that she didn't yet know about?

That's how it had been for her. Making love with Edward, becoming his secret lover, all the excitement and illicitness of it, for the weeks before they were forced to marry, hurried out of Kildare for Australia – yes, she had loved every second of it.

He had made her feel powerful. In charge of herself. Independent. Her relationship with him had given her a new sense of herself, a new identity, separate from her parents. He had made her feel like a woman, not a girl any more. Made her realise that she was attractive, that she was desirable. She'd never needed a psychologist to help her recognise that her father had done all he could for years to belittle her, to keep her hopes low, her aspirations small town. Or to remember that her mother had never praised her, never given her any reason to delight in her own looks, her height, her personality.

But being with Edward had done all of that and more. She felt sure he'd never been aware of his effect on her. She had been too busy marvelling in it herself to think of telling him. Even from the start they had never confided in one another. That real mixing of mind and desire with a man had only come to her when she had met Alex, her dear Alex, so many years later in Melbourne. But being with Edward physically had released something in her, set her free in some way.

Lola leaned her head back against the chair. The tears had stopped. Her chest hurt. But she felt lighter, somehow. As if something that had been stopping her from remembering too much had gone. She realised what it was. Fear. Not fear of bad memories. It was a fear of remembering that there had been good times with Edward as well as their many bad times.

She hadn't allowed herself to remember that. How could she have gone on as a single mother if she had constantly revisited the good times they had shared? It was only by remembering the bad times, his drinking, their fighting, that she'd been able to keep going, known that it was best to stay away from him.

But what was she to do with any good memories? Was it permissible to even have happy recollections of their time together? Or did that betray all she'd done to find her own independence? Absolve him in some way? Had he been an evil man, or had he been as much a victim of his own upbringing, his own difficult family life, as she had been?

In a room less than ten kilometres from where she had first met him, and for the first time in so many years, she allowed herself to remember their early days together.

CHAPTER TWENTY

They had spoken only briefly the first day, after Lola accidentally tripped him up. She knew very few boys – or young men – her own age. She was at an all-girls convent school. Her father kept too close an eye on her. Her mother wasn't going to initiate social outings either.

She was still allowed out, now and again. Occasionally there were dances in the parish hall or in nearby Blessington. Her parents would usually attend too. Lola was always conscious of them watching her. She often talked about it when she visited her mother's friend Elizabeth, to help with childminding.

'How will I ever meet someone when my parents are spying on my every move?' Lola asked Elizabeth one afternoon. She'd called in to see her on the way back from teaching piano at the Bayfield estate. It was a week after she had first spoken to Edward.

'They just want the best for you.'

'What best? I'll be lucky to get the scrapings of the barrel around here, let alone the best. I've already got the odds stacked against me. Half the eligible men around here only reach my knees.'

Elizabeth laughed. She and Lola often laughed together. They also spoke more honestly than she ever did with her own mother.

'Shall I just give up?' Lola said, dandling Elizabeth's youngest daughter, Helena, on her lap, making her gurgle with pleasure. 'Declare myself a spinster and come and live with you and mind your children for the rest of my days?'

'You would be far too bad an influence. Thank heavens my older two are safely away with the nuns, out of your reach.'

'This is my special one, anyway. Aren't you, Helena?' She kissed the baby. 'We'll run away together as soon as you are old enough to walk and you can be my maid. If you haven't run away to work at one of the estates before then.' Many local girls had taken jobs on the estates. The work was hard but sought after.

'The word is that Bayfield is in trouble. The lord and master is gambling again.'

Lola loved that Elizabeth always knew about the happenings in their area. 'I'd better finish teaching the girls their scales before the piano is sold.' She put the now sleepy baby into her nearby cradle. She casually crossed the room and just as casually poured a glass of water for herself and Elizabeth. 'I suppose the staff will be the first to be let go?'

'As always,' Elizabeth said.

'Who is the gardener there at the moment, do you know?'

'There are several of them. Old Mr Quinlan is there now, I believe. He was out of work a good while, I heard. One of his sons too, the youngest, I think. Another older fellow —'

'The Quinlan son? Would he be taller than me? Dark hair?'

'That would be him. Fine-looking boy.' Elizabeth smiled. 'Lola, why are you asking?'

Lola explained. 'I apologised for tripping him up. Then he walked me to the end of the drive and I walked on and he went back to work. Even Father couldn't see any harm in that, surely?'

'I wonder.'

When Lola returned to Bayfield for the next lesson, she watched for him. As the little girls happily practised – they much preferred the livelier tunes – Lola positioned herself so she could glance regularly out the large window of the music room. She could see figures working in the gardens. One seemed too stocky. The other too short. But as she was walking home there he was in the driveway. As if he'd been waiting for her.

She didn't imagine it this time. She felt a jump in her heart to see him.

He tipped his head in greeting. She smiled back at him. He was older than her, perhaps in his early twenties. Taller. Muscular. Jet-black hair.

'I should escort you to the gate again,' he said, falling into step beside her. 'There's fierce dangers here sometimes. Only last week I was attacked out of nowhere by a wild beast and sent flying.'

'Is that right? It must have given you a terrible fright,' she said.

'I enjoyed it,' he said.

'Did you?'

Another exchange of smiles, another faint hum of attraction.

'I'm Louisa Delaney,' she said. 'But my friends call me Lola.'

'I've just met you so I'd better call you Miss Delaney.'

'No, Lola is fine.'

'Edward Quinlan,' he said, with another polite tip of his head.

'From?'

He pointed. 'Beyond Kilcullen. My father is the gardener here. Myself and another fellow help him.'

They were getting close to the gate. She slowed her pace.

'I teach the children piano.'

'I know,' he said. 'Twice a week, for the summer, until they go back to boarding school in England. You're the only daughter of the Ballymore Eustace headmaster and his wife.'

'How do you know all that?'

'I asked until I found out.'

With that he turned and walked up the drive. If he looked back, she didn't know. She was too busy being determined not to. But the few days until her next lesson there never passed so slowly.

Over the next two weeks, she would finish her tuition and begin to walk home, only to find Edward beside her with a wheelbarrow or a rake, something to make it seem that he was working. Only once did they meet someone else, one of the other gardeners. Without any fuss he veered away from her as if it was pure coincidence they were side by side.

It was during the fourth conversation that he asked her if she would meet him outside Bayfield.

'Just us? Or all the other gardeners too?'

'Just us.'

That hum, that sudden sense of anticipation. 'My father wouldn't approve.'

'Your father doesn't need to know everything you do, does he?'

'No.'

Standing there, he reached over and gently stroked her cheek, for just a second. The daring of it took her breath away.

'I'll be at the tearoom by the lake next Saturday,' he said.

'So will I,' she said, raising her chin. As she walked home, she could still feel where he'd touched her.

It was easier to get away than she thought. Lola was often invited to Elizabeth's house to mind Helena and help with the cooking. She had planned to ask her if she could break from her duties on Saturday even for half an hour. Elizabeth finished with her earlier than expected. It was as if whatever was about to happen was meant to be, the path ahead being cleared.

It took her ten minutes to find him in the crowds at the tearooms. She saw people she'd gone to school with in Ballymore Eustace, at her father's school. Others she saw each week at mass. Several girls from the convent in Naas. All in summer clothes today. The long spell of good weather was making everyone more relaxed. She saw one of his older brothers. At least, he had to be one of his brothers. He looked so like Edward that her heart gave that little thump again. But then he turned and she saw it wasn't him. When she did definitely see him, she felt another sudden quickening of her pulse. He was laughing, talking to a woman about Lola's age, pretty, dark-haired. Lola's chin rose. Fine. So he was already spoken for. He saw her, waved, that smile again, that look in his eyes, as if he had a secret for her, which he'd share as soon as they had a moment alone.

She felt different near him. Excited. As though she was waiting for something. Longing for something. A hunger. There was never any direct talk at school about sex or relationships. Her parents had never spoken about such things to her either. But Lola had talked to her friends about it a little. Desire, it was called. Or lust. Whatever its name was, Lola didn't care. It was a new, special sensation. It was a force telling her that the only place her body should be was near his. Pressed against his. This Edward Quinlan to whom she had barely spoken, of whom her father would most definitely not approve. Uneducated gardeners? She could imagine his scorn. She didn't care about that either.

'Miss Delaney,' he said with that polite tilt of his head again.

'Mr Quinlan,' she said as politely.

'This is my sister, Margaret,' he said, gesturing towards the young woman. 'We call her Peggy.'

More greetings, as Lola's smile grew wider. His sister. She was his sister.

They only spent ten minutes with each other that first day. It was too crowded, too many people they both knew, several stopping for brief conversations, interrupting the humming connection that Lola could feel between them. She was sure Edward could feel it too. He left her company first, joining a group of fellows his own age, all noise and attention-seeking confidence. As he walked away, he looked back over his shoulder at her. A look, and then a wink.

A wink! She felt like smiling for the rest of the day.

The following week, there was another conversation at Bayfield, brief – too brief – but long enough to arrange another meeting. This time not at the tearooms but down by the river, at the swimming spot where everyone in the area gathered on warm evenings. It took her less than five minutes to find him. Again, Peggy was with him.

It had been sunny for three days in a row, the warmth sending everyone outdoors, not just young people, but families, children, even elderly folk, relishing the rare good weather. The three of them walked further down the river path to a quieter spot, took off their shoes and dangled their feet, as so many others around them were doing.

Lola had been here on other sunny afternoons, sat on this same riverbank, dipped her feet into the water as she was doing now. But the feeling of the cool water rushing over her feet, between her toes, over her bare calves, had never been so exciting. She was sitting beside Peggy. Edward was on his sister's other side, but that didn't seem to matter. That feeling was still humming back and forth between them, his jokes made for her, not his sister, his laugh, his voice affecting her in a way his sister surely wasn't even noticing.

Finally, finally, Peggy stood up, called over to a friend, promised her brother that she'd be back shortly. Now it was just the two of them, Lola and Edward, side by side on the riverbank, bare legs inches apart under the cool flowing water.

Lola moved first. She couldn't bear to not be touching him when he was so close and she felt so . . . so alive, that's what it was. She moved her foot as if it was accidental and it brushed against his. He looked at her.

'Is the water too cold for you?'

'Only a little,' she said.

His foot brushed back against hers. 'Is that better?'

'Much better,' she said. 'Thank you.'

The next fifteen minutes were among the best of her life. She had tried to imagine what it would be like to sit close to a man like this, what they would talk about, whether she would feel nervous or shy or tongue-tied. She had never expected it to be as easy as this. Edward wasn't nervous or shy or tongue-tied. He was full of chat, and jokes, telling her easily about his job. 'Sure, it's just rows of cabbages and carrots. I don't get to do any of the fancy flowers but it's just for now after all. I won't be here for the rest of my life.' Then he surprised her, telling her his plan.

'You're going to Australia?' she said, turning towards him, still making sure their dangling feet could easily, thrillingly brush against each other's.

'Why not? There's nothing for me here.' Two of the other lads from the village were out there already, he told her. There was plenty of work there, everyone knew that.

If even then she'd thought he was overly confident, full of bluster, she'd chosen to ignore it. What was a bit of boasting? Especially when it was wrapped in so much optimism for the future. His plans stretched far beyond the tight boundaries that had been set for her, by her father in particular.

She didn't mind too much when two of his friends came over and indulged in a good bit of teasing. She didn't mind when they produced several bottles of beer, drinking them as they lay sprawled on the grass beside Edward. They offered her some, but she declined. She definitely didn't mind when for a minute – one thrilling minute – he reached over and put his arm around her, a sign of ownership, claiming her in front of his friends.

She was the one who reluctantly had to leave. She was expected home. The last thing she wanted was for someone to come looking for her here. Worse still, for her father or mother to arrive and see her, Louisa Delaney, the headmaster's daughter, lying here beside Edward Quinlan like a – she searched for the words and then found them – a wanton woman. *Who was he anyway?* she could imagine them asking.

She'd found out a little more from him, before his friends arrived. Edward, his parents, his sister Peggy and four older brothers had lived in a house on one of the other estates in the area for five years, a fine house, he told Lola. Then the estate owner had gone broke. 'Not that he was ever here. He spent most of his time at racetracks in England,' Edward told her. They had to leave, along with the other staff. They now lived crammed into two rooms in a small cottage a mile out of Kilcullen. His father didn't like working at Bayfield, but a job was a job. And it was better than having him around the house all day, Edward said. She noticed something change in his voice. There were obviously problems at home. She would ask Elizabeth. She might know more.

As she reluctantly took her feet out of the water, she felt him watching her. There was something so . . . intimate – that was the word – about her feet drying on the grass bank, her toes wriggling, until they were dry enough for her to put her shoes on again. Her body had always just been her body, she thought. But today something had happened to it. She was suddenly intently aware of herself, of her bare skin, and of Edward looking at her bare skin.

His friends were taking turns throwing stones into the water, laughing loudly. Under the cover of their chatter and noise, he leaned towards her.

'I'll see you next week,' he said.

She paused.

'At Bayfield,' he said. 'I'll walk you to the gate again.'

She smiled at him, then left.

He was there the following Tuesday, waiting for her. They didn't touch at all. He walked alongside her, teasing her and talking more about his plans, about the cost of the sea voyage to Australia, how long it would take. He talked nonstop. If she didn't get to speak much, if, once again, there was a sense of boasting about him, she chose to ignore it. She liked hearing him talk. She didn't have anything to tell him, after all. Now and again, she made a cheeky remark and was rewarded by a burst of laughter.

On the Thursday, knowing there'd be another weekend gathering at the riverbank, she deliberately slowed her step as they approached the gate. That was the point where he would turn back and run, back to the garden and the sheds. She knew he ran because she had started turning to watch him. He was a fast runner. Strong. Athletic.

'Have you got a boyfriend?' one of her piano students had asked her that morning.

'We saw you walking with him,' the other added.

'Of course not,' Lola had said, feeling a blush rush into her face. 'He's an old friend from the village.'

'We don't have any friends from the village,' one of them said mournfully.

'We're not allowed to go down there,' the other had added.

At the gate, Edward surprised her by reaching for her hand, just for a second. 'Will I see you at the river tomorrow?'

'I don't know. Will you?'

'I'd like to.'

'Then you will.'

'But not the same place again. Do you know the other spot, further down?' He named it, two bends of the river further south than the last place they'd met. It wasn't as popular, involving a scramble through a hedge and a longer walk to reach it.

She nodded.

'I'll be there at three,' he said.

He turned and ran back to where he should be working. She found herself doing the same thing, running out of the gate, along the road towards her house, needing to do something with all the energy that was suddenly coursing through her.

She spent that night and the Saturday morning in fear of her parents noticing something different about her. They were fortunately preoccupied themselves, her father marking a pile of copybooks, her mother diligently helping him. Lola busied herself with her household chores, head down, before slipping to her room and choosing her brightest summer dress. Her choice was limited but she found a yellow one. She stood for a moment in front of the mirror, smoothing down the fabric, feeling her own hands on her body and thinking of someone else's hands.

'I'll be back by five,' she called from the hallway.

'Are you meeting Una and Triona?' Her mother named Lola's two closest friends from school.

Lola just waved from the gate, neither a yes nor a no, her conscience clear.

He wasn't there. Two other small groups of people were, laughing, sitting on the riverbank. She stood still, disappointed. More than that. Flattened. And then he was behind her, his hands over her eyes, touching her. After that, it seemed the most natural thing in the world to take his hand, pull it from her eyes and not let go. For the two of them to keep walking, to find a shaded spot of their own further down the river. And to once again take off their shoes and dangle their feet in the river, even if the weather wasn't anything like as warm as it had been the week before. They talked. And teased one another. And laughed. And moved closer. When his hand moved over hers, and his other hand gently touched her face, it was the easiest, the most natural, the best thing in the world to do to lean forward and meet him halfway so it wasn't just his hand on her face but his lips on her lips, and his hand on her shoulder, then her waist, and her own hand on his shoulder. She could feel the strength of it, the muscles, from all the hard work gardening. She touched the skin of his arm and she felt his touch in return, as her cardigan somehow slipped down, baring her skin to the sun and to him.

They kissed. Again and again. How much time went past? An hour? Ten minutes? Did other people walk by and see them in their hideaway among the trees? Lola didn't know, didn't care. All she cared about was the feel of his lips on hers, the extraordinary sensations she was experiencing, the deep longing, the feeling that there was no way she could ever feel closer to him but wanting even more.

He was feeling it too, she was sure. They stopped, abruptly. His face was flushed, as hers must have been. Again, his chatter began. She was recognising it now as nerves. He talked his way through any awkward moment, filling the air around him with opinions, words, boasts. Again, she didn't mind. Let him talk all he liked. As long as there was a possibility of him touching her again like that, kissing her again like that. She would let him talk all day long if he wanted.

Once again, the arrival of several of his friends changed the mood. It seemed everyone knew him. Lola was shyly introduced. She sat quietly and watched again as drink was produced. She said no again, imagining her father's reaction if she was to return home not only looking as if she had spent the day in the sun, but with the smell of drink on her breath too.

For the next three weeks, they followed the same pattern. He knew of even more private spots along the river. If anyone was asked, yes, it would be said that they had both been there, in the crowd. But did anyone ever notice that they would then slip away out of sight?

It was no longer enough to sit side by side kissing. On the fourth weekend, they found a spot even further from the others, down by the second stone bridge. It had all the privacy they needed, a secluded bend of the river, hidden by overhanging trees, turning the sunlight into dappled fragments. He was nervous. Was this all right here? he wanted to know. Not too far away from everyone? The words were spilling from him. She was very happy, she told him. Are you sure? Yes, Lola was sure. They both knew the real question he was asking.

This was the freedom she had wanted, the thrill she had yearned for. She might be the dutiful daughter, the disciplined piano teacher, during the week. But when she was here, by the river, alone with Edward, this was when she was really herself, in her own body, her own skin, every inch herself.

The previous week they had gone beyond simply kissing. She had shocked, then delighted him, she knew, by unbuttoning his shirt, by making it very clear he could remove her cardigan, then unbutton her dress. She'd been wearing a slip but that had easily been unbuttoned too. The first time she felt his hands move onto her bare skin, onto her body, she had tensed. He had kissed her again. She had kissed him back. Then she had relaxed and his fingers had found her breasts, caressed her and she had sighed with pleasure. And in turn, he had shown her where to put her hands, what to do, and her own deep sigh had been echoed by his. She had wanted more. She knew he did too. She knew enough to know they had to be careful. Then, before anything more had been possible, they'd heard voices. She'd realised the time. She'd left, her skin still flushed, every part of her feeling alive.

Today they wouldn't stop. She knew it. He knew it. It was clear in the way they looked at each other when they met at the bridge, among the crowd. Today felt different. She had thought of little else all week. What would happen today was what she wanted, what she needed. She was going to do nothing to stop it happening. It was urgent now. Time was running out. He had been talking about Australia again. The ticket had been bought. In nine weeks' time, he would be on his way to the other side of the world.

That morning, before she left the house, she had fought with her father. He had heard of a clerical position he wanted her to apply for. In a store in Naas, managing their accounts. She might as well be sent to prison, she told him. She wanted to do more with her life, with her music – teach piano in Dublin, perhaps, or study more, try to get a teaching job in a school.

'With whose money?' her father had shouted.

'I'd rather be poor than die of boredom,' she shouted back.

Back and forth it went between them, her mother retreating to another room, ignoring Lola's pleas to support her.

Lola left the house in a temper. The argument gave her a new recklessness. Edward was waiting for her. They walked down the river path. The sun was shining. She could feel the heat of it on her skin. She took off her cardigan, baring her arms to the warmth. To his gaze. She was walking in front of him, feeling his eyes on her body.

They began to kiss even before they reached their secret place. They were kissing as they moved through the overhanging leaves, kissing as they lowered themselves onto the grass. They had no rug with them. He spread his jacket on the ground for her, shrugging out of it, still kissing her, still holding her. She knew she was surprising him with her kisses too, with the way she was touching him.

She couldn't say she led him into it, because he wanted it as much as she did. She had also long stopped caring how he knew exactly how to touch her. If he had been with other girls before her, so be it. She was glad of his experience.

There was more kissing. More caressing. The feel of his skin. The touch of his hands on her body. She whispered, 'We have to be careful,' and he whispered back, 'I'll be careful,' but then there was too much else to do and think about as she felt his bare skin on hers, and the weight of him on top of her and then more than on top of her, pushing against her, between her legs, and she wanted him there as much as she knew he wanted to be there. The pain lasted less than a second and then it was only pleasure, pure pure pleasure that lasted, and if she cried out loud in her ecstasy, she didn't know, because they were kissing too fiercely for her to be aware of any sound.

Afterwards, they had no words. She lay there, eyes closed. She was a woman now. Their breathing slowed. They looked at one another, smiled. There was some quiet talking, then some laughing. She stroked his face. He kissed her neck. She felt so happy. So alive. She was the one who began to kiss him again. And then he kissed her back and then it happened again. It was even more wonderful.

She didn't know which time Jim was conceived. But she was always sure it was that day.

CHAPTER TWENTY-ONE

In Clare, Carrie was in a tizz. There was no other word for it, she'd decided. She had been that way for five hours, ever since she'd received an email from the TV producer. Short and to the point. Rafe Ascot was in Clare now. He'd moved his trip forward for personal reasons. Would Carrie like to interview him for her blog?

By phone? She'd emailed back.

No, in person. Tonight.

Tonight!!??

It's tonight, or nothing, I'm afraid.

She'd immediately said yes. A publicist had emailed her, telling her when and where to go. He was staying at one of the Valley's finest guesthouses.

'I hope the council isn't paying for it,' Matthew said.

He'd arrived early to get the feel of the Valley before filming started, the publicist said.

'To get lots of free wine, more like it,' Matthew said.

'Are you jealous?' Carrie said, as she came out into the living room in her third outfit.

'Of course not. He sounds like a big poser, that's all.' Matthew picked up the glossy gossip magazine on the sofa beside him and flicked through to an inside story. He started to read aloud. '"Rafe

Ascot seems oblivious to the fuss about his latest relationship as new photos of the loved-up couple enjoying romantic Paris emerged this week. He tweeted: *Love knows no borders, no boundaries, no barriers*." How corny can he get?'

'It's how celebrities talk these days. Should I get a Twitter account as well as a website, do you think? Or an Instagram account? Or even Snapchat?'

'I have no idea what you're talking about and I don't want to know. I'll be outside.'

'Matthew, come back. Does this look okay?'

There was no reply. A minute later she heard the shed door creak open. He'd be in there polishing the car. Still, better he hit the polish when he was in a bad mood than the beer, she thought, inspecting her appearance in their bedroom mirror. Thankfully the kids were having a sleepover with a friend of hers in town. She just wished Matthew would stop being so silly about this interview and help her decide which of her few decent pregnancy dresses looked the best. Not that anything would possibly happen between her and Rafe – not only was she married and pregnant, but he was also in a very public relationship, and anyway, what would a famous English actor find at all attractive about an ordinary South Australian entertainment investigative journalist?

Her phone chimed. A text from Bett in Ireland: *Just checked emails, saw the one from the producer.*

Carrie frowned. How had Bett seen that? She quickly checked. Bett had been copied in. Damn. She'd been looking forward to breaking the big news to Bett herself. She read on.

Great news about the interview. Let me know if you need any help with your questions.

She certainly didn't need Bett's help. Not with the questions, anyway. She took a quick selfie and sent it to Bett's number. *Questions fine. Does this look okay?*

A few minutes went past, then another chime.

Are you in full makeup? And is that an evening dress? It's a ten-minute interview, isn't it?

She quickly typed back. *I've decided to video it and put it up as a vlog rather than just write it up.*

Ping. *Carrie, I've asked you to write for me not vlog for me.*

Okay, then. I'll write up the interview for you and post the vlog on my website for me. Send.

Ping. *What website????*

There wasn't time to go into it. She had to be at the guesthouse in twenty minutes. But maybe Bett was right. Maybe the dress, bought to wear to a friend's wedding, was a bit much. She hurriedly changed into her next-best outfit – a more casual flowing top over capri pants – slipped her feet into strappy silver sandals and went out to find Matthew.

Sitting in the back seat of Des's car in Kildare, Bett stared down at her phone, waiting for a reply from Carrie. Nothing. Her sister could be so infuriating sometimes. She hoped Carrie wouldn't make a fool of herself doing this interview. Bett also did her best to damp down a ripple of jealousy that was unfurling inside her again. If she hadn't been here in Ireland, she'd be interviewing this English actor about the TV series. She was definitely more interested in real news, like council meetings and regional politics, but it wasn't every day someone as famous as him came to town. There was no way she would have said no to accompanying Lola on this important journey home, either. Except that this trip wasn't happening as she'd expected. She'd imagined being by Lola's side as she rediscovered special places from her childhood, sharing memories with her, growing even closer to her grandmother. Instead, here she was, sitting with Ellen in the back of a broken-down car, on the side of an unidentified country road in Kildare, Lola back at the hotel on her own, while Des was outside calling the RAA or whatever the Irish equivalent of the roadside assistance was.

After she'd made sure Lola was truly happy on her own, Bett had joined Ellen and Des downstairs. She'd explained that they really didn't want to visit Lola's home places without her. It didn't feel right. Des had suggested an alternative destination. A nearby shopping village of some kind. A designer label mecca, he said. That had sounded just as unattractive to Bett. Clothes shopping was never her favourite pastime. But Ellen had seemed quite interested and they needed to go somewhere. Then, less than ten minutes from the hotel, fate or the gods of car engines had stepped in. On a back road, the car's engine had suddenly cut out. Despite Des's numerous and increasingly panicky attempts, it wouldn't restart.

It could be worse, Bett thought. It could be raining. And at least Ellen seemed happy enough beside her. Busy on her phone, naturally. Without Lola to police her on the daily allowance, she hadn't been off it since they left the hotel. They could be driving through an Amazonian jungle or African safari park, for all the attention Ellen was paying to her surroundings.

While, back in Clare, Carrie was about to go and interview one of the most famous, and infamous, actors in the world. As for Daniel . . . he was behaving oddly too.

When the car had first broken down, Bett had taken the opportunity to contact him. After checking the time, she'd texted him first, rather than phone, in case the twins had just gone to sleep.

All fine here but Lola still not herself. It's a homecoming trip without a homecoming so far. All okay there? Xx

She'd got the briefest of messages back: *All fine. Hope Lola better tomorrow.*

Can you talk? She'd texted.

Not right now, sorry.

Are you at work? Are the twins with Jane?

Nearly home. Will text again asap.

Nearly home? From where? And where were Yvette and Zachary, with him or with Jane? He wasn't supposed to be working today, she knew that. So where had he gone that he was nearly home from?

She quickly tapped out a message. *Where are the twins?*

A minute later, a two-word reply: *Sound asleep.*

But where? She started to text him again, then stopped herself. She was being ridiculous. It was anxiety about Lola turning into anxiety about Daniel. He was allowed to go out without telling her where he'd gone. Maybe he'd nipped into Clare to get some milk. If he had, he would have brought the twins with him. He'd never leave them on their own. She had to calm down.

She was congratulating herself for being so sensible and rational when, beside her, Ellen held out her phone, made a strange pout and took a selfie.

'Ellen, what are you doing?'

'Talking to my friends.'

'No, you're not. You're pulling faces and sending photos. That's not talking.'

Ellen ignored her and just tapped away at her phone.

Bett felt a rush of frustration. Enough was enough. It was a beautiful sunny May day. They were in Ireland, surrounded by green fields and little lanes. Lola always went on about the value of a good walk. At least this way they'd be able to tell her they'd done something.

Bett leaned across and took her niece's phone out of her hands, ignoring the squeak of protest. 'Your phone time is up. Well up and you know it. Come on, kiddo, come and see Ireland.'

'But I want to go shopping.'

'No, you don't. We have enough shops in Australia. We're going exploring.'

'We don't even know where we are.'

'That's what exploring is.'

That was a great idea, Des said, apologising yet again for the breakdown. He'd wait here for the repair van and text when the car was fixed.

Ellen sulked for the first part of their walk, steadfastly refusing to be interested in or excited about anything Bett pointed out. They had walked along the road for a few minutes before an even narrower road appeared to their left. That would do nicely, Bett decided. Only two cars had passed them since. Both drivers had given them friendly waves.

Bett attempted to make conversation at first, pointing out stone walls, flowers – 'Look, Ellen, see that pink one there? It's called a fuchsia' – and receiving a shrug in reply. After a few minutes she decided she was content with silence too.

She allowed her mind to drift back to the last time she'd been in Ireland. She'd been a different person then. Single, still confused and hurting after her break-up with Matthew, her big row with Anna and Carrie, the ongoing rift. To think back to all that had happened in the five intervening years . . . Moving from Clare to Melbourne to Dublin and then to London, working for that record company. Coming home for Lola's eightieth birthday. Or being summoned home, more accurately. Staging Lola's musical for her. Meeting Daniel again. Falling in love with Daniel. And then —

Then Anna dying.

It hit her again. The punch of grief. She felt a sudden welling of tears. She stopped in the middle of the road. Five years on, and she was still grieving so much for her sister. Would it ever get better? And if she was still struggling, how must it be for Ellen?

Beside her, Ellen spoke. 'Bett? Are you all right?'

She told the truth. 'I started thinking about Anna. And this happened.' She gestured to her tears.

'Oh, I cry all the time. Don't worry,' Ellen said. She started walking again.

'You do?'

'Of course. She was my mum, remember. Not just my sister.'

Bett let that go. Ellen was right. If there was any hierarchy to love and grief, mother and daughter surely won out over sisters.

'Do you remember lots about her?' Bett asked as she caught up with her.

Ellen nodded. 'But sometimes I don't know if I'm remembering my own stories or if they belong to other people. Like the time Mum swallowed a fly when she was singing with you in the Alphabet Sisters. That makes me laugh when I remember it but I wasn't there. So that's not my memory, is it?'

No, but it was a great memory, Bett agreed. It had been hilarious. Anna had fallen off the stage in shock at the fly. Their whole performance was abandoned.

'But I do definitely remember lots of other things,' Ellen continued. 'Like Mum reading to me when I was a little kid. And being in the car with her when we came to Clare. And doing lots of lying around with her when she was so sick.'

Bett wished she could think of those times as cheerfully as 'lots of lying around'. For her, each day after Anna's diagnosis had been frightening, watching Anna lose weight so rapidly as the disease spread and took hold of her already slender frame. Watching her get so tired, sleep so much, either from exhaustion or from the effects of the powerful cancer medication.

'Do you remember that, Bett?' Ellen asked. 'Before Mum died, when we all used to take it in turns to lie on the bed beside her? I loved doing that.'

Another spike of grief. 'I'm glad.'

They walked on in silence for a few minutes.

Bett spoke first. 'And is everything okay at home?' She hesitated. 'Do you like Denise?'

A shrug. 'She's okay. Dad likes her more than I do.'

'I guess that's why he married her and you didn't.'

Ellen gave a little bark of laughter. 'Lily's cool enough, though. I don't mind having a stepsister. Though I might call her my little sister. She calls me her big sister. I like that.' Ellen stopped abruptly. 'What's that? Bett, is that a castle?'

It was the ruins of something, perhaps a small castle. A big house, at least. Two fields away, glowing almost golden in the warm sunlight. Bett reached for her phone to google 'Kildare castle ruins' and then stopped. Some example that would show Ellen. If there were no signs beside it, they'd ask someone later what its name and history was. Like people would have done in the olden days. In Lola's time.

There was a gap in the stone wall beside them. A few black-and-white cows were grazing on the other side of the field. They didn't look bothered by their presence. 'Shall we go and explore?'

'Like *The Famous Five*?'

The previous year, Bett had sent Ellen Anna's collection of old Enid Blyton books. They'd unearthed them when they were helping their parents pack up to leave the motel. She'd assumed Ellen had put them on the bookcase and returned to looking at her phone.

'You've read them?'

'All of them.'

'Which one are you? George or Anne?'

Ellen rolled her eyes. 'George, of course. Anne just cleans and sweeps.'

'I always wanted to be Julian,' Bett said.

'Then be Julian,' Ellen said matter-of-factly. 'Come on, let's go catch some smugglers.'

'And then have a lunch of boiled eggs and ginger beer?'

'Exactly,' Ellen said, in an excellent English accent. 'If Timmy hasn't got to it first.'

Bett was smiling as she followed her niece across the field.

Their timing was perfect. They reached the ruins as the sun came out completely, warming the stone to a glow. After walking around the circumference, peering through the window gaps into a courtyard filled with grass and stones, they took a seat on an upturned stone ledge, leaning their heads back against the wall.

Bett shut her eyes, enjoying the sunshine on her face. 'I always feel like a cat when I do this.'

'If you're a cat, I'm a kitten,' Ellen said.

They were both silent for a moment. Bett opened one eye and saw to her dismay that Ellen had quietly taken out her phone and was tapping on the keyboard. She'd already told her off once today. She couldn't do it again.

'Lola would kill you,' she said instead.

'If she was here. But she's not. I'm not on Facebook or anything, I promise.'

'No?'

'Only because there's no wifi here.' She grinned. 'I'm joking, Bett. I'm looking for something else.'

'Angry Birds?'

'Nope, and not Candy Crush either,' Ellen said. 'Bett, would you like to hear Mum's voice?'

Bett couldn't keep up with the butterfly mind of a teenager, talking about online games one minute, her mother the next. 'Are you missing her badly today, Ellen?'

'I always miss her. But you didn't answer my question. Would you like to hear Mum's voice?'

'Of course I would. And talk to her. And have dinner with her.'

'I can't do the talking or the dinner but shut your eyes and listen.'

Bett started to protest.

'Come on, now,' Ellen said. Again, a perfect replica of Lola's Irish tones. 'For once, Bett, would you do what you're told?'

Bett shut her eyes. At first, the only sound was the trilling of a bird nearby, a far-off sound of a tractor, a car. Then something else. Music. Gentle piano music. Followed by something else.

Anna's voice.

Talking about dishcloths.

Bett's eyes snapped open.

Ellen was holding out her phone. She had her eyes shut. Bett stayed still, listening as Anna's cheerful, deep tones voiced a dish-washing ad. A tinkle of music and then her voice again, this time in low confiding tones, asking the listener to phone a particular num-ber if they had any money worries. Then the piano music, followed by Anna again, her voice bright and cheerful, giving details of an amazing new range of fridges and freezers for sale in the super sum-mer sale. One advertisement after the other, Anna's voice changing in tone and speed each time. A final note of music and then Ellen pressed a button.

Bett stared at her. 'How? When?'

'It was a present from Dad for my thirteenth birthday. He got in touch with his friends in agencies around Australia and asked them to send him any ads Mum had done the voiceovers for. Then he edited them together for me.'

'Can I hear it again?'

'That was only some of them. There are heaps more. I listen to a few every day. Sometimes twice a day.' She pressed play again.

Bett put her head back and shut her eyes once more, feeling the presence of her niece beside her, while her sister's voice filled the air. After a moment she felt something else. Ellen's hand creeping into hers. She took it and held it tight.

Anna's voice became deep, growling as she pretended to be a

bear for a toy store commercial. Beside her, Ellen giggled. Bett felt an unaccustomed sensation in her chest. The grief was still there. It always would be. But listening to Anna, holding Anna's daughter's hand, she felt something else.

A kind of peace.

In Bett and Daniel's house in the Clare Valley, the washing machine was going. The dishes were done. The twins had finally settled. All Daniel wanted to do now was slump onto the sofa, turn on the television, maybe have a beer and relax for the rest of the night. He was exhausted.

When he'd rung his neighbour Jane to say he was on his way home and would be there shortly to collect the twins, she'd offered again to keep them overnight. They were already fast asleep, she said. Her daughter Lexie had loved helping to look after them, adored them, and she'd been begging to have them for a sleepover. Daniel had thanked her but put the offer on hold for the time being.

It would have been easier, definitely, just to go home, knowing Yvette and Zach were sound asleep – as he'd truthfully texted to Bett when she'd asked – in Jane's house a kilometre away. He wouldn't have had to disturb them, or go to the trouble of carrying two heavy toddlers out to the car.

The truth was, he didn't want to miss waking up to them in the morning. He loved them all the time, but especially when they'd just woken up, when they were still sleepy, their dark curls all tousled, chatting away to each other in their hilarious twin-babble from their adjacent cots or, as was more usual, roaring at him to come in and get them. There was nothing like walking into their room and being greeted by the sight of two beautiful little kids, his kids, literally jumping up and down in excitement, their arms outstretched, as if seeing Daniel was the best thing that had ever happened to them. It made him laugh every morning. Yes, they were messy, yes, he still wasn't mad about the whole idea of nappies, and no, he hadn't had a full night's sleep for months, but he still wouldn't change anything about being their father.

He was secretly pleased with how well he was managing without Bett. And right now, it also suited him for other reasons that she was on the other side of the world. He'd never have been able to do what he was trying to do if she was at home with him.

Unfortunately tonight's visit to Audrey hadn't worked out as well as he'd hoped. He had thought he'd found what he was looking for when he first saw her ad. They'd talked via the chatroom first, then exchanged emails, and more photos. After several missed calls, they'd arranged for him to come to her house on the outskirts of Adelaide tonight, after work. Within minutes of her bringing him inside, he'd known it was a wasted journey. He was back to square one.

Ignoring the siren call of the couch, he opened his laptop and keyed in the site's address. Usually he bookmarked pages he visited often, but he'd had to be careful with this one. Not that Bett would be able to check his search history from the other side of the world, but just in case.

The familiar site came up. So many photos, so many glowing sales pitches. They all looked so beautiful. How was he supposed to choose? He'd have to go through them again one by one, and then decide.

CHAPTER TWENTY-TWO

In the drawing room of the Valley's finest guesthouse, Carrie was still waiting to interview Rafe Ascot. She'd been waiting for two hours. Each time the door to his suite had opened, she'd looked up in anticipation, only to be disappointed when his publicist appeared alone. Once, she was with a woman dressed in what looked like a nurse's uniform, until Carrie saw the insignia on her top pocket and realised she was from a beauty spa in Adelaide.

'A long way to come to give a facial,' she said with a friendly smile.

The woman didn't even acknowledge her as she hurried past. Either she was rude or she'd signed a confidentiality clause, Carrie decided.

There had been two other journalists waiting when Carrie first arrived, right on time. She was disappointed. She'd been under the impression this was an exclusive interview for her blog. The producer had made it sound like that. But, no, she was just one of a stream of interviewers apparently, some in person, some on the phone. The publicist, a well-groomed woman in her late twenties called Sophie, kept apologising for the delay. The interviews were running over time.

'But I always think that's a good sign, don't you?' Sophie said with a clearly fake smile. 'Like when it happens at the doctor. If everyone else is getting that extra time, then you will too.'

Carrie hoped she wouldn't. She'd only prepared a few questions. The longer she waited, the more nervous she was getting.

'Do they always run this late?' she asked the journalist waiting next to her.

'It depends.'

'On what?'

'How rude the person is. How many drugs they've taken. Whether they're trying to seduce the interviewer. Whether they've passed out from jet lag.' She laughed at Carrie's expression. 'How many have you done?'

Carrie swallowed. 'This is my first, actually.'

'And you've been let loose on Rafe Ascot? Good luck!'

'What do you mean?'

There wasn't time to find out. Sophie appeared. 'Carrie, Rafe will see you now.'

'Have fun!' the other woman said with a mischievous smile.

'Thanks,' Carrie said, smoothing down her top, wishing she'd worn something completely different. Like her dressing-gown.

She was glad to see it was a suite with a separate seating area. She'd had a disturbing mental image of the two of them perched side by side on a double bed.

Sophie made the introductions. Carrie tried not to stare. That was *the* Rafe Ascot lying there on that modern sofa by the window. He was wearing sunglasses, indoors, at night-time. Carrie said hello. Rafe nodded without speaking.

'I'll leave you to it,' Sophie said.

'No!' Carrie said. 'You're welcome to stay.'

'I need to make some calls. I'll be just outside.'

Rafe stayed on the sofa, his hands now covering his face. Carrie waited.

After a moment, she spoke. 'Hello again.'

Nothing.

She tried again. 'Hello, I'm Carrie Quinlan. I write a blog for the local paper.'

'Good for you, Carrie Quinlan.' His voice was immediately recognisable. Low and rich, like treacle, as someone had described it in a magazine she'd read during her online research. Like a finger trailing down your back, another writer had said.

He moved his hands away from his face. She saw the cheekbones he was famous for. You could hang your nightdress off them, another gossip magazine writer had said.

He yawned loudly. 'Go ahead, Carrie-who-writes-a-blog-for-the-local-paper. Ask me a question.'

'Um, sure. I'll get my list.' She reached into her handbag. It slipped through her clammy hands and deposited all the contents on the floor.

He didn't move to help as she scrabbled on the floor, cramming everything back in – car keys, lipstick, tissues, an apple core, a dummy. Finally, there it was, her list of questions.

'So, what do you think of the Clare Valley?' she asked, blushing inwardly. She sounded like a five-year-old reading her work aloud in class. She asked it again, in a more normal voice.

'Nothing,' he said.

'Nothing?'

'I haven't seen it yet. I got here late last night. It was pitch black. I'm so shagged from the flight, I haven't left the room yet. What's out there? You tell me.'

'Vineyards. Hills.'

'Is it beautiful?'

'Very.'

'The Clare Valley is very beautiful,' he said. 'Especially the vineyards and the hills.'

'What do you think of your role in the TV series?'

'I like that I'm being paid for it. Beyond that, I don't know. I haven't read the script yet.'

'But you start filming soon, don't you?'

'I don't know. I haven't seen the schedule either. Someone will come and get me when they need me. They usually do.'

She read through her notes again. 'Why did you decide to become an actor?'

'It was better than being a butcher.'

'Were you a butcher?' She hadn't seen anything about that in her research.

'No. But it wouldn't be a great job, would it? Cutting up dead animals all day. Next question.'

'What was it like performing in the Globe Theatre in London?'

'The same as anywhere. A stage. People watching. Except they didn't care one bit about the play. All they wanted to do was film me and that kid —'

One of the stars of the *Harry Potter* films, Carrie recalled.

'— and upload it to YouTube. So, frankly, it sucked. Most jobs do, at the end of the day. This one will too, I suspect.'

Carrie bristled on behalf of her home town. 'Why did you take it, then?'

'I told you. I'm being paid to do it.'

'But you haven't even read the script. Do you even know what it's about?'

'Wine. Australia. Murder. Do you need me to say more than that? Give me a moment.' He suddenly sat up, startling her. He took off his sunglasses and opened his eyes. His piercing blue eyes that she'd seen in close-up on TV screens, at the cinema. Those eyes and those cheekbones, together. She gasped. He either didn't notice or was so used to it he didn't care.

'From the local paper, did you say? Are you taping me or doing shorthand?'

She held up her phone. She'd been recording the entire exchange. He held out his hand. She passed him her phone.

He spoke directly into the tiny microphone. 'I've enjoyed the pleasures of Clare Valley wine for many years, especially its world-renowned crisp, sharp riesling. So I didn't hesitate when I was offered this role, which will have me on location not only among the beautiful vineyards and rolling hills of this boutique wine area, but in autumn, one of the most glorious times of the year here. And what a role. My character appears on the surface to be a straight-forward, honest, hardworking wine buyer. But in the ingenious, twisting, turning plot it quickly becomes apparent that like good Clare Valley soil, there is plenty hidden beneath the surface. As the poet Horace said, "Skies change, not cares, for those who cross the seas." That's exactly what happens to my character. He thinks he's leaving his problems back in London but they've all followed him, as the good people of the Clare Valley and a worldwide TV audience are about to discover. Blah blah blah blah blah. Is that enough, Carrie-from-the-local-paper? I can go on with more of that kind of nonsense if you like.'

She took the phone back, taking care not to touch him. 'No. No, that's fine, thanks.'

He lay down again, shut his eyes and called out. 'Sophie? Sophie?'

She appeared in the doorway.

'Get me a drink, there's a love.' He'd lapsed into a mock Cockney tone.

Sophie hesitated. It was then that Carrie noticed two empty wine bottles on the table. One glass. She was glad to see they were Clare Valley wines, at least. The fine riesling he'd mentioned, in fact.

She pretended to be looking at her questions as there was a whispered conversation between Sophie and the actor.

'You do have three more interviews,' Sophie was whispering.

'I'm concerned, between the wine and the jet lag, on top of such a long flight, and you did say you'd taken a sleeping tablet or two as well, that perhaps —'

'Get the wine, Sophie. Get it or I won't talk to one more fucking journalist, whether they're from *The New York* fucking *Times* or the *Clare Valley Bugle* or wherever the fuck this woman is from.'

Carrie gasped. So did Sophie.

'How rude,' Carrie said. She couldn't help herself. Enough was enough. She stood up, deciding to be gracious even if he had no manners. 'Thank you for your time,' she said in as icy a voice as she could manage. 'I hope you enjoy your stay here.'

His eyes were shut. He was asleep again or else he'd chosen to ignore her. Either way, there was no movement and no reply.

Sophie left the suite with her. The area outside was empty. The other journalist must have given up waiting or stepped out for a moment.

'I'm so sorry,' Sophie said to Carrie. 'Jet lag and sleeping tablets can be such a terrible combination. I can try and reschedule it for another day if you like?'

'I have all I need. Also, I'm on a deadline,' Carrie said, liking how it sounded even if it wasn't true.

'Please do excuse him. He's really very charming. He's just had a hard time lately, all the gossip, people repeating lies about him. He wants to be known as an actor, not a "star".' She made quotation marks with her fingers. 'He really is so talented. The producers are blessed to have him. It's quite a coup.'

'You don't mean a word of that, do you? I bet he's been really rude to you too.'

For a moment, Sophie's professional face dropped. Carrie was sure she was about to hear the truth. Then the other journalist returned and up came Sophie's guard. 'The producers are thrilled to have him as the star of the series. It really is a shot in the arm for

Australian drama. You can quote me on that.'

'I might need to quote you on everything,' Carrie said gloomily. 'I'm not sure my phone was recording properly.'

'You will send me the blog post before you publish it.' It was a statement, not a request.

For God's sake, Carrie thought. First Bett and now this Sophie asking to check her work as if she was a schoolkid. She answered in her best haughty tone. 'Do you ask everyone that?'

'Yes,' said Sophie, steely now. 'That's what you agreed to when you came in and signed the form.'

Carrie hadn't read it. She thought she was just adding her name to a mailing list.

Sophie produced it again. There it was, clause 14. In legal talk but basically insisting that the producers had right of approval of any interview done today. Should she take a photo of it to email to Bett? Carrie wondered. She reached for her phone and realised then that she didn't have it. She'd left it in the actor's suite.

'I'm sorry,' she said. 'I think I've left my phone in there. May I?'

She hurried in, shadowed by Sophie. Her phone was on the table. She could see Rafe was back on the sofa. He was snoring loudly. An empty wine glass dangled from his hand. His other hand was tucked inside his trousers. As Carrie picked up her phone, doing her best not to stare at him, Sophie's own phone rang. She turned away to answer, immediately launching into a hurried conversation under her breath, clearly about the actor.

Carrie couldn't resist it. Quickly as possible, out of Sophie's line of sight, she snapped a photo. Yes, in regard to her blog, she'd have to obey Bett and Sophie and write something positive and fake. But she hadn't signed anything about photos for her private use, had she? Wait until her friends saw this one!

CHAPTER TWENTY-THREE

As Ellen and Bett walked back across the fields, they could see Des and his car, with a repair van parked beside it. There was no point rushing back yet.

Instead, Bett suggested to Ellen they follow the field down to what seemed to be a stream. They could hear the sound of it in the distance.

'It's funny to think of Lola living around here as a little girl, isn't it?' Bett said. 'She might have walked across this very field when she was your age. Paddled in that very stream.'

Ellen gave a little shiver at a sudden cold breeze. 'I hope it was warmer back then.'

The stream was in full flow, the water a deep-brown colour, tumbling over rocks. The edges were lined with lush ferns and long, bright-green reeds. There was a tree trunk on its side, covered in moss. It was slightly damp but still a good natural bench. Bett and Ellen sat side by side. Bett had gathered a handful of stones as they walked along the water's edge. She handed them to Ellen. For a few minutes the only sound was the water rushing over rocks, punctuated by the occasional 'plop' as Ellen threw the stones one by one into the water.

'Do you think Lola did this as well?' she asked.

'Maybe,' Bett said. 'We'll ask her when we go back to the hotel.'

'Why doesn't Lola want to see all the places when the reason she came here was to see all the places?'

'I don't know,' Bett replied honestly. 'She's had only memories in her head for sixty-five years. She might be worried that the memories are better than the real pictures.'

'I felt like that when I came back to Clare for the first time after Mum died.'

Bett waited as Ellen threw in another stone.

'But it was okay,' Ellen continued. 'Dad talked to me about it and said my mind could hold new and old memories at the same time, and that the new ones wouldn't cancel out the old ones so I didn't have to worry.'

'That's very wise of him.'

'He is wise sometimes. Not always. He and Mum were fighting before she died, did you know that?'

Bett had always dreaded this topic coming up, hoping that Ellen would ask Lola, not her, if the memories ever surfaced. 'I knew a little,' she said cautiously.

'It was about me sometimes,' Ellen said. 'You know that scar on my face? Where the dog bit me?'

Bett nodded. The whole family had been horrified when the accident happened. They'd all seen how self-conscious it made Ellen as a young girl. The treatment she'd had and the healing of time had made it virtually invisible.

'They fought about that a lot,' Ellen said. 'Dad said Mum should have looked after me better. Mum said Dad should have spent more time with me.'

'Would they fight in front of you?'

Ellen shook her head. 'After I went to bed. But I'd open the door so I could hear.'

Bett vowed never to argue with Daniel in earshot of the twins.

She had no memories of her own parents ever fighting.

'Were Mum and Dad going to get divorced, Bett? Before Mum died?'

'I don't know.' It felt like a necessary lie. She did know. She chose her words carefully. 'I do know they'd decided to have some time apart. But whatever they'd decided, they put it to one side when your mum got sick. Do you remember, your dad came to Clare as soon as he heard, to be with you and your mum? Because you were the person they were most worried about. They both loved you so much they wanted to make sure you were okay, no matter what happened to —'

Bett suddenly couldn't speak. She couldn't relive that moment again, of Anna dying.

Ellen comforted her again. 'It's okay, Bett. We have to remember all our memories of her.'

'I'm sorry, Ellen. I shouldn't be like this in front of you.'

'Why not?'

'Because I'm the adult and you're the kid.'

'I'd cry too except there aren't any tears in my eyes at the moment. Dad said I wasn't to worry about that. When I first stopped crying all the time I was scared it meant I didn't miss Mum any more but Dad said it's just that tears were like rain. Sometimes it rains and sometimes it doesn't but the feelings are always there.'

'Your dad's right about that too.'

'He's a good dad.'

The matter-of-fact statement nearly made Bett smile. 'I'm glad.'

'I thought at first that I might come and live with all of you but it's better that I stayed with my dad.'

She was remarkable in her calm knowledge, Bett thought. She was right too. There had been discussions about Ellen coming to live in Clare, all of them needing to keep a part of Anna, her daughter, close to them. It was Lola who'd helped them see that the best place for Ellen was with her father, wherever that might be.

'Can I take a photo of us here, to show Dad?'

It was the first time either of them had mentioned taking photos, Bett realised. Perhaps Lola was right. It was a good idea to be in the world for real now and again, not always via a screen.

'Do you want me to take it?' she asked.

'No,' Ellen said. She reached into her little backpack and pulled out a selfie stick.

'Lola would kill you if she knew you had accessories as well as your phone.'

Ellen grinned. An echo of Anna, again. 'What Lola doesn't know won't hurt her. Smile, Bett.'

Bett smiled.

Des texted Bett shortly afterwards. The car was fixed. As they returned, he was handing the mechanic a business card and receiving one in return.

'I was just explaining to Ray here how mortified I was, to break down when I'm supposed to be showing two charming young ladies around our beautiful country,' Des said, after introducing them. 'Still, all working now. It was the fuse in the fuel injection pump of all things, Bett and Ellen, imagine! I'll let you go, Ray, and thanks again. Great talking to you. Here's hoping I never lay eyes on you again.' He laughed merrily.

Bett wondered if she imagined the look of relief in the mechanic's expression as he walked to his own van. He'd obviously discovered for himself how much Des could talk.

Des clapped his hands together. 'So, ladies, off to the shopping village! Better late than never.'

Bett and Ellen had made a decision as they walked back. They wanted to be with Lola, not out on their own. Bett explained to Des that they'd like to go back to the hotel.

Des was puzzled. 'But it really is an excellent shopping experience, I believe.'

'Thank you, but no,' Ellen said in an upper-class accent. 'Home, James, and don't spare the horses.'

Des's lips twitched. 'Your wish is my command, milady.' He bowed as he opened Ellen's door. She climbed in, giving him a gracious nod as she did so.

He was amused by Ellen, Bett could see. So was she. Ellen was definitely her mother's daughter. But she was growing into something special all of her own.

CHAPTER TWENTY-FOUR

Back at the hotel, Lola wasn't in her room, or in the lobby people-watching, or in the bar enjoying a gin. She was strolling in the grounds. The weather was warm enough that she needed just a wrap, not a coat. She'd chosen her most colourful one, bright blue with yellow swirls. It was what she had always done – the lower her mood, the brighter the colours. It usually worked to lift her spirits. But it wasn't working today. Her mind was still drifting too far back, burrowing through six and a half decades of Australian memories and unearthing the most difficult of her Irish memories.

She took a seat in the sunniest area of the hotel's gardens, beside the fountain, out of sight of the wedding party. She could hear birdsong, some soft chatter from the nearby guests, but mostly the soft repetitive sound of water falling on water.

All she could think about was Edward.

Had she loved him at all, back then? She wished so much she could say that she had. That she could justify her behaviour by believing it had been sparked by wild emotion, fervent infatuation – what she was sure she could call love. That it was only later she realised how wrong she had been about him. But she couldn't. The truth was she had never loved Edward. She was also sure he had never loved her.

She'd desired him. That had been a kind of drug, to her and to him, during those passionate early weeks of that summer. They'd stolen all the moments together they could. She had marvelled in how he could make her feel, how her body would long for his touch.

It was constant. Even during moments at the piano with her students, or at home with her parents, out with her friends, or helping Elizabeth with her daughter, she felt it. A pulsing sense of being alive, of imminent pleasure. No, it wasn't love. It was pure lust or pure animal attraction or whatever the right word for it was.

He felt it, she knew. Amazement too, at how readily she accepted his invitations to meet, how quick she was to initiate physical touch. They'd both grown up being told behaviour like this before marriage was strictly forbidden, a mortal sin. Those warnings weren't for them. They'd long put the idea of sin from their minds. What they had was so special, felt so good – was getting better each time, in fact – that the condemnation of others was the last thing on their minds.

Until everything came crashing down around them. In the space of a week. Perhaps the worst week of Lola's life.

They weren't caught together. Her parents never guessed where she was going, all those times. They'd met whenever it was possible, either at the river or, more daringly, once in the grounds of Bayfield. They would fall upon each other hungrily, hurriedly. They barely spoke. Lola had slowly realised that she had little to say to Edward, and that most of what he said to her was nonsense, boastful talk. She found him so physically attractive that she didn't care about conversation. There was so much else to enjoy.

Had she known much about contraception? No. There'd been giggling talk at school, about how babies were made, how to avoid it, but she felt what they were doing was beyond sensible thinking. Perhaps she also thought that, like her mother, she might have trouble becoming pregnant.

She was wrong. She was more than able to fall pregnant. She suspected it when her period was a fortnight late. When she felt sick in the morning. When her body began to feel different. When there was a strange new taste in her mouth. She waited another month to be sure. She kept seeing Edward, still enjoying their secret meetings as much, her body still able to ignore any sense her mind was trying to impart. When a second month passed without her period, when there were even more clues – a new roundness to her body, more nausea – she knew for sure.

She didn't tell Edward. Not at first. Or her mother or her father. She told Elizabeth.

Elizabeth had already guessed.

'I've heard you getting sick, Lola. I've also seen you slip away and I've seen you slip back, and I've hazarded a guess what might have been happening. It's the Quinlan boy, isn't it? The gardener?'

Elizabeth was serious, worried. Lola couldn't lie to her. She nodded.

'How long has it been going on?'

More than two months, Lola admitted. She told her everything.

'He's going to Australia very soon, isn't he?'

Lola nodded. 'What do I do, Elizabeth?'

'You have to tell your parents.'

'It's going to be terrible.'

'Yes. But you still have to tell them.'

It was worse than she could have imagined. She was glad and grateful that their house was outside the village, that there were no neighbours to hear the roars from her father, or the sound of the vases, glasses and plates being thrown. They all missed her, but one of them glanced off her mother. He flung insult after insult at

Lola, at the shame she would bring on them, the wickedness of her behaviour. He shouted at her mother as well, for letting this happen, for being an incompetent mother. But he would deal with it. All of it. Lola would be sent away to Dublin. The nuns there would take care of everything. He would tell people she'd got work up there. She would stay away until the baby was born. After a suitable time, after she'd given the baby away, she could come back. But in the meantime she would work for the nuns. It was the punishment she deserved.

There was no support from her mother. None. 'How could you do this to me?' was the most she said to Lola. There wasn't just disappointment on her face. Fear, too. They both knew that if Lola went away, it would also be bad for her mother. People in their village, their county, the whole country, always knew why young girls left home so suddenly, no matter if it was spoken of as an unexpected job opportunity or even as a holiday. Everyone also knew why those same young girls sometimes came back looking sadder and thinner, as if they had a secret that had broken their hearts.

Lola had seen those girls around town herself. She had no intention of becoming one of them.

The arguments lasted for two days. She was banned from leaving the house. Her childminding and piano lessons could 'be damned', her father said. On the third day, he returned home after a morning away with the name of a convent in Dublin. It was all organised, he said.

No, it wasn't, she told him. She was trembling, nauseous, but she clenched her fists and stared her father in the eye. 'I'm not doing that. I'm going to go to Australia with Edward.'

The words fell out of her mouth. She hadn't spoken to Edward about it. He had no idea that she was even expecting his baby. She doubted he would even have cared too much when she didn't turn up at their assigned place two days earlier. He might have waited for a little while but before long he would have gone back to Kilcullen to meet his friends, she was sure.

But as she said it aloud, talking over her father's shouts, even stamping her foot at one moment, standing firm as he raised his fist at her, threatening but not hitting her, she became more determined with each word. She would make it happen, somehow.

She was smarter than Edward, she knew that. It wasn't vanity. He was good-looking and strong, and he could tell a joke and a story, but she knew that they were no match intellectually. He wanted fun, an easy life, friends around him. But he also had religious parents. If she spoke to him, she knew she could convince him that her idea was the best one, the most responsible one. The only possibility.

She was proved right. It took three more terrible days, more shouting by her father, even threats to lock her away, before she convinced him to let her go and talk to Edward. She tried to ignore her mother's constant tears.

When Edward left work at Bayfield that evening, she was waiting at the end of the driveway. After checking there was no one nearby to see, he reached for her. She stepped back from his embrace, even as her body yearned again, still, to be close to his. They needed to talk, she said.

Edward was horrified at the news of her pregnancy. Even more horrified about the idea of her coming to Australia with him. That hurt. In her mind she had expected some opposition, but she'd hoped he might see it as an adventure. She was trying to shape it that way herself.

'Get married? To you? You come to Australia with me, as my wife?'

She nodded. 'We're having a child, Edward.'

'So? I didn't want that.'

She hid another unexpected stab of hurt. 'Nor did I. But it's happening and you're responsible too.'

The next night, she met his parents, in the company of her father. There were more terrible scenes. She stood her ground, trying to ignore Edward's ashen face beside her. He didn't care about her, she knew that. He would have been happy for her to be sent up to Dublin, to have their baby, give it away, to come back when it was deemed socially acceptable. He said as much to her, more than once. 'I don't want a baby.'

But she did. She didn't know what exactly was happening inside her as each day passed, but she felt sure something extraordinary was. She knew she wanted to keep this baby.

The priest was called. More words of shame rained down on her. She found a quiet place deep inside her mind, a place of refuge when she was being insulted, shouted at, threatened. It was a skill she hadn't known she possessed, honed by the years of being told by her father that she wasn't good enough, well behaved enough, demure enough.

In the following days, she met Edward again, secretly. She didn't beg or plead, but she slowly persuaded him. She had some savings, she told him. She would make life in Australia better for him. Easier. And then, yes, she kissed him, touched him, and the same passion flared between them, regardless of all else that was happening. That's what persuaded him in the end, she knew.

There was a hurried, secret wedding ceremony in the Ballymore Eustace church. A perfunctory ceremony, with only the priest, Edward and Lola, her parents and his parents present. Elizabeth wasn't invited. Only two photographs were taken. No one was smiling in them. There was no celebratory meal or gathering afterwards.

The next day, she and Edward left Kildare. Her parents said goodbye to her at the front door of the house. There was no hugging. No tears. Her father still radiated anger, her mother stayed silent, cowed beside him. They didn't walk her to the front gate.

She went down the path on her own, carrying her suitcase. Halfway down, she looked back. They had already gone inside.

Lola had arranged to meet Edward at the bus stop in Ballymore Eustace. She was deliberately early. The bus wasn't due for another half-hour. She had one more farewell to say.

It was early, but she knew Elizabeth would be awake. In the short time they had, she told her everything. She cried all the tears she hadn't dared cry at home. Elizabeth hugged her as tightly as she needed. She asked Lola to write to her, as often as she could.

'Of course,' Lola said, still crying. 'As often as I can.'

'And you'll come back and visit one day, won't you?'

'I promise,' Lola said. 'I promise.'

She and Edward barely spoke on the journey to Dublin. They stayed in a cheap hostel near the bus station. They ate a bad meal in a noisy cafe, and slept together for the first time as husband and wife. There was little conversation. Nor did they make love. They tried to sleep, backs to one another. Just after ten, she felt him get up, dress and leave the room. He came back four hours later. She could smell the drink. She pretended she was asleep.

The next day, they boarded the mailboat to Holyhead. A train to London. Another train to Southampton. They were two among many, the pier crowded with travellers, sailors, people hurrying up and down gangplanks with supplies, the shouts all around them, as the ship was readied for the long journey. Ahead was five weeks in the smallest, cheapest cabin on board, with the new husband she didn't love and who didn't love her. But there wasn't only a baby growing inside her, day by day. A new feeling was growing in strength each day too. Yes, she was scared. Yes, she was sad, about her parents most of all. But she was determined to make the best of this situation. She would somehow try to make their marriage work. She would be the best mother she could. Her child would never feel as her parents had made her feel, never —

'Lola!'

A voice calling her name stopped her memories with a jolt. She turned to see her granddaughter and great-granddaughter walking across the grass towards her. They looked so beautiful. So full of life.

'Well,' Lola said as they reached her. 'Tell me everything.'

'Your house is incredible,' Ellen said before Bett had a chance to answer. 'Someone has painted it bright pink and there are sculptures of cats and dogs in the front garden. And your old school was amazing too. We went inside and there was an old teacher in there, a white beard down to his knees, and he said he remembered you, that you were the most disobedient student he ever had.'

Lola's eyes widened at first, before her expression changed. 'He's still alive? Good. I cursed him. I told him I was a witch and I'd make sure he lived forever as punishment for being so mean to me.'

Bett sat beside her. 'You may have guessed we didn't actually get to your house or school.'

'So no cat and dog sculptures? I'm sorry to hear that.'

Bett explained what had happened with the car breaking down, their decision to come back.

'We didn't want to go without you, Lola,' Ellen said. 'We came to see it all with you, not on our own.'

'You're right. My apologies. I wasn't thinking straight. Of course we should see it together.'

'Now?' Bett said, reaching for her phone. 'Des's waiting in case we need him again today.'

'Not today,' Lola said. 'I'm still too tired. It must be delayed jet lag. Please tell him he's free to go home, Bett. But I'd like him here at ten in the morning. We'll have a busy day tomorrow.'

'Visiting your village and your house and your school?' Ellen asked.

'All of it,' Lola promised.

'But what will we do now?'

'Did you bring your bathers?'

Ellen nodded. So did Bett.

'There's a pool here, did you know that? And a sauna. And a spa. I think we should make sure they're all up to scratch, don't you?'

'Do you wear a bikini, Lola?' Ellen asked as they walked towards the hotel entrance.

'Often, darling. But only when I'm not skinny-dipping.'

Soon after, Bett was walking down the corridor with Lola and Ellen on their way to the pool, when her phone chimed. It was an email from Carrie. She must have been up late.

My interview for your approval. He was HORRIBLE!!

She'd better read it now, Bett decided. She could even sub it and put it online, so it was there waiting for early-morning readers in the Valley. She explained as much to Lola and Ellen, arranging to meet them down at the pool as soon as she could.

Ellen put her hands on her hips. 'Don't be long. This is supposed to be a holiday, remember.'

Back in her room, Bett opened and read Carrie's blog. It was very short.

Rafe Ascot looks just like he looks in the magazines and films. His eyes really are that blue, but I suppose he might have been wearing contact lenses. I asked him if he was looking forward to the TV series and this is what he said.

'I've enjoyed the pleasures of Clare Valley wine for many years, especially its world-renowned crisp, sharp riesling. So I didn't hesitate when I was offered this role, which will have me on location not only among the beautiful vineyards and rolling hills of this boutique wine area, but in autumn, one of the most glorious times of the year here. And what a role. My character appears on the surface to be a straightforward, honest, hardworking wine buyer. But in the ingenious, twisting, turning plot, it quickly becomes apparent that like good Clare Valley soil, there is plenty hidden beneath the surface. As the poet Horace said, "Skies change, not cares, for those who cross the seas." That's exactly what happens to my character. He thinks he's leaving his problems back in London but they've all followed him, as the good people of the Clare Valley and a worldwide TV audience are about to discover.'

He also said he thought the vineyards and hills were beautiful and that if he hadn't become an actor he would have been a butcher.

The End.

Bett frowned. That was it? An anodyne statement that could have been written by a publicist? Nothing about what it had been like for Carrie to meet him? Bett had expected this particular blog to go for hundreds of words, for Carrie to gush about how handsome and charming and funny he was. About to email her back, she decided against it. It was late, but hopefully not too late to phone.

Carrie answered on the second ring. 'I knew it would be you. Edit it as much as you like, I don't care. Edit it to nothing.' In a rush of words, she told Bett what had happened. 'I know I'm not a proper journalist but he was so rude and condescending, Bett. He's nothing but an old drunk. If I could only write what he was really like. But I promised you I wouldn't and I've already run this blog past his publicist and she approved it, but you don't have to even use it if you don't want to. And I know I signed a Secrets Act thing, but I'm still allowed to talk about him to my friends, aren't I?'

'It's better if you don't. I'm sorry, Carrie. Sometimes famous people can be really difficult.' Bett had had similar experiences while working in the music industry, interviewing egotistical musicians and manufactured pop stars. 'But I'll still use it, don't worry. The mayor will love it, in any case. Did you take any photos of him?'

'Just one, but it's not good enough for this.'

'Okay, no worries.' She'd get one off the internet easily enough. 'Thanks again, Carrie.'

'Thanks for nothing, more like it.' Carrie sighed. 'So how is everything there?'

'Fine. Good. We're in Kildare now. Just up the road from where Lola grew up.'

'Any nasty family secrets yet? Was Lola exported to Australia for stealing a loaf of bread?'

'Wrong century, Carrie, but I'll ask her later. They're waiting for me in the pool.'

'The pool? Are you still trying to make me jealous? Because it's working. Poor Daniel, home playing Mister Mom while you're floating around in luxury.'

Bett winced at the Mister Mom tag. She knew Daniel would hate it too. She forced herself not to react. 'I'd better go,' she said instead. 'Talk to you soon. I'll post your blog now.'

In Clare, Carrie hung up. Should she have said anything to Bett about Daniel and that phone call from the mysterious Audrey? No, it was probably better that she hadn't. She'd keep an eye on Daniel as much as she could until Bett came home. She'd relax tonight, though, now that her Rafe Ascot interview was over. Even if she couldn't share all the details, she knew her friends would be impressed she'd actually met him. More than Matthew had been, at least.

When she'd finally got home, he'd hardly listened, just said it was no surprise he'd been horrible, all actors were, as if he met actors every day of the week. She'd teased him one more time.

'You really are jealous, aren't you?'

'Of course I'm not.' A pause. 'I don't want you falling for anyone else, that's all.'

'I won't. At least I'll try not to. But if you give me a foot rub, I promise I never, ever will.'

'Okay.'

'You will?'

He nodded. 'I'll get it ready while you're writing your blog.'

She'd kissed him on the cheek. 'I love you, Matthew.'

He'd looked delighted at that. Men were such simple creatures sometimes.

She heard him calling out as she hung up from Bett. He was ready to do the foot rub.

'I'll be out in a second,' she answered.

She had a quick look at the photo of Rafe on her phone. He was so out of it. Still handsome, though. As she enlarged it, she noticed his eyes were open just enough that you could get a glimpse of that amazing blue. There was no mistaking those cheekbones of his either. But he really was wasted. The producers would hate anyone to see a photo like this, with that empty glass of wine in one hand, his hand down his pants. There was a large pile of paper beside him. She pressed the enlarge button again. It had to be the TV script. She could see the words on the page and everything. What was even more obvious was a big red wine stain on it. He'd obviously been enjoying a Clare Valley shiraz or cabernet sauvignon as well as a Clare Valley riesling. Good luck learning your lines when you can't even see them, she thought.

Still, how amazing! She'd not only met but interviewed a real-life famous Hollywood actor, here in Clare! She quickly opened her email account, keyed in the names of her ten best friends, attached the photo and wrote a quick message: *LOOK WHO I MET TONIGHT!!!! HE'S HORRIBLE!!!*

She pressed 'send' with a flourish, then went into the living room to get her feet rubbed.

CHAPTER TWENTY-FIVE

The sound of her phone ringing woke Bett at five a.m. She didn't recognise the number, only the area code. It was someone calling from Sydney. She answered.

'Bett, it's Denise.'

Still half-asleep, Bett repeated the name. 'Denise?'

'Denise Green. Glenn's wife. In Sydney.'

'Denise, I'm so sorry. I've just woken up.'

'I know it's early there, I'm sorry. I had to ring. It's Glenn —'

Bett sat up properly. 'Denise, no, what —'

'It's all right,' she interrupted. 'He's okay. Well, not okay but he's fine. He's had a heart attack. He's in hospital. They're operating on him tomorrow, as soon as his temperature goes down enough.'

Bett was now wide awake. She listened intently as Denise explained. Glenn had thought it was severe indigestion or food poisoning. His pain had got worse. They'd called the ambulance, worried it was a possible heart attack. They'd been right.

'But he'll be okay, won't he?'

'We hope so, but he's in intensive care. His temperature keeps spiking. The doctors are doing all they can, trying to get it under control, but they think there might be a secondary infection —'

Nearby, Ellen stirred, then sat up, sleepily pushing the hair out of her eyes. 'Bett?'

'Back to sleep, honey. It's still early.'

Bett didn't want Ellen to hear any of this yet. She moved into the bathroom, quietly closing the door.

Denise was still talking. '— what to do, Bett. Glenn keeps asking about Ellen. I don't know if she should be here or stay there with you and Lola. What if something happens to Glenn and she's not here with him? I'm sorry, but the thought of her so far away, if —'

It was immediately clear to Bett. 'She'll be on her way home as soon as possible. I'll come with her.'

'But Lola's big trip —'

'She'll understand. We'll have Ellen back as soon as we can. I'll look for a flight as soon as I hang up.'

'I hoped you'd think that, Bett.' Denise was tearful now. 'Thank you so much. Glenn will want to pay for everything, I know that. Whatever you need to do to change the flight, we'll cover it.'

Bett told her not to worry about that, about anything. She asked her to tell Glenn they were all thinking of him, and promised to call back with their flight details as soon as she had them.

Ellen was fast asleep again. Bett stood in the middle of the room, trying to decide what to do. Wake Ellen and tell her the news? Go online and try to change their flights? Tell Lola first or ring Daniel?

A moment later, she was knocking on Lola's door. It took several minutes before Lola opened it, her white hair askew, in her long shimmering nightgown. 'Darling, what is it?'

Bett filled Lola in even before they'd sat down at the table overlooking the gardens. The sun was starting to rise, an edge of light along the horizon. They spoke in hushed tones.

'Did I make the right decision, Lola?'

'Yes, you did. For Ellen's sake and Glenn's sake. Just in case.'

'It would just be too cruel. For her to lose her mother and —'

'Glenn's not going anywhere, Bett. Stop that. He's in hospital, he's having treatment, his prognosis is good, Denise told you that.'

'What would we do if he did die? Would she come and live with me or Carrie? Or Mum and Dad? Oh, poor Ellen. It would be too much —'

'Stop it!' Lola's voice wasn't a shout but it had the same effect. 'Calm down, Bett, even though there's no proof in all the history of people being told to calm down that anyone ever has. But I've distracted you from your panic, which is what I wanted. You need to get organised. Flights first. Then wake Ellen and tell her the news about her father, and then about going home, as calmly as you can. She'll be upset. The last thing she'll need to see is an upset you or an upset me.'

'But what about you, Lola? Everything's spoilt for you. Your big trip, your homecoming. We haven't even seen your village or your old house or your school yet.'

'I'll stay here. Glenn doesn't need me there, in the way. I'll go to the old places on my own. And I'll show you my photos when I get home again. I'll have a slide night in the Clare Town Hall.' Lola held up a hand. 'Bett, I'm an elderly but still mobile woman. I can manage. What I wanted was to come home to Ireland with you both and so I have. It's just been cut short, that's all.'

'It's my fault. We should have come straight to Kildare, not wasted those two days in Dublin.'

'Bett, we couldn't have foreseen this happening. Now, ring the airline. There might even be a flight leaving later today. Then ring Daniel and Carrie. I need to make a phone call myself.'

'Who are you ringing?'

'Your father. My son.'

Bett hadn't even thought of her parents yet. 'Thanks, Lola.'

Lola's room was soon like an office. Bett in one corner speaking to the airline, confirming, to her relief, that yes, they could change their existing business-class seats to a flight leaving Dublin airport at noon that day. In less than seven hours.

Bett's next call was to Des. He wasn't due to collect them until ten a.m. She woke him but he was instantly professional. Yes, he could be there by eight o'clock, he told her. Yes, he'd have them to the airport in good time for their flight.

Denise was calmer and very grateful when Bett called her back to confirm everything. 'I'm at the hospital now. Glenn's still asleep but I'll tell him as soon as they let me in to see him.'

Daniel was next. The words spilled out of her as soon as he answered, telling him she was coming home, but not to him and the twins yet, but to Sydney for the time being.

He was as calm as Lola. 'Everything will be fine, don't worry. You've made the right decision.'

She knew that now. How could they possibly have continued with their trip? Sightseeing, sitting in the back of a fancy car driving around Ireland, knowing Glenn was so ill and wanting his daughter nearby? And Bett couldn't possibly have put her young niece on the plane alone.

She phoned Carrie next. Her sister started talking before Bett even had a chance to say hello.

'Bett, I'm so sorry. Please don't get mad. It's not my fault. I don't know how they got it. Well, I do. I mean, I took the photo, but I just sent it to a few of my friends. I forgot to tell them not to send it on to anyone but some of them did and they sent it to others and on and on, which must have been how that radio station and the newspaper got it. And when the radio station rang late last night, I thought they had read my blog, not seen the photo, so I said, sure I can talk. Then suddenly I was on air and they were asking me what he was like and had he made a pass at me? And I said no, of course not, I'm pregnant, and they made a really bad-taste joke. It was disgusting. And now it's all gone mad and I don't know what to do. Is this going viral? Because it's awful. How do I stop it?'

Bett blinked. Was her sister drunk? 'Carrie, what are you talking about?'

'The photo I took of Rafe Ascot. That's why you're ringing, isn't it?'

'No. I'm ringing to tell you Glenn is in intensive care and Ellen and I are flying home.' She hurriedly explained, with a reassurance that Glenn would be okay. 'Now you. What photo? What radio station?'

'My photo of that actor. A terrible photo. And now it's all over the internet. I'm so sorry, Bett.'

Bett's phone started to vibrate, alerting her to other messages and emails. It could be Denise, or the airline, or Des. An actor's antics seemed trivial. 'Carrie, I have to go. I'll call back as soon as I can.'

'I'll be here. I'm not going anywhere. I'm not answering the phone to anyone I don't know, either. I'm sorry if I've got you into trouble too, Bett. But I'm not sorry for saying he was horrible. He was.'

Bett had four new voice messages. She listened, frowning. They were all from the TV producer, once again furious with Carrie. The latest, left a minute earlier, informed her that the actor was now threatening to leave the series. 'Call me immediately,' she said.

Bett bristled. Who did this woman think Bett was? Her personal assistant? Whatever Carrie had or hadn't done didn't warrant such rudeness. She heard Lola finishing her call to Jim. She decided not to mention any of this to Lola or to call the producer back. She'd let her calm down first.

'I'll wake Ellen,' she said after Lola had hung up. 'Is Dad okay? He agrees we should come home?'

'Completely. He's ringing Denise now. He wants her to know we're all thinking of them.'

Bett was glad to hear that. Her father's calm, reassuring personality was always good at times like this. 'And he isn't worried about you being here on your own?'

'No, not at all. As he said, it's only for a day or so.'

At the door, Bett stopped. 'Oh, Lola, I'm so sorry. I can't come back again. I don't think it makes sense, much as I'd love —'

'Darling, I know you can't. I wouldn't expect it of you.'

'Then who —' Bett stared at her. 'Do you mean Dad? Dad's coming to Ireland?'

Lola nodded. 'It was his idea. If he can get a flight tonight, he'll be here in twenty-four hours.'

Ellen reacted exactly as Bett and Lola had expected. Shock, then tears, even panic. They'd been right to put the arrangements in place first. After much reassurance, she slowly calmed down. 'But what about you, Lola? Your big trip, it's all ruined too.'

'I'll be fine, Ellen. Every cloud has a silver lining. I'll have a day or so on my own and then your granddad, my Jim, is arriving to look after me.'

Ellen's eyes widened. 'With Grandma too?'

'No, darling. Just Granddad this time.'

For the next hour, Bett's phone kept buzzing. She ignored any messages from the producer or unfamiliar Australian numbers. She quickly googled Rafe Ascot and winced. Carrie was right. It was a terrible photo and it had gone viral. He looked not only drunk, but lecherous as well.

She helped Ellen pack, then packed her own case. They had a

hasty breakfast in the dining room. It seemed impossible it wasn't eight a.m. yet. Des arrived early, his concern a comfort to them all.

Ellen was tearful as she hugged Lola tight. 'I'm sorry, Lola. I don't want to go but I don't want Daddy to be sick without me.' She'd only started calling him Daddy, not Dad, in the past hour.

'He'll be fine, Ellen. Keep telling yourself that. And as soon as he sees you, I bet he'll feel even finer. So you enjoy all those movies and snacks on the plane and have a big sleep. Aunty Bett will be right beside you all the way. Before you know it you'll be back home with him.' Lola reached up and took a butterfly hairpin from her own white locks. 'And I want you to have this so that you know I'm watching over you too. Every step of the way.'

'Will you put it in for me?'

'I'd love to.' Lola gently smoothed back her great-grand-daughter's hair and positioned the hairpin. 'There. If ever you want to know if I'm thinking of you, touch that.'

Ellen touched it now.

Bett hugged her grandmother tightly too. 'I'm so sorry, Lola. All your plans. I didn't even get to see your house, your village —'

Standing nearby, Des coughed quietly. 'I'm sorry to eavesdrop, but it's not too late. I could take a detour, Bett. Lola, you could come with us. We could go to the airport via Ballymore Eustace. There's time. I could even bring you to the airport, then back here. It's no problem at all.'

'No, Des,' Lola said. 'Getting my girls to the airport is more important than me. I'll look forward to seeing you back here again with Jim tomorrow instead.'

The new arrangements had all been made. Jim had managed to get the last seat on a flight leaving Adelaide that night. Des would meet him at Dublin airport on arrival and bring him straight to Kildare.

Bett and Ellen would probably pass him in the sky, Lola said.

Ellen liked the idea of that. She'd wave out the window now and again, just in case, she said.

'And before you ask me again, Bett,' Lola said, 'yes, I really am fine on my own until he gets here. Thank you for everything. You have managed it beautifully for me, from the very start. Now, off you all go. Safe travels, and be sure to give Glenn and Denise and Lily my love.'

Bett and Ellen climbed into the back seat. Lola leaned in to wave once more. She noticed Ellen reach for Bett's hand, and saw Bett give it an answering squeeze.

Des slowly drove away. Lola stood in the hotel courtyard waving until their car was out of sight.

CHAPTER TWENTY-SIX

It wasn't until they were in the airline lounge and Ellen was occupied with a game on her phone that Bett could concentrate on the fuss about Carrie's photo. She decided to get the worst call over first.

Moving to a quiet corner, keeping Ellen in sight, she phoned the producer. An email would have been easier, but this way it would be quickly over and done with. It was a brief, chilly conversation. The producer was still angry. Bett held her ground. She was in charge of a newspaper, not a public relations agency, she said calmly. No, she agreed, Carrie shouldn't have taken that photo, or sent it to her friends, but it was equally unprofessional of the actor to be so drunk and so rude, Bett argued. The producer barely said goodbye before hanging up.

Bett took a deep breath and returned to her seat. She sent Carrie a soothing email, telling her it would all soon blow over, that before long another celebrity would do something even more outrageous. Rafe Ascot would quickly be forgotten.

Afterwards, she did another quick Google search, wincing again. It was nowhere near blowing over yet. The photo was everywhere, on gossip sites, Twitter, Facebook, and on many newspaper sites too. Not just the tabloid ones either. Serious newspapers were using it as an excuse to lament the loss of good manners. Columnists were using it as a hook to write about the dangers of excess drinking or too much fame. The only positive that Bett could see was that the Clare Valley and the TV series were being mentioned in nearly every post.

She glanced over at Ellen. She was doing a drawing on her phone, as if she was a little girl, not a thirteen-year-old. It was for her dad, she told Bett. A Get Well Soon message. She would email it to Denise to give to him tonight. It was a drawing of Ellen and Glenn, hand in hand. No sign of Denise or Lily, Bett noticed. She hoped Denise wouldn't mind.

As she returned to her googling, a new Rafe Ascot article appeared. His publicist had put out a statement, explaining that a combination of jet lag and anti-migraine medication mixed with one glass of fine Clare Valley shiraz – another plug, Bett noted – had brought about this unfortunate situation. Rafe Ascot had apologised, with a perfect blend of contrition and humour: *In my wonderful role in this exciting new TV series I play not just a wine-loving cad, but an Englishman misbehaving in Australia. Apologies to anyone I may have offended. I really must stop this method acting.* The website had of course posted the photo again.

As Bett went to close the site, something in the photo caught her eye. There was something beside him. A pile of paper. She enlarged it until the front page filled the screen. It was the script, the title barely readable under a red wine stain. *Murder in the Vines.* Below it, the scriptwriter's name. Tom Nikolić.

Tom Nikolić? Why was his name familiar? There wasn't time to google it. Their flight was being called.

In Kildare, Lola was also on her phone. It had rung as she walked back into the hotel lobby. Tom, calling from Sydney. She'd taken a seat in one of the lobby armchairs and listened, enthralled, as he told her all about Carrie's viral photo. Bett hadn't even mentioned it. Understandable, with all else that was going on. What a mess, Lola said to him. She hoped he wasn't too annoyed?

'Annoyed?' he said. 'Not at all! It's fantastic publicity. And your granddaughter is right. He is horrible. With any luck, this public shaming will make him behave. That's what we're all hoping, anyway.'

'I'm so glad to hear that,' Lola said, closing her eyes. It was only morning, but she was suddenly exhausted.

'Quite a family affair, this,' Tom said. 'You as my secret script advisor. Your granddaughter a brilliant worldwide publicist. You know, the winery whose wine he was drinking in that photo has record hits on their website today? And orders from all over the world. There's no such thing as bad publicity, Lola. But enough of my frivolous world. How is Ireland?'

This unexpected day on her own would hopefully give her the answer. 'Green and beautiful, as it always was. Now, you better go. But please do keep me posted.'

After she'd said goodbye she keyed in Rafe Ascot's name on her phone. The photo appeared instantly, again and again. Good Lord, she thought. He did indeed look horrible.

What a morning. Lola was used to quick thinking, to dealing with situations swiftly, easily. But events had moved too fast for her today. Life seemed to be moving too fast for her. In Australia one day, Ireland the next. Bett and Ellen here one moment, gone the next. Now, Jim was on the way. And all the while, her family house, her village, her old school, were only kilometres away, while she sat here in a hotel lobby – a very nice hotel lobby – twiddling her thumbs.

As if she was an invalid, a helpless old lady, needing an escort. How ridiculous.

She was still independent, not helpless yet. She was old, yes, but she wasn't sick. She didn't need Des to drive her. She didn't need someone to accompany her, either, be it Bett or Ellen or Jim.

She had been on her own when she made the promise to Elizabeth. She could keep it on her own.

She walked over to the reception desk.

'Could I order a taxi, please?' she said to the smiling young woman. 'For now, thank you.'

She'd waited sixty-five years. She wouldn't wait any longer.

In the Adelaide Hills, Geraldine and Jim were in their bedroom. The bed was covered in piles of his clothes, an open suitcase beside them. Jim had just hung up from talking to Carrie. He'd expected her to be upset that she was the only member of the family not going to Ireland. He'd been relieved when all she'd wanted to talk about was some photo of hers getting a virus or something. She'd talked too quickly for Jim to be able to keep up, he reported to Geraldine. But she'd sounded happy and excited and had cheerily asked him to give Lola her love, as if he was going for a short drive, not taking a sudden unexpected twenty-two-hour flight.

Across the room, Geraldine wasn't happy or excited. She was folding his clothes and pointedly not looking at him.

'Gerry,' he said, using the nickname he only used when they were alone. 'Don't be like this. It makes sense that I go. Lola needs me. We can afford it. Please don't be angry.'

'I'm not angry with you.'

'You can't be angry at Lola either. She didn't suggest it. I did. And you can't be angry at Glenn because he had a heart attack.'

'He drinks too much. Eats fatty foods. Or he used to.'

'We'll bring that up with him when he's out of intensive care, will we?'

Geraldine didn't answer.

'Please don't be in this mood,' Jim said. 'I need your help to pack. I could also drive myself to the airport and leave the car there for the next ten days, but I'd much rather you drove there with me.'

Geraldine ignored that. 'She still rules over us, doesn't she? We've moved away physically but emotionally all she has to do is crook her little finger and you come running.'

'She's my mother, Geraldine. My eighty-five-year-old mother. Yes, I'll do whatever I can to help her, whenever I can.' A note of steel had come into his voice. 'I love her. I will always love her. I love you too. I will always love you. I'm also a grown man. I am capable of loving my wife in one way and my mother in another. And you know I am always on your side but right now I'm disappointed in you.'

Geraldine's chin lifted. 'And I'm disappointed in you. We're so busy and you're leaving me alone to manage.'

'What would you prefer? I leave my elderly mother on her own on the other side of the world?'

'She has a driver. She isn't on her own.'

Jim didn't answer, just kept putting clothes into the suitcase.

'I bet you still won't even tell her, will you?' Geraldine said.

Jim kept packing. 'If it comes up, and it feels right, yes, I will. If it doesn't, I won't.'

'You've been saying that for years.'

'Because it's what I've felt for years.'

'I've half a mind to tell her myself. Ring her and say, "Lola, there's something Jim needs you to know. I need you to know."'

He looked up then. 'It's not your business, Geraldine. You're my wife, but this is about me and my mother.'

'Your mother and your father.'

'Yes. Both of whom are my business.' He checked his watch. 'I'm going to the kitchen to get us both a cup of tea. I hope when I come back you'll have stopped thinking like this. And that I'll get to say goodbye to you and be able to tell you that I love you and I will miss you, but I also hope you understand that this is important to me. I'm going anyway but I would prefer to go knowing I have your blessing, not your disapproval. That you can put this jealousy aside, even for the week or so I'm away, and let me have this time with Lola. It might be the longest she and I ever get to spend together again. Speech over.' He left the room.

Geraldine sat on the bed, her fists clenched. They often were when she and Jim spoke about Lola.

'You don't have to love her,' Jim had said many times. 'You don't even have to like her.'

'What's left?' Geraldine said.

'I'll settle for tolerate at this stage,' Jim had said.

She forced herself to feel that tolerance now, before Jim returned. Perhaps he was right. Lola was a schemer and a mistress of manipulation, but even she couldn't have set in train all the events that had somehow conspired to bring them to this point. And she also hadn't asked Jim to go with her in the first place. Geraldine had secretly thought Jim was hurt by that. And perhaps it would be a special thing for them to spend time together, in Lola's native country, before she died.

Geraldine felt an inner glow from being so reasonable. Her final thought helped too. Lola wouldn't be around forever. The day would surely come when Geraldine would finally have Jim to herself, without the constant invisible unbreakable bonds linking him so tightly to his mother.

Jim returned, carrying two cups of tea. Hers was in her favourite cup. She gazed up at his kind face. He was not only her husband, he was her best friend. He had asked her to try to be understanding. She could at least pretend, for his sake.

'Tea, love,' he said.

'Thank you.' She took it. 'Sorry, Jim.'

It was all she needed to say.

He sat down beside her. 'No worries, love,' he said.

CHAPTER TWENTY-SEVEN

Lola was in the hotel courtyard when the taxi pulled up. A young black man was at the wheel.

She got into the front and introduced herself. 'Lola Quinlan from Australia.'

He introduced himself in return. 'I'm Emmanuel.'

She asked him to take her straight to Ballymore Eustace. 'I may need to go on to other places as well. It may be for the whole day. Would you be able to do that?'

'Of course, madam,' he said.

Even before they reached the end of the hotel's long driveway, she'd asked him a dozen questions. He'd moved to Ireland from Nigeria five years earlier with his family, he told her. Yes, he loved Ireland, yes, there was occasional racism, but they were still happy to be here. She'd told him that in her day, back in the 1930s – 'So long ago,' he said – there hadn't been any black people in the area at all. Black men had been known by the Irish term *'fear gorm'*. Blue men. Ireland had become so multicultural since then. In Dublin she had seen Chinese people, Indian people, a family from the Philippines, the children with strong Dublin accents. Nothing new for Bett or Ellen, or for Lola now, but a new image to overlay her old memory of her home country.

'I haven't been back to Ireland for many years,' she told him. 'I want to see how much it's changed.'

'That is why you are here?'

It was one of many reasons, she knew that now. She nodded.

A sign informed her Ballymore Eustace was twelve kilometres away. She sat up straighter in her seat as they drew closer with each minute. It was in a beautiful setting, she appreciated now. Fields and hills on either side, tall trees lining the winding, narrow road. There was little traffic.

She tensed as they met the sign announcing the village. It was in English and Irish. Ballymore Eustace. *Baile Mór na nIústasach*. She knew the River Liffey was to her left, winding past the town, out of sight. The first building she saw in the distance was the handball alley, still here after all these years. Across from it would be the national school, where she had attended primary school. Where her father had been headmaster for more than forty years, as Des had discovered.

'Stop. Please.' She said it as they came around the bend. 'Sorry. I might need you to stop quite often.'

'The more warning you can give me, the better,' he said, calmly. He stopped across the road.

She didn't get out of the car. It was enough to look from afar. The building was no longer a school, but a kitchen showroom. As they sat there, a smartly dressed couple came out of the door holding a handful of brochures, in the company of someone Lola assumed was the salesman. Everyone was smiling. She could ask Emmanuel to drive over. Ask that smiling salesman if she could take a look around. It hadn't changed much from the outside. Two storeys, two rows of windows. Even the same front door was in use. The boys had sat in one big room, the girls in another.

But the last thing she wanted to do was set foot in that building again. She remembered the school records Des had found. She still hadn't looked at them. She wasn't going to.

She asked Emmanuel to drive on. Over the stone bridge they went. Almost instantly there was another landmark on her left. The church she'd attended every Sunday throughout her childhood. Where she'd made her First Communion. Her first Confession. Her Confirmation.

Where she'd married Edward.

It, too, looked the same, with the silver bell tower in front. She pictured the altar, the stained glass, the rows of wooden seats, the choir loft. She wouldn't go in there either. There was no need.

At her request, Emmanuel drove slowly on, turning into the main street. On top of the hill was a stone archway in the centre of the intersection, with flagpoles, a lamppost and a small pond beside it. Nothing like that had been there in her day. She asked Emmanuel to please keep driving, to go back down the hill, on the other side of the street.

She started to breathe more normally. It wasn't that different from the image she'd carried in her head all these years. What had she expected, skyscrapers and shopping centres? It was simultaneously a relief and a disappointment to see that the terrace cottages that had been there when she was a child, a teenager, were still there. Some now had colourful doors, windowboxes filled with flowers, but they were much the same. The pubs were still there. There was a chain convenience store, but it was in the same spot that the general store had been in her youth.

As Emmanuel kept driving, she noticed more changes. A grocery shop where there had only been a house. A Chinese takeaway. A pharmacy. A restaurant, opposite the pub where the bus stop had been. Where she and Edward had left for Dublin all those years ago. It was still a bus stop.

It wasn't yet ten a.m., but people were already out shopping, talking. She sensed Emmanuel glancing over at her, waiting for her to ask him to stop again. She didn't feel the need. This was the right way to do it, an anonymous drive through.

If she had done this journey the previous day, with Des driving and Bett and Ellen in the back seat beside her, there would have been question after question. Des may very likely have produced folders of information that he'd spent the evening before googling.

At the edge of the village they stopped at pedestrian lights near the new school. Traffic lights in Ballymore Eustace. Who would ever have thought? A mother and child crossed in front of their car. Might she have known the woman's mother or grandmother? Or was she from another place altogether?

Lola felt another pang. Of regret? Disappointment? Perhaps she should have taken Bett's advice, and placed an ad in the Kildare paper. Asking if anyone remembered her, letting them know she'd be back in town. Who would have replied?

No one, she realised. Who was left here who knew her? Elizabeth had died twenty years earlier. They had continued to write to each other for many years, at least once a year. Lola had noticed Elizabeth's handwriting become more spidery. The sentences were often disjointed. Once, she had received a card from Ireland that had no writing in it at all, just a blank card. Had Elizabeth's mind been going? she'd wondered. There had been no way to find out, no one she could ask. The following Christmas, there was no card at all. Lola wrote to her, as normal, but there was no reply the next year either. Or the next. She sadly came to the conclusion that Elizabeth had either died or become too infirm to write any more.

Her assumption was confirmed, but not for some time. Eight years after she'd received the last blank Christmas card from Elizabeth, an envelope arrived at the Valley View Motel with an Irish stamp and airmail sticker on it. A card from Elizabeth, finally! She'd eagerly opened it, only to find a Mass card inside, with a photo of Elizabeth, now an old woman, the dates of her life and an

289

Irish prayer: *Ar dheis Dé go raibh a h-anam dílis*. May her faithful soul be seated at God's right hand. Underneath that, another line: *Dearly loved and missed by her family and friends*. There was no note enclosed. A family member must have gone through her address book while responding to sympathy cards, and Lola had somehow been included on the mailing list.

Fighting sudden tears, Lola turned her face to the car window. She had an intense longing to see Elizabeth, to speak to her one more time. To say to her, after sixty-five years, 'Here I am, Elizabeth. I kept my promise.'

She wondered where Elizabeth's children were now. If they were all still in Ireland, or had emigrated. If they had gone on to marry, have children of their own. If they were all still alive, even. The little girl, Helena, whom Lola had once dandled on her knee, would be in her sixties. Perhaps with children or even grandchildren of her own. Perhaps even living in Elizabeth's old house?

She directed Emmanuel to her street on the edge of the village. Even as they turned into it, she knew the answer. Elizabeth's house was gone. The whole row of cottages was gone. In its place, modern houses. Another pang. She didn't ask him to stop. There was no point.

There was one more place to visit and then she would go back to the hotel.

It was only a short drive from the village. As Emmanuel followed her directions, Lola realised she had never made this journey by car. She had always walked or cycled it. Back then it had taken her fifteen minutes. Less than two minutes after leaving the village, here they were.

Her family home.

She asked Emmanuel to park down the road. Telling him she wouldn't be long, she took her stick and slowly walked back to the house. She stood in front of the gate, holding on to it for support.

From the outside, it hadn't changed. Two storeys, a large garden around it, that old oak tree still out the front. The fields on either side and across the road were empty, apart from a few sheep, their bleating the only sound.

She didn't go any further. She didn't open the gate, walk up the path or knock on the door. She stood there, looking at the house.

It was occupied. She'd hoped it would be. It would have been sad if it had gone to ruin or been left empty. From what she could tell, it was no longer a guesthouse or, if it was, they didn't advertise it. The sign was gone. It looked like a family house now. There was a set of swings in the side garden. A ball on the front lawn. The sight of that ball gladdened Lola's heart. To think of this house filled with the sound of children playing, being happy . . .

She stood at the gate for several minutes, deep in thought. She'd expected to feel sorrow. Heartache. She didn't. Instead, she recalled the many times she had opened this gate. She'd walked up that path so often, never knowing what mood might be waiting inside. If her mother would be cheerful, in the kitchen cooking, perhaps, or even playing the piano in the front room. Or if she would be in bed, the curtains closed, crying or lying silently, deep inside herself and her mood. Deep in her depression, as Lola had eventually named it, many years later. Other days she'd walked up the path feeling a different dread, knowing her father was home, preparing herself, tensing instinctively against the words he might throw at her, his stern manner, the constant disapproval.

She remembered the last time she had stood here. The day she and Edward had begun their journey to Australia. The day she reached to hug her mother, and her mother began to raise her arms, then stepped back. Her father hadn't managed even that. It was clear in every aspect of his body language that he felt no sorrow about her leaving, only more disappointment in her.

Standing there, looking at her childhood home, Lola realised something. None of those events was the house's fault. She could no longer even blame her parents for everything that had happened. They'd surely been victims of their own upbringing as much as she had been. The difference was that she had escaped. Run away, as fast as she could, to the other side of the world. Under the only circumstances available to her at the time.

She hadn't known how it would feel seeing her home again. It was why she hadn't been able to come here with Bett or Ellen. She hadn't wanted to break down in front of them. She knew what would have happened if they'd been with her today. Bett, her dear, kind Bett, would have insisted they knock at the door. She could easily imagine her words. 'I'm sure they wouldn't mind you taking a look. Even if you don't want to, I'd love to. Please, Lola, can I knock on the door and say hello, get a look at the hallway?'

Ellen would have been as eager. 'Please, Lola!'

And so perhaps the three of them would have walked up the path, knocked at the door. And perhaps the new owners would have been lovely people who would have invited them in, given them tea, asked for the history of the house, marvelled that Lola hadn't been back to Ireland in so long. They would have been given a tour. She would have shown Bett and Ellen where her room had been, where her parents had slept – until they had started sleeping in separate rooms, the year Lola turned ten. Would she have told them about that? No.

Would she have told them about the huge fight they'd had in the front room, the one that now looked out over the swings? When her father shouted at her and called her a slut and a tramp and threw objects at her, while her mother cowered in the corner, waiting for him to turn on her too?

No, she wouldn't have told them about that, either.

She would have stood there, or more likely sat there, and smiled and pretended that she had spent the happiest days of her life here in this house, so that the new owners wouldn't have felt strange knowing that once upon a time their much-loved home had been an unhappy house.

She would have declined an offer to come back another night for dinner, to meet the children, the rest of the family. Irish hospitality might have changed a little over the years, but Lola wouldn't have been surprised if such an offer had been made.

They would have taken a brief walk around the garden together. Lola pointing out the oak tree that was there when she was a child too, and the corner where her mother had grown hollyhocks and foxgloves. Perhaps the new owner would have smiled and said, 'How beautiful. I love those old-fashioned flowers. I must plant some. They can be in memory of your mother and of you, Lola.'

'That would be lovely,' Lola would have said. And she would have meant it. She loved those old-fashioned flowers herself.

And then what? They'd have taken a photo, probably. All of them in front of the house, the photo taken by the kind new owner, not just one shot, but more than a dozen, from different angles.

And Ellen or maybe Bett saying, 'Please, can we send one back to Australia now, Lola? Everyone would love to see it, you in front of your old house in Ireland.'

Lola didn't need it to have happened to be able to picture every moment of it.

Coming here alone had been the right decision. She was sure of it as she walked back down the road to where Emmanuel was waiting.

'All done, madam?' he said.

'All done, Emmanuel, thank you.'

As he drove back to her hotel, she shut her eyes. In her bag, she heard the sound of a phone. She checked it. Des. She let it go to voicemail. She'd ring him back soon. She needed to do some thinking first.

She was feeling so many emotions at once. There was disappointment. Sadness. Even a relief, of sorts. There was enough that was familiar to make her know she was back home, but so much that was new too. Neither the village nor her house had stood still, waiting for her return.

So much would have happened while she was away. Not just births and deaths and marriages. Accidents. Scandals. Far worse than the one she had caused with her sudden, unexpected marriage to Edward Quinlan, before their equally sudden emigration to Australia. Of course, there would have been gossip at the time, speculation about whether she was pregnant. It might have mattered back then, but it would hardly have stayed in anyone's minds. Who would even remember one little flurry of gossip from sixty-five years earlier? Who was left behind who'd even know who she was?

She felt the truth settle even more deeply inside her.

No one.

Because there was no one left here for her. No one and nothing.

CHAPTER TWENTY-EIGHT

On the other side of Ballymore Eustace, on the Brannockstown road, the phone was ringing in an office attached to a small garage. The young woman at the tidy desk answered it, taking down details. It was the AA, the Automobile Association in Dublin, booking her boss for a job. A broken-down van on the nearby motorway. Their garage was the closest. It was always the way. It had been quiet for days and now they'd had two outside jobs in a row.

Aisling hadn't been working the day before, but she'd heard about the fancy car that had broken down near the old ruins. Her boss, Ray – who also happened to be her big brother – had got them back on the road quickly enough. Aisling was completing the follow-up paperwork. She worked three days a week, the part-time arrangement keeping the money coming in for her and her husband Sean, the office organised for Ray, and also letting her spend most of the week with her baby daughter, Holly. Her mother minded her while she was at work, doting on her grandchild. It was a great arrangement all round.

She went out to the workshop and gave Ray the details for this new job. She was returning to the office when he called her back. He was holding a business card. 'Sorry, I meant to give you this. It's the fellow I rescued yesterday. The one that wouldn't stop talking. File it somewhere, would you?'

Aisling glanced at it. It was a thick white card, with embossed gold writing. 'Wow, very flashy.' She read out the name. '"Desmond Foley, Chauffeur of Excellence". Who was he chauffeuring? A Hollywood star back in Ireland tracing her Irish roots?'

'Not this time. I don't think his passengers were famous, but what would I know? Australians, a mother and daughter, I think. I suppose it could have been Cate Blanchett in disguise. Has she got a teenage daughter?'

'I'm impressed you've even heard of Cate Blanchett. Was the woman tall with blonde hair?'

He shook his head. 'Tallish. Dark curly hair, I think. I only met them briefly. I needed to get away before the driver started telling me about his childhood. Or his first day at school. Or his lunch on his first day of school.'

'It'd be a nice way to travel, wouldn't it? Sitting back in the lap of luxury, being driven around.'

He shrugged. 'If they get to see any of it, with him constantly yapping. He told me he should have had three passengers in the car, and it was just as well the third lady had decided not to come, as she was nearly a hundred years old or something like that.'

'He's driving a hundred-year-old woman around Ireland?'

He nodded. 'The old lady grew up near here, is back for the first time in decades, he told me. Her name's Leila or Lola or something like that.'

'And where was she yesterday?'

'Back at their hotel. I was cursing her the rest of the day too. I started thinking of that Kinks song "Lola", after I left them. Couldn't get it out of my head for the rest of the day. You don't know it? Too young?'

'I'll google it later,' Aisling said. 'The hundred-year-old lady is originally from around here, did you say? When did she leave? Mum might know her.'

'He told me, I'm sure, but I can't remember. I tuned out after the first half-hour. I was too busy doing my job to be able to waste time standing around and chatting about people I didn't know.'

'Very subtle,' she said.

She worked steadily through until lunchtime, taking the opportunity while Ray was out on the latest AA job to google the Lola song he had mentioned. It was now stuck in her head too. The name Lola was also tugging at her memory for some reason. Something to do with her mother, or even grandmother? It'd come to her. Perhaps. Since she'd had Holly and started living on half her usual sleep, her poor brain had definitely slowed down.

Ray got back just after twelve. At one minute to one, as usual, she called out to him that she was heading home. 'Back at two,' she called to the figure half under a car. He grunted in response.

It was only a ten-minute walk to her house. She could hear music as she came up the path. Nursery rhymes playing from the TV, her mother and Holly singing along. Well, Holly was trying to sing along. Babbling along, at least.

'Hello, my little darling,' she said, coming inside and sweeping her up into her arms, smothering her face with kisses. She was rewarded with more giggles and a big kiss in return.

'Has she been good?' she asked her mother.

'An angel. Takes after her grandmother. Lunch is ready.'

'What did people do before mothers came along?' Aisling asked as they sat at the table. A bowl of homemade vegetable soup, fragrant steam rising off it, was waiting for her, alongside a plate of freshly made ham, cheese and salad sandwiches. She balanced Holly on one knee, bouncing her up and down as she ate.

They exchanged the latest news, about her husband Sean's promotion at the big computer company in Newbridge, about her father's latest success in the bridge club, her mother's latest meeting of the local history group. They made arrangements for a shopping trip to Dublin the following week. Yes, it was busy enough at work, she told her mother. Ray had been called out by the AA again, second time in two days. A handy extra earner for him. Which reminded her —

'You know that journal of Grandma's that I'm typing up for you?'

Her mother raised an eyebrow. 'The one we mustn't mention? The one I gave you a year ago? The one you'll finish as soon as you can?'

Aisling grinned. 'I will, I'm sorry. Blame your beloved grand-daughter, coming along and interrupting me. I did get to page one hundred before Holly was born. And I did another ten pages last month. Just another ten thousand to go.'

'My mother was nothing if not prolific. Why do you ask?'

'Ray was telling me a story today, about a woman who used to come from here called Lola. It's been driving me mad why the name rang a bell but I remembered on the walk home. There was a Lola mentioned in Gran's journal, wasn't there? I remember thinking it was a nice name when I came across it when I was pregnant, but we'd already decided on Holly. Would that have been a common enough name back then?'

'I only ever heard of one when I was growing up. Not that I remember her myself but Mammy talked about her a good bit. She used to help her with childminding, I think, before she emigrated. All before I came along. Why?'

Aisling explained. 'Wouldn't that be weird if it was the same Lola, back home for a visit? All these years later. Isn't that right, Holly?' she said, leaning down to kiss her little daughter again, speaking in a singsong voice. 'Wouldn't that be weird?'

'What was this Lola-from-yesterday's surname?'

Aisling shrugged. 'I don't know. Ray only remembered her first name because he said it reminded him of some song.'

'And she was here in Kildare but now she's gone? Where was she staying?'

'Mum, I don't know. It was just a casual conversation.'

'You've got me wondering about her now too. Where's the journal and I'll have a look myself.'

'I was hoping you wouldn't ask. I'm sorry I'm taking so long. I know you want to get started on editing it, and you're right, it is quite interesting really, all that stuff about the food people ate back then, and the way of life —'

'It's all right, love, there's no rush. Don't worry. But let me take a look anyway.'

Aisling handed Holly over to her mother and found the journal. It was safely in the cardboard box it had been kept in for years. Aisling knew how precious it was to her mum. Her grandmother had presented it to her with some ceremony, a few months before her memory had completely gone. It had been so sad for her mother, Aisling knew. She'd heard lots of stories about how lovely her grandmother had been, how interested in people she always was. Aisling was sorry her own memories of her were only of an old lady in the nursing home, content but truly away with the fairies most of the time. She had lived at home with Aisling's mother for several years, until her dementia had got so bad they'd all agreed it was best she go into a nursing home. She hadn't even known her own daughter's name by the end. It had been a hard time for her mum, with one of her sisters dying a few years later as well.

Aisling carefully took the journal out of the box and handed it to her mother. She retrieved her daughter and continued to eat her lunch, as her mother began to leaf through the pages.

The paper was thin, the writing crammed, but it was still readable, with each entry preceded by a date and, to the family's amusement, a one-word description of the weather that day. Most of the time, the word was 'grey'. It seemed the weather in Ireland hadn't been much better back then. Her mother wanted to reproduce extracts from it in their local history magazine and on the society's website. The journal covered nearly sixty years of the previous century. Her grandmother had begun it as an eighteen-year-old and written it up until she was in her seventies.

Her mother seemed to be looking for a particular section. 'Here it is,' she said. 'My sister Helena, God rest her soul, would have been two at the time. I haven't arrived yet.' She began to read aloud.

> *Lola came to say goodbye today. She is doing her best to*
> *be excited about all that lies ahead in Australia, I know,*
> *but I couldn't stop the tears, and once I started, so did*
> *she. She has promised to write as often as she can and I*
> *made her promise to come home too if it was ever possible.*
> *Her parents aren't even accompanying her and Edward to*
> *Dublin. I pleaded with Alice – not that I told Lola – but she*
> *said Charles had forbidden it. She'll regret it, I'm sure.*

She looked up at Aisling. 'It's dated sixty-five years ago. About a Lola going to Australia. It must be her. There can't be two people with that name from here, surely? It's incredible she's still alive. What would she be, in her nineties? Is she even able to walk? Did the driver mention a wheelchair or anything?'

'Not that Ray told me.'

'I can remember Mum talking about her. I remember her letters arriving from Australia when I was a kid too. They're probably still in those boxes of Mum's somewhere.'

'Those boxes stored in my attic that you promised three years ago would only be for a few months?'

'My, how the time has flown,' Jean said, smiling. 'You and Sean don't mind, do you? There's no room in the apartment at all for storage.'

'That will teach you and Dad to be trendy and downsize. We don't mind at all. I don't think I've been in the attic myself since we put your boxes there.'

'I must take a look at them again. I'm curious now. That Lola was great fun, by all accounts. Lively. Mum seemed so fond of her. And so sad for all that happened with her and her parents.'

'What happened?'

'If you'd finished typing up the journal, you'd know. That can be your incentive to keep going. I wonder, did she try to find anyone round here that might remember her?'

'There'd hardly be anyone left, would there? And where would you start after so many years away? Even if she'd tried to find any of Grandma's family, it would be too hard, all of you getting married and changing your surnames. See, Mum, that's another reason why women should keep their own names when they get married. It will make life easier in the future when people come looking for old family skeletons to rattle. If you'd stayed an O'Connell, no problem, she could have looked you up in the phone book. Except there's no such thing as a phone book either, is there? How do people find people these days? Do you hope everyone you're looking for is on Facebook?'

Her mother wasn't listening. She was gazing down at the journal, still slowly turning the pages. 'She was using a chauffeur, did you say?'

Aisling nodded. 'With an expensive business card and all. Shame he spent all his money on his card and not on his car, if you ask me.'

Her mother looked up at the clock on the wall. 'It's nearly two. Shouldn't you get back to work?'

'And leave this little pet? How could I?' She showered kisses on her daughter's face, as the little girl laughed. 'I better go, you're right. Considering he's my brother, that boss of mine is very strict.'

'Would you mind looking up the name of that chauffeur when

you get back? And texting it to me?'

'What, and break all the rules of garage confidentiality? Sure. I'll do it straight away.'

There were customers waiting in the office when she arrived. Ray, behind the desk in his oil-covered work clothes, handed them over to her with relief. It wasn't until she got a reminder text from her mother an hour later – *Chauffeur's name please?* – that she remembered.

She found the card again and quickly texted back: *Oops sorry. Frantic here. His name is Desmond Foley.* There was a website address and phone number on the card too. Aisling sent it all to her mother. *But don't tell Ray I told you LOL. xxx*

Back at Aisling's house, Jean spent a half-hour playing with Holly before putting her down for her afternoon nap. For the next hour, she sat quietly reading. Not the *Kildare Nationalist* or the *Ballymore Bugle*, both of which she'd brought to the house with her. She started re-reading her mother's journal.

The small taste of it earlier had given Jean an all-too-familiar longing for her mother. She still missed her so much, even after twenty years. She'd been such a lovely woman. Jean wasn't being biased either. Everyone in the area had loved Elizabeth. One of the kindest, most generous, least judgemental women in the world, one of the mourners at her funeral had said. It was true. She'd always accepted people as they came, been hospitable to them. Growing up, Jean's memory was of a house filled with visitors. The Ballymore Eustace church had been packed at her funeral. Jean and her sisters had sent out hundreds of Mass cards afterwards to the many people in her mother's address book, the many people who had sent sympathy cards.

How extraordinary if the Lola who'd hired the car was the same Lola mentioned in the journal. Jean had already found nearly a dozen mentions of her in the section she'd just read. She and Elizabeth had obviously been very close. Her mother had also been quite candid about Lola's own parents. She had liked Lola's mother, Alice: *A sweet lady, but so timid. It's hard to believe Lola is her daughter. She must have been a changeling!* There had been little affection for Lola's father: *I don't like to find ill in anybody, but I can't help myself in regard to Charles Delaney. A bully at the school and a bully at home. Poor Alice, my heart goes out to her with all she has to put up with*, she had written in one entry.

Flicking back and forth, Jean began to piece together more of Lola's story. Her mother had chronicled every aspect of the unfolding drama around Lola and her pregnancy. The father was a local boy, Edward Quinlan, a gardener at Bayfield, one of the big estates. The first mention of Australia appeared two entries later. This Edward had been planning to go to Australia, to join friends there. He would still be going, with one change in plan. Lola would be going with him, as his wife. His pregnant wife.

> *I tried to talk to her about it, but she said she couldn't see any other way out. She sounded excited, I must admit. She's seeing it all as an adventure. As it will be, on the other side of the world, with a husband she barely knows and a baby to rear on her own, no family or friends nearby to help. But she was as spirited as she always is. She said her parents are extremely upset and angry. An understatement, I'm sure.*

As Jean read on, her mother's entries became more concerned with her own family. Once again, she found the entry relating to her mother discovering she was pregnant again: *It is such wonderful news.* Jean smiled at the words. She was the baby in question. How special to have this handwritten proof of how happy her mother had been at the thought of her coming into the world.

'Ah, Mammy,' she said aloud. 'I miss you so much.'

It felt like a gift to read her words again. Perhaps she would type it up herself, rather than rely on Aisling to do it. She had the time now she was retired from the bank, after all. She could even do it here when she was babysitting, in the quiet times while Holly was sleeping. She could also use the time to go through all those boxes she'd stored in her daughter's attic.

While they were cleaning through her mother's house after she died, they'd found not only a great deal of fine china packed away, all unused, but also every letter, Christmas card and birthday card she'd received over the years. All the sympathy cards she'd received after Jean's father had died had been carefully packed away too. Jean hadn't been able to throw out any of them. They'd been so touching to read, proof if she had needed it of how many people had been fond of her parents.

Jean checked on little Holly again. Still fast asleep. She quietly climbed the stairs to the attic. The boxes were easy to find, three small ones, in a neat stack. Within minutes she had them down at her feet in the living room. One was filled with the sympathy cards. The other two boxes were letters her mother had received over the years, from friends all over Ireland and beyond. They were sorted into bundles. Her mother had always been very organised. The ones from this Lola were easy enough to find. She had been her mother's only correspondent from Australia, the envelopes bearing bright stamps. The letters inside were still in good condition, from all their years of being nestled away.

Jean opened one of them, eager to read. Then something stopped her. These letters hadn't been written to her. If she had known for sure that Lola was long dead, yes, it would be different. This would feel like another of her local history projects, looking through archives, discovering facts about lives from long ago. But if the Lola who had written these letters was the same Lola who had been or perhaps still was in the area . . . it wasn't right. It would feel too much like prying.

There were certainly plenty of them. Checking the date stamps, it appeared Lola had written once or twice a year. Had Lola in return kept all of her mother's letters? Jean wondered. More importantly, she wondered if Lola – if it was the same woman – would want to re-read these letters she'd sent from Australia?

Jean tried to put herself in Lola's shoes. Would she want that? Yes, she would. But if Lola had wanted to make connections with people from her past, surely she'd have got in touch with someone either online or through the council? Even the history group, Jean's own organisation. It would be so easy these days. She could even have contacted the newspaper. Perhaps Lola simply hadn't thought of it. Perhaps she'd decided to wait until she got here and then try to track down people from her past? Or perhaps Jean had it all wrong, and the Lola with the chauffeur wasn't the Lola from the letters at all?

There was only one way to find the answers to her questions.

She picked up her phone.

Fifteen minutes later, she finally hung up. Good Lord, that chauffeur could talk. She'd introduced herself and explained the situation as briefly as she could.

'So then,' he'd said, 'my client might be someone mentioned in your late mother's journal, did you say? Well, that is interesting. Not that I can give you her phone number yet, discretion is my middle name, but I'm sure she'll be keen to hear about it, especially now she's on her own. Her son is arriving from Australia tomorrow, mind you, because her granddaughter and great-granddaughter had to go back to Australia suddenly, due to a medical emergency. But I can certainly give her a message, if you give me all the details first.'

Jean spelt out the facts in question – her name, her mother's name, her old address. 'I thought she might like to read some of the journal,' Jean said. 'She's in it a good bit, the early part at least. From the 1930s.'

'In it a good bit. The 1930s,' the chauffeur repeated, obviously writing down everything she was saying. He read it all back, repeating her phone number too. 'I can't promise anything,' he said afterwards. 'She does seem to be a very private person —'

God help her, travelling with you, Jean thought.

'— but I'll do my best.'

There was nothing she could do until she heard back. She picked up the journal and read, until her granddaughter started to stir. She settled her quickly, then returned to the living room, restless now.

She could understand that the chauffeur couldn't give out his clients' names and numbers, but it was so frustrating, especially when she'd just read the journal again. She wanted to find out for sure if it was the same Lola. Even if the chauffeur did pass on her message, if Lola did decide to call her to hear more details, it would be difficult to have a private conversation tonight. Jean had to go out to a fundraiser at the parish hall. She was helping out in the kitchen from six o'clock, and would be busy serving sandwiches and tea till all hours.

But perhaps she didn't have to wait to hear back from Des. If this woman was her mother's friend, wouldn't her mother want her to get in touch?

'So what will I do, Mammy?' she said aloud.

There was no answer, of course. But Jean didn't need supernatural help.

If Lola was travelling in a chauffeur-driven car, she was hardly staying in backpacker hostels. There were several five-star hotels in Kildare. She'd start with those, then move on to four-star hotels. Easy. All she needed was Lola's surname. She picked up the letters from her mother's collection. There it was, written on the back of every envelope. Lola Quinlan.

Feeling like a detective, she took out her phone, and googled 'Kildare' and 'hotels'. She dialled the first one. Jean had never had cause to ring this five-star hotel before, let alone visit it.

This is fun, she thought, as a professional-sounding young woman answered.

'Oh, yes, hello. I'd like to speak to one of your guests please. Her name is Lola Quinlan.'

CHAPTER TWENTY-NINE

After Emmanuel dropped her back to the hotel, Lola had decided not to go up to her room. She'd been out in the garden since then. It had rained a little that morning, but the sky was blue again. She'd taken a seat on one of the many benches. She could hear birds in the bushes nearby. The marquee was being moved from one part of the garden to another. Another wedding due in the next day or two, Lola guessed. Good. She hoped this next one would be as easily visible from her bedroom window.

She shut her eyes, feeling the warmth of the May sun, hearing the breeze in the leaves behind her. The accents of the workmen putting up the marquee. Not Irish; Polish, perhaps. Eastern European, at least. One of their phones rang. That reminded her.

She took out her phone and listened to Des's message. Everything was fine with collecting Jim, he assured her. He had something else he wanted to discuss. He sounded quite excited. She called him back, getting his voicemail. She left a brief message. As she hung up, she saw her battery was nearly dead. She'd meant to charge it that morning. In all the activity with Bett and Ellen she'd forgotten. She'd try Des again once her phone was charged.

Picking up her stick, she slowly made her way along the path to the hotel.

In Dublin, Des frowned as he dialled Lola's mobile number, getting only her recorded message again. Why wasn't she answering? It was so frustrating. He was bursting to tell her about the call he'd got. He couldn't even tell Breda. She'd worked a night shift and was asleep upstairs. He knew well not to wake her before her alarm went off. He couldn't even ring Bett and ask her to try to contact Lola. Her flight was still in the air, many hours away from landing in Sydney.

What could he do? Drive down to Kildare again and find Lola in person? He didn't have another job on, after all. The Quinlans had negotiated a ten-day fee for his services. Officially, he was still their employee. So as part of his role he really should pass on this message as soon as possible, shouldn't he? What else could he do, sit here and twiddle his thumbs? He liked the road to Kildare, in any case. If Lola rang him back while he was driving, well, he'd pull over, tell her what he needed to tell her and head home again. He left a note on the table for Breda. *Quick trip to Kildare, back by dinnertime, Love D xx*

Five minutes later, he was on the road.

In Aisling's house, Jean checked the clock. Her daughter would be home in an hour. Holly had woken again and was now happily playing with her toys in the playpen, gurgling and chewing the ear off her favourite toy. There was no harm in trying a couple more numbers, surely. She'd had no luck with the five-star places, or the first three of the four-star hotels either.

She'd actually been to the next hotel on her list. She also passed it three times a week, on her way from her and her husband's new apartment in Naas to Aisling's house. Before becoming a hotel it had been a boarding school, and a private hunting lodge before that.

She dialled. 'Oh, hello there. I'm hoping to speak to one of your guests if I may? Lola Quinlan?'

There was a pause. 'Certainly, madam. Putting you through. Please hold the line.'

Jean's heart started beating faster.

Halfway up to her room, Lola remembered – with the prompt of a sudden rumble from her stomach – that she hadn't had lunch yet. That was no way to carry on, a woman of her age, needing all the sustenance she could get. The hotel had a bright little cafe in a conservatory downstairs, with a lovely view of the gardens. She'd have a sandwich, she decided. A pot of tea. Then she'd charge her phone and try Des again.

The young waitress greeted her with a smile. 'Table for one?'

'Lovely, thank you.'

Upstairs in her room, the bedside phone rang and rang.

Jean waited. Eventually, the receptionist came back on the line.

'I'm sorry, madam. There doesn't seem to be any answer. Can I take a message?'

Jean thought quickly. No, it was too complicated. 'Thank you but no. I'll try again later.'

She hung up. Moments later, Holly started to howl. Jean picked her up and soothed her. Perhaps it was as well Lola hadn't been in her room. It would have been impossible to talk with this racket going on. Or perhaps it just wasn't meant to be.

An hour later, Lola was leaving the cafe. Her quick late lunch had turned into a long late lunch. At first she'd sat quietly, enjoying her tea and sandwich. She'd chosen a good table, in view of the latest marquee construction. The men were fast workers. It was nearly finished. They were now doing the decorating. Another van had pulled up and more than fifty large pot plants unloaded. They were being arranged around the marquee. Any more and it would be like a greenhouse, with no room for the guests, Lola thought.

She'd even met the bride. A young dark-haired woman had come into the cafe, walked to the window, anxiously watched the work in the marquee and then looked up at the sky. There were now more clouds than blue patches. She had sighed heavily.

'Don't worry,' Lola said. 'I heard the forecast. It's supposed to be dry for the next two days.'

The young woman turned around. 'My mother's done nothing but pray for dry weather since my fiancé and I announced our engagement a year ago. She's got a hotline to heaven at this stage.'

'Let me guess,' Lola said, smiling. 'You're the blushing bride?'

'The fretting bride.' She pulled a face. 'Everyone says I won't notice the weather, I'll be so busy.'

'I'm sure you'll have a wonderful day, rain or shine,' Lola said.

'Thank you very much,' the young woman said, with a quick grin.

Lola had the cafe to herself after that. She was so sorry, of course, that Glenn had got sick, and that Bett and Ellen had left so suddenly. But the old saying was true. Every cloud had a silver lining. She had needed this time on her own. Not only to make the return journey to her village and home in her own way. She'd also been given unexpected thinking time. Decision-making time. If Bett and Ellen had stayed, they'd have been with her now, talking. Or she would have been in her room, expecting them to visit. She'd have loved that. She loved her family.

But today, right now, she wanted to be on her own. With her own thoughts.

Tomorrow, around eleven, if Des had a good run from the airport, Jim would be here with her. Everything would change again. She knew she couldn't put it off any longer. It was time.

She had finally realised it this afternoon, when she was being driven back to the hotel. Her head was filled with thoughts of her childhood. Her parents. Edward Quinlan. Their courtship. Her pregnancy. Their hasty marriage. Most of all, with memories of all that happened after they arrived in Australia. She had kept so much of that time to herself, for so many reasons. Good reasons. But she didn't need to keep it to herself any more. She wanted to share it. And she would.

As soon as Jim had recovered from his flight, she was going to tell him the truth about his father.

Des was halfway to Lola's hotel when his phone rang. He used the hands-free. Safety was number one with him. 'Desmond Foley, Chauffeur of Excellence, Des Foley speaking.'

It was an old friend of his, another chauffeur. He was in a fix. A morning job had turned into an all-day job. He needed several clients collected from the airport that afternoon, off different flights. He was sorry to ask Des at such late notice, but was there any way possible at all . . .

Des saw a sign for a slip road coming up. It was his best chance to turn back. This surprise job would be a handy extra deposit into their Asian trip savings account too. He could always try calling Lola again from the airport. And deep down, he could also too easily imagine Breda telling him off if she heard about this trip of his: *You drove down all that way to pass on a message? Rather than try ringing her again first? Desmond Foley, what a waste of petrol. You have to stop doing everything on the spur of the moment.* Sometimes the Breda who told him off in his head was even scarier than the real Breda.

'I'm your man,' he said to his friend. 'On my way to the airport now.'

Just before Aisling came home, Jean made a decision. She wouldn't phone Lola's hotel again. For all she knew, Lola might be hard of hearing, making it difficult for Jean to explain why she was ringing. Or even worse, Lola might not even remember Jean's mother. That's if it was the right Lola at all.

She'd take a different approach. She found a sheet of paper, and with the now-happy Holly on her lap, wrote Lola a note. She enlarged her handwriting, in case this Lola had bad eyesight too.

> *Dear Mrs Quinlan,*
> *You don't know me, but I hope you don't mind me writing. I think you may have known my mother, Elizabeth O'Connell. It's a long story but, Ireland being Ireland, I understand you are back in Kildare and might be interested in meeting people who knew people you knew when you were still living here. I've left a message with your chauffeur too.*
> *If you are the same Lola who my mother spoke and*

*wrote about so fondly, it would be lovely to meet you. She
died twenty years ago, and I miss her every day. It would be
a pleasure to talk to someone who knew her before I was
born (I am now sixty-three years old).*

*If you are not the same Lola, or would prefer not to
respond, that is fine, of course. Otherwise, please do get in
touch with me.*

She signed her name, added her mobile number, put it in an envelope and wrote LOLA QUINLAN on the front. She'd drop it off on
her way to the fundraiser.

In her room, Lola was watching the evening news. She'd been surprised that it started at 6.01 p.m. to accommodate the ringing of the
Angelus church bells at six o'clock. How extraordinary to see such
a Catholic prayer ritual still broadcast in modern Ireland. Times
had changed in some ways – her taxi driver Emmanuel had told her
he attended a mosque in Dublin each week.

Lola hadn't heard back from Des yet. She checked her phone.
It was surely charged again by now. She frowned as she noticed it
was still flat. She checked the plug. All fine. She checked the connection to her phone. It had come loose. How annoying, but easy to
replace, she hoped. Jim would be able to help her find a new one in
Naas or Newbridge. What a comforting thought. In the meantime,
perhaps the hotel had a spare one.

She phoned reception and was pleased to hear that they had
one. The porter was helping unload the luggage from a busload of
new guests, but he'd bring it up to her room as soon as possible.

'I'll come down and collect it myself,' she said. The exercise
would do her good.

The foyer was filled with people. Lola found a comfortable chair and waited. The new arrivals were Italians, she thought. Or French? Excited, either way. Off to the races at the Curragh, it seemed. Perhaps she and Jim could do that too.

If he was still talking to her after all she planned to tell him.

Eventually the crowd thinned. There were now just a few people waiting in front of the reception desk. Lola rose from her seat, reached for her stick and took her place behind a woman in her sixties.

'Good evening,' the woman in front said when it was her turn. 'Could I please leave a letter for a guest?'

'Certainly, madam,' the receptionist said. 'The guest's name?'

'Lola Quinlan.'

Had Lola heard right? She stepped forward.

'That's me,' she said.

Less than five minutes after meeting Lola, an excited Jean was back in her car, on the phone to her friend at the parish hall.

'I'm very sorry, but I can't make the fundraiser. Something unexpected has come up.'

Soon after, she surprised her daughter by reappearing at her front door. She started talking as Aisling opened the door, Holly in her arms.

'It's her, Aisling! Mammy's friend! The same Lola! She's not a hundred, she's eighty-five. But she could be seventy, she's so full of spark still. And you should see her clothes! Quick, I need the journal. And the letters. She'd love to see every single thing tonight.'

Aisling watched as her mother hurriedly gathered it all. 'But aren't you working at the fundraiser?'

'Not any more!' Jean called over her shoulder as she ran back out to her car.

Lola was still in the hotel foyer. Groups of people were arriving for pre-dinner drinks, new guests checking in. She was glad of the distraction. Her head was whirling.

At the front desk, Jean had introduced herself and started to explain, the words tumbling out of her, before simply handing over a letter to Lola. 'Please, read this. I'll wait just over there.'

Lola took a seat again and read the letter. Once, twice, then a third time, as it slowly sank in.

That woman, Jean, was Elizabeth's daughter. Her Elizabeth.

When she'd looked up and nodded, Jean had hurried across to her.

'You're the same Lola?' she said.

'I'm the same Lola. And I loved your mother dearly too.'

Jean had sat down beside her, smiling, breathing out in relief. 'Oh, I'm so glad.' She spoke in a rush again, explaining about the afternoon at her daughter's house, her son the mechanic, the broken-down car. 'This was meant to be, wasn't it? It could have been any garage that came to fix your car!' She told her about the journal, the letters, how she had been looking through them all that afternoon. She was delighted when Lola told her she would love to see them.

'I can drop them here to you tomorrow, as early as you like.'

'My son is arriving tomorrow morning. From Australia. It's his first time in Ireland.'

'You'll be far too busy, then. And you can't possibly wait until tomorrow anyway. I know I couldn't. Are you free tonight?' At Lola's nod, she smiled. 'I'll be right back.'

As Lola waited, she thought of all the questions she had for Jean. About Elizabeth, first and foremost. But also about Jean's sister, Helena, the little girl she'd minded all those years ago. She wondered if Jean had read the journal and the letters herself? Did she already know all of Lola's story?

A man walked by talking loudly into his phone. It reminded Lola. She collected the charger from the front desk and found a power point near her chair. She'd just plugged in her phone when it rang.

'Lola!' It was Des. 'Thank God you're all right! I was starting to worry!'

'I'm grand, Des, thank you. I'm sorry, my phone ran out of battery.'

'I'm at the airport, collecting clients for a friend of mine. But you're always number one with me. I'm tracking your son's flight constantly, let me assure you. I'll have him down to you tomorrow as soon as I can.'

Lola didn't get a chance to thank him for the update before he continued.

'Now, it's entirely up to you, and you can of course say no and I'll happily ring this lady back and tell her you're not interested, but a Kildare woman rang me today to say she thinks her mother may have had a connection to you back when —'

'Des —'

'— you lived here in your younger years. It's such a small world. Her son was the mechanic who fixed my car. I'm still mortified it broke down. And I know this is a private visit, as I told her too in no uncertain terms, and so you —'

'Des —'

'— might not want to take it any further, and that is —'

'Des, it's fine. I've met her.'

'— completely understandable and I will call her.' He paused then. 'You've met her? How?'

Lola explained.

Des didn't sound happy about that. This had been his big scoop, Lola realised.

'But you did the right thing, Des. Thank you for respecting my privacy.'

'Fat lot of good that did. She tracked you down herself. What if she's a psychopath?'

'She doesn't seem to be so far,' Lola said mildly. 'She seems very nice, in fact.'

'Well, then, I'll leave you both to it. My client's just landed. I'll see you with your son in the morning.' With that he was gone.

Jean walked into the foyer again, carrying a large bag. It seemed natural to hug one another this time.

Lola gazed at her. 'I can see Elizabeth in you. How marvellous. Oh, I was so fond of her, Jean. Someone in your family sent me a Mass card after she died. I was very grateful. It helped to have definite news.'

'We had to print hundreds of Mass cards. She was so popular.'

'And how is your sister Helena? The one I used to babysit.'

A shadow passed over Jean's face. 'She died seventeen years ago. A stroke.'

Lola felt a ripple of sadness, remembering that lively little girl. 'I'm so sorry. You've had difficult times.'

'Yes. But the best of times too. I have five grandchildren.' She named them, finishing with Holly. 'It's Holly's mother, Aisling, who set all of this in train.'

'I'd love to meet her too.' She glanced down at the bag in Jean's hand. She wanted to read everything in it. But that could wait.

'Have you time to talk to me tonight, Jean?'

'All the time in the world, Lola.'

It was nearly eleven by the time Lola was back in her room. Her head was filled with stories. She'd had three wonderful hours hearing about Elizabeth, about Jean and her family, about life in the village, the county, the country over the past six decades. Not only was Jean involved in the history group, but through her children she had connections with schools and sporting clubs in the area too. Her husband played bridge and was in the Lions Club. They had a wide circle of friends. Any time Lola mentioned a name from her childhood, it had taken Jean just a moment to recall a fact about either the person themselves or their family.

Until Lola asked about the Quinlans.

Jean frowned. 'I didn't know them, Lola. Not personally, I mean. I'm sorry, I know more about you and your parents and your life than I should, really, through Mammy's journal. But I don't remember any of the Quinlans working at that estate. Not that it's a private house any more. It's a successful stud farm now.'

Lola mentioned Edward's sister then. Margaret, known as Peggy, married name Hegarty.

Again, Jean shook her head. 'I'm sorry. But I can ask around if you like?'

'Thank you but no,' Lola said. If any information came to her, so be it. But she wasn't going looking.

It was Jean who noticed how late it was. They hadn't sat unrefreshed for all that time. Lola had ordered sandwiches and tea. But it was time Jean left.

She smiled at Lola as she stood up. 'My fundraiser is probably just kicking off. We're night owls around here. I might still be in time to pour a few cups of tea.'

Lola gazed up at her. 'Thank you, Jean. For so much.'

'Oh no, it's me who should be thanking you, Lola. Mammy would have loved this, wouldn't she? The two of us sitting here talking about her for the past three hours?'

'I'm sure of it,' Lola said.

In her room, Lola got ready for bed. If she was at home she would have poured herself a gin and tonic. Perhaps put on a CD of quiet classical music. Not tonight. All she needed now was her bed, a lamp and her reading glasses. Sending up a prayer of thanks to Elizabeth – if there was a heaven, that's definitely where Elizabeth would be – she settled herself comfortably in bed, placed the journal at close hand, picked up the first letter and began to read.

CHAPTER THIRTY

Four hours later, Lola lay back on the pillow, feeling the tears still drying on her face. The journal and all the letters surrounded her, spread over the soft white quilt. She had cried often while reading them, not just at Elizabeth's words but at her own.

Her many letters had been sorted into date order, by Elizabeth or possibly Jean. Lola had never kept a diary, but these letters read like one. She'd relived her early years in Australia, from the long and difficult ship journey with Edward to their struggle to find somewhere to live when they finally arrived in Melbourne. About finding unexpected ready support among the many Irish immigrants already in the city. They'd lived in cheap rooming houses at first, until they'd been able to rent the ground floor of a rundown but liveable house in Richmond. Edward's Irish connections had helped him find work too. Nothing permanent, but enough short-term jobs to keep money coming in to pay their rent and buy food. Slowly, she'd started to earn some money too, cleaning, teaching piano.

She told Elizabeth about her relationship with Edward. How, on the ship, it had become clear that they were barely compatible. That he resented her. His feelings didn't change when they arrived in Melbourne. But she'd still sounded optimistic in her letters, writing about her new life, the feeling of freedom. She would keep trying to make everything work out, she told Elizabeth.

As the letters continued, she began to write about Edward's drinking. Her dawning realisation that her husband wasn't just a social Friday-night or a sunny-afternoon-by-the-river drinker. It was all there, alongside the events and impressions of her early days in Australia. She remembered sitting alone at night in their tiny kitchen, while Edward was out. Working, he'd told her. Drinking with his friends, she knew. But she'd never felt alone while writing to Elizabeth. She wrote as she'd talked to her, quickly, with lots of detail, sharing her hopes and fears, the day-to-day difficulties but also the surprising joys of this new life. The vivid colours of the Australian flowers, the birds. The bright light. The huge sky. The space. So much space.

She had written to her parents too. She didn't need to have those letters in front of her to remember what she'd said, so formally, every word carefully chosen. Lies, mostly. She'd made it sound as though she and Edward were the happiest couple in Australia. She increased Edward's pay packet, his working hours. She described their small living quarters as twice the size. It rained more often in Melbourne than she had expected, but she avoided mentioning that too. She spoke of sunshine, blue skies, exotic wildlife, a lively neighbourhood, people from all over the world living happily and harmoniously side by side. She'd barely written about her pregnancy, she recalled.

She was the opposite with Elizabeth. Re-reading her letters, Lola was almost shocked by the detail. She'd written about how changed physically she felt in Australia, how all the space and light and sunshine in Melbourne made her somehow different in herself. She described her pregnancy in detail too. How she felt drifting and dreamy some days, and possessed with a furious kind of energy on others. She told Elizabeth she'd made friends with a Scottish woman called Edith three streets away who ran a lodging house.

She could never have known at the time how important Edith and that lodging house would become to her.

She'd taken a break from reading the letters then. She knew what was coming. Instead, she picked up Elizabeth's journal. She read not from her own entrance into Elizabeth's life in the 1930s, but from the beginning, learning about Elizabeth's early days as a married woman, in that small but happy house in Ballymore Eustace that had become Lola's second home.

She discovered more about Elizabeth's life than she might ever have known, even if she had stayed in Kildare for the rest of her life. Elizabeth had written about everyone in her immediate circle: her husband, her children, her family, her husband's family, her neighbours, all with a compassionate eye. It wasn't just a chronicle of a family. It was a chronicle of Irish life in the twentieth century. It was no wonder Jean was so keen to have it transcribed and shared with her history group.

It was also a chronicle of Lola's parents. Elizabeth had observed them closely too.

At the house today, Lola had been flooded by memories of life as a young girl there. She'd felt so powerless, an observer of the daily reality of her parents' unhappy marriage, but too young to fully understand. Why was her mother always so sad? Why was her father such a bully? She'd only ever been able to see them from a daughter's viewpoint, caught between their warring factions, fighting her own battles with her father, unable to help her mother or connect with her in any meaningful way, before or after she'd left for Australia.

Through Elizabeth's eyes, via Elizabeth's pen, Lola discovered more about her own parents than she would have thought possible to know. Yes, her father had been known throughout the area as a bully. Not just at home to Lola and her mother, but in the school and village too. His students got good results, but he ruled the classrooms with fear. He was quick to mock anyone less clever than he was. He kept himself apart, imagined himself superior. *I've tried for Alice's sake,* Elizabeth had written, *but he is very hard to like. Impossible, in fact.*

There were many entries about her mother too. From what Elizabeth described, it appeared Lola's own retrospective diagnosis was true. Her mother had suffered from depression, perhaps linked to her miscarriages, perhaps to something genetic. Not that the term 'depression' had been in use during Elizabeth's journal-writing days. She used terms like 'nerves' and 'melancholy'. Lola's mother had visited Elizabeth more often than Lola had known, often while Lola and her father were at school. The visits had continued after Lola had gone to Australia.

Elizabeth had written about them with her usual honesty.

Alice visited today, to ask if I wanted help with the children but of course it was to ask if I had heard from Lola. I hadn't but she seemed content for me to read out parts of one of Lola's early letters, even though I had read those to her before. What had I written back? she wanted to know. News from here, I said, of the family, of the village. I kept telling her, write to her yourself, I'll send it with mine, Charles need never know. He'll find out somehow, she would say in return. 'How?' I would ask. 'Has he spies in Australia as well as here in Kildare?' It is a terrible thing to see the fear she has of him, another human being. And equally terrible to see how nervous she is of the whole world. I can see it in her face, in the way she moves. She reminds me of a dog that has been whipped too often. It sits there shivering, waiting for the next blow to fall. How that self-important bully of a man and that poor nervous woman managed to produce a girl as fearless

and generous and kind as Lola I will never know. Poor
Alice, she has no strength or confidence. No backbone.
She can deal only with what is in front of her, in small steps.
Yet she still visits me here so regularly, and she always sits
so still, so attentively, anytime I read aloud any of Lola's
letters to her.

Lola imagined that scene, the two women in the kitchen together, Elizabeth's children playing nearby, food being prepared, the warm mood so different to the cold heart of Lola's family house.

She read on.

I know Alice wants me to send a message to Lola too.
I know she loves her daughter. As much as she can, in
her own way. I also feel sure she wishes everything was
different. She is just too fragile to be able to show it or
speak of it. Her life has been too hard, trying to please that
difficult, selfish man who will never be pleased. He wants
everything for himself. He has left her unable to be herself.

Lola read that passage several times. Could that be true? Had her mother loved her?

Lola had put down the journal then and shut her eyes. During her long life, she had met many other women like her mother. Women who found life overwhelming. Who lived their lives in fear. Others who found themselves trapped in difficult relationships, for emotional or physical reasons. Those women had been common in those early days in Australia. She'd met too many of them, as she and Jim moved from guesthouse to guesthouse, town to town. Men returning from the war came back damaged, changed forever, in their minds or their bodies, sometimes both. The women in their lives often bore the brunt of their anger and frustration. As the years passed, Lola learnt to her sorrow that it wasn't only war that could turn men violent. Far too often, she recognised a look in the eyes of a female guest, or a woman of her acquaintance. She'd see the nerviness, the way the other woman seemed to shrink into herself. That, as much as any bruises or marks, betrayed what was happening or had happened in that woman's life.

Lola knew she could have been one of those women herself. If she hadn't done what she'd done. Taken the risks she had. If she had obeyed her parents.

Her mother had never had the chance to change her life. Elizabeth's journal underlined the fact. Her father's domination continued after Lola left. Right until the end of her life. Her mother died first, her father just months later. Alice had never lived as an adult without her husband ruling over her.

'You poor, poor woman,' Lola said aloud into the lamp-lit room.

She didn't cry. Perhaps her tears might come later. She had not cried about her mother for many years – a deliberate, difficult choice. But she felt pity, more than ever. She wished, once again, she'd been able to help her in some way. Talk honestly to her. But that had been impossible enough before she left Ireland. Even more so afterwards, when everything happened with Edward.

She re-read the line in Elizabeth's journal: *I know she loves her daughter. As much as she can, in her own way. I also feel sure she wishes everything was different.*

Elizabeth wouldn't have written that if she didn't believe it was true. She would have had no way of knowing that all these years later Lola might be in Kildare again, reading her journal. That for many years – too many years – she had needed to see those exact words.

She reached up and turned off the bedside lamp. She stared out into the darkness, remembering.

326

CHAPTER THIRTY-ONE

Edward hit her for the first time when she was five months pregnant.

The tension had been building between them for days. He was drinking too much after work. She would try to get him up out of bed in the morning, to get to his new job as a gardener on time. Hungover, he'd ignore her calls, shouting at her when she eventually resorted to pulling back the covers. She was a nag, he said. A bitch. Inwardly she flinched, but outwardly she ignored him, keeping her voice calm, reminding him they needed this money. He muttered more insults. But she still managed to get him out the door. She also managed to get his weekly pay packet off him when he came home each Friday night. A sixth sense made her do something else. When she divided up his weekly pay for rent and food, she took a small amount for herself. She gave him whatever was left. He replied with more insults. How could he shout his friends a drink on a pittance like that? He would manage, she told him. The state he was in when he came back from the pub was proof.

She'd started helping out in a guesthouse three streets away. She'd seen a sign in the window: *Cleaner Needed*. The Scottish owner, Edith, had looked down at her growing belly. Lola had quickly assured her that she was still fit, healthy and hardworking.

Between the money from that work and her piano lessons, her savings steadily increased.

Each week the tension at home grew worse. Edward constantly criticised her, her appearance, her personality, her behaviour. One Friday night, he surprised her by coming home early. She hadn't cooked for him. He helped himself to the last of the bread, roughly pulling at it with his fingers. When she asked for his paypacket, he laughed.

'You're too late,' he said. He made a show of turning his pockets inside out. 'All gone!'

It was then she realised he was already drunk. 'Did you even go to work today?'

He didn't answer. Instead, he mimicked her, repeating her words.

She tried to reason with him. She told him he had to stop wasting money on drink, that she was doing all she could to make things as good as she could before the baby arrived, before —

'Shut up!'

She kept talking, trying to get him to see —

'Shut up, I said!'

She didn't see it coming. She felt just the rush of air as his fist came towards her. Into her face. Once. Twice. The force of it pushed her back against the wall. She gasped, too shocked to scream.

'Shut up!' he kept saying. 'Just shut up. I didn't want you here anyway.'

She put her hand to her face, silent now. In shock. In pain.

He kept shouting, his fist still raised. She cowered back against the wall, trying to protect her body, her baby. It was all her fault, he kept saying. Everything was her fault: she had trapped him, he didn't want a wife or a baby, this was his adventure and she had ruined it for him. On and on he went, while she stood still, her cheek aching now, her legs unsteady, so unsteady that she had to slide down against the wall until she felt the floor beneath her.

He left, slamming the door behind him. She stayed where she was, for thirty minutes, perhaps more. When she finally stood up she slowly moved between their two small rooms, taking what she needed.

On the way out, she noticed something on the floor. A roll of notes. He hadn't spent it. He'd somehow dropped it as he came in or went out. She pushed the money deep into her pocket.

She went to Edith's guesthouse. She began to explain but the older woman stopped her. She didn't mention the red mark on Lola's face. It was already starting to bruise. Yes, she told Lola, there was a room out the back, not nice, but cheap. Lola tried again to explain. Again, Edith stopped her. 'The way I see it,' she said, 'you'll be an even better worker than you already are, if you live here too.'

The next day, she wrote to her parents. This time she told them the truth about her marriage. She pictured the letter making the month-long sea journey from Australia to her home in Kildare. She pictured them reading it.

Two months passed. Two months of seeing her body slowly swell into the final months of her pregnancy. She didn't miss Edward once. Slowly, she felt the tension drain from her. She worked even harder than before, was given more shifts. She was safe here with Edith. She was even happy.

Then the letter from Ireland arrived.

It was waiting on the hall table when she came in from giving one of her piano lessons. She took it into her room. Her name and address was in her father's handwriting – dark, fierce strokes on the envelope. Her hands shook as she opened it.

It wasn't just from her father. Her mother had included a page too.

She read her father's first. He was, predictably, angry, full of bluster, ordering her to return to Edward, to get over this 'nonsense' as he called it. His words barely touched Lola.

Her mother's letter was different. She wrote about the coming baby. She implored Lola to understand that a baby needed a mother and a father. *Edward is just immature. He'll change when he sees the baby, his own son or daughter. Please, Lola. Do this for our grandchild.*

Grandchild.

The word went straight to her heart. She'd been making decisions for herself and her baby. But it wasn't just about her. Her mother was right. This baby deserved not only a mother and a father but grandparents too.

Lola obeyed them. She went back to Edward, ten weeks to the day that she had walked out. He seemed happy enough to see her. He'd never liked his own company. He was sober the day she returned. It was only later that she discovered it was because he had no money and his friends had grown tired of funding him.

There was no mention of him hitting her. No apology. She gave no reason for returning. Somehow, they simply went back to living together, as if it had never happened, as if she had never been away.

She kept as busy as possible. She was fit, young, able to keep working all through her pregnancy. Edward was offered labouring work, outside of Melbourne, clearing bushland near Castlemaine. He was soon away more often than he was home.

She wrote to her parents to tell them she and Edward were together again. She wrote about the coming baby, about Edward's work. A formal letter, a complete contrast to the ones she continued to send Elizabeth. Weeks later, a reply. One line from her father at the end of a one-page stilted note from her mother: *I'm relieved you came to your senses.* Her mother said much the same.

Edward arrived back in Melbourne ten hours before Jim was born. He waited outside the hospital, smoking with the other expectant fathers while she experienced the worst pain of her life and then the most joyous moment of her life, when her baby was given to her, wrapped and cleaned. Her son.

Something changed in her at that moment. It was only years later that she was able to put it into words. She became fierce. She knew she would do anything to protect this child.

A nurse came to her in the ward. 'Will we get your husband to come in?'

'Not yet. Thank you.' She'd wanted to have as much time alone with her son as she could.

By the time Edward came in, he'd enjoyed too much good cheer. Two of the other waiting fathers had brought hip flasks of whiskey, to help pass the night. It was cold out there, Edward said, as if Lola had been inside napping, not going through the agony of labour. 'I needed a drink.'

'Needed.' She'd heard it so often.

He continued drinking when they returned home a week later. He told her he needed it to help him sleep when the baby, whom they had named James Edward, was crying.

Lola sent a telegram – expensive, but she felt it was worth it – to her parents. Three weeks later, there was a letter of congratulations in her mother's handwriting. *Please send a photo if it is possible*, she wrote. Lola was taken aback at how happy that simple, ordinary request made her feel. Her mother cared about her baby! She wanted to see him!

It was the photo session in a studio in the city centre that brought everything to an end. By the time the photos were developed and ready for collection, Lola's marriage was over. This time, for good.

Jim was nearly two months old. Edward was late arriving at the studio. She could tell even as he walked in that he'd been drinking. Not a sway, but a swagger. He'd brought a friend. Lola tensed. He was inclined to show off around his friends. To put her down, to make remarks about baby-minding being women's work. It was true, in their case. He certainly never lifted a hand to help.

Jim was unsettled and cried from the moment the photographer began to arrange them into position in front of a painted garden scene. Lola and Edward were instructed to stand side by side, Lola holding up Jim, his chubby legs visible. Edward was to have his hand resting on her shoulder. His breath stank of drink and cigarettes and something stale, whatever he'd last eaten. His friend grew bored of calling out insults and teasing them from behind the photographer and left the studio. Jim kept crying.

Afterwards, they barely spoke a word, Lola pushing the pram home as fast as she could along the uneven footpath, her anger increasing as she heard Edward deliberately slow his steps, whistle loudly, knowing it would annoy her. She reached their house first. Their neighbour, a nosy Polish man called Josef, was at his front fence.

'Lovers' tiff?'

She gave him an icy smile.

Edward stayed back to talk to him. They both liked to put money on the horses. Edward would boast that he knew more than the usual punter about good horses. Hadn't he grown up in Kildare, after all – great horse country? Hadn't he worked at one of the finest estates in the country, where the horses were stabled in grander stalls than the houses most people lived in?

Lola had long lost patience with the stories of his supposed life in Kildare. Edward had rarely gone near a horse, to her knowledge. But he could talk himself up, she'd give him that. She'd seen money change hands once too. Edward had given Josef a sure tip, she learnt afterwards. But such bad luck – the horse had lost for the first time in many races. Still, there was always a next time.

'Are you pocketing some of his money?' she'd asked Edward. Of course not, he said. She hadn't believed him. A week earlier, she'd stopped to talk to Josef's wife. Lola brought up the subject of horses. 'I wouldn't believe everything Edward says to you,' she'd said.

In the pram, Jim was still crying. His cheeks were bright red. Colic? Something else? She leaned into the pram and kissed him. 'I'm sorry, Jimmy, I'm sorry. You poor little mite.' She was still trying to soothe him when Edward came in. Something had happened. She felt that charged air around him.

'What have you been saying about me to Josef's wife?'

'Nothing.' Then she lifted her chin. 'Nothing untrue, at least.'

'Don't you ever talk about me behind my back like that again.'

'I wouldn't need to, if you weren't trying to rob our neighbours.'

He pretended to ignore that. 'And don't you ever look down your nose at my friends like you did today, Miss Snob.' It was his latest insult.

Lola pulled herself up to her full height. 'I'm the one who should be complaining. You're the one who turned up late today. And I don't have to talk to your drunk friends any more than I need to talk to you when you're drunk. Like right now.'

That time, he didn't use his fists. The leg of the chair hit her in the face. Jim started to cry louder even before she fell onto the floor. Edward moved towards him while she was still trying to get up. She could feel blood on her cheek. She was lucky, she remembered thinking. It was just the leg that had hit her, not the back of the chair.

Lucky.

'Shut up. Just shut up.' It took her a moment to realise he was screaming it at Jim, not at her.

She moved as fast as she could. She wasn't fast enough. Edward reached into the pram, pulled Jim out roughly, so roughly —

'Don't touch him!'

Edward ignored her shout. He was shaking Jim. He was shaking her baby. He was raising a hand. She moved, as if propelled by a mighty engine, by fury. She still wasn't fast enough.

Edward hit Jim. Hit him across the face. There was a moment

of quiet, of shock, and then a cry she had never heard from her son before.

A rage engulfed her. She couldn't remember grabbing Jim, but he was now in her arms. The room was filled with his screams.

'Get out of this house!' She roared the words.

'It's my house.'

'Get out or I'll call the police.'

'Don't be ridiculous.'

She watched as he went across the room, to where a bottle sat on the sideboard. She spoke again, not shouting now. 'If you touch that bottle —'

He touched it. 'You'll what?'

She felt calm. As if her whole life had come to this moment. She thought fleetingly of her parents, of her father's anger, her mother's frailty. Only Jim mattered now. She stared at Edward. She spoke again, her voice low, powerful. 'Get out of this house. Now. Get out.'

He left. He went straight to the nearest pub. She saw him there half an hour later, through the open door. He was in the bar, laughing with his friends, old ones or newly met. He was laughing and talking, as if he hadn't just thrown a chair at his wife and hadn't just hit his baby son.

Lola stood outside for less than five seconds. She didn't say goodbye. She simply looked and then walked on, pushing the pram, which held not only her baby but all she could fit in it. In her spare hand she carried the largest suitcase they owned, filled with everything else she had calmly, quickly removed from drawers and cupboards.

She returned to the same guesthouse. To Edith. She didn't need to give a reason. They negotiated a long-term price. There was some money from the jewellery she pawned over the next month. She kept herself busy, working hard for Edith, looking after Jim, continuing her piano lessons, Jim in tow.

deposit on her own guesthouse, in a small coastal town in Victoria. She had to paint it herself, but she enjoyed painting. When Jim was thirteen, they moved again, this time to a motel near the border of Victoria and South Australia. The next move, three years later. Jim was by her side throughout. Her assistant, she called him. The best son in the world, she also called him. Hardworking, reliable, kind. All the traits she'd hoped he'd have. She watched anxiously for signs of his father in him: the quick temper, the fondness for a drink. She had nothing to worry about, she slowly realised.

He occasionally asked about his father. It wasn't unusual to be a boy without a father in the postwar years, sadly. She told him his father had died during the war, adding more detail each time. For a brief while, she considered returning to her maiden name, changing their names by deed poll. But she liked the sound of Jim Quinlan more than Jim Delaney. She'd grown to think of herself as Lola Quinlan too, or Mrs Quinlan, as her guests called her.

The year she turned forty, she realised she had lived in Australia for as long as she had lived in Ireland. She continued to write to Elizabeth. Elizabeth continued to write to her. There was nothing from her parents. She stopped writing to them, forcing herself not to think about them. If anyone asked about her family in Ireland, she would simply say how hard it was to be so far from them.

She and Jim continued to work together after he finished school. He loved it, he told her. He was an even better manager than she might have hoped: calm, organised, friendly. When he turned twenty-one, after yet another move, she started giving herself occasional nights off, leaving him in sole charge, going off to Melbourne to meet Edith and other friends from her early days.

The year Jim turned twenty-five they moved again. They had a choice of two motels to manage. It came down to the toss of a coin. It was extraordinary, Lola often thought later. If she had thrown heads and not tails, they wouldn't have moved to Warrnambool.

They wouldn't have taken over the small country motel in which Geraldine was working as an assistant cook. Jim wouldn't have fallen in love with her. They wouldn't have had three daughters. Her three Alphabet Sisters. A toss of a coin had brought them into being.

The year she turned forty-seven, everything changed again, wonderfully. Jim told her that Geraldine was expecting their first child, the baby that would be Anna. Lola was going to be a grandmother. She didn't much like Geraldine and Geraldine didn't much like her but that didn't seem to matter now. There was going to be a baby!

As Christmas approached, she found herself thinking of her parents. Of Ireland. Of Edward. She had no idea where he was, if he was still in Australia or back in Ireland; if he was dead or alive. All she knew was a sudden urge to speak to her mother, to tell her she was going to be a great-grandmother.

She knew from Elizabeth that her father had recently retired as headmaster at the school. She knew that her mother still taught piano occasionally. As the December days passed, she felt a sensation growing. She recognised it. Homesickness. She tried to rationalise why it was so strong. She always felt a little melancholy at Christmas, after all, recalling Irish traditions, thinking of frosty mornings, short days, candles burning in the windows on Christmas Eve. She still found hot summer Christmases a novelty, even after the decades. But it wasn't just a longing for Ireland she was feeling. It was a longing for her own family.

She had asked Elizabeth in her last letter if her parents had a phone. In her reply, without any questioning or fuss, Elizabeth had said yes, they did. She'd written down the number.

Jim and Geraldine were away the night she decided to do it.

The motel was quiet, just four guests in their ten rooms. Evening in Australia was morning in Ireland.

She spoke to the operator. An international call. It seemed akin to booking a ticket to the moon. The cost would be astronomical.

She gave the operator the number. A long wait followed. Twice the operator asked if she was still there. Once she almost hung up. Why, after all these years, was she doing this?

Because it was her parents. Because there was a child on the way. A new member of their family. Her father had never and would never approve of her, even like her, let alone love her. But her mother . . . Surely she had thought of Lola often over the years? Wished there hadn't been that rift?

She had a sudden jolt of doubt. She hadn't thought this through properly. What if Edward had returned to Ireland, to Kildare? What if they had seen him in the streets of Ballymore Eustace, or in Kilcullen, or Naas? Would they have spoken to him? Would that be even more appalling for her father, his daughter's husband back on their doorstep, with no sign of her?

A moment of wavering, and then she stood up straighter, holding the phone more tightly. She would not let other people's judgements and opinions dictate the way she lived her life. She'd been determined to become her own woman here in Australia, behave the best she could, but express herself too. She'd done it with her clothes at first. They had become more colourful and, yes, more flamboyant with each year. Too bad, she'd thought, if she ever saw someone laugh at her colour combinations or a flower she had put in her hair for no other reason than she liked the brightness of it. Her first twenty years had been lived under a small-town sensibility: *Don't do this, Don't do that, What will people say?* She was not a slave to that any more, and it amused Jim, she knew. And too bad if Geraldine thought her too showy, a figure of fun —

'Caller?'

Her heart started beating faster.

'Go ahead, please,' the operator said.

Lola spoke first.

'Mammy?' She hadn't said the word in twenty-seven years.

A long pause. An echo. 'Hello?' A soft Irish accent.

'Mammy, it's me. It's Lola.' She was suddenly twenty again. No longer the woman who had made a new life for herself, but the young woman who had left her husband, who was scared, with a small child, who needed her mother. She had to choke back a sob.

'How are you, Mammy?'

A too-long pause. More echo. Then one word.

'Grand.'

Her mother's voice. Across the world, across those oceans, down phone lines from Australia to Dublin to Kildare, to her parents' house on that country road. Where was their telephone? In the hallway? The front room? She heard herself asking that question. Twenty-seven years of not talking to her mother and she was asking her where the phone was. It seemed so important. Because now she was actually talking to her, she was terrified there was nothing to say.

'How is Father?' she asked, when her mother finished telling her the phone was in the front room, by the door, on a side table.

'He is well. He's retired from the school but he's still tutoring.'

Ask me something, Mammy. Ask me how I am. Ask me about Jim.

Nothing.

'I write to your friend,' Lola said. 'To Elizabeth.'

'Yes, I know.'

'Is Father at home?'

'Not yet. Any moment.'

Lola realised then. Her mother was nervous. She was worried that her father would come home and find his wife talking to the daughter he had insisted they disown. Their only child.

What could she say in the limited time they obviously had? *I miss you, Mammy.* But she didn't always, not after this long. *I wish things had been different.* Yes, that was true. She said it out loud, longing for something back from her mother in return. Longing for her to say, *Yes, Lola, I do too.*

Her mother didn't. She said something else instead. 'Your father's home. I can hear the car.'

'A car? You have a car?'

'Lola —'

'Mammy, you're going to be a great-grandmother. My son, Jim, he and his wife are having a baby.'

Nothing. Had her mother even heard her? Lola waited. There was one more word from her.

'Goodbye.'

So formal, in case her husband heard? In case he said, 'Who was that?' An anonymous goodbye so she didn't have to say, 'That was our daughter ringing from the other side of the world'?

Lola put down the phone before the operator came back on. She could imagine what she was thinking. All that money, all that organisation, for that short conversation? What a waste.

What a waste.

But what had she hoped would happen? So much, she realised. She'd wanted her mother to cry, to say, 'I miss you, Lola. I've missed you every day since you left. I wish I had your courage. I wish I had left my husband too, that I hadn't let him control me and my life. I wish I'd found the courage to travel to Australia. To meet my grandson. To see what your life has been like.'

And she would have said, 'It's too far for you to travel, but I can come back. I can come and see you and Father.' Jim and Geraldine would manage without her for a few months. She'd make sure she was back before their baby was born. She would bring photos of the motel, the trees, the birds, show her parents what her Australian life was like, tell them about her jobs, all the guesthouses over the years, tell them that she was still playing piano, still teaching piano.

She hadn't done any of that. She had never spoken to her mother again, or to her father. For the next month or more, she'd waited for a letter from Elizabeth. When it finally arrived, she had ripped it open, expecting – longing – to read the news that her mother had visited, that the first thing she had told Elizabeth was that Lola had rung, that she wished so much she hadn't been taken by surprise, that she had been able to talk to her.

There was no mention of the phone call in that letter. No mention in any subsequent letter either. There had been nothing about it in Elizabeth's journal today. Lola had read through that time period with even greater care than the other entries. If Lola's mother had confided in her friend, surely Elizabeth would have mentioned it? Phone calls were so rare and expensive, especially from Australia. But there was nothing. There was only one conclusion she could reach. Lola's mother hadn't told Elizabeth. Had she even told her husband about the phone call? Lola had no way of knowing.

All she had were those lines in Elizabeth's journal: *I know she loves her daughter. As much as she can, in her own way. I also feel sure she wishes everything was different.*

All Lola could do was hope, somehow, that they were true.

CHAPTER THIRTY-TWO

Bett and Ellen arrived at Sydney airport in the early morning. As soon as they collected their luggage, they hurried to the taxi rank. Bett had spoken briefly to Denise once they'd landed. She sounded calm. Glenn was conscious and eager to see his daughter.

Arriving at the hospital, they walked quickly through the foyer, past a cafe with a TV on the wall.

Ellen stopped. 'Look, there's Carrie.'

'Where?' Bett turned left and right.

'Not here. On the TV, look.'

As they watched, a photo of Rafe Ascot flashed onto the screen too. They moved closer but the segment finished. A music video began to play. There wasn't time to phone Carrie. After a quick conversation at the reception desk, they made their way to the lift, up three floors, along a wide, busy corridor, then along another smaller, quieter corridor to intensive care.

Before they were allowed in, they were asked to disinfect their hands and put covers on their shoes. Bett deliberately stood back as the nurse opened the door, but she still saw Glenn's face light up as Ellen ran across the room to him. At Glenn's bedside, Denise smiled too. She looked like she hadn't slept for days. Glenn managed a smile for Bett as well, before his attention returned fully to Ellen.

Denise joined Bett in the corridor. They hugged.

'How is he?' Bett asked.

'This morning's been better,' Denise said. 'Yesterday wasn't so good.'

Glenn's temperature had kept spiking during the night, she explained, and his blood pressure had fluctuated. Thankfully, in the past few hours he'd started to show signs of improvement. The doctors were continuing to monitor his heart and run a range of tests. They'd told Denise the prospect of a full recovery was good. They'd also determined the cause of his bacterial infection and it was now being treated. He'd be in hospital for some days yet. But she was feeling much more optimistic.

At Denise's invitation, Bett came into Glenn's room. He and Bett exchanged a smile as Ellen continued to chatter away to him.

'— and then we saw a leprechaun without its head on and a ruined castle but we didn't see any of Lola's places so Grandpa is going to take her instead of me.'

'That's good,' Glenn whispered. 'And did it rain all the time?'

'No, but it's really green,' Ellen said, appearing relaxed with the drips and bandages. It was Glenn who seemed different. So vulnerable, Bett thought. It wasn't just his body that appeared frail. His normal boisterous voice had been weakened by the illness too.

As she leaned down and gave him the gentlest of hugs, she saw tears in his eyes. She realised then how frightened he had been.

'Thank you, Bett,' he said softly.

'You're welcome, Glenn,' she whispered back.

It was just after dawn at Dublin airport. Des was keeping a close eye on the arrivals door. He had his iPad ready, JIM QUINLAN written on the screen. He'd called Lola that morning to say the plane was on time. He'd asked for a description of Jim, so he could easily spot him. Tall and smiley, Lola said.

'I'll have him to you as soon as I can, Lola.'

'You're a gem, Des.'

He'd felt himself blush at the words.

The first passengers off the Australian flight appeared, the tags on their luggage the giveaway. Des always loved this moment before he collected a new client, not knowing what they might be like, what he might get to discuss with them, what he might overhear them talking about. Breda had given him her normal warning that morning, telling him to be sure to stay quiet, reminding him that it had been a long flight for Jim Quinlan, and an unexpected trip at that. Another reminder to be sure to give Lola and her son all the peace they needed. It was quite a lecture. But in the next breath, she'd asked Des to be sure to ring her as soon as he could to fill her in about him.

'You're as bad as me,' he said, laughing.

'Not quite,' she said. 'You're one of a kind.'

Two compliments in twenty-four hours. A fellow had to be happy with that.

A tall man carrying one suitcase joined the crowds streaming through the arrivals doors. He had a ruddy complexion. An open and – yes, Des instantly decided – a cheerful face. It had to be Jim Quinlan. There was also something about his stature and his bearing that reminded him of Lola. The height but also a dignity. That was it: he looked dignified.

The man saw his name on the iPad and smiled in recognition, coming towards him. Des stepped forward, smiling too, and holding out his hand.

'Welcome to Dublin, Mr Quinlan. Desmond Foley, at your service.'

*

344

In Clare, Carrie wasn't happy. She'd thought it would be a great thing to go viral. She'd imagined it would be a combination of thrilling and empowering, knowing that a part of her was whizzing around the world, that people she didn't even know were reading her words or looking at her photo.

It was awful.

If she could turn back time, she would. She would delete that photo of Rafe Ascot. She wouldn't have taken it in the first place. She wouldn't have agreed to write the blog for Bett. She would have stayed perfectly happy living the life she'd been living before this TV crew chose the Clare Valley to film in and ruin her life in the process.

Beside her, the phone rang again. She ignored it. She'd started screening her calls, answering only Matthew and a few friends, though not the ones who'd forwarded her photo, causing this mess in the first place.

She ignored the voice that reminded her she was the one who'd first sent the photo to her friends. And that she was the one who had accepted the most recent media invitation.

She'd thought it would be good fun to be on TV. That's why she'd said yes when that morning show in Sydney got in touch, though she still didn't know how they'd got her number. They'd asked her if she would be able to travel to a studio in Adelaide or Port Pirie to do a link. Even the word 'link' had seemed exciting. She'd said yes straightaway, choosing Port Pirie. She could do with a shopping trip there anyway. She was more than happy to call into the TV station first.

Matthew had stayed in the car with the kids. She'd expected to be taken to have her makeup and hair done, but there'd been no such thing, only time to give herself the quickest dusting of powder and a hurried brush through her hair, before she found herself sitting at a desk with a blue screen behind her. Suddenly a man wearing headphones pointed to her, a red light appeared on top of the camera in front of her and she heard a woman who she couldn't even see asking question after question. So, what had Rafe Ascot been like? Had he made a pass at her? Were there other even worse photos? Had he asked for her number? All the time, she'd been able to hear the woman's co-hosts giggling and interjecting in the background, as if they weren't taking it seriously at all.

She'd stuttered and stammered her way through it. They'd said goodbye to her in less than a minute, obviously disappointed with her. But what else could she have said? He hadn't made a pass at her. There hadn't been any other photos. That one alone had got her into enough trouble.

The interview had gone to air yesterday, and been shown on repeats today. The phone calls had kept coming, and so had the emails. Whoever had received her forwarded email with the photo of Rafe also had her email address. Normally she got about two emails a day, if that. In the past two days she'd received one hundred and twenty, all from strangers, and some of them really disgusting.

She'd been counting down the hours until Bett arrived home. She'd have welcomed her sister telling her off. She hoped even more fervently that Bett would somehow take control of it all again. But Bett had only rung quickly to say they were back in Sydney, at the hospital, that Glenn was doing well and that he seemed happy and relieved that Ellen was back home again.

Carrie already knew Glenn was okay. She wasn't that self-obsessed. She'd been texting Denise and getting all the updates. But this photo business kept taking over. What a mess.

She'd had lots of emails from that cranky TV producer too. She'd decided to ignore those. She was also trying to ignore all the comments that had started appearing under her posts on the news-paper website too. At the start, they'd all been from her friends in the Valley, leaving lovely supportive messages: *Great blog, Carrie!*

SOOOO jealous, Carrie! Can't wait to read more, Carrie!!

In the past day, the whole mood had changed. Complete strangers were saying the meanest things about her and her blog: *Who writes this drivel??? A six-year-old?? Don't give six-year-olds a bad name!! WTF??? Is this supposed to be journalism? No wonder newspapers are a dying breed.*

She'd stopped reading them after that, but not quickly enough. She'd seen a really disgusting comment, not about her article but about her photo, from someone called HotDude96 telling her what he'd like to do to her. In graphic detail.

That was when she phoned Luke, Lola's computer guru. He was now here beside her, in their living room, at her computer. He was so calm, so smart. She wanted to adopt him, she felt so grateful.

'Okay, Carrie, step one done,' he said, still typing on the keyboard. 'I've disabled the comments function, so no one can leave any more. I'll delete any that have already been left.'

'All of them? Can you keep the nice ones? The ones from my friends?'

'I think it's better if we delete the whole lot.'

'Can I take a screen shot of the nice ones first, though, so I can —' She stopped. 'Okay. Sure. Yes, delete them all, please.'

More clicking on the keyboard. All the comments disappeared.

'I'll disable your email address as well,' he said. 'That means if anyone emails you they'll get a bounce back telling them that the email address is no longer in use.'

'But how will I get emails?'

'You'll have to set up a new one.'

'What about my old emails?'

'I'll put them in an archive. You can access them later.'

He was so quick, his fingers flying across the keyboard as he set up a new email address and imported her contacts. It was a relief to see that shiny new empty inbox.

As Luke watched beside her, she wrote a quick message to everyone on her list.

Dear Friends

In light of recent events, I've had to close down my old email address. Please use this one for me from now on and PLEASE PLEASE don't pass it on to anyone else. Thank you!!!

Carrie xoxoxox

'So was he really that horrible?' Luke asked her as she pressed send.

'I can't remember. Too much has happened since. Luke, can you please google me. I don't dare to any more.'

'Is that a good idea? You might not like what I find.'

'I think it's better I know.'

She shut her eyes while he started googling. This was so weird, she thought. She could hear Matthew outside playing with the kids. In here, her whole life was being ruined through a computer screen. The panicky feeling started to rise again. She patted her stomach protectively, sending an ESP message to her baby: *I'm sorry, little one. I promise this will all be over by the time you arrive.*

'Okay, Carrie,' Luke said. 'There is quite a bit of new stuff about you. It's not great, to be honest.'

She opened one eye, saw the images on the screen and shut it tight again. 'What the hell was that?'

'It's called a meme,' Luke said. 'It's when people take a photo and add a funny caption to it.'

'How did they get my photo?'

'Off your blog.'

'Not that one. The other one?'

'I think that's from the TV interview you did. It looks like a freeze frame or screen shot.'

She quickly peered at it again and winced. 'That is gross. That's horrible. How sexist.'

'Trolls usually are.'

'Trolls did this?'

He explained what the term meant: anonymous people who took pleasure in insulting and threatening people – usually women – online.

'What can we do to stop them?' Carrie asked.

'Nothing.'

'Nothing?'

Luke gestured at the screen. 'It's a big world out there in the internet, Carrie. No one is in charge. There are no laws or rules, really. But don't worry. Someone else will soon make a silly mistake like you and they'll be the new target. Everyone will forget about you.'

There were more insults in those words of his than she wanted to hear. 'This is a nightmare.'

'Have you told Bett?'

'Some of it,' she said in a small voice. As if Bett had been eavesdropping, Carrie's phone rang.

She snatched it up. 'Bett! Hi! How are you? How's Glenn? Any change?'

'Not since last time I spoke to you,' Bett replied. She explained that she was at Denise and Glenn's house. Ellen was still at the hospital with her dad. The staff had been so kind to her.

'How are you?' Bett asked. 'How are things there?'

'Oh, fine,' Carrie said. 'It's pretty quiet.' She had to lie. Bett had just arrived home after a long flight, a long unexpected flight. She might not be thinking straight yet.

'Really?' Bett said. 'You haven't been busy appearing on TV shows while I was in the air?'

Carrie didn't try to defend herself. 'Bett, I'm so sorry. I know I should have said no. It's awful. I'm —'

'Carrie, stop apologising. And don't worry.'

'Don't worry? I thought you'd be furious with me.'

'Not yet. Let's sort it out first.'

Her sister's calm reaction was the best Carrie could have hoped for. In a rush, she poured out everything that had happened since they'd last spoken.

'It's as if it's my fault he's a rude drunk!' she said. 'No one is saying anything about him online. I'm the villain for taking the photo and sending it to a few friends. It's so not fair.'

'Welcome to the internet, Carrie. Welcome to being a woman on the internet.'

'It's vicious out there. Thank God Luke's been amazing. He's here, fixing everything up for me.'

'Luke is there now? Can you put him on?'

Carrie handed over the phone and sat back as Luke and Bett had what sounded like a very technical conversation. Luke handed back the phone to her.

Bett was still calm. 'Okay, he's got everything possible under control. Good call, getting him in.'

Carrie swallowed. 'I've also had some emails from the TV producer. I haven't read all of them, but —'

'I have. She copied me in. She's been in touch with me directly too.'

Carrie could just imagine what she'd said. 'I'm sorry, Bett,' she said again.

'Don't worry. Leave her to me. You know the saying, there's no such thing as bad publicity.'

'That's what they think? That this is all okay? That it's been good for the TV series?'

'Not completely. Rafe has apparently left Australia. Said he didn't fly all this way to be humiliated.'

'Oh, no. Oh, no! What does that mean for the TV series?'

'Presumably his agent will try to calm him down. I don't know. I don't really care about him. Are you okay? It can't have been much fun for you.'

Carrie couldn't stop herself. She burst into tears. 'It's been horrible. Can you please come home?'

Fifteen minutes later, Bett was still sitting on the bed in the spare room of Denise and Glenn's very nice house in Mosman.

After she'd hung up from Carrie, she'd sat quietly, thinking. Normally, she would have rung Daniel straightaway to share the latest update. But these weren't normal circumstances. She'd already spoken to Daniel twice since she got home, and also spoken – as much as possible – to the twins. They'd burbled down the phone to her, the sound filling her with joy, with a longing to see them, for everything to go back to normal. Nothing had happened as she'd expected lately. She wasn't in Ireland. She wasn't with Lola and Ellen. She was here in this strange house when her own husband and children were just a two-hour flight away. And now her sister was in the middle of a nasty piece of internet bullying, her own fault, admittedly, but still . . .

Bett hadn't told Carrie everything that the TV producer had said in her email, or everything that Rafe had said about her. For some reason, the producer had felt it necessary to share his words in full with Bett: *Some two-bit, useless, brainless, pregnant bimbo local reporter has wrecked my career. Well, fuck her and fuck the lot of you. I'm going home.* Carrie was right. He was horrible. But Bett still felt sure it would all blow over once another internet scandal arrived. She also suspected the actor wouldn't be allowed to walk away. Surely contracts were involved? Carrie was upset now too, but in a day or two it would all be forgotten. In the meantime, Bett had urged her to stay off the internet and concentrate on Matthew and her children. The real things in her life.

'You're right, Bett,' Carrie had said, her sobs finally subsiding. 'Who wants to be part of that shallow entertainment world, any-way? Not me, that's for sure. I'm still going to keep doing a blog, but I'm going to make it all about real life, family and food and living the country dream. Would that work as a good name for my website, do you think? "My Country Dream"?'

It was a perfect name, Bett had told her, fighting an urge to scream.

Bett suddenly wished she could click her fingers and be back home in the Valley, with Daniel beside her, her babies in her arms, feeling safe, secure, loved. But could she leave Ellen yet? Just a few hours after arriving back in Australia?

There was a knock at the door. It was Denise with a cup of tea. 'I thought you might need this.'

Bett smiled. 'More than you could know.'

They sat side by side on the bed. Bett had never spent much time with Denise. Not for any bad reason. She'd been genuinely happy for Glenn that he had found love again after Anna. Especially knowing what she knew about Anna and Glenn's marriage. Denise hadn't been the cause of that breakdown. She had only met Glenn two years after Anna had died. And she was good for him, Bett had seen that. They had a strong marriage. If Ellen had to have a stepmother, Denise was a fine choice. Her daughter, Lily, was a fine stepsister too.

'It must have been such a frightening time for you all,' Bett said to Denise.

Denise nodded. 'The shock of it. Thinking it was indigestion and it all happening so quickly – the ambulance, the hospital, intensive care. I'm sorry for spoiling your trip, Bett. He seems so much better now but we just didn't know what might happen.'

'You did exactly the right thing. Ellen needed to be here.'

'I'm very fond of Ellen. I hope you know that.'

'I do, Denise. You're doing a great job with her. She can be a handful.'

A wry smile. 'Tell me about it.'

They had a brief exchange of Ellen stories. The battle with the phone. Her disappearing act. In return, Denise shared tales of spectacular temper tantrums, followed by complete contrition. Teenage moodiness, followed by rushes of affection.

'I suspect a career on the stage is ahead of her, would you say?'

'I'd bet my two firstborn on it,' Bett said.

There was a moment of silence before Denise spoke again. 'What was Anna like, Bett?'

Bett wasn't sure how to answer.

Denise continued. 'I know what she looked like. I've talked about her with Glenn too. But what was she like as a sister?'

The question was suddenly too much for Bett, on top of the long flight, feeling responsible for not just Ellen but Lola too, being away from her husband and children . . . She did her best to keep her voice steady. 'She was wonderful. Kind. Funny. She was infuriating. She was always right, you see. It was maddening. She was so elegant too, so beautifully groomed, at all times. And she was so thin. Annoyingly thin.' Bett was laughing softly now. 'I know it wasn't effortless, but she never put on any weight. Ever. We used to joke that her share of the world's kilos always somehow found their way to me.'

She turned serious again. 'She balanced us. Me and Carrie. It's hard to explain, but she always made it better between us. And I loved her so much. And I miss her. Every day.' She took a deep breath. 'I'm sorry. It's been five years now, and I thought that it would stop hurting, but it hasn't. Look at me. I still can't talk about her without wanting to cry.'

'I'm sorry, Bett,' Denise said quietly.

The mood between them was gentle. Bett asked something she'd wanted to know for some time.

'Does Ellen talk about Anna much?'

'A lot.'

'And is that okay for you?'

'Most of the time, yes. Sometimes, when she's in a temper, it's not quite so okay.'

Bett could imagine what Ellen might shout in one of her tempers.

'But I try to talk about it with her afterwards. And I tell her that I know she misses her mum so much and I also wish she hadn't got sick. And then I always promise to try to be the best friend for her that I can be. I use that word, friend, rather than stepmother. And it feels right. For us both, I think. I care about her very much, and I hope she is growing fond of me too.' Denise turned to Bett then. 'Did you know Glenn made a tape of Anna's voice for her?'

Bett nodded. 'She played it for me in Ireland. Did you mind?'

'Was I jealous, do you mean?'

'Yes.' She admired Denise for asking so honestly.

'I was at first, yes,' Denise said. 'Anna was so beautiful. So talented. Glenn had obviously loved her very much, in the beginning at least. But – this might sound terrible, Bett, and I'm sorry if it does – I think it would be even harder for me if Anna hadn't died. If she and Glenn had divorced, if she was still here in Sydney, sharing custody of Ellen with Glenn, in contact with him —'

Bett had to hide a sharp intake of breath. How could Denise say that to Anna's grieving sister? She forced herself not to react, to keep listening. She knew Denise had been without much sleep for days.

'Glenn loves Ellen so dearly,' Denise continued. 'He'll do anything for her. And at first I was envious of that too. But I decided it was one more thing to love about Glenn. That it was wonderful to see a father care so deeply for his daughter. That I couldn't see it as a bad thing. That helped me.'

'And Lily?'

'Lily loves Ellen to pieces and thinks Glenn is the bee's knees. And he says she's the cat's pyjamas.' She smiled. 'Her own father lives in America. He never sees her. Glenn is so kind to her. She congratulated me the other day for finding Glenn, as if I'd gone out foraging in a market.'

'I'm glad you found him too.' It was the truth.

'Thank you, Bett.'

After Denise left the room, Bett knew her question had been answered. Ellen would be fine here. She was safe. Happy. Loved.

Bett could go home to her own family.

CHAPTER THIRTY-THREE

Two hours after farewelling Denise, Bett was on her way back to Sydney airport. She'd got a seat on the last flight to Adelaide. En route to the airport, she had briefly visited Glenn and Ellen in the hospital to say goodbye. Glenn was looking even better. He understood completely that she wanted to go home. So did Ellen. They hugged each other tightly.

In the taxi, she called Daniel again. She'd tried him earlier and got only his voicemail. This time he answered.

'You'll be back tonight?' he said, when she explained. 'In just a few hours?'

'Is that okay?'

'It's fantastic. Great.' He'd taken her flight details and then abruptly hung up.

She stared down at her phone. Admittedly, she was jet-lagged, tired, her nerves jangling. But she also knew she wasn't imagining it. He'd sounded strange again.

As her taxi arrived at the airport, another wave of exhaustion hit her. Another urge to cry. What would Lola tell her if she was here? She could easily imagine the words: *Calm down, Bett. You've got more than an hour before your flight leaves. Enjoy it, you silly girl. It might be the last peaceful hour you have for the next ten years. If I were you, I'd check in, then go and have a gin and tonic. It always works wonders for me.*

She did as she was told. Lola was right, once again. A G&T had never tasted so good.

Des and Jim were halfway to Kildare. Jim was in the front passenger seat. At the airport, he'd laughed at the idea of travelling in the back seat.

'I'd feel like you were being my chauffeur.'

'I am your chauffeur.'

'I've never been driven around before. That's novelty enough for me, thanks, Des.'

Des had felt relaxed with him straightaway. Jim seemed happy to answer all his questions, and asked plenty in return. Even before they'd got onto the motorway, Des had told Jim about his and Breda's travel plans. He'd also heard all about Jim's flight – the movies he'd watched and all that he'd eaten. The meals in economy sounded pretty delicious, to be honest. He'd asked Jim all about the Clare Valley, and heard about all its Irish connections. He'd heard all about Jim's new guesthouse in the Adelaide Hills too. If he and Breda ever made it to South Australia, they'd come and stay, for sure.

Des loved knowing all the answers to Jim's questions too, about the bilingual road signs, the green fields he'd seen from the plane before they landed, the car registration plates that showed not just numbers but also the initials of counties. He reeled off the names of all twenty-six Irish counties, then the six counties of Northern Ireland. He gave Jim the briefest history of the Troubles that he could, a quick rundown of the Easter Rising, about the War of Independence, the signing of the Treaty that had resulted in the creation of Northern Ireland, the civil war that had followed . . .

Jim seemed really interested too. Usually Des cursed traffic jams on this motorway. Today they were great.

Once again, he remarked on the fact this was Jim's first trip to Ireland. A double homecoming, for him as well as Lola, he said.

'I guess so,' Jim said. 'I've always thought of myself as Aussie through and through, though. Even with an Irish mother.'

'She's one in a million, isn't she?'

'She is. Always has been.'

'What about your father? Was he Irish too?'

Jim nodded. 'From the same part of Kildare as Lola.'

Des frowned. Now he thought about it, had there been any talk at all about Lola's husband? He didn't think so. That was odd. Especially if he had come from the same area. 'Were they married long before they emigrated?'

'About a day, I think.' Jim grinned. 'Not that I've ever spoken about this much with my mother, but I think it might have been what we used to call a shotgun marriage. I arrived six months after they were married. Maybe I was premature.'

'What age were you when your father died?'

'Just a baby.' Jim seemed to hesitate. 'He died during the war.'

'In the Irish Army? But we were neutral.'

'No, the Australian Army. He joined up after they emigrated.'

'Where was he killed?'

'I don't know exactly.'

'But it's all online these days, isn't it? I saw a TV documentary about it. I mean, the one I saw was about the Irish Army, but it would be the same with the Australian Army, wouldn't it? Photos of all the soldiers, copies of their paperwork, all of it. You could even find out exactly where he's buried, not just which cemetery, but the exact location in the cemetery.'

Jim made a noncommittal sound.

'Sorry,' Des said. 'None of my business.'

'You're okay, Des. But I might try for a bit of a nap, if you don't mind, until we get to where Mum is.'

'Go right ahead. You won't miss much scenery. It's pretty much motorways from here.'

See, Des! He imagined Breda again. *You've bored the poor man to sleep and him just off the plane.*

At the next set of lights, he sent an update text to Lola: *ETA twenty minutes from now.*

He glanced across. Jim was fast asleep. Or if he wasn't, he was doing a good job pretending.

Lola was getting ready to go downstairs and wait in the foyer for Jim's arrival when her phone beeped. It was Des, letting her know they were getting close.

How wonderful. It was all simply wonderful, the way everything was working out.

She had thought her Irish homecoming had been a terrible mistake. But in the space of a day, it had all changed. What unexpected turns life could take. She had Des to thank for it all too, she'd realised. Because the truth was, if his car hadn't broken down, Lola would never have got to read Elizabeth's journal or her own letters. How else would Jean have learnt that she was back in Kildare? It was meant to be. Lola had to believe that fate or some other higher being was at work at times like this.

She had slept surprisingly well. She'd expected to lie awake the rest of the night, her head filled with the conversation with Jean, with all she had read in the letters and journal. But it was as if everything had nourished her, not exhausted her. She'd woken up feeling better than she had in months. She'd also woken up knowing something else.

She was going to give her letters to Jim to read.

It was all there, after all. The truth about the early years of his life. The truth about his father, the drinking, the violence. Why Lola had left. But the letters had contained other stories too, about Jim. As a baby. A boy. A teenager. Stories about his sunny personality, his sense of humour. How affectionate he was. How much she loved him. *My lovely boy*, she often called him.

She hoped Jim would enjoy reading all of that about himself. She also hoped it would make reading about his father easier.

Elizabeth must have asked in one of her letters if Lola would ever tell Jim the truth.

I will when and if the time feels right. For now, he doesn't need to know more.

She'd checked the date. She'd written it fifty-three years ago. The right time had taken a long while to arrive. But it was here now. This was also the best place to tell him. In Ireland. Just the two of them.

Bett already knew some of the truth, of course. Five years earlier, she had read the letter from Edward's sister that had arrived unexpectedly at the Valley View Motel. Lola had been forced to admit to her that Edward hadn't died in the war, a revelation that Bett had promised to keep secret. There was so much more Lola hadn't shared. Perhaps down the track, she would tell Bett – and Carrie – the whole story.

But it was Jim who would hear it first.

Fifteen minutes later, she was waiting in the foyer. She'd changed into the brightest outfit she could find among her travelling clothes. A red taffeta skirt. A yellow-and-green-striped shirt. Her green shoes. She'd put on more makeup than usual. She caught a few amused glances from other guests, and smiled back at them.

She saw the car arrive. She saw the two men inside.

She was waiting at the front door as Jim, her lovely boy, got out of the car and walked towards her.

*

In a small house in a southern suburb of Adelaide, Daniel was sweating from his exertions. He thanked the woman again, handing over six hundred dollars. It was more than he'd expected to pay, but it was worth every cent.

It had all happened so quickly. He'd thought he had at least another week before Bett came home. But that had all changed in the past twenty-four hours. He'd had to move everything forward, call in favours, not just from his neighbour Jane, but from Len the butcher in Clare. Len was the only person he knew who had a van the right size. He could have hired one but it would have cost even more dollars. He didn't have them to spend.

But it was now done. It was loaded safely in the van. Len had promised – sworn on his mother's life, in fact – that he would drive slowly. Jane had the house key and would let him in. Two of Daniel's friends, both strong country footballers, had agreed to be there to meet Len. He'd told him twice exactly where it had to go.

And while all that was happening – as smoothly as possible, Daniel hoped – he'd be making his way to Adelaide airport to collect Bett. She'd sounded a bit odd on the phone today. He'd started to wonder if she'd guessed he was up to something. He'd tell her the whole story soon. But not yet. Not until she had seen it for herself.

He turned and thanked the woman again. She was in her seventies, a retired teacher. Once he'd seen her photo on the website, he'd known for sure. He liked that it had been used to teach many children over many years. He knew Bett would like that too. So would Lola.

He'd have liked to ask Lola for her advice. No one knew more on the subject than her. But he hadn't wanted to ring her, especially when all her Irish plans had turned upside down, with Bett and Ellen back here, and Jim on his way there. He was probably landing around about now, in fact.

Len slammed the back door of the van shut. 'All set, Danny. All secure.'

Daniel thanked him again. 'And you'll drive slowly?'

'You betcha. It couldn't be in safer hands.'

Daniel just hoped it wouldn't smell of chops and sausages once he got it home. He watched as Len slowly reversed, then drove off towards Clare, giving a cheery few blasts of his horn in farewell.

Now, to the airport. To Bett. He couldn't wait.

He walked over to the car, smiling in at the back seat. 'Ready, kiddos?' Yvette and Zachary smiled back at him, safe in their car seats. 'Let's go and get your mum, will we?'

In Kildare, Lola half-expected Des to come into the hotel, sit down and join them. She'd grown fond of him, but he was inclined to overstep the mark occasionally. Thankfully he was being a model driver today, carrying Jim's bag in, helping him check in and then saying he'd leave them to it.

'You get over the flight, Jim, and just give me a call whenever you both want to be driven anywhere. I'm at your beck and call and I can be back here before you know it.'

After he had gone, Lola hugged her son again. 'Thank you for coming, Jim.'

'As soon as my brain rejoins my body, I'll say no worries, Mum.' He laughed. 'It's a long way, isn't it?'

She smiled. 'It certainly is.'

Tea was in order, she decided. They could sit here in the foyer until his room was ready and he could take a shower.

'How is Geraldine?' she asked. 'I hope she knows how grateful I am that she let you come away at such short notice?'

'She's busy but she'll be fine. How are you, Mum? Has the

homecoming been all you expected?'

She told him briefly about her solo trip the previous day, how she hadn't been able to go there with Bett and Ellen. 'I hadn't expected that. I could have saved them the bother of the trip. Not that they had much of a holiday in the end.'

'Short but sweet. And Glenn is still improving?'

'Getting better every day,' Lola reported.

'I'll understand if you don't want me to go to any of the places with you, either. But I'd still like to see them. On my own if I need to.'

'No, Jim. I'd like to show you everything.' She hesitated. 'I've so many stories to tell you.'

'I'm all ears,' he said.

He'd read an entire Irish tourist guide during the flight, he told her. He'd been surprised to realise Ireland was only the same size as Tasmania. He was hoping to see as much of her Kildare as he could, as well as anything to do with his father, but he hoped they'd get to see more of the country too. He mentioned his father so casually, so easily. Lola hoped it wasn't obvious how tense she'd become. Perhaps they could hire a car, he said. Go sightseeing. But it was all up to her.

No need to hire a car, she told him. They had Des at their disposal, already fully paid for the week.

Jim grimaced. 'I'm not sure I can handle that. Not for a whole week. He talks a lot, doesn't he?'

'He does,' Lola agreed.

'Maybe we could come to some arrangement with him,' Jim said. 'Hire our own car, or even hire his and I'll do the driving. Just the two of us. I wouldn't mind trying some of these terrible Irish roads I've been reading about.'

'It's all motorways now,' she said, already enjoying that he was taking charge.

'We'll leave them behind,' Jim said. 'Go off the beaten track. An Irish road trip – what do you say?'

'It sounds wonderful,' she said.

It did. She hadn't even thought of the possibility of Jim driving, of the two of them heading off on their own. What a special thing to do, tour her home country with her beloved son. Making up an itinerary as they went along, perhaps to Cork, to Kerry, to Clare, to Galway. All that time together.

All that time to talk.

The journal and letters were upstairs on her bedside table. Everything she wanted to tell Jim was in them. But she couldn't simply hand them to Jim, could she, and say, *There's something I've been meaning to tell you, but the right opportunity never seemed to arise. But it's all here if you'd like to have a read. I'll be across the hall if you have any questions.*

The receptionist called their names. Jim's room was ready. He'd go up and shower, he told her. Unpack. They arranged that he would call at Lola's room in thirty minutes.

Exactly half an hour later, back in her room, she heard a knock on her door. He was always so punctual. He'd changed his clothes. His hair was still wet from the shower. She couldn't stop smiling at him. 'Are you exhausted, darling?'

'No, I feel great. I haven't sat that still for so long in years. I feel like I've had a holiday already.'

'I'm delighted to hear it,' she said. She gestured towards the table and two chairs overlooking the gardens. The latest wedding was in its early stages but Lola knew she wouldn't be watching this one.

Now. Tell him now.

'Sit down, Jim darling, would you? I've got something to tell you. Something important.'

'There's something I need to tell you too,' he said.

She had a hunch what it was. He and Geraldine had decided to sell the motel, not just lease it. But there was plenty of time to discuss that.

'Could I please go first?' she said.

'Of course,' Jim said.

He sat down, waiting.

CHAPTER THIRTY-FOUR

Bett's seat was at the back of the plane. It took twenty minutes from the time they landed in Adelaide before she was making her way up the ramp into the airport building. The gin had helped her mood. So had the hour's sleep on the flight. She'd been away for less than a week, but it felt like months. She scanned the waiting people, looking for Daniel, longing to see him. She looked left. No sign of him. Right. Still no sign. She checked her phone. No message either.

'Bett!'

She wasn't the only one who turned around. Daniel was running towards her, pushing a double pram. In it were her son and daughter. All three were smiling.

They met halfway. Daniel swept her up in his arms and she found herself laughing and crying at once. He spoke, then she spoke over him, in between the hugs she was giving him and then her babies, both still alert even this late at night. They wrapped their little arms around her neck, Yvette giving her a sloppy kiss, Zach reaching straight up to grasp a lock of her hair, as he'd liked to do since he was a tiny baby.

She looped her arm in Daniel's as they made their way to the baggage collection, talking nonstop. She stayed close as they walked to their car. It felt so normal, all she'd hoped for. The twins suddenly succumbed to tiredness. Yvette was asleep as they put her into her car seat. Zachary reached up for one more tug of Bett's hair before he fell asleep too.

It was only once Daniel had negotiated their car out of the car park, through the city outskirts and onto the main road north to Clare that she stopped talking. She reached across and took his hand. He held it tight for a moment, kissed it, and continued to hold it.

'I've so much more to tell you but I might just shut my eyes for a minute,' she said.

'You go right ahead,' he said.

Moments later, he looked across. She was fast asleep.

Ninety minutes later, a few kilometres from their house, he pulled in to the side of the road. After making sure Bett and the twins were still asleep, he quickly tapped out a text to Len: *All okay?*

Roger, Len texted back. *As in Roger, Daniel. Not that your name is Roger LOL!!!!!!*

Thanks, Daniel texted. Then he had a thought. *Have you left yet?*

Five minutes ago. Did you want us to be there too?

No, he shot back. *No thanks*, he sent a moment later.

Bett woke as he drove into their front yard. He asked her to please stay in the car. Dozy still, she obeyed him. He lifted first Zachary and then Yvette out of their seats and carried them inside to their cots. He came back for her luggage. It was only on that trip that he quickly checked the living room. It was there. Exactly where he'd asked Len to put it. It looked perfect.

Bett was still in the car. He opened the passenger door, asking her to keep her eyes shut. She got out carefully. They were standing close. Before they moved any further, he leaned down and kissed her, on her mouth, on her closed eyes, on her forehead. 'I missed you, Bett Quinlan.'

'I missed you too, Daniel Hilder.' She put her arms around him.

'It's no fun without you here,' he said. 'Please don't ever go away with Lola to Ireland again on a last-minute trip that gets cut short for sad reasons that turn out to be okay reasons.'

'I promise,' she said.

There was another quick kiss that turned into a longer kiss. She pressed against him, feeling his long, strong body, his hand on her back, his hand reaching up under her T-shirt. It was like being a teenager again. These were like stolen kisses, out in the darkness, her eyes tightly shut. The longing rose inside her, as his lips left her mouth, moved to her neck, to her collarbone, back to her lips.

They still had a spark between them. Thank God, she thought, giving in to it as he kissed her neck again, as his hand stroked her back, as she in turn lifted his T-shirt, felt his bare skin, as they pressed closer against each other. This was where she wanted to be. Back home, back with her darling, her babies inside, safe and —

Cold. He'd stopped kissing her and moved away.

'I really didn't want to do that,' he said. 'That was really difficult. But I need you to come inside.'

She felt dreamy, dazed. 'You're right. It's too cold out here. And we're too old to get back in the car and do it there.'

He laughed then, a low laugh that had the same effect on her as his kisses had. '"Do it"? I am officially seventeen again. If you're good, I promise we'll "do it" properly later in a proper bed, like the grown-ups do. But there's something else I have to show you first. Shut your eyes again.'

She did, letting him lead her inside, asking questions but being silenced. She heard the back door creak, felt the floorboards in the kitchen under her feet, then the carpet as they went down the hall and turned right into their living room. Had he painted it while she was gone?

'Eyes shut still, please,' he said as he released her hand. She sensed him move away from her. 'Okay. You can open your eyes.'

She opened them. He was across the room. The ceiling light and every lamp in the room was on.

He was standing beside a piano.

A beautiful upright wooden piano.

She stared at it. She put her hand to her mouth. She could only speak in single-word sentences. 'Where? How? When?'

He smiled. 'I found it in Adelaide. Via the internet.' He checked his watch. 'When? About three hours ago.'

She walked over to it. She opened the lid. Stared down at it. A piano. Her own piano.

He knew what she was thinking. 'They're fast asleep. I shut their bedroom door. Play it.'

She took a seat on the polished stool, placed her hands on the keyboard and felt the keys, the soft wonderful keys, beneath her fingers. She played a note. Another note. Another. A tune began to form, the notes so sweet and perfect in the lamplight of the room. It was as if she had been playing every day for years. She didn't need sheet music, she didn't need to think. Her head was full of songs, classical pieces, pop songs, traditional Irish music, vaudeville tunes. Lola had made sure she could play anything. She skipped between them, a little bit of Chopin, a little bit of West Side Story, a chorus of 'Down by the Salley Gardens', even a line or two of a Justin Timberlake song. She only played for five minutes but she could feel the music in every cell of her body. She stopped abruptly, put her hands on her lap and turned to her husband.

'This is what you've been doing? The wiped internet searches? The odd phone calls?'

He nodded. 'This is what I've been doing.'

She stood up, gently closed the lid and moved to her husband instead. She put her hand on his cheek and kissed him as he'd kissed her outside. She kissed him first on the mouth, then on each cheek, then on his forehead. Before she kissed him on the mouth again, before everything began to build between them, as she knew they both needed, she whispered her thanks and told him what he already knew. That she loved him very, very much.

CHAPTER THIRTY-FIVE

Lola had never truly imagined having this conversation about Edward with Jim. But now, here it was.

There could be no prevaricating. No grey areas. She asked him to hear her out, to listen before he asked questions. She promised him she would answer anything he asked, as truthfully as she could. Then she began.

'Jim, I've lied to you all your life. I told you that your father was a soldier and that he had died in the war. That wasn't true. He was a drunk, and a bully, and he hurt us. So I left him. I left him once when I was still pregnant with you, and then I returned to him, under pressure from my parents. And it was worse, and so one day, when you were two months old, I left for good.'

He didn't move. He didn't speak. He sat across from her, watching her, listening. She couldn't read any reaction in his face. He was just listening.

She kept talking. She told him about the kind guesthouse owner, who had run a refuge as much as a business. She told him about standing outside the pub seeing Edward drinking, laughing with his friends, less than an hour after he had hit them both. She told him about the decision to lie and say she was a war widow. The decision to keep moving, determined to stay away from Edward but also worried that one day he might come looking for her. Jim already knew the stories of their early moves. They were his stories too.

She told him about her parents. How they had been ashamed enough of her before she went to Australia. How they had disowned her when she left Edward. She told him about her phone call with her mother. Her last contact with her. How that had made this trip home even more difficult.

She told him about her letters to Elizabeth, telling her everything. How she had read those letters only the day before, read Elizabeth's journal only the day before, when fate, happenstance, had brought her into the orbit of Elizabeth's family again.

She stopped then. He still hadn't spoken.

'Please, Jim, ask me anything. Be angry at me if you need to. I can't apologise, because I can't fix any of it, or change any of it. All I can do is finally tell you the truth and hope you understand.'

His face was still. She couldn't read anger or disappointment. He was just watching her. As if he was seeing her for the first time? As if he had been let down, completely let down, by the mother he thought he had loved? The mother he thought he could trust?

No, it wasn't that. He was calm. Not angry.

'Have you got the letters here?' he asked. 'The ones you wrote to Elizabeth?'

'Yes. Her journal too.'

'Can I read them?'

'Now?'

'We've got time, haven't we?'

'Yes. Yes, we do. All the time in the world.'

She fetched them from the drawer behind her. The bundle of letters. The journal. She had already marked the pages that mentioned her, not in preparation for this moment, but for her own memory aid. She explained as much to Jim.

He nodded. 'Thank you.'

'Do you want me to leave you alone?'

'No, I'd like you to stay.'

He didn't speak again for more than an hour. He quietly opened each envelope, read the letter, folded it again and returned it to its envelope. One after the other. He picked up the journal. He turned to each of the marked pages, read slowly, then turned to the next entry. No comment. Barely any movement. She watched his face but he was still giving nothing away.

At one stage, she made them both a cup of tea. She placed his on the table beside him. He thanked her without looking up, and took a sip. She sat back at the window overlooking the gardens and drank her own tea. The wedding was underway below. The sky was blue. All those prayers had worked. The bride looked beautiful.

Finally, she heard the journal being shut, then a rustle as he straightened the pile of letters.

'Thank you,' he said.

'Thank you?' she echoed.

'Thank you for telling me. For letting me read all of these.' He gestured at the journal, the letters.

She was wary, waiting for – for what? Anger? Disapproval? No. That wasn't Jim's way. He was not that kind of man. He hadn't been that kind of boy. For all she had waited for elements of his father to emerge, they never had. He had arrived his own person and he had stayed that way, all his life.

'I'm sorry I lied to you,' she said.

'Don't be. I don't blame you. I can understand completely why you lied.'

'Just from the letters?'

He shook his head.

'Then how? If I'd known you'd take it like this, I'd have told you years ago. How can you be so calm?'

'Because I know exactly why you did what you did.' He paused. 'Because I met Edward too.'

CHAPTER THIRTY-SIX

Lola could only stare at Jim. Had she misheard? Misunderstood? 'You mean as a baby?'

'No,' he said, still calm. 'I met him as an adult. The year I turned twenty-one.'

Lola had a sudden sensation that she was falling. A strange dizzying feeling. She couldn't have heard that. It wasn't possible.

Jim began to speak. It was her turn to sit quietly. To listen without interrupting.

'We had just moved to Portland in Victoria. To that ten-room guesthouse, with the verandah that had the sea view. We'd been there a month, perhaps six weeks. You were going to Melbourne for the day, to buy new linen. You said you couldn't let our guests use the old sheets any longer, or our good reputation would be tarnished forever. Then one of your friends from your hostel days rang. There was a musical on in that big Melbourne theatre – would you go see it with her, and stay the night?'

Lola remembered it as clearly as Jim was telling it now.

'You tried to say that we couldn't afford it, not just the linen, but the theatre ticket, a night's accommodation. I insisted. I told you I could look after the guesthouse on my own for one night. We only had three guests booked in. I eventually convinced you.

'It was past eight when I heard the bell ring. I'd checked in the other guests and thought this was a late arrival. I opened the door. It was a man in his fifties. An Irishman. Dark hair. Overweight.'

Lola waited, tensing.

'It was a cool night, but he was sweating. I remember thinking that was odd. I welcomed him. Asked was he looking for a room? Not exactly, he said. He was looking for a person. For people. Who? I asked. A woman called Lola Quinlan nee Delaney, he said. And her son James.

'I nearly said, "I'm James." I nearly said, "Lola is my mother but she's not here at the moment." But something stopped me. I asked him who he was. I can't explain it but even before he spoke, I knew he wasn't going to say he was an old friend of yours from Ireland, or a friend from your early days. I had only ever seen your wedding photo. The man in front of me couldn't have looked more different. But I knew who he was.

'I asked him his name. I still hadn't said I was James. I needed to hear him confirm it first. He stuck out his hand. "Where are my manners? My name is Edward Quinlan." And I shook his hand and said, "I'm James Quinlan."

'He barely reacted. He didn't say, "Son, my long-lost son!" He didn't say anything about not having seen me for nearly twenty years. He asked could he come in? I said yes. He asked if it would be possible for him to have something to eat. I said yes. Then he asked me if he could have something to drink.

'Yes, I said. I had tea, coffee. Soft drinks.

'He laughed then. "I mean drink drink."

'There was only the whiskey you kept in the pantry for cooking. And a half bottle of sherry. He followed me as I went into the kitchen. He took the whiskey. I asked him did he want ice or water? "Neither, thank you," he said. He was polite. But his hands were shaking. And he was still sweating.

'He had just taken a seat at the kitchen table when I heard a voice outside. One of the other guests, calling for me. The lamp in their room was broken. I excused myself, went to the store room, got the new light bulb, got the lamp working again.

'By the time I came down again, half the whiskey was gone. I don't know for sure, but I think there was less sherry than there had been too. "I'm your father," he said then.

'I didn't say, "But I thought you were dead. I thought you'd died in the war." I sat there and I listened. He talked and he drank. Then drank some more and kept talking. I put out bread and cheese, but he didn't touch it. Sometimes I wasn't even sure if he was talking to me, or talking for the sake of it.'

Lola had a thousand questions but didn't dare interrupt. She could only watch her son and listen.

'He said you had walked out on him. Walked out and taken his son, his firstborn, with him. That it had been a silly tiff, a little "domestic", but you had always been overdramatic. That you'd had tickets on yourself. That you'd always thought you were better than him. That he'd had every right to have a few drinks with his friends whenever he wanted – didn't he work hard enough, hadn't he done everything for you since you'd arrived in Australia? He said his first thought when you left,' Jim corrected himself then, 'when you and I left, was good riddance. That he had never loved you, that it was a shotgun marriage and it should be put out of its misery. I remember him saying exactly that, because he seemed to find it very funny, telling it to me again, that the marriage was like a half-dead animal that needed to be put out of its misery.

'But then he drank some more. And the tone changed. He started to get louder. I had to ask him to be quiet several times, remind him that I had other guests. He asked again where you were. I told him again you were in Melbourne for the night. Then I asked him how he had found us.

'He went into a long story. A long, rambling story. How he had spent the past years travelling around Australia, picking up work wherever he could. He spoke a lot about how talented he was, how he could turn his hand to anything. Gardening, carpentry, plumbing – you name it, he could do it. He asked me did I need any work done, there in the guesthouse? I said no thank you and asked him again how he had found us.

'A friend of a friend, he said. The friend had known the previous owners of the guesthouse. Had done some work in it over the years. Always good for odd jobs, he said. When Edward had mentioned he was thinking of heading down the coast, his friend had given him the address, said it was worth a try. Said he'd heard the place had been sold, but that it had been sold to an Irishwoman, one of his own, a woman called Lola and her son. "Actually, the friend said, now I think of it, she has the same surname as yours. Common enough for you Paddies, I guess." He started to act out the whole conversation with his friend. "Lola?" says I. "Not Lola Quinlan? And is the son named James?" The friend didn't know. Edward had thrown his arms out wide, nearly knocking over the bottle of whiskey. "There couldn't be two Irishwomen in Australia called Lola with a son called James, I said to myself. It was time to remake our acquaintance. And here I am."'

Lola spoke then. Her voice didn't sound like her voice. 'Did he stay?'

'He wanted to. He argued for it quite vociferously, in fact. Said his friend had told him there were plenty of bedrooms. I said unfortunately they were all being renovated and the only ones that were ready had guests in them already. All he needed was a patch of floor, he said. He had a sleeping bag. He'd never needed many home comforts. Hadn't he lived the life of the gypsy traveller for years? He hadn't let life fence him in. Australia was built by people like him: adventurers, hardworking men who had risked everything they had known back home to cross the seas.' Jim stopped there. 'You get the general idea.'

Lola nodded. Jim had always been able to do a good Irish accent. She hated hearing it, coming from her son, but he was also capturing Edward's boastful way of speaking.

'He insisted I let him stay. I said again it wasn't possible, unfortunately. But there was a caravan park down the road and I knew they had vacancies. He ignored me, reached for the bottle again, poured himself another drink. Himself, not me. I didn't have a glass in front of me. And he kept talking. It was past one before he finally stopped, before I managed to get him outside. It took me more than thirty minutes to walk him to the caravan park. I had to wake up the manager. He wasn't happy, with Edward or with me. Told me I should have put him up, rather than palm him off on him.

'I came back, tidied the kitchen, went to bed. I was up five hours later, to cook breakfast for the guests. They were all gone by ten. Then you rang. You'd had a great night with your friend. The musical had been wonderful. You were going to go shopping together. Your friend knew a warehouse out beyond Williamstown, filled with everything any guesthouse owner could want, all at a good wholesale price, not just linen, but crockery, cutlery . . . They even did country deliveries. It was worth a look, at least, you said. Would I mind if you caught the last train back, not the noon one you'd planned? I didn't mind at all, I said. Then I reminded you we didn't have any guests booked in for that night. Why didn't you stay a second night? You could pay for your accommodation with all the money you'd saved at the warehouse.'

'I remember,' Lola said, her voice soft.

'You said you would. You were really happy, I remember that too. You said you felt like you were playing hooky from school. "What did that make me?" I said. "The schoolmaster?" "I am a lucky woman," you said. "To have a son like you." I always remembered you saying that too.

'Edward came back just before two in the afternoon. I was expecting him. He was more sober than he'd been the night before, but not in good shape. Shaking. Sweating again. He asked if you were back yet. You'd been delayed, I said. I didn't say you'd be away for a second night. He asked for a cup of tea. Something to eat. This time he ate it all. He was different. At the start, anyway. Not as boastful. He didn't talk as loudly. But he still talked. About Ireland. How much he missed it. That his sister kept telling him to come back, but what was the point? he'd said. The place was in a bad way, from all he'd heard. He was more interested in seeing America. He had a friend there. A fella he'd met when he first came to Australia. He'd worked as a labourer with him. He'd saved a fortune. Bit of luck on the horses helped too.

'He was in Texas now, Edward had heard. American wife, American kids. He'd look him up. He just needed a bit of money for his fare and away he'd go.

'I asked him is that why he was here? To ask you for money? He got belligerent then. Told me he didn't like my tone. Said he was offering an honest day's work for an honest day's pay. That you owed him, after all. That you'd never have got the opportunity to come to Australia if it hadn't been for him. That none of this – he'd waved his arms around – would have been possible for you without him in the first place. You were the one who had walked out. She didn't even leave an address, he said to me. He kept calling you she.

'I let him talk for another hour. I don't know how, but he remembered the sherry that he'd seen the night before. Could he possibly have any of it? he asked. Just to settle his hands. He had a nerve disease, he said. He was hoping to get that looked at in America too. The doctors were far more advanced there. Australia was backward. He had a lot to say about how terrible Australia was. Back of beyond. Too hot.

'The sherry must have been ten years old. Do you remember we used to laugh about it, Mum? That we'd used it in ten years of Christmas puddings? He didn't seem to mind. He started dropping hints again about staying. Said that you'd surely be longing to see him, talk about old times. And he wasn't on the scrounge. He'd said that in an exaggerated Australian accent.

'I asked him had he ever joined the army? He laughed at that. Did I think he was mad? Cannon fodder, that's all those boys were. Ireland had the right idea, staying neutral. And the sooner this country became a republic too, the better.

'I offered him work then. He seemed surprised. I said that if he mowed the back lawn and weeded the flower beds at the front, I'd pay him. But he had to do it now and he had to be finished and gone by nightfall.

'He started to do it. Then he said the mower was broken. I couldn't start it either. It wasn't until I took it to be repaired a week later that I was told it had been tampered with. He spent an hour weeding. An hour pulling up plants, at least. Including all the seedlings you'd planted.'

'You told me a dog had dug those up,' Lola said.

It was as if she hadn't spoken. Jim was far away in his recollections now.

'He came back in. Asked for a drink again. He didn't mean water. I said I was all out. It was true, I'd tipped it down the sink.

'While he'd been weeding I'd gone into town, to the bank. I had the notes ready in my pocket. I asked him what I owed him. Then I asked him how much the fare to America was.'

Lola couldn't stop herself. She gasped.

'It was my savings, not yours, Mum. My bank account, not yours. By boat was the cheapest, he said. Terrible long journey, but a man had to do what a man had to do. How much? I asked him again. He told me. I had taken out just enough. He was lying, of course. I looked it up in the newspaper the next day. It was half the price he'd told me. I gave it to him. I said he had to go. And I said he was never welcome here again. That if he came back again, I would call the police and report him for stealing. He blustered. I wasn't lying. He hadn't seen me notice, but he'd taken the silver sugar bowl and spoon that you kept on the kitchen sideboard. Other things too, probably. I never knew for sure.

'He left. A new guest arrived an hour or so later. I cooked their evening meal, served them breakfast the next day. Then I went to the station and collected you at noon.'

'But you didn't say anything. Why didn't you tell me?'

'At first, it was a kind of shock, I think. It was him, I didn't doubt it. The longer I spent with him, the more I could see the younger him in the older, battered version. He was Irish. He knew about you. The little he said about Ireland seemed to tally with what you'd said.'

'But you gave him money. A lot of money. You told him to go.'

'Yes.'

'Why?'

'Because he didn't ask me a single question. Not one. His son, the son he hadn't seen in more than twenty years. He took drink from me, food from me, money from me. He talked at me for six hours. I counted. Six hours. He had plenty to say against you, against Ireland, against Australia. Plenty to say about his own brilliance, his own talents. All of that but he had nothing for me.

'I gave him a second chance. That's why I let him back in the house the next day. He'd been drunk the first time, I told myself. Disorientated. Surprised, perhaps, to have found where you and I were living. But nothing changed during his second visit. It was as if I was —' Jim stopped. 'I was nothing to him. And I realised that's exactly what I was to him. Nothing.'

'But why didn't you tell me?' she asked again.

'I could ask you the same question. Why didn't you tell me the truth about him? Why did you tell me he had joined the army? That he had died in the war?'

She told the truth now. 'To make our lives easier. And because I was embarrassed I had married a drunk, a bully. A fool. Somehow, miraculously, he and I had produced a boy who was clever, generous, kind – everything his father was not. I wanted to keep you away from him. Not just from his fists, or his drinking. From him. From the weak man he was. It was easier to say he was dead, Jim. I'm sorry. But it was.'

He nodded. He still wasn't angry, she could see that.

'I understand,' he said. 'I did then and I still do. It had always been the two of us. I loved you. I admired you. I saw how hard you worked. I knew you would do anything for me. Because you did do everything for me. Worked long hours in the guesthouses, taught piano to all those students, extra jobs to put me through school. You think I didn't notice all that? Admire you for that? I knew you wanted the best for me. And then when I met Edward —'

She realised then he had never called him Dad.

'— I knew you had made the best decision for us about him too. He had his chance with me. He'd found me. I was there, on my own. He knew I was your son. His son. Yet he couldn't think of one question to ask me that was about me and my life, not about money, or drink.'

'You've known the truth for forty years.' It was a statement, not a question.

'Yes.'

'Does Geraldine know?'

'Yes. I told her the year we were married.'

'And all these years, hearing me telling people we met – the girls,

Ellen – that their grandfather, their great-grandfather, was killed in the war. You went along with it.' She didn't mention Geraldine.

'I went along with you. Not it. Not him. With you.'

'When you were last in Clare, you mentioned that you were thinking of visiting the Canberra war memorial. That you were going to look up his war record.'

He nodded. 'I wanted to see how you would react. The truth is, I'd already done it. I had the crazy notion, out of the blue one day, that the man who had come to our guesthouse was a con-man, someone pretending to be Edward. That perhaps the other Edward had been a soldier. That he actually had died fighting for the Australian Army. But there was no record of him, of course.'

There was a long silence. He broke it.

'Geraldine's wanted me to talk to you about it for years. She feels strongly about it. I wasn't even sure if I would bring it up during this trip. She wanted me to. We argued about it.'

'Why didn't you want to?'

'I thought about that on the flight. I realised it was for the same reason I didn't tell you forty years ago. I decided it didn't matter. You'd left him all those years ago, and I knew it must have been for good reasons. You'd decided not to tell me the truth. Once I met him, I understood why. I also realised you can't miss what you've never had. I hadn't had a father. But I hadn't needed one, not when I had you. I never felt lonely or unloved. You were all I needed in a parent. You spoiled me, in fact.' He smiled then. A cheeky quick smile that instantly reminded Lola of him as a ten-year-old.

'No, I didn't,' she said. 'I was a very strict authoritarian mother.'

He smiled again. 'You spoiled me rotten and we both know it. Geraldine's often said it. She said I was like a sultan with my own harem, you adoring me, the three girls too. She was the only one who kept my feet on the ground, she said. And she was right.' He gave an affectionate laugh.

Lola kept her expression neutral. 'You didn't feel anything for Edward? Any kind of bond at all?'

He shook his head. 'Apart from pity, perhaps. And a strong urge to get rid of him before you arrived home. Mum, I'm not rewriting history to make you feel better. I can't pretend something I didn't feel. All my life, I had you, someone who believed in me, who made life interesting, fun. Who taught me how to work hard. Who not only helped raise my three daughters, but brought so much colour and life and music into their lives. Could that man have done any of that? I knew within minutes of meeting him that he couldn't. I don't know his life story. Perhaps it would make me pity him even more if I did. But I don't need to know. All I learnt from those two sessions with him was I didn't need him in my life. He didn't want to be my father. He wasn't interested in me. He didn't have even one question for me.'

It was the third time he had mentioned it. Edward's lack of interest had stung, Lola realised in that moment. For all Jim was saying, in his careful, measured way, it must have hurt. To be a twenty-one-year-old man, to meet your father – believed dead – and for him to behave like that. If she hadn't decided long before to stop wasting her energy on feeling ill will towards Edward, she would have cursed him anew.

Jim gestured then to the letters. 'So now I know both sides. Yours as well as mine. And so do you. I know something else now too. About him. Not that I really had any doubt.'

'You do? What?'

'We both had a lucky escape.'

She stood up. She wanted to walk towards him, but she couldn't. She was trembling too much. He came to her instead. Her tall, kind, gentle boy crossed the room and enfolded her in his arms.

She didn't cry. She had never cried in front of him, not even when Anna died. She couldn't start now. But she did need to say something else to him.

'I'm sorry, Jim.'

She didn't elaborate. She was sorry for so much, and he knew that, she felt sure of it. Knew that she was sorry for all the times his life had been hard without a father, no matter what he'd just said. That she was sorry for not having told him the truth long before now.

'Don't apologise. I kept a secret from you too, remember. Like mother, like son.'

She knew then that everything would be all right. That he still loved her as much as she loved him. That nothing would change that. The relief gave way to a slow building of happiness. She smiled up at him. At her dearest son.

'So we're even?'

'We're even,' he said.

He hugged her again.

CHAPTER THIRTY-SEVEN

Carrie was impressed to hear the news. 'A piano! Wow! But when will you get time to play it?'

'I'll find it somehow.' Bett was trying to have a phone conversation with her sister while giving the twins their breakfast. Daniel was still in bed. She'd crept out early that morning, happy to give him a sleep-in while fighting an urge to stay under the covers for more of that beautiful, long-needed lovemaking they'd enjoyed the evening before. More than once.

'I must buy you a piano more often,' he said after the second time, as they lay in the tangled sheets, limbs entwined. 'I had no idea they were such aphrodisiacs.'

Bett had rung Carrie as soon as the twins were occupied with their food, if by 'occupied' she meant 'smearing cornflakes on one another'. Not that she minded. Not today. Today she thought she'd never seen anything quite as adorable as the two of them making a big mess.

'I'd love to hear you play it,' Carrie said. 'Are you there all morning? Can I drop over after I've taken the kids to school? I want to hear all about the trip, of course, but I need to show you something too. It's top-secret at the moment but it's so exciting!'

Bett told her she'd love her to visit. It was true. She also knew she had to stop expecting Carrie to somehow miraculously change into Anna, to be the sister to Bett that Anna had been. Carrie could only be Carrie. And perhaps there were times when Carrie also wished Bett was more like Anna. It wasn't a pleasant thought, but Bett had an uneasy feeling it was true too.

Daniel was up and in the garden with the twins when Carrie arrived. He'd told Bett in detail the evening before all about the barbecue with Carrie and her family, and how much Carrie's joking term for him had driven him crazy. Bett met Carrie at her car, hugged her and whispered, 'Just a quick tip – no Mister Mom, for your own safety.'

'But it's funny! Matthew thought so too.' She called over to Daniel in a teasing tone, 'God, Daniel, there was me thinking you had a good sense of humour.'

'I do,' he said. 'That's why I didn't laugh at it.'

Carrie rolled her eyes. 'Talk about oversensitive. Thank God you're back, Bett.'

Inside, Bett made coffee and put out the golden biscuits that Carrie had brought with her. Homemade, delicious Anzacs, she'd announced.

'When do you find the time to bake?' Bett said, instantly annoyed with herself for slipping straight back into their 'who is the best mother and homemaker?' rivalry.

'I didn't say homemade by me,' Carrie said. 'I got them at a street stall yesterday. I bought everything they had. It was in aid of the refugees' fund. All of Lola's crew were behind the table. Those old ladies might be shaky on their pins, but they sure can bake up a storm.'

Bett laughed. There really was no one in the world who could infuriate and then entertain her as quickly as her younger sister.

They managed an entire forty minutes of conversation without interruption, catching up on all that had happened in Ireland, in

Sydney with Glenn, with the TV series and Rafe Ascot. Bett was able to let Carrie know she'd had an email from the producer that morning. She'd written that the actor had fortunately agreed to 'rise above the recent unfortunate events' – 'Honour his contract, in other words,' Bett said – and would be filming in the Valley during Gourmet Weekend at the end of the month, as scheduled. He had, however, decided to stay in Adelaide rather than Clare for the duration of the filming, travelling back and forth from the capital city each day.

'He's obviously terrified I'm going to chase him down the main street,' Carrie said. She shuddered theatrically. 'What a creep. I hope he's the one who gets murdered in the TV series.'

Bett suddenly remembered something. She asked Carrie if she still had the photo of him.

'Are you joking? That photo nearly ruined my life. Thank God that American pop star got caught taking drugs and all the heat went off me. I deleted it. Well, Luke did, at least. Off my camera, off the blog, everywhere on the internet he could find it.'

Bett remembered she had it stored on her own phone. She located it, slowly enlarging it until she'd found what she wanted. She held her phone out to her sister. 'Look at this.'

Carrie shut her eyes. 'I don't want to see it again, I told you.'

'Not the actor. The actor's script. Look what's on the front of it.'

'A wine stain, I know. He had wine stains all over everything. Your twins are cleaner than he was.'

Bett let that one go by. 'As well as the wine stain, Carrie.'

Carrie looked. 'It's a name. The scriptwriter. Tom someone?'

'Tom Nikolić.'

Carrie stared blankly at her. 'Should I know him? Has he won an Oscar or something?'

'Don't you remember him – Lola's protégé? When we were teenagers? That young guy who lived at the motel for a while, doing odd jobs?'

Carrie frowned. 'Was he Greek or Russian or something? God, he hit the jackpot. Odd-jobs man one day, scriptwriter the next.'

'I suspect he didn't quite leap from one to the other, Carrie.'

'Whatever. No need to be so snarky about it,' Carrie said. She brightened. 'That was snarky, wasn't it? Brilliant, now I get it. Because I'm thinking about occasionally being snarky on my new blog.'

'New blog? I thought you told me you didn't want to write for my newspaper any more.'

'I don't. I've had it with that TV series. This is different. I got Luke to help set it up. I've only done a few trial pages so far, but I'm loving it. Remember, I told you about it when you were in Sydney?'

Bett's mind was trying and failing to locate that particular piece of information.

Carrie reminded her. 'I'm calling it "My Country Dream". It's all about my life here in the bush.'

'We're not in the bush. We're less than two hours from Adelaide.'

'That's close enough to the bush for overseas readers. It's still country, isn't it? Or maybe I should call it "My Rural Dream"? No, "My Country Dream" definitely sounds better.'

Bett blinked, trying to keep up. 'But what will you write about?'

'Whatever I want, that's the fun of it! The kids, Matthew, the meals I cook, the interior decorating I do. All my hobbies. My wide circle of friends. I'm going to post lots of photos too. I'm having a great time with it already. Want to see?' Carrie tapped in an address, then handed over her phone.

Bett scrolled through the blog, frowning. She read the first entry aloud. '"Hi and welcome to My Country Dream! My name's Caroline and I can't wait for you to get to know me!" But you never call yourself Caroline.'

'Well, I can't call myself Carrie, can I? Not after the disaster of my last blog.'

Bett read on. '"I love life, my kids, my hubby (my hot hubby!!), my kitchen and my 'me time'. I hope you'll enjoy coming on this journey with me, as I share my days here on the farm with you all!"' Bett looked up again, puzzled. 'Carrie, what farm? You live a few miles from town.'

'You're so nitpicky. Skip the words for now. I'm still finding my own voice anyway. Apparently that's the key. Just look at the photos instead. I've read all the child protection guidelines too, before you ask. I'm only using photos that show them from the back. Apparently that's the safest way.'

Bett flicked through more than a dozen photos. Her frown grew deeper. 'But this isn't your house. Or your kids. You only have three kids, not five. You also don't have identical twins.'

'But look how cute they are! And five sounds better than three, don't you think? Especially when I'm going for a kind of "bohemian chaos" mood.'

Bett didn't even know what 'bohemian chaos' was. She kept scrolling. There were photos allegedly of the children's bedrooms, with stencilled walls, handpainted cupboards, patchwork quilts. Each photo was beautifully lit, impeccably styled. The kitchen photos showed an enormous room, twice the size of Carrie's actual kitchen. It looked like something from a villa in the South of France.

It was from the South of France, Carrie confirmed cheerfully.

The final shot was a photo of a family banquet. On display was a large crispy-skinned roast chicken, four dishes of colourful vegetables, beautifully arranged striped napkins and an elaborate table decoration of berries and twigs. It was taken in close-up, so it was impossible to tell if it was Carrie's house or not. Bett took a guess. 'You didn't cook this either, Carrie, did you?'

'Of course not. When would I get time? Anyway, I've given up on healthy eating for now. I'm too tired. We've had fish fingers for the past three nights. I tried taking a photo of those but they looked like yellow clothes pegs.'

'So where did you get these photos?'

'Off Google images. It's incredible. Have you ever used it? You type in whatever you want, like, for example, I did "roast chicken dinner" for that one and, voila, all these photos appear. I've already got all the ones I need for next month's blog. My Winter Wonderland, I'm calling it. I found the most gorgeous photo of a roaring open fire, with all these people warming their feet in front of it. There's even a dog asleep with his paws out. It's so cute.'

'But you don't have an open fire. Or a dog.'

'Stop being the journalist all the time, would you?'

'But a blog is supposed to be about you, Carrie. Showing photos of you and your life, not random people and houses off the internet. Which you probably have no right to use anyway, without paying some kind of copyright fee.'

'Who's going to know? Besides, if they don't want people to look at their photos, they shouldn't put them on the internet, should they?'

'That would really stand up in court.'

'Come on, Bett. You know I can't use my own life. Matthew would kill me. And it's too boring at the moment. All I seem to do is wash the kids' clothes, tidy the kids' rooms, cook the kids' —'

'Fish fingers,' Bett said.

'Exactly. This is much more fun. The glamorous life I'd like to have.'

'You wouldn't consider calling it "My Make-Believe Country Dream"?'

Carrie gave it some thought. 'Would that keep you off my back?'

'Me and the lawyers, I suspect.'

'I could still write all I wanted, couldn't I? Actually, that might be even more fun. Because I could have us flying around the world on holidays, skiing and sailing, and getting loads of pets too, couldn't I? Not just a boring dog – exotic pets, like iguanas. That might get me even more readers. What's that called? An aspirational lifestyle? I was definitely too close to my real life as it was.'

Bett glanced down again at the fake roast chicken feast and said nothing.

Carrie stood up. 'I can't wait to get back to it. Thanks, Bett. Welcome home. Any more word from Lola and Dad, by the way?'

Bett shook her head. 'Not since Dad texted to say he'd landed. Lola's probably banned him from sending anything else.'

Carrie laughed. 'They'll have such a great time together. It's much better that it's Dad there with her than you, isn't it?'

Yes, they would have a great time, Bett agreed, as she walked her sister to her car. She also decided not to take exception to Carrie's other remark. She had a strong feeling it was true.

CHAPTER THIRTY-EIGHT

Lola and Jim met for dinner in the hotel restaurant. After their long conversation that afternoon, they'd gone their separate ways for a few hours: Jim for a jet-lagged nap, Lola to walk and read in the hotel grounds. She'd spoken to Des, explaining they were still unsure about the next day's plans.

'No pressure at all, Lola,' he'd said. 'Call me in the morning once you know. I can be there in an hour. You just have to say the word.'

Over dinner, there was no more talk of Edward. It would come, Lola felt sure. But for now, as always, there was so much else to discuss. Jim had dozens of questions about Ireland he'd never thought to ask. About the history, the language, the geography. Lola did her best to answer, eventually having to laugh and remind him she'd left the country when she was twenty years old. 'I'm much better on Australian history, if there's anything you want to know?'

They discussed his guesthouse. Bett. Carrie. Glenn. Ellen. They talked about everyone who mattered in their lives, except Geraldine. Lola felt sure Jim knew of the tension. Surely Geraldine had never been shy expressing her true feelings about Lola to her husband? If she had, Lola didn't want to know. This was too special, being here in her home country with her son. Why spoil it by introducing a spectre like Geraldine to their feast?

As if she'd been somehow mind-reading, a text from Geraldine arrived on Jim's phone. She must have been awake very early. Lola watched as he scrolled and scrolled. Had she sent a text or an essay? she nearly asked. Jim and Geraldine's relationship was between them. Even if she nearly had to swallow her serviette to stop herself from saying anything.

'All okay?' she said brightly, when he finally finished reading.

'Great,' he said. 'She's rushed off her feet. Just how she likes it.'

'She's a wonderfully hard worker,' Lola said. It was true too.

Jim asked the waitress to take a photo of them to send home to Bett, Carrie, Ellen and Geraldine. They raised their glasses. It was easy to smile. Lola felt as if a huge weight had been lifted from her.

Had Jim felt the same about his secret? She was on the verge of asking him when something stopped her. She knew the way he thought. He didn't go over and over a subject, examine it from all angles, as she was inclined to do. As most women of her acquaintance were inclined to do. An event took place, he dealt with it, and then moved on. She had seen him do that all his life. Until Anna's death. That had devastated him in ways he was still recovering from, Lola knew. All of them had changed after Anna died. But her instinct told her he didn't need to talk more about his father. Not yet.

They were finishing their coffee when Lola's phone pinged. It was Bett. She – or at least the twins – were early risers too.

Her message wasn't only in response to Lola and Jim's photo. She'd sent a note long enough to rival Geraldine's. She had also attached a photo.

'I think Daniel has just won husband of the year,' Lola said. She showed Jim the photo of the piano. 'If I could have waved a magic wand and got exactly what Bett needed, I couldn't have done better. She needs to be playing music again. I need her to be playing music again.'

395

She typed back a response. *How wonderful! Start practising. I want a one-hour concert when we get back home.*

Home.

To Australia.

But not before she finished what she needed to do here.

'Jim, will you do something with me tomorrow?' she asked.

'I told you, I'm at your beck and call.'

She gave Jim a list she'd drawn up that afternoon.

'That's some itinerary,' he said when he'd finished reading it. '"This is your life, Lola Quinlan." Or should I say Louisa Delaney? No worries, Mum. Will I ring your driver and book him for the morning?'

Lola shook her head. 'We need someone quiet for this trip.' She gave him Emmanuel's phone number. Her taxi driver friend. Jim rang him. Yes, Emmanuel could be at the hotel for nine a.m. Jim rang Des next to let him know he had another day off.

Des was cheery. 'No worries at all, as you Aussies say. All the young ones say that here in Ireland now, too. From watching so much *Neighbours* and *Home and Away*, apparently. That and the fact that most of them have spent a few years in Australia. The world's a small place these days, Jim, isn't it? My neighbour's kids are in Canada, New Zealand . . .'

'I think you made the right decision,' Jim said to Lola after he eventually managed to hang up.

In the foyer after dinner, on their way up to their rooms, Lola heard her name being called. It was Jean. She was passing by, she said, and had decided to drop in rather than phone. They hugged. She felt like an old friend. Lola introduced Jim and then, guessing why Jean was there, offered to fetch the journal and letters for her.

'Oh, I don't need them back yet,' Jean said. 'Please, hold on to them for as long as you like. I've come to deliver an invitation. You told me you and your son might be heading away to see the sights, but you can't go before we've had you over as our guests. My mother would kill me, God rest her soul. Everyone wants to meet you. My husband. My children. The grandkids. In fact, so many that we're going to have it at my daughter Aisling's house. We wouldn't fit in our new apartment. There's going to be some crowd tomorrow night.'

'Tomorrow night?'

'Is that too short notice? Did you have other plans?'

Lola glanced at Jim. He was smiling. She knew he was enjoying every bit of this, from Jean's accent to the generous hospitality. She realised then she should have brought him to Ireland long before now. But they would make up for that lost time while they still could.

'We'd love to join you,' she said for them both.

Emmanuel arrived right on nine a.m. They were waiting outside. He greeted Jim with the same quiet courtesy he'd showed Lola. She handed him her list. Yes, he said, he knew where all those places were.

They began at Bayfield, the estate where she and Edward had met. It was now a horse stud, closed to the public, yet on Lola's urging when they saw the gate was open, they drove up the avenue all the same. They were stopped by a groundsman before they reached the main house, but there was still time to take in the magnificence of the grounds, the estate buildings, the mansion itself.

'It's like Buckingham Palace,' Jim said. 'Look at the size of it. There must be twenty rooms, surely? And you actually spent time in it?'

'Thirty-five rooms, in fact. And I was a lowly servant, remember, not an honoured guest.' She wondered what had happened to those two young girls, if their lives had gone on to become any happier. Or if either of them played the piano any more.

The next stops were in Ballymore Eustace. The old village school. The church. She pointed out the shop where she'd bought sweets as a child. She showed him where Elizabeth's house had been.

She asked Emmanuel to follow a road out of the village, towards Naas. She hadn't been back here yet. She used to cycle or walk this route, she told Jim. After driving for several kilometres along a winding, tree-lined road, at her request, Emmanuel stopped just before an old stone bridge. Jim and Lola both got out. Using his arm as support, she walked to the top of the bridge. The River Liffey flowed strongly beneath them.

This had been the village meeting point in the summertime, she told Jim. She pointed to a grassy area, now overgrown. It wasn't as popular any more, it seemed. There was also a new fence blocking the way to the next section of the riverbank – the area she'd always thought of as hers and Edward's. She stopped short of telling Jim that this was where he had been conceived. A mother needed to keep back some secrets. Then she decided against any more secrets and told him.

Jim raised his eyebrows. 'I think that's what Ellen would call TMI, Mum. Too much information.'

She patted his hand. 'Better late than never,' she said.

They drove to her parents' house, beyond the village. She still thought of it as that, she realised. Their house, not hers.

They walked from the taxi to the front gate. The house looked even more beautiful today than it had on her first visit. The soft blue sky and spring sunlight cast a glow over the garden. There were clothes on the line, sports uniforms. Two footballs on the grass this time.

'Would you like to see inside?' Jim asked. 'I can go and knock if you want me to?'

She shook her head. She didn't need to explain why not. He now knew it hadn't been a happy place for her. 'But I'm glad you've seen it for yourself,' she said.

They were nearly back at the car when they heard a voice. 'Excuse me! Hello!'

A woman in her thirties was walking down the path from the front door. 'Can I help you at all?'

About to say no thank you, Lola was beaten to it by Jim.

He smiled and said hello. 'Sorry, you probably thought we were stalkers.' He introduced them both. Before Lola could stop him, he explained further. 'My mother grew up in this house. It's her first time back in Ireland in sixty-five years. She's showing me around.'

'How wonderful!' the young woman said. She introduced herself as Niamh, then turned to Lola. 'You were here before, weren't you? I wanted to speak to you then too, but I had a sick son inside.'

'How did you recognise me this time?'

Jim glanced at his mother's bright-orange tunic top, purple culottes and the yellow rose in her white hair and said nothing.

'You do stand out a little on a quiet Irish lane,' Niamh said with a smile. 'I've just boiled the kettle. You must be dying to come in and see what it looks like now. Have you got time?'

'We couldn't possibly intrude,' Lola said.

'We'd love to,' Jim said.

Niamh looked from one to the other.

'Mum?' Jim said. 'Wouldn't you like to see it again?'

Two days ago, she couldn't have stepped back inside. Now, with her son beside her, everything felt different. 'Yes, I would,' she said.

It was like a new house. In every way. In Lola's time all the walls had been painted stark white. They were now rosy pink, buttery yellow, even a cornflower blue. Her parents had only had dark, heavy furniture. Now, it was all light wood, practical, stylish.

'Ikea,' Niamh said cheerily. 'We spent so much on the renovations we couldn't afford anything else.'

The entire back of the house had been transformed. Lola remembered a small kitchen, with windows that barely let in light yet still managed to send out a chill. There was now a warm, light-filled area with a long wooden dining table, cream fitted cabinets and a wall of windows.

'Excuse all the handprints,' Niamh said. 'Three boys under ten, each one dirtier than the next. All at school today, luckily, or they'd be following us around now too.'

Upstairs and, again, it was barely recognisable. Two new bathrooms. They'd already been there when they moved in two years earlier, Niamh told them. 'It was a B&B for a while, as far as we know.'

Lola didn't say anything.

The guesthouse people had done a lot of the hard work, Niamh said, as she showed them the five upstairs bedrooms. The master bedroom was still at the front of the house. Her father had slept on his own in there for most of Lola's life, her mother choosing to sleep in the smaller room at the back. Lola had been told it was because it was quieter. In later years, she'd realised it was because her parents didn't want to sleep in the same room.

Back then, the bedrooms had been gloomy, with heavy drapes on the windows, and dark timber floors. They were changed completely too, filled with colour and warmth, bright bedspreads and curtains, colourful rugs on the floor. The two older boys' rooms had full-length shelves crowded with toys and books, their quilt covers a riot of colour, both depicting movie characters, Lola noticed.

The final room they visited was Lola's old bedroom. Niamh's youngest son slept there, she told them. The only similarity Lola could see was the shape of the room. That, and the ceiling cornice. It had been an unexpectedly elaborate feature in an otherwise austere house. It was there when they moved in, Lola had been told by her mother. She knew her father would never have allowed such extravagance. Made from plaster, it was a tumble of leaves, flowers and birds. Lola had a vivid memory of lying in bed and looking up at it, counting the flowers and birds. There had been twelve of each.

Niamh saw her looking up. 'It's beautiful, isn't it? The auctioneer told us it was original but we didn't know whether to believe him.'

'It's original,' Lola told her.

'My son loves it. He always counts the birds and flowers before he goes to sleep. There are twelve of each.'

'I'm happy to hear that,' Lola said.

Back downstairs again, Niamh offered tea, coffee, lunch even. They declined it all.

'But you'll want to take photos to show your family back home? You're most welcome to.'

'No, thank you,' Lola said.

'Yes, please,' Jim said. 'My wife would love to see it. So would our daughters, I'm sure.'

'How many daughters do you have?'

There was the faintest hesitation from Jim. 'We had three, but sadly my eldest, Anna, died nearly five years ago. From cancer.'

'I'm so sorry.'

Jim thanked her. Lola appreciated her quiet sympathy too.

Niamh was happy to be photographer, taking their photos in the main rooms, and then outside, in front of the house. Several of Jim and Lola together, then several of Lola on her own. And then, at Jim's invitation, one of the three of them, selfie-style. Niamh insisted Lola check them all, to make sure she was happy. She was.

Jim walked to the taxi to ask Emmanuel to drive up. Niamh and Lola waited for them at the front gate. Leaning against it for support, Lola was jolted by another memory. As a child, waiting for her parents, she would often stand here and push the gate open and shut, listening to the rhythmic squeak. She tried it now. It didn't make a sound.

Niamh noticed. 'That gate made such a racket when we first moved in. The boys used to swing on it. The shriek drove me mad. It was the first thing we fixed.'

'I don't blame you,' Lola said. 'Thank you again, Niamh. You have been so hospitable.'

'I'm glad I was here today. I told my husband last week that I'd seen an eccentric-looking old woman outside, and I wished I'd —' Niamh realised what she'd said. 'Lola, sorry.'

Lola patted her hand. 'I'm definitely old and I'm happy to be eccentric, don't worry. And it was much better today, having my son with me.'

'What a special trip this will be for you.'

Lola agreed. Again, as the taxi pulled in beside them, it seemed natural to hug a near-stranger.

Back in the car, Lola was about to ask Emmanuel to drive them to the hotel, when Jim surprised her. 'I'd like to go somewhere else first, if you're not too tired?'

'I'm fine,' she said. 'Where?'

'The cemetery. To your parents' graves.'

It shocked her to realise that it hadn't occurred to her. She'd thought about visiting Elizabeth's grave. She'd even planned to ask Jean tonight where it was. But not her own parents.

'There are several Catholic cemeteries around here. I don't even know for sure where they are.'

'I do,' Jim said. He reached into his coat pocket and took out a piece of paper.

She put on her glasses and read it. Written in Jim's firm handwriting were her parents' names, and the name of a cemetery. There was a third name on the page. Edward James Quinlan. Beside it, the name of a different cemetery. Lola felt a small jolt to see all three names. All dead. All buried.

'How did you find this?' she asked.

'A website called rip.ie. All the death notices in Ireland, going back for decades.'

The same website Luke had found, Lola realised.

'I think we should visit your parents' graves first,' Jim said. 'Then my father's.'

My father's. Not Edward this time.

Her parents' cemetery was small. Lola sat on a bench near the entrance while Jim went looking. It didn't take him long. Holding his arm for support, she made her way across the uneven grass.

The gravestone was simple. Inexpensive, Lola guessed. Their names, birth dates and death dates. Rest in peace. No mention of her. Nothing about 'beloved by their daughter'.

It hurt. She hated admitting it, and hated feeling it, but it hurt. In life and in death, her father had disowned her. The wording would have been his decision, she was sure of it.

It was a longer drive to the cemetery where Edward was buried, across to the other side of the county. Again, Lola was glad Emmanuel, not Des, was driving. The car was silent, each engrossed in their own thoughts.

The cemetery was down a country road. It took them a few minutes to find Edward's grave. It was plain: his name, the dates. He was buried beside his sister Margaret, known as Peggy. There was mention of her five children. Lola read their names aloud.

'My cousins,' Jim said.

Her nieces and nephews by marriage. Bett and Carrie's relatives too. There was a whole Irish family here that they would never meet. 'Do you want to try to find them?'

He shook his head.

She saw Jim make a sign of the cross. He'd been baptised but to her knowledge hadn't been to Mass in years. Nor had she. But together, they found themselves saying a Hail Mary and the Our Father.

'Rest in peace, Edward,' she said after the prayers.

'Rest in peace, Dad.'

Lola turned to him in surprise. 'That's the first time you've called him that.'

'He was my dad. In one way, at least. I wouldn't be here if it wasn't for him.'

Jim was right. If she could be grateful to Edward for anything, it was that.

They returned to the car. This time, Jim agreed when she asked Emmanuel to go to the hotel.

CHAPTER THIRTY-NINE

'You're sure you're not too tired?' Lola asked several hours later, as she met Jim in the foyer. They were being collected by Jean's husband at seven. 'I'm sure they'd all understand if you'd rather not come.'

'And miss an Irish family gathering? No way. If I do fall asleep, throw a potato at me, would you?'

'You might try to get those corny Irish jokes out of your system,' Lola said. 'As quickly as you can. Here's Jean's husband now.'

Midway through the evening, Lola felt as though she was starring in an Irish film. She suspected this wasn't a normal get-together for Jean's family either. Unless they really did live their lives with this much music, singing, food and conversation, night after night.

From the moment she and Jim arrived, they'd been swept up by the entire family. She was introduced as an old friend of Grandma's, all the way from Australia. Everyone knew it was her first time home in sixty-five years, and Jim's first time in Ireland. The questions flowed from all directions. What did they think of Ireland? Of Dublin? Of Kildare? Had Lola noticed many changes? Was Jim impressed or disappointed? Wasn't the weather terrible, and it was supposed to be summer! They should have brought some of that Australian sunshine over with them!

Lola met Jean's daughters, their partners, her grandchildren. She also met Jean's oldest son, Ray, the mechanic. The man she had to thank for this whole reunion, she realised.

'Don't thank me,' he said shyly. 'Thank your driver's dodgy car.'

Lola had been feeling guilty about Des. She'd rung him that afternoon to explain about her and Jim's road trip, telling him she would still pay his retainer, of course, but if there were any other jobs on offer, she hoped he'd take them.

He was as chatty and cheery as always. As it happened, yes, he had been offered another job and he would accept it, if Lola was sure? Definitely, she said. And yes, indeed, she would also be sure to ring him if she and Jim needed any directions or travelling tips. And yes, indeed, she would also ring him to say goodbye before they flew home. It had been hard to get him off the line.

'You're the very man I need to speak to,' Lola said to Ray now. 'My son and I want to hire a car and go touring. Could you recommend a rental company?'

He did better than that. He had a courtesy car at the garage, he told Lola. For customers whose cars were taking more than a day or two to repair. She and Jim would be welcome to use that. He'd sort out the insurance. He wouldn't dream of charging her, either. She was practically family, after all.

Soon after, for the first time that evening, Lola found herself sitting alone, in the most comfortable chair in the house. The room was abuzz with conversation and laughter. She saw Jim talking to Jean's husband, laughing. He didn't look in the least jet-lagged. She realised then what he did look like. As though he belonged here. It had never struck her before, not in multicultural Australia, but Jim truly was Irish-looking.

There had been several questions about their surname. Were they related to the Quinlans who were horse people? someone wanted to know. No, my late husband was from a different family,

Lola explained simply. There were no further questions. No one asking how long they had been married, or if it had been a happy marriage. No need tonight for stories about soldiers and deaths on battlefields. Time had done its job. The idea of a woman being pregnant before she was married would have caused no scandal either. Two of Jean's three daughters – both there with their partners and children – weren't married.

'It must be time for another, surely?'

She turned. It was Jean, with a fresh gin and tonic, in what looked like a Waterford Crystal glass. Lola accepted with pleasure.

Jean took the seat beside her. 'Are you coping with my rabble, Lola? Not too much, I hope? Your son looks as fresh as if he stepped off a bus, not a long flight.'

'He's always loved company. You've made us so welcome, Jean, thank you.'

'Mammy would love to see it. We'd always have a gathering like this for her birthday. She'd sit where you're sitting now. In her final years, she couldn't really take it all in. But she'd still smile away at us. The grandkids adored her. They spent one of the parties doing her hair and makeup. You've never seen such a sight!' Jean laughed at the memory. 'Ah, I still miss her so much. I was sad when my Daddy died, but it was different with my Mam. It's like a part of me is still missing.'

Lola couldn't empathise. She tried but she couldn't feel the emotions Jean was describing. Yes, she had known that feeling of missing her mother, of longing for things to be different. But she had felt it all her life, not just when she had learnt her mother had died. Yet Lola could easily imagine how it felt to miss Elizabeth. She'd felt her spirit, and her absence, from the moment she stepped into the house. There were many photos of her amid the big display on the wall. Not just as an elderly woman, but from her younger days too. Lola's eyes had been drawn to them immediately.

The Elizabeth she'd known. She'd felt a kick of grief then. What a friend Elizabeth had been to her.

'She must have been so proud of you all, Jean. Of her wonderful family. I only have to look around tonight to see how close you all are, and how well you get on.'

'Oh, she was proud of us all right. But we're like any family, Lola. The things I could tell you.'

'Please do,' Lola said. 'You know all my skeletons. It's your turn to tell all.'

For the next while, speaking in a near-whisper, Jean pointed out different people in the room. The two sisters-in-law standing at opposite ends of the room loathed one another and never spoke, she said. Her daughter's partner, the man there with the black hair, had had an affair the year before. He was on his last chance. Jean's own husband had recently had a cancer scare. They'd detected it early enough that the treatment had worked, but he'd need to have more tests in six months. As for the grandchildren, the girl with the long red hair had recently been cautioned for shoplifting in Naas. It was a new dare with the girls in her class, apparently.

'I'll stop before you think we're a nest of criminals altogether,' Jean said. 'I used to tell Mam everything like this too, even after her mind had gone. She'd smile away and pat my hand and say, "Isn't that lovely," no matter what I told her. It was the ideal situation. She wouldn't remember anything and I would feel like I'd unloaded my worries.'

'I'm on Skype. Feel free to call anytime. My lips are always sealed too.'

'I just might, Lola.'

'I once made a promise to your mother, Jean. That I would come back to Ireland one day. It's taken me far too long, and I've only done it by the skin of my teeth, but I've done it.'

'What do you mean, "by the skin of your teeth"! Look at you, full of beans yet. As my youngest grandkid said, "How can that lady be nearly ninety? She hasn't got nearly enough lines yet."'

'The wonder of pancake makeup, Jean. Never underestimate it.'

'Now, can I get you anything else, Lola? Or even better, can I persuade you to join in the singsong? Your son was telling me you love music and singing. That you even wrote your own musical.'

'I've a voice that can skin cats, Jean. But if you can all bear it, I will too.'

Jean didn't even call order, or announce that the singing was starting. She simply went across to one of her daughters and whispered in her ear. Moments later, the young woman started singing from where she was, not moving into the centre of the room. She started low, tone perfect. Lola knew the song immediately. 'She Moved Through the Fair'. One by one, people fell quiet. She sang three verses, the room still by the time she finished, then erupting into applause. One of the grandchildren was next. Completely unselfconscious, stepping forward to sing a song in Irish. It was followed by three other songs, from an in-law, another daughter, then Jean herself. Not an Irish traditional one, but a Tom Jones hit, 'Delilah'. Everyone joined in on that.

Jim had made his way across to Lola. 'If I was younger, I'd hire the lot of them and take them on the road,' he whispered. 'The von Trapps have nothing on them.'

'You'll be next,' she said. 'I hope you're ready.'

She had never known Jim to sing in public. She had done her best to teach him piano before realising to her astonishment that she had somehow produced a completely unmusical son. As he was called upon now, he insisted, laughing, that he was doing them a favour by not singing. But he did know a poem, if that counted as a party piece? He recited it, standing beside Lola: 'Clancy of the Overflow'. He'd loved it since he was a boy. He'd even had a print of it in the motel office back in Clare. She hadn't realised he knew it off by heart. He was greeted by whoops and cheers afterwards.

'Your turn, Lola,' Jean called.

'My voice comes with public health warnings,' Lola said. 'You might think I'm being modest, but for your own wellbeing, cover your ears. If the dogs in the area start howling, that's my fault too.'

She saw Jim take out his phone. Usually, she'd ask him not to take photos, and especially not to record this. But why not? she decided. Perhaps Bett and Carrie might like to see this. Ellen too. A glimpse at what their lives might have been like if they had grown up in Ireland.

Lola knew many Irish songs. 'Molly Malone'. 'Grace'. 'The Foggy Dew'. But what was right for tonight? What was her signature song? It came to her then.

She began. It took a moment for everyone to realise what she was singing. A few of them started to laugh and were shushed. Lola continued. She wasn't being modest. Her voice would strip wallpaper. But then, kindly, some of the others joined in on the chorus: 'L.O.L.A. Lola.' The song by The Kinks.

She stopped before the final verse. 'I've punished you enough,' she said, taking a bow from her seat.

Across the room, Ray put his hands to his head. 'Oh, Jaysus. Now I'll have that song stuck in my head for another week.'

It was past midnight by the time they left. They'd been issued with an invitation to come and see everyone again before they returned to Australia. They'd do their best, they said. Once everyone heard they were taking a road trip, they'd been given a long list of must-see places. Jim had been given warnings about the state of the Irish roads, the unreliable road signs, the traffic jams. They received apologies in advance about the weather, even though Lola had seen the seven-day forecast and it was supposed to be mostly fine.

'Don't mind that. They always get it wrong,' one of Jean's daughters told her solemnly.

The goodbyes took nearly an hour, as everyone came up to say a few words. Last of all was Jean. Again, a close hug. 'We'll see you again before you go, Lola.' A statement, not a question.

'You will,' Lola said. 'Thank you. Such hospitality to a stranger and her son.'

'Stranger! Nonsense. You're one of us,' she said.

But she wasn't, Lola realised, as they were being driven home. Jim was in the front seat with Jean's husband. She was in the back, with her own thoughts. Yes, Ireland was her birthplace, but it was no longer her home. It was a place full of memories and stories, wonderful music, warm people, as well as all the difficulties that every country in the world had. But Australia was her home. It was where she had made her life, had her son, ended her marriage. Begun friendships, some lifelong, some short term. Where she had fallen in love with her three granddaughters. Fallen in love with her dear Alex. Where she had known love and laughter alongside heartbreak and sorrow, loneliness and hardship. Ireland was a place of memories for her now. She truly was only a tourist here. A tourist with closer links than many, certainly, but a tourist nevertheless.

She had a momentary flash of sorrow but, swiftly, another thought occurred to her. Perhaps that was a good thing? Because what did a tourist do but see the highlights of a place? Flit like a butterfly from one scenic spot to the next. And she was even luckier than most, for who did she have as her guide but her son, who was not only endlessly patient, kind, generous and even-tempered, but an excellent driver and navigator. If she was going to get lost on Ireland's back roads, there was nobody she'd rather be with.

After waving goodbye to Jean's husband out the front of their hotel, she took Jim's proffered arm and they walked into the foyer. Yet another midweek wedding was in full swing in one of the hotel's function rooms. Lola saw a glimpse of the bride, in deep conversation with one of her bridesmaids. Nearby was a woman in a frankly astonishing fascinator that looked like she was being chased by wasps. Lola wondered what Jim would say if she was to announce she was happy to spend the next week here in the hotel, wedding-spotting. No. The poor fellow had flown all this way. He needed to see Galway Bay, at least. And the Cliffs of Moher. Perhaps the Lakes of Killarney and the Ring of Kerry. And Cork. They had to go to Clare, of course, with all its connections to the Clare Valley. And then there was Mayo. Lola had always wanted to go to Westport. Donegal was supposed to be magnificent. The wildest county of all, apparently. There was so much to see. Jim would have to drive like a demon.

'What a great night,' Jim said, as they made their way up the stairs, Lola insisting on the exercise. 'It was all put on for us, I suppose? Usually they sit around eating pizza and watching box sets?'

'Exactly,' she said. 'And I did hear you right, did I? Doing your best to keep up Australian stereotypes with that story about your pet kangaroo? The one I don't remember you ever having?'

He grinned. 'It was for the kids. They wanted it to be true. I couldn't let them down.'

'Of course not. But couldn't you have come up with a better name for it than Skippy?'

'I'm still jet-lagged. Go easy on me.'

They reached her room. 'See you in the morning, Jim. Thank you again.'

He gave her a courteous bow. 'One of the best nights of my life, Mum. I mean that.'

'I'm so glad to hear that. You looked right at home there tonight.'

'So did you,' he said.

In the Adelaide Hills, Geraldine was in the dining room, serving her latest guests the sumptuous breakfast promised in their brochures and on their website. Her own muesli. Homemade brown bread. Organic bacon and free-range eggs. She thought back to the mornings in the motel when she sometimes had to cook up to eighty eggs. Cooking for four guests was such a luxury. She and Jim should have done this years ago.

Her phone chimed from where it was tucked out of sight in her pocket. She checked it once she was back in the kitchen. Jim! He must have been up late. Her guests would be busy with their bacon and eggs for a while. She could phone him back now.

He'd just got back from a great party held in Lola's honour, he told her. Geraldine listened as he described the warm welcome, the crowded room, the singing, his own recitation, Lola's song . . . She knew immediately that he'd had a few drinks. More than a few, by the sound, but she wouldn't say anything. There were other things to discuss.

'And is everything okay? With you and Lola, I mean?'

'Yes. Yes, it is. It's fantastic, Ger. I know everything. Mum knows everything now too.'

'About you meeting your father?'

'Everything. I didn't even have to ask. She's wanted to tell me for years, she said. She's been waiting for the right moment. The way I've been waiting for the right moment.'

'But it's not the same, Jim. She lied to you. Deliberately invented an entire false story. For years. That's not as simple as you not telling her something.'

Jim went silent. If it was possible to feel a chill down a phone line, Geraldine felt it.

'Mum had her reasons. I had my reasons. Don't make this bigger than it is, Geraldine, please.'

There it was again. Jim-and-Lola once again. It took all of Geraldine's self-control not to put the phone down. She forced her voice to sound normal. 'Of course not. I'm glad to hear you sorted it all out, so easily too. So what are your plans now?'

To her own ears, she sounded so fake. But he answered as if there'd been no bump in their conversation, telling her about the sightseeing trip they were going to take, no set itinerary, just driving around the country together.

'How wonderful,' she said, fighting a sudden rising of jealousy. She should be the one doing road trips with Jim. They were in their sixties, not getting any younger themselves. Any time left should be for the two of them, not for him and Lola. *When will your mother ever let us have our own lives?*

She didn't say it. She murmured encouraging responses about their travel plans. How lucky they were to be making it up as they went along. 'Ring me as often as you can, won't you?' she said. Every day, he told her. And yes, she assured him in turn, all was going great at the guesthouse. Very busy but she wouldn't have it any other way.

She forced herself to sound like the perfect wife and daughter-in-law. What choice did she have? Lola and Jim had worked it out between them. She had lost, yet again. It was never going to change or get better. Not until the day Lola died. And it was starting to look as if that day would never come.

She heard a burst of laughter from the dining room. It was time she checked on her guests. 'I'd better go,' she said. 'I miss you. And I love you.' It was how they always finished their phone calls. It was still true.

He echoed it. He should go too, he said. It was late there and they were hoping to make an early start, be on the road by ten. There was so much to see.

'How wonderful,' Geraldine said again, the words like ashes in her mouth. 'Say hello to Lola from me, won't you? Give her my love.'

'Of course. I'm sure she'd say the same back to you.'

Geraldine knew they were both lying.

CHAPTER FORTY

Bett was at Adelaide airport waiting for her mother. They'd arranged to meet at six p.m. in the cafe near international arrivals. Bett had driven from Clare. Geraldine was coming from the Adelaide Hills. Bett had offered to meet Lola and her dad and drive him home before going on to Clare, but Geraldine insisted on being there too.

'It's not every day my husband gets back from his first overseas trip.'

'But you'll have to get someone in to look after the guesthouse for a few hours.'

'I don't mind. I'm going to be there, Bett.'

Bett knew better than to argue with her mother when she used that tone of voice.

She couldn't wait to see Lola and her father herself. Over the past week, there'd been only brief messages from them, saying all was well. There'd been no more photos. Lola's ruling, Bett was sure.

Bett took her coffee to a quiet corner of the cafe, glad she'd arrived early. It seemed impossible that it was only two weeks since she and Lola were here, flying to Sydney to meet Ellen, before travelling on to Ireland together. So much had happened in that time. Her and Ellen's unexpected return. Glenn's illness and, thankfully, his ongoing recovery. Daniel's beautiful gift of the piano.

The closure of her newspaper.

She'd heard the bad news two days earlier. It was still a secret, but she knew it wouldn't be long before everyone in town heard. It wasn't immediate. They would print paper editions for another two months. They would then go online only. It was the future, the manager in Sydney had said during the conference call. Sales of print newspapers were plummeting. People wanted news at their fingertips, on their phones, tablets, computers. This was seizing the day, reshaping new media. On and on he'd gone. They would keep up local content, he assured her. Her job was safe. No, it wasn't, her union friend Rebecca told her when she rang afterwards. The same company had gone through the same process with other regional newspapers in their stable. First the print edition was stopped. Then, weeks or months later, the online news was centralised. In several cases, junior reporters had been kept on. In none of the cases had the editor stayed.

'I wish I could be more positive, Bett, but the precedent is there. I don't think they'll make an exception in your case. Even if you are living in a hotbed of Hollywood gossip at the moment.'

The articles about the TV series had perhaps given them a few more weeks than they might have had. Certainly, they'd had stronger sales since the TV people arrived. Her most recent main street post-publication walk had been a pleasure. She'd been treated like a showbiz correspondent, an insider. She'd discovered exactly why Carrie had enjoyed it so much.

As Bett had received her bad news, Daniel heard good news. A pay rise. The paper he worked for was independent, a family business. His job was still secure. The irony was that the closure of Bett's paper would make it even safer. His paper would pick up advertising from the Valley now. He'd also been asked to photograph three more weddings later in the year. They were often long, difficult days, but he was good at them. Nervy brides and panicky grooms appreciated his calm nature.

They had stayed up late for the past two nights talking about their work, their future. Bett kept thinking about going freelance. Carrie's new blog had given her the idea. The Clare Valley was full of people living busy, productive, inventive country lives. Perhaps there was a market for feature or business articles about them. She'd made some calls to journalist friends, one now the editor of a glossy lifestyle magazine, the other working on the business pages of a national paper. They'd both agreed to look at any of her story pitches. She'd started drawing some up already – one on the wine industry, the burgeoning olive oil businesses, specialist food companies, the impact of Airbnb on boutique tourism operations . . .

She'd also discovered another possible new string to her work bow. Her piano. The evening before she'd been sitting at it with Zach and Yvette on her lap. It had been a tight squeeze, and noisy too. They loved hitting the keys, laughing, using one finger and then their whole hands, crashing down on the keys. She'd steadied them on her lap and, with one hand, played a series of nursery rhymes they already knew from the musical lamp in their bedroom. They'd both gone still. Zach had looked up at her, eyes wide. So had Yvette. 'Again, Mummy. Again,' they insisted.

She played them all. 'Ring a Ring o' Roses', 'Jack and Jill', 'Sing a Song of Sixpence'. More wide eyes, and smiles too. They'd insisted on playing the keys themselves then. She saw they were actually trying to pick out notes, childishly and unsuccessfully, but they'd stopped simply thumping the keyboard.

'It's never too early to start, I guess,' Daniel said, coming in.

They'd talked about it that night. She'd probably been as young as them when Lola first started teaching her. Her grandmother had always made her lessons fun, Bett remembered. She had school friends who'd told stories of being taught by scary nuns with rulers poised to hit their fingers whenever they made a mistake. Lola had made it a joy, encouraging her, letting her make errors, talking as much about the feeling music gave a person as the skills necessary to be note perfect.

The seed of an idea was planted. She'd teach the twins, definitely. But perhaps there were other children in the Valley who'd like to learn piano too. She and Daniel did some sums, trying to calculate what her income might be. It would be tight but it was possible. It would also make life easier in many ways if one of them was mostly home, they agreed. Would she miss being in an office? he asked. Yes, she confessed. She'd loved it. But the office was being taken away from her. And perhaps it was time for something else.

On the drive from Clare that afternoon, she'd moved from anxiety to excitement and back again. In the airport now, she decided it was nervous excitement. She had her notebook out and was toying with names for her music teaching business – Bett's Beats, Daniel had suggested – when she heard her name. It was her mother.

They hugged, briefly. They only ever did hug briefly. Bett had grown closer to her mother since Anna's death, certainly. They spoke several times a week. But Geraldine had never been an affectionate mother. As Bett took her coffee order and waited at the counter, it occurred to her that the two of them, in fact, rarely spent any time together. Either her dad was always there too, or Daniel and the twins, or the whole family.

Returning with the coffee, she smiled. 'Just the two of us for once. We can have that heart-to-heart you've always longed to have.' She was joking. Bett and her sisters had long ago realised that the last thing their mother wanted with them was a deep conversation.

'I do want to talk to you about something, Bett. Something important. Before they arrive.'

She was serious, Bett realised. She sat down opposite her, wary, glad their table was in a quiet corner of the cafe. 'Are you okay? Is Dad?'

'I'm fine. Your dad is fine. But there's something you need to know. Something that's been kept a secret in our family for too long. And I think that's wrong. And so I've decided to tell you. And when I see Carrie next, I'm going to tell her too.'

'A secret about you?'

'Not me. About your grandmother.'

Bett frowned. 'Then shouldn't she be the one to tell us?'

'She never will. But enough is enough. I won't let it go on any longer.'

Bett had never seen her mother like this. So agitated. 'Mum, are you okay?'

'No, I'm not, Bett. I've had a week on my own, a difficult, lonely week. And why? Because your father is still at his mother's beck and call after all these years. Because he dropped everything at the spur of the moment because of her. Again.'

'Mum, he had to go to Ireland. She couldn't have been left over there on her own.'

'It's as if it's what she wanted all along. The two of them jaunting around Ireland, having a wonderful time, sightseeing and —'

'But that's great, isn't it? I think it's perfect that it was Dad there with her instead of me and Ellen.'

Her mother's lips tightened.

Bett realised then how serious this was. She had always known of the tension between her mother and Lola but it had stayed unspoken. Not any more, it seemed. 'Mum, please understand. Lola left Ireland when she was still a child, really. I'm sure she'd have loved to have gone back before now. I can't imagine not being home for sixty-five years. This was truly a once-in-a-lifetime trip for her, can't you see —'

'You're always on her side too, aren't you? You're as bad as Jim.'

'As bad? Mum, it's not about taking sides. She's my grandmother.'

She felt a shimmer of unease. 'I love her but I love you too. It is possible to love more than one person, you know.'

'Even though she's a liar?'

Bett went still.

'And that she has been a liar for nearly every day of your father's life, and every day of yours? That's acceptable, is it? I should go along with it as you all have, saying, oh, that's just Lola, eccentric Lola, oh, she's such a character.'

'Mum, please —'

'I'm going to tell you the truth, Bett, because I won't let this lie be perpetuated for another day.'

'Mum —'

'It's about Lola's husband. Jim's father. Edward Quinlan. He wasn't in the Australian Army during the Second World War. He didn't die on a battlefield somewhere.'

'I know.'

'What?'

'I know he didn't.'

'You know?' Geraldine's voice rose. A woman at a nearby table turned around. 'You can't know.'

'I know, Mum. I've known since just after Anna died.'

'No.'

'I found out accidentally. It was difficult. Very difficult, actually.' She explained about the letter from Edward's sister arriving with the sympathy cards, and the conversation with Lola. She kept her voice low, trying not to react to the raw emotion coming off her mother. 'I found it hard too, but Lola helped me understand that she'd done it for all the right reasons. To protect Dad. To give them respectability. She had to leave her husband, Mum. He was an alcoholic. Abusive. She couldn't stay with him.'

'We don't know if any of that is true. Whose word do we have?'

'Why would Lola leave him if she didn't have to? She came

421

across the world with him, to a new country, with no family to help her. It must have been so hard, Mum, so lonely for her. All during the war years, on her own with a baby, having to earn a living —'

'Yes, I know. Saint Lola. I've heard these stories for years, Bett. I don't need to hear them again.'

There were a few moments of tense silence. Geraldine broke it. 'Does Carrie know any of this?'

'Not yet. And I don't think she needs to.'

'Of course she does. He was her grandfather too. Yet Lola chose to keep you all away from him.'

'She didn't have a choice. She had to do it, for her own safety. For Dad's safety.'

'Your father met him.'

Bett wasn't sure if she'd heard that right. 'Pardon me?'

'Your father met his father.'

'No, he didn't. At least, not since he was a baby.'

'He did. He was twenty-one. Edward Quinlan came looking for him. For him and Lola.'

'No, Mum. Lola would have told me.'

'Lola didn't know. She only heard about it herself this week for the first time.'

Bett's eyes were wide. 'But I don't understand. Why didn't Dad ever tell us?'

Geraldine sniffed. 'It seems keeping secrets runs in the family.'

'But you always knew?'

'I've known since the year we were married.'

'Why didn't you tell us?'

'It wasn't my story to tell.'

'So why is it your story now?' It sounded rude, but she had to say it.

'Because I'm sick of this, Bett. I'm sick of everything in this family being run as Lola wants it run. I've waited patiently while she meddled in my marriage, my children, my business. This week I decided I had run out of patience.'

Bett could only stare at her. 'You hate her, don't you? You actually hate Lola.'

'Hate is a very strong word.'

'You dislike her. Very much.'

Geraldine lifted her chin. 'Yes, I do. I always have.'

Bett swallowed. 'Mum. I can't understand. She's Dad's mother. She's an elderly woman. Who knows how many more years she has left?'

'Another twenty or so the way she's going. She's indestructible.'

Bett felt as if a mask had slipped off her mother. As if the reserved, even shy woman she'd always known her mother to be had vanished, revealing a different person. One Bett wasn't comfortable seeing.

Was Geraldine going to ask Bett to choose between her mother and grandmother? Bett wouldn't do it. She could not be party to another rift in her family. The three years she'd spent not talking to her two sisters had been the worst of her life. She couldn't go through anything like it again.

She checked her watch, calmly, obviously, giving herself time to think. Their flight was due to land in five minutes. This was the only chance she would have to say all she needed to say.

'I can't do it, Mum. I won't take sides. I love you and Dad. I love Lola. I love Carrie. I loved Anna. You are my family, all of you, and I'm not letting us break into pieces again. Anna's death was hard enough on us all. It still is. I can't let your jealousy make it worse.'

'Have you any idea what it's been like? For me and your father? For every day of our marriage?'

'Yes. Because I was there too for a lot of it.' Her own temper was rising now. 'I saw every day of my life how much you and Dad love one another. I know he is your favourite person in the world.

423

And that has been a wonderful example in many ways, but it was also hard at times. There were times when I wish you'd had as much time for us as you had for Dad, and for your work.'

The words were pouring out of her. 'But Lola always explained it to us, Mum, that motels didn't run themselves. That we were lucky to have parents who loved one another. That we should be grateful that you and Dad suffered her constant presence, because otherwise the three of us would have run riot, grown up as savages, and how terrible that would have been. She made a joke about it but she was serious, we knew that. She never once said anything bad about you. She never once made us feel like we were burdens on her time, that there were things she'd rather be doing than look after three little girls while their parents were at work.

'And if it wasn't for Lola, Mum, I am sure that Anna, Carrie and I probably wouldn't have talked again and Anna would have died without us getting the chance to say goodbye to her.' Unbidden tears sprang into her eyes. 'So I won't do this for you or with you. I won't be part of it. If Dad ever wants to tell me about meeting his father, then I want to hear it from him. But only for the right reasons, because he thinks it's time to tell me. I don't want to hear it if it's being used as a weapon.' She stood up. 'We better go. They're about to land.'

They were silent as they walked to the gate.

They were silent as they stood there, as the crowd grew around them.

The first passengers started coming out. Tired, rumpled, greeted by enthusiastic family and friends. Bett could see the airbridge through the large glass windows. She spotted them, at the back of a long queue of slow-moving passengers, Lola standing tall, probably using her stick, Jim beside her.

'There they are,' she said to her mother. Her first words since the cafe.

'I'm sorry, Bett.' Her mother's voice was so low Bett wasn't sure if she'd heard it.

There were only minutes before they would appear. Before the hugs and greetings and stories would begin.

Bett fought back her own resentment. 'I'm sorry that you feel this way.'

'I've thought about it. I won't say anything to Lola. Or to Carrie.'

Bett looked at her mother. She seemed exhausted. Sad. A rush of feeling came over Bett. Confusion, love for her mother, pity. Understanding. Because her mother was right, Bett knew that. Lola was the centre of their family. She always had been. Life had always revolved around her. Bett loved being in her orbit. She truly dreaded the day Lola wouldn't be there for her. But now she saw, more clearly than she would have liked, how that might have made her mother feel.

Second best. Left out.

Lonely.

She didn't reach over and hug her mother. She couldn't. It wasn't their way. But she could do the next closest thing. She reached for her mother's arm and she squeezed it. Her mother looked down, and she put her own hand on Bett's. An answering squeeze. It was the best they could both do.

They were both somehow smiling as Lola and Jim appeared.

CHAPTER FORTY-ONE

The eight p.m. news came on the radio as Bett and Lola drove along the main north road on their way back to Clare. Jim and Geraldine would be halfway home too, Bett knew. The airport hadn't been the place for an extended catch-up. They'd decided to meet in Clare soon for a proper 'debrief', as Lola dubbed it.

Even before they'd reached the city outskirts, Lola's eyes had begun to close. She was now asleep. No wonder, Bett thought, glancing across fondly. She could only imagine how emotional the entire Irish trip must have been. She had dozens of questions, but they would have to wait.

They were nearly home, passing through Sevenhill, the nearest town to Clare, when she was startled by Lola's voice in the darkness.

'Darling, could we make a detour before you drop me home?'

'Of course. Where to, the bottle shop for gin?'

'No, I stocked up in duty-free. I need to talk to you and it would be better if you're not driving.'

'That sounds serious. You're going to tell me I'm not really your granddaughter?'

Lola didn't reply.

Bett realised then this was serious. 'Did you have somewhere in mind?'

'Billy Goat Hill, perhaps?' Lola said, naming Clare's lookout spot.

The car park at Billy Goat Hill was empty, Bett was glad to see. It was occasionally used as a courting spot, or even as a teen drinking spot, but Clare's cold frost had kept everyone away tonight. The town below looked pretty, the street lights glowing yellow, the hills around it a dark smudge.

Bett switched off the engine and turned in her seat. The troubling conversation with her mother was uppermost in her mind. She wouldn't mention it to Lola, she'd decided.

Lola spoke. 'I'm sorry to seem so dramatic, and to carry on as if we're in a John le Carré novel, but I decided on the flight that I need to come clean to you about a number of things. So I am striking while the iron is hot, before the jet lag sets in.'

Bett waited.

'Do you remember I told you that I found out I was pregnant after I left Edward?' Lola said.

Bett nodded.

'That was a lie. I married Edward because I was pregnant. By the time I arrived in Australia I was nearly three months pregnant.'

'Oh.' Bett couldn't think of anything else to say.

'You already know that Edward didn't die during the war. But I didn't tell you the truth about me leaving him. I told you that he had hit me once, and I had left him there and then. I made it sound like I was brave and fearless. But the truth is, I wasn't. I told my parents I had left him, and they wrote to me and told me I had to go back to him. And even though I was on the other side of the world, I obeyed them. I went back to Edward, for the rest of my pregnancy, and for Jim's birth and for the first weeks of his life. Until it happened again. Edward hit me again. And he also hit Jim. A baby of two months old.'

Bett's gasp was loud.

'I left him for good then. Again, I wrote and told my parents. They punished me as a result. I was disowned. I never heard from my father again. I spoke only once again, briefly, to my mother.' Sparely, in a low voice, Lola told Bett about her phone call home to Ireland.

Bett sat silently, imagining that phone call, picturing her grandmother and her infant father with a drunken Edward, cowering as he —

She stopped. It was too terrible to think about.

'I should have told you all of this before now, Bett,' Lola said. 'But the truth is that I was always ashamed of myself for going back. I know my life only began properly when I left him. When we left him.'

They were quiet for a moment, before Lola spoke. 'There's something else. I may regret this, but I have an urge for you to know everything possible about your family. Your father may decide to tell you in due course, but my instinct tells me to share it with you. And perhaps you'll do me the honour of pretending it's news to you, if Jim does say anything.'

Bett's own instinct advised her to stay quiet. She listened as Lola told her all that had happened in Ireland, the conversation with Jim, his revelation that he had met his father. She asked for more detail. Lola told her everything, about the letters, Elizabeth's journal too.

When she had finished speaking, Bett reached over and held her grandmother's hand. 'I'm sorry, Lola. I'm sorry things were so hard for you back then.'

'Thank you, Bett.' It was all she needed to say. She squeezed Bett's hand. 'And that is all my skeletons out of the closet now, my darling. Every last one of them. You might be glad to hear that.'

'I think there's one more left.'

'One of yours, do you mean?'

'No, it's still about you. You didn't have shares to sell, did you? Or a diamond ring?'

'No, I didn't. I had a painting. One I'd had for many years and loved for many years.' She explained what she had done. 'I did intend to leave it to you all in my will, not waste it on airfares. I'm sorry, Bett. Especially considering your big overseas trip lasted less than a week.'

'I remember that painting. You loved it. I'm so sorry you had to sell it.'

Lola shrugged. 'It was gathering dust. Forest scenes are so yesterday, anyway.'

'But please don't say the trip was a waste. It didn't go as we expected, but it was even better in some ways, don't you think?'

'I don't just think it. I know it.' Lola reached across to tuck one of Bett's curls behind her ear. 'And now you better take me home, put me to bed and leave me to sleep for at least twenty-four hours.'

Bett started the car. 'Your wish is my command. As always. As ever.'

'Someone did raise you well,' Lola said.

CHAPTER FORTY-TWO

It was the first day of the Clare Valley Gourmet Weekend. Lola had been home for a week.

Bett always loved the mood in the Valley during 'Gourmet', as it was known by the locals. Crowded buses travelled from winery to winery. Every pub, restaurant and cafe was filled with people. This year, the merry mood was heightened by the presence of the TV crew. They were more low-key than everyone expected. They'd hoped for blocked-off roads, security guards, helicopters and police cordons. Instead, it was just an actor or two being filmed walking amid the crowds, or strolling through the autumn-coloured vineyards.

Bett, Daniel and the twins met Lola, Carrie and her family in the Lorikeet Hill vineyard on the main road. It was their favourite spot in the Valley, run by Maura Carmody and her husband, Dominic. Maura had lots of Irish connections and always hired an Irish band to provide the background music. Bett was secretly pleased it wasn't one of the locations for the TV series. It meant they could enjoy their visit without feeling self-conscious about possibly being filmed.

As they met friends and other family groups, it was soon clear that Carrie was still queen of the Valley, basking in the reflected glory of her Rafe Ascot experience. She'd perfected her response,

Bett observed. 'I'd love to say more but legally I can't,' she answered each time.

Bett was doing her best to keep an eye on Lola too. Her grandmother hadn't been behaving as expected since she returned home. Bett had felt sure Lola would organise a slide night in the Town Hall at the very least – a chance to tell all about her travels. Instead, she'd been living quietly, staying at home. Bett had visited her several times, Lola assuring her that she was fine, just jet-lagged, that she wanted to wait until the family was together before she shared all of her and Jim's travel stories. It was very long-lasting jet lag, Bett said to Daniel, especially considering she'd flown home business class.

She'd been heartened when Lola rang and asked if they could have a small gathering at Bett and Daniel's house. Just family, Jim and Geraldine too, to talk about the trip and show some photos.

Bett was glad to hear she'd actually taken some. 'You don't want to invite Margaret? All your friends?'

'Not this time, darling.'

At six o'clock the following Wednesday, it was all set up. Bett and Daniel had moved the furniture in their lounge room so it was theatre-style. They connected the laptop computer to their marginally bigger-screen TV. Bett knew Lola had asked Luke to move all her photos onto a memory stick. Lola had also asked Bett to provide piano accompaniment as the photos were displayed.

'Can I see them first?' Bett asked.

'That would be boring, darling. You'd have to see them twice. Just play whatever comes to mind.'

Shortly after seven, the show began. It was a full house: Carrie, Matthew and their children, Bett at the piano, Daniel by the computer, Yvette and Zachary on either side of him. Jim and Geraldine were on the sofa, side by side. Holding hands. In the centre of the room, in an armchair, was Lola.

'Please begin, Daniel,' Lola called.

Having seen Lola's photography in the past, Bett's hopes weren't high. But as she played the piano and watched the images flash onto the screen, she changed her mind. The photos were glorious.

There was a dramatic one of the Cliffs of Moher in County Clare: waves crashing, the sky a swirl of stormy clouds. A photo of Blarney Castle in County Cork, the stone golden in sunlight, the sky an unexpected vivid blue. Photo after photo of the Irish landscape: green fields sweeping down to the sea, stone walls, bright-pink fuchsia, delicate orchids and other wildflowers. Small thatched cottages with whitewashed walls and red doors. Black-faced sheep, their fleece daubed in bright splashes of colour, posing on clifftops, with small bays and glittering sea beneath them. A funny photo of a small flock of sheep blocking a country laneway, a picture-postcard image.

Bett played on as instructed, encouraged by Lola's tapping foot. She moved between jigs and reels to snatches of ballads and more poignant Irish songs. The photos continued. One showed shafts of sunlight hitting a castle ruin. A graveyard filled with Celtic crosses, with a rainbow in the background. A beautiful snow-covered field with just one tree standing upright in —

Bett stopped playing. A snow-covered field? In the Irish summertime?

'Daniel, stop there, would you?' she called. 'And could you please put the light on?'

Bett glanced over at her father. He was smiling.

'You brat,' Bett said to Lola. 'You didn't take any of these, did you?'

'Not a single one,' Lola said.

'What about you, Dad?' Bett asked.

'I don't even have a camera, Bett.'

'Lola!' Carrie said. 'What's going on?'

'I didn't want to disappoint you all,' Lola said. 'I know how obsessed you are with seeing photos. So I downloaded these from Irish tourism websites. Well, I didn't. Luke did. I told him what I wanted and he found them for me.'

'So you didn't take any photos at all?' Bett asked them both.

'Just the ones at Lola's old family home,' Jim said.

'The waitress took the one of us in the hotel restaurant,' Lola added.

'Did the two of you actually go anywhere in Ireland?' Carrie asked. 'Or did you stay put in that fancy hotel?'

Jim looked at Lola. Lola looked at Jim. 'You tell them, darling,' Lola said. 'It was your idea.'

'I made an executive decision,' he said. 'We did plan to go on a road trip, trying to see all the sights in a week. But I didn't think it was fair on Mum, having to pack up and move every morning. I thought she needed it to be a holiday as much as anything.'

'So what did you do?' Daniel asked.

'As Carrie guessed,' Jim said. 'We stayed put in that fancy hotel. And some days we went for drives and did a little bit of sightseeing.'

'And some days we didn't,' Lola added.

Carrie frowned. 'But I thought the whole idea of the trip was to see Ireland?'

'No, the whole idea of the trip was for Lola to go home,' Jim said. 'And she did go home. Her old home, at least.'

'So you went all that way and you didn't see any cliffs, or castles, or thatched cottages?' Carrie said.

'Bett lived there for several months and all she saw was the inside of Dublin music clubs,' Lola said.

Bett stayed silent. It was a good point.

Lola continued. 'But we did see plenty. The Irish distances were nothing to Jim. We took day trips to Galway, and Kilkenny, and across to County Clare, of course. Not that we got to see the Cliffs of Moher. There was too much fog, even in May. They're only visible a few weeks of the year – imagine that. Then the weather turned bad the final few days. Rained nonstop. So we decided it made far better sense to stay in the hotel and talk and play Scrabble.'

'You crossed the world to play board games?' Carrie said.

'We watched a few weddings too,' Lola said.

'And as Lola kept reminding me,' Jim added, 'Geraldine and I can see all the sights together when we go back next year.'

Geraldine's head shot up.

Both Carrie and Bett echoed his words. 'Next year?'

Jim smiled at his wife. 'What do you think, Ger? We close the guesthouse for a few months and go to Europe? Start in Ireland, perhaps go on to France and Italy?'

'We've won the lottery, have we?'

'Not exactly. But yes, we will have the money.'

'So you finally decided?' Geraldine said.

Jim nodded.

Carrie was looking back and forth between them. 'Decided what?' she asked.

At a nod from Geraldine, Jim explained. 'I was planning to talk about it with you all later. But now is just as good. Your mum and I think the time has come to sell the motel, not just lease it. Tourism is on the up. The TV series might help even more. We're not getting any younger. And I have a taste for travel now. You'll have to thank Lola for that, Ger. I'd never have found out I can handle long-distance flights if she hadn't forced me into it.'

'Thanks, Lola,' Geraldine said.

'My pleasure, Geraldine,' Lola replied.

Bett was surprised not to see icicles sprout from the ceiling above the two of them. But any tension was forgotten as they all started asking questions about the motel sale, about Jim and Geraldine's travel plans. As Carrie began to complain that she would be the only member of the family not to have been to Europe, Bett moved away from the piano to sit beside Lola.

'Did you talk Dad into selling while you were away?'

'We never discussed it. It was his to sell, anyway. I signed all my voting rights away years ago.'

'But you still have a share in it. You might not have needed to sell your beautiful painting.'

'It was time someone else enjoyed it. I can frame all of my beautiful photographs of Ireland instead.'

'And you really didn't mind not going on the road trip?'

Lola shook her head. 'Jim made the right decision. It was much better this way. We had all the time in the world to talk during our day trips. And we had time to ourselves too. The perfect holiday.'

'But you travelled all that way, so did Dad —'

'We still couldn't do and see everything, Bett. If I've learnt anything at my ancient age, it's that I need to be selective now. There won't be time for me to do everything I want. I'll have to choose carefully. It was the same in Ireland. We could have rushed from one place to the other, but I wanted to savour what we did see. So I drew up a list and chose my top-three places. And I couldn't have been happier.'

'Was it your idea for Dad to take Mum there?'

'I may have mentioned how much I thought she would enjoy it. And how an overseas holiday would do her the world of good.'

Bett gazed at her grandmother. 'You really are much kinder than you pretend to be, aren't you?'

'I'm an angel on earth, darling. Haven't you realised that by now?' She held out her glass. 'Now, please fetch me another drink before I die of thirst.'

EPILOGUE

Eight months later

Once again, the Quinlans were gathered together, this time with many friends around them. It was a special event. Their first viewing of *Murder in the Vines*.

Questions were flying around the room.

'Why did it take so long to be shown?' someone asked.

Bett knew the answer. 'A combination of editing problems and program scheduling.'

'Is Rafe Ascot back to do publicity?' another asked. 'Will he be in Clare again?'

Bett didn't share that answer. She'd heard via Lola, who'd heard it from her friend Tom, that Rafe Ascot had declared he'd never set foot on Australian soil again. Lola had edited out his swear words.

Tom had invited them to fly to Sydney for a private screening a month earlier but Lola was having problems with her left hip and preferred to stay close to home. There'd also only been room at Tom's screening for three of her friends. She wanted to bring at least thirty. It was much better for them all to watch it together, she'd decided. As word spread, her guest list kept growing.

Tom had then offered to send them a preview DVD. Thank you but no, Lola said. They'd decided they wanted to watch it at the same time as everyone in Australia. On the ABC at seven-thirty on a Sunday night.

There were now over a hundred people gathered in the function room at the Valley View Motel. Len the butcher had helped Daniel set up a large TV screen. The chairs were lined up in rows. People began to hush one another as the clock ticked towards the starting time. Up on the big screen, the opening credits appeared, with the title *Murder in the Vines* in elaborate script, vine leaves winding through the letters. There was a wide shot of the Valley with its vineyard-covered hills, stone cottages and tall gum trees. A funeral cortege appeared, making its way along the curving road from the church to the cemetery. There were close-up shots of the key characters – the winemaker, the restaurant owner, the politician. Everyone whooped at a glimpse of familiar faces amid the crowd of extras.

The scriptwriter's name came up. Tom Nikolić. Another whoop. Lola patted Tom's arm. He was sitting beside her. She was so glad he'd been able to make it to Clare tonight. Then they all fell quiet as the drama unfolded.

An hour later, the room erupted into applause.

'Oh my God!'

'Who did it?'

'Which one is the killer?'

'It's fantastic!'

Tom basked in the attention as people came up to him, begging for a hint about the murderer. He couldn't possibly say, he said.

Bett was busy doing interviews and taking photographs. Not for her paper. That had closed down four months earlier, as expected. It was now only online, under the editorship of her former assistant, Sam, the young man she'd hired as a cadet eighteen months earlier. She had been made redundant, also as expected.

She'd had a week of feeling sorry for herself, of wishing it was like the old days when she first started in journalism, when it seemed as though 'real' newspapers would always be needed. By the second week, she'd been too busy for self-pity. Sometimes she was busier as a freelancer than she'd ever been as a full-time editor. She averaged six articles a month for the various magazines and online sites she contributed to, producing business stories, tourism features, personal profiles. This article on the hometown screening of the TV series would be a colour piece in the state's daily newspaper the following day.

She also spent six hours a week teaching young piano students, in her own home. That was working out even better than she had hoped. She was able to cook, or put on a load of washing before her students arrived. She'd have an enjoyable – mostly enjoyable – half-hour teaching them their scales and a few simple tunes. Afterwards, she was able to hang out the washing, or take the meal out of the oven. It felt so efficient.

She and Daniel had had a few problems as they became accustomed to their new working and home lives. Occasionally she'd had to remind him that they hadn't time-travelled back to the 1950s – that she wasn't a full-time housewife. That just because she was at home most of the time didn't mean she was lazing about on the sofa having her nails done or watching soaps. That she worked as hard as he did in his Gawler office and so he needed to do his share of the housework and the cooking. And in his calm way, he often had to point out to her that just because she now had a number of bosses, not one boss, that didn't mean she had to work even longer hours at home than she used to when she was in an office.

But the fights were rarer than the good times. It seemed to Bett as though the trip to Ireland had been a watershed. She often thought of her life as 'before Ireland' and 'after Ireland'.

She wasn't the only one who had seen big changes. Carrie's baby had arrived safely on her exact due date. A little girl. Keeping up with the alphabetical naming they had started years before, she had been baptised Harriet. She'd been given a special middle name too. Louisa. Carrie had been so surprised to find out that Lola hadn't always been called Lola that she wanted to record her grandmother's 'real' name for posterity. Not that anyone called the new baby by her official name. From the day she'd been brought home, her big sisters and brother had called her Harry. It suited her.

Harry's christening had been an excuse for another family gathering. The whole family had come to Clare for the weekend: Glenn, Denise, Ellen and Lily from Sydney, and Jim and Geraldine from the Adelaide Hills. Glenn had been almost back to full health, but still mindful that he needed to watch his weight and exercise more. They'd all teased him when he announced he was off for a jog. Bett had asked Carrie if she was going to use the christening as inspiration for a post on her 'My Country Dream' blog. 'What blog?' Carrie had replied. She'd forgotten all about it.

Bett stood at the edge of the room now, trying to decide who else to interview for her article. She'd spoken to the motel's new owners already about the expected tourist boom for the area. They were the same couple who had previously leased it. They'd been happy to make the arrangement permanent. Jim and Geraldine had got a good price for it. Better than expected. They'd surprised her and Carrie, and Lola too, with a share of the proceeds. That windfall was now earning interest in a special bank account Bett and Daniel had set up. A holiday fund, they'd decided. When the twins were a little bit older, in a year or so, they'd take a proper, long holiday. Not as far as Ireland. Possibly not much further than Queensland. But a sunny, relaxing few weeks together.

Not just the four of them. By the time they took that holiday, there could possibly be five of them. She and Daniel had decided soon after she returned from Ireland that they were ready for another baby. They'd had some very enjoyable times trying to make that happen. It hadn't yet, but they were hopeful. There might even be six of them on that Queensland trip. Not another baby. Another adult.

Lola.

'I'd only get in the way,' her grandmother had said when Bett visited one afternoon, soon after they'd received the windfall. 'You and Daniel and your twins need a holiday on your own, not with some ancient old hag of an Irishwoman slowing you down.'

'We'll need a babysitter. That's the only reason I'm asking you.'

'So it's a paid gig?' Lola said. 'In that case, send me the employment contract. I'll get my lawyer to talk to your lawyer and we'll see what we can agree.'

Her father's announcement about the overseas holiday was also coming true. Her parents had already booked their flights. They'd be leaving for Europe in five months' time, via a week in Hong Kong. They were joining a guided tour for some of it, one that promised the highlights of Ireland, England and Scotland. He might get to see the Cliffs of Moher this time, Jim said.

'Check the weather forecast first,' Lola said.

There'd been no thawing in the relationship between Lola and her mother, Bett had been sad to see. She'd done all she could, inviting them both for lunch one Sunday, and regretting it within minutes. The tension was awful. She tried a second time, bringing Lola to visit her parents in their guesthouse. Her mother had barely sat down, dusting and polishing, until it was Bett herself who suggested they all go for a walk around the town of Aldgate, rather than feel they were at a housework demonstration.

'You're wasting your time, darling,' Lola said to her as they drove back to Clare. 'You can't fix everything. You can't make everyone you know like everyone else you know.'

'You're my grandmother. Mum is my mother. I hate it that you don't get on.' It was a relief to talk openly about it.

'I'm sorry about that. But do you really think you can change it?' Lola asked.

'No. I've tried but I can't.'

'Then suck it up, princess.'

'Lola!'

'I do like those modern sayings, don't you?' Lola had said.

Bett came over to her grandmother now. For the first time all evening, Lola was alone. Most of the night she had been sitting like a queen receiving her subjects, as one after the other came up to say they'd always guessed she had something to do with the TV series, or to beg for clues about what would happen in the following episodes. Bett hadn't been the only person surprised to see Lola's name at the top of the thankyous in the closing credits.

'Did you tell Tom all our secrets?' she'd asked.

'Of course not,' Lola had replied. 'I mostly advised on the technical aspects of winemaking and the geographical and geological elements of the Clare Valley landscape.'

'Can I get you anything?' Bett asked her.

'Not a thing, darling.' Lola patted the chair beside her. 'Sit there for a minute. I need some peace and quiet. If anyone comes up, tell them you're interviewing me and we can't be disturbed.'

'Are you tired? Do you want to go home already?'

'Not just yet. Tell me, what did you think of the first episode?'

'I loved it. Rafe Ascot might be horrible but he's a great actor. It'll bring in lots of tourists, won't it?'

'I hope so. Even if they are just in search of a murderer.'

'You do know who did it, don't you?'

'I certainly do,' Lola said. 'Myself and Rafe Ascot, in cahoots. Like Bonnie and Clyde.'

'You're impossible.'

'What a mean thing to say. And all these years I was sure that you loved me.'

They sat in silence for a moment, watching the crowd, enjoying the hubbub of conversation. They'd spent many evenings in this room over the years, working at weddings, business meetings and other motel functions. The highlight had been a family gathering, Lola's gala eightieth birthday party, nearly six years earlier.

Bett guessed Lola's thoughts. 'Don't tell me, you want to have your next birthday celebration here?'

'I don't think so, Bett. I'll hold off on the big guns for my ninetieth.'

'That's four years off. So you're going to stick around a bit longer?'

'If it's possible,' Lola said. 'And if you'll have me?'

Bett leaned over and kissed her grandmother on top of her head. It was hard to find a spot that wasn't covered in a jewelled clip or a fake flower. Lola had pulled out the stops outfit-wise tonight.

'Oh, I think we can put up with you for a little bit longer,' she said.

Lola smiled. 'I was hoping you'd say that. And now, if you don't mind, I'd like to go home.'

'Are you sure? I heard talk of a singalong. You don't want to stay for a bit of that first?'

'And steal the spotlight? No, darling. I really must give others their chance to shine.'

As Daniel went outside to get their car and bring it to the front of the hotel, Bett helped Lola gather her belongings.

'Do you want to say goodnight to everyone?' Bett asked. 'Make a little speech, even?'

'Nothing, Bett, thank you. I'm going to slip out without anyone noticing.'

Bett glanced at her grandmother's gold kaftan, silver wrap and six necklaces and said nothing.

On their way out, Lola had a quick whispered farewell to Tom, arranging to see him for lunch the next day. Daniel escorted her, arm in arm, to the car. It was only a short journey from the hotel to her house. She was first home. Margaret was staying on for the singalong.

At the front door, Lola reassured Daniel that she felt fine, she was just tired. No, she didn't need any more company tonight, she was perfectly capable of putting herself to bed. He was to go straight back to the party and have a knees-up, she insisted. And he also had to make sure to take note of every song sung and who by. She would want to know it all the next day.

She waited, waving from the doorway, until he had driven off. His car lights disappeared around the corner. She didn't go inside. It was a cool evening, but her wrap was warm. She took a seat on the bench Margaret had placed on the verandah to catch the morning sun. There were houses on either side, and the main street was in walking distance, but from here it was like being in the countryside. In front of her was a hill covered in gum trees. In the day time, the sound of birds filled the air. Tonight, all was quiet. The sky was cloudless, lit bright with stars. She felt quite alone.

Alone. Not scared. Not lonely. Simply alone.

With her thoughts and with her memories. Where once her mind had been filled with plans and hopes, she now found herself looking back more often than forward. A phrase occurred to her: 'Her best years were behind her.' Were they, in her case? There was no way of knowing. She could have one more night left on this earth, or many more years.

Once, that thought might have made her sad. Now, it didn't. She recalled Bett's words when they had first been planning the trip to Ireland. Bett had been so puzzled, unsure why Lola hadn't wanted to arrive in Kildare in a blaze of glory. 'But you've had a wonderful life, Lola. A big, beautiful life.'

The words had resonated. Bett was right. It had been a big, beautiful life. One of many layers. Good times and bad. Full-colour and black-and-white. Sadness. Happiness. Despair. Hope.

A life that had taken her from her childhood home in Ireland all the way to Australia. She had thought she was starting a new life here. But that was impossible, she knew now. You didn't start afresh when you moved house, or country. You brought yourself with you everywhere you went, experiences, faults and all. All you could do was try to be the best version of yourself. Show compassion. Be kind.

She couldn't say when her time would finally come, but she now knew one thing for sure. She wanted her life to end here, in this town, among her family, her friends. She hoped she would live in Margaret's house for as long as possible. If that became difficult, she would ring that nice friend of Bett's and ask if there might be a room in the old folks' home. Perhaps by then she might even enjoy singing 'Shine On, Harvest Moon', over and over again.

But not yet. Not for some time, she hoped. For now, she would try to keep living her life. Her big, beautiful life.

A phrase of Irish leapt unbidden into her head. A phrase she'd used as a child at school, one that generations of Irish children had used to end their school essays about outings and holidays: *Ag deireadh an lae, bhí gach duine tuirseach ach sásta*. At the end of the day, everybody was tired but happy.

She lifted her face to the night sky, breathing in the clean, crisp air. That was it exactly.

She was tired but happy.

She had so much to be grateful for. She had loved many people. Seen many beautiful sights. Lived in many places. All those moves and all those moments leading her to where she was now, right here, tonight.

She had taken the long way. The scenic route. But she was here, at last.

She was home.

ACKNOWLEDGEMENTS

My warmest thanks to the following people, who helped me in many different ways with *The Trip of a Lifetime*.

Firstly, Sheila Peacocke, a remarkable County Kildare woman, who shared her great memory and childhood stories so generously during hours of conversations with me. (Lola's story is fictional, and any historical errors are mine, not Sheila's.) My big thanks, too, to Sheila's niece, my dear Irish–Australian friend Sarah Duffy, for being a wonderful research assistant/driver/detail-checker and so much more with this novel. *The Trip of a Lifetime* is dedicated to Sarah, with my love and thanks.

Thank you to Mark and Heather Baxter and Jo and Brett Cowley, Australian visitors to Ireland who arrived with perfect timing as I was writing about Lola's visit to Ireland; my sisters Lea McInerney and Marie McInerney; my niece Mikaella Clements; Gerard Duffy; Rod Quinn of ABC *Overnights*; Susan Owens of the SewZone in Dublin; Frances Brennan; Alan Duffy; photographer Ashley Miller; and Roisin McFadden of Killashee House Hotel in Kildare.

Thanks, as always, to my friends in Australia, Ireland and beyond, especially Kristin Gill, Carol George, Clare Forster, Sinéad Moriarty, Noëlle Harrison, Karen O'Connor, Jane Melross, Brona Miller, Sarah Conroy, Maria Dickenson, Stephanie Dickenson,

Austin O'Neill and Kayleigh Scally.

Thank you to my dear agents in Sydney, London and New York: Fiona Inglis, Jonathan Lloyd, Lucia Walker, Kate Cooper, Nadia Farah Mokdad of Curtis Brown, and Gráinne Fox of Fletcher & Company.

To all at Penguin Random House around the world. In Australia – Ali Watts, Julie Burland, Nikki Christer, Ben Ball, Amanda Martin, Saskia Adams, Emma Schwarcz, Alex Ross, Samantha Jayaweera, Lou Ryan, Karen Reid, Chloe Davies, Jake Davies, Ellie Morrow and Jackie Money. In the UK – Maxine Hitchcock, Matilda McDonald and Clare Bowron. In Ireland – Michael McLoughlin, Cliona Lewis and Carrie Anderson.

My thanks and love to my two families, the McInerneys in Australia and the Drislanes in Ireland and Germany.

As always and as ever, my love and thanks to my two first readers, my sister Maura and my husband, John, for the constant help, support and many laughs they both give me.

BOOK CLUB QUESTIONS

1. '*But you've had a wonderful life, Lola.*' Do you think this is true? To what extent do you think Lola's life has been a happy one?

2. Des tells Lola that home is not about places, but about people and memories of families. How would you define 'home'?

3. Is it possible to start life over in a new place, or do you inevitably bring parts of the past with you?

4. '*Lola had hoped the most difficult of her Irish memories had lost their power by now . . . But it was as if all her memories had been waiting. The trip had prised open a trapdoor in her mind, letting them out one by one.*' Did Lola do the right thing going back to Ireland? Is it best to confront difficulties from the past?

5. Lola is devastated when she arrives in Ireland and convinces herself that there is nothing and no one left for her there. On the contrary, she receives the greatest gift of all. Discuss.

6. Bett believes that Lola lied about her past for all the right reasons. Is there ever a good reason to lie?

7. Was Lola right to sell her valuable painting, or was it a foolish act for the short-term benefit of a few?

8. Discuss the significance of the two settings in the novel, the Clare Valley and Ireland, and their similarities and differences.

9. Lola likes to be the centre of attention in the Quinlan family. Is this character trait a blessing or a curse?

10. Geraldine tells Bett that 'keeping secrets runs in the family.' Discuss.

Also by
MONICA McINERNEY

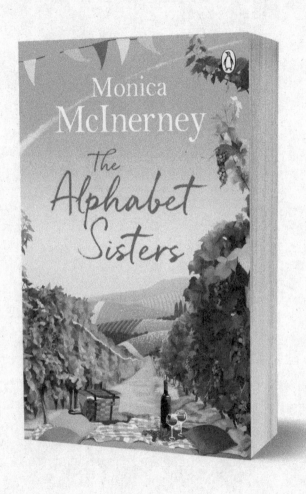

Available to order now

Also by
MONICA McINERNEY

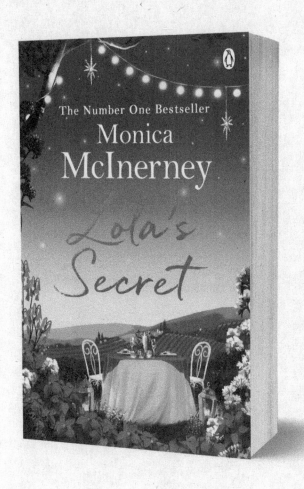

Available to order now